PART B

Janey Grange

Copyright © 2024 Jane Smedley

All rights reserved

The characters and events portrayed in this book are fictitious. Any similarity to real persons, living or dead, is coincidental and not intended by the author.

No part of this book may be reproduced, or stored in a retrieval system, or transmitted in any form or by any means, electronic, mechanical, photocopying, recording, or otherwise, without express written permission of the publisher.

ISBN: 9798333247902

Cover design by: Jane Smedley
Library of Congress Control Number: 2018675309

For Matt and Lottie

CONTENTS

Title Page
Copyright
Dedication
Chapter 1   1
Chapter 2   4
Chapter 3   7
Chapter 4   13
Chapter 5   18
Chapter 6   33
Chapter 7   38
Chapter 8   46
Chapter 9   57
Chapter 10   64
Chapter 11   74
Chapter 12   90
Chapter 13   105
Chapter 14   114
Chapter 15   127
Chapter 16   141
Chapter 17   154

Chapter 18	167
Chapter 19	174
Chapter 20	183
Chapter 21	192
Chapter 22	204
Chapter 23	212
Chapter 24	220
Chapter 25	227
Chapter 26	235
Chapter 27	239
Chapter 28	247
Chapter 29	255
Chapter 30	263
Chapter 31	270
Chapter 32	279
Chapter 33	286
Chapter 34	297
Chapter 35	304
Chapter 36	309
Chapter 37	316
About The Author	321
Praise For Author	323

CHAPTER 1

It was a Monday morning on set with Erin, the show's stylist, when Sam realised that she couldn't speak.

'This gorgeous mini,' Erin had cooed the minute before as she adjusted the sleeves of a model's dress, 'is stunning. Neon green is having a moment. Love the neckline. Love it with chunky heels or trainers. Layer it with this tie skirt and you've got a midi for an everyday look. Love.'

She held up a flat palm in approval as the next model pranced onto the carpet. This was Sam's cue to walk over and comment on the colour or cut, but her mind was in a different place, and she only managed a few steps forwards and a glazed nod.

'Who says because it's beachwear that it can't be an investment buy?' Erin asked the camera. 'Love this jumpsuit. Wide leg so you can move. Take it from the pool to the dance floor. And tie straps make it suitable for different body types. Gorgeous.'

Erin gave a little clap as the final model emerged. 'My fav piece of the collection. Love the signature Ella shape in a new print. Love the little slit – gives it some sass. Such a fab look. And,' she winked at Sam, 'the stretch fabric's great for pregnancy.'

Sam stood still. It felt like she had been submerged in icy water. She knew that she was due to say something. The phrase 'fab look' was her cue to plug her pick of the outfits and send their millions of viewers into a shopping frenzy. But she couldn't.

Silence descended like an invisible mist. She opened her mouth to speak but her heavy tongue wouldn't budge.

Erin raised a tattooed eyebrow, and Keira, the producer, cleared her throat.

'That's fantastic, Erin.' Martin strode over from the sofa. 'You've done an amazing job getting those together. And they're available to buy online now?'

'Absolutely. There's nowhere else you'll need to shop this summer.'

Martin waited a split second for Sam to lead the transition to the next segment. She showed no signs of movement so he seamlessly read her line.

'And now, ladies and gentlemen, from summer outfits to the diets we need to fit into them. Let's give a hearty *Wake Up!* welcome to Graeme Stark, who's going to demonstrate fresh recipes for summer salads.'

The studio's entrance music played, and cameras panned to the kitchen area where a sinewy man was leering over purple cabbages and multi-coloured tomatoes.

'What the fuck, Sam?' Martin hissed. 'You missed your cue.'

It was all she could do to breathe and keep standing. Her body twitched with the adrenaline that pumped through her veins, and her throat felt like it was swelling.

'Welcome, Graeme!' The cameras followed Martin as he paced across the studio. 'Talk us through what you're preparing.'

'Ok, hun?' Erin shuffled over to Sam, hands clasped under her chin. 'Morning sickness kicked in?' she whispered. 'I think it's so *great* you're sharing your story. So many people do IVF these days. It's all over socials.'

Sam felt dizzy. She tried to back up against the wall, but it was further away than she had accounted for.

'Someone did once mention to me freezing my eggs,' Erin went on, smoothing her sleek ponytail, 'but I feel like it'll happen if it happens, you know? And I'm younger than you – plenty of time!'

Sam knew she should take a deep breath, compose herself and join Graeme and Martin in the kitchen to discuss the best way to serve chicory or whatever, but she couldn't. She was hot and thirsty and jittery. Her hands were clenched in a fist as each muscle felt as tightly wound as a compressed spring.

Erin knew. Who had leaked it? Martin? Her agent, Louise? She wouldn't, surely. And, God, she darted her eyes about the room, what would she do now? Deny it? Tell the truth? Turn it into a shallow segment on the show to be um-ed and ah-ed over where people grimaced in pity about how *brave* she was?

A surge of anger burst in her brain, and she charged straight past a blinking Erin and ripped out her earpiece. She stormed across the living and presentation sections of the set, past the dark mess of wires and gormless blinking camera operators and out through a double fire door, letting the heavy metal clang shut behind her.

And there, on a crowded street under the high sun of a London June morning, she screamed.

CHAPTER 2

A handful of ruck-sacked tourists looked up in surprise, but most people just continued on their commutes: nonplussed, eyes down, headphones in – a crazed woman in the city was nothing they'd not seen before.

Sam crossed the street and made a beeline for the river, weaving past the merry-go-round and performers and stands selling tacos and coffee and candy floss and bao buns, until she grasped the wall looking over the water. It rushed beneath her, deep and brown and cold. She took a breath. Her muscles relaxed as she watched the ripples glint in the sun.

She could do this.

Head back to the studio, get miked up and slip back onto the sofa ready for the next segment. Any questions asked and she'd say she had a funny turn.

All was fine now. She was a professional.

So professional that you walked out of a live recording, a voice inside her mocked.

She gave her head a sharp shake and tried to remember the segment up next. Wasn't it an interview with a new reality star? She could cope with that. Of course she could cope with that. She was Sam Elton, the woman who'd once been a coveted young political reporter – nimble, sparky and with an acid-like ability to slice through spin. The woman who, before they'd moved to a morning lifestyle show, had been hounded by producers in the search for a female political presenter to support audience favourite Martin Bailey.

She'd been fearless, jostling to the front of every barrier, raising her hand highest at every press conference, asking the most difficult questions. She'd met every deadline, every word count and was early to every event. On the rare occasions she went out with colleagues, it was to snap up the fresh, unsaid Westminster news slipping from drink-loose tongues. She didn't use her holiday allowance for the first five years of her career and endlessly badgered contacts for a scoop. And rather than it exhaust her, she'd thrived on the thrill.

So she could certainly glide into the studio and smile sympathetically as a 22-year-old made almost entirely of plastic explained the challenges of swanning around in a bikini before being voted off a reality show after a week.

Of course she could. She steeled herself, counting to ten as she watched a packed pleasure boat bob over the water.

But, as she turned to head back, she felt a hand on her arm.

'Oh wow, Sam Elton?' A soft, moon-faced woman beamed at her. 'I'm *such* a fan!'

Sam smiled tightly. She never took her privilege for granted; having a few strangers who cared where you ate, lived, holidayed, dated might be annoying, but it was evidence of success.

'I was *so* inspired to read your story today.' The woman looked straight at her with bright, earnest eyes. 'People just don't talk about it. All those years that everyone thought you were just a career woman. And then to find out that you'd been going through IVF.' She squeezed Sam's arm, which bristled beneath her touch. 'Wow. An inspiration.'

Bile rose in Sam's throat. Her head started to float as if it was detached from her body. This couldn't be right. How could people know?

'When are you due?' The woman opened a gossip magazine website on her phone and held it up for Sam to see.

'This here says a winter baby.' She stared pointedly at Sam's stomach. 'You're not showing yet.'

Sam's mouth almost dropped. There it was in stark letters accompanied by a photo of her and Martin at his sister's wedding a few years ago. It was taken in front of an enormous white flower wall before Martin had insisted on making an impromptu speech and having Sam drag him away from leading his fifth conga on the dance floor. That world of trivial problems felt a lifetime away.

'FINALLY, it's Baby Joy for *Wake Up!* Co-Stars and Couple, Sam Elton and Martin Bailey,' the headline read.

Sam felt like she'd been punched in the stomach.

'Urm,' she stuttered. Things started to spin, the sounds and crowds and smells merging like a zoetrope.

She couldn't go back to the studio. She couldn't see anyone. She didn't have a phone on her or any money.

She dived past the woman and stumbled in her heels towards the other side of the pavement. She would walk back to her and Martin's flat. She would shut the door behind her. And she would climb into bed and never get out.

CHAPTER 3

'Well thank the fucking Lord,' Louise announced as she kicked open Sam's bedroom door a few hours later and threw her white blazer over a chair. 'Look who's here.'

She was stoney-faced, her legs in a wide stance and arms crossed over her large chest. Sam had several times met Louise's mother, who had five children, six noisy grandchildren and a stare more effective than Medusa's. Louise had inherited her expression.

Sam sighed and rolled over. 'Go away,' she mumbled into her pillow.

'Charming. That's what I get after four fucking hours looking for your sorry ass. We can call off the dredging of the Thames.'

Louise had been Sam's first and only agent. The relationship hadn't come easily. They'd met at a networking event where they were simultaneously the youngest and most driven people in the room. Naturally competitive, both were wary of the other slick and confident 23-year-old. But when Sam wanted someone to represent her who knew what it meant to fight to be seen in an industry where you could easily be overlooked, only Louise fit the brief. They'd fought bitterly over the years – about which job to take, which contract to sign – but they'd also become close friends, and there was no one Sam trusted more. But Louise wasn't the ideal person to be there when all she wanted was to wallow in self-pity, a concept that was simply not in her lexicon.

Sam pulled the duvet up closer round her neck. 'I only came home.'

'Yes.' Louise dropped onto the bed, her chunky mules slipping to the floor. 'I noticed. With a load of people saying you'd been staring gloomily at the river and your bag still in your dressing room, we hadn't guessed you'd be tucked up in bed. You really fucking freaked us out.' She paused and let out a deep breath. 'How *did* you get in?'

'Spare in the plant pot.'

'You're joking? In *London*?'

Sam shrugged.

'Jesus.' Louise flopped back, her long curls splayed out around her. 'Well.'

Sam tried to tighten herself into a ball as far away as she could.

Louise sighed. 'Babe, look.' Her voice was quieter. 'I went to the toilet when I got in. I know I should have checked that you were here first, but I was legitimately about to piss myself.' She paused. 'I saw the tests.'

Sam stared blankly at the white wall in front of her. She didn't want to talk about this. Not now, not ever.

'The line's faded, huh? I'm so sorry.'

Sam swallowed back a lump in her throat. She mustn't cry. She wasn't the kind of person who cried.

'I just never even considered the prospect of you miscarrying, you know? After all you'd been through to get there. It's fucking rough.'

'I didn't,' Sam snapped. 'Not really. It was a chemical pregnancy. Doesn't count.' It was what she'd repeated to herself each morning over the past few days as the pink line on the tests became fainter and fainter, and something in her – that silver bullet of hope – faded with them.

'Shit, babe,' Louise rolled onto her side and put her hand

on Sam's shoulder, 'of course it counts.'

The women lay there in silence for a few minutes, neither knowing what to say. Sam focused her attention on clamping her eyes and lips shut, desperate not to allow any tears. Her head throbbed and she pulled her knees closer to her chest.

'Is there anything I can get you?' Louise finally asked. 'Tea? Lunch? An exotic, far-flung holiday?'

'Ibuprofen,' Sam mumbled, holding her temples in one hand. 'In the drawer.'

Louise reached over and took out a packet. She propped herself up on her elbow as something caught her eye. It was a scrawled-on napkin lying on top of a notebook embossed with the phrase '*Be stronger than your excuses.*'

'I remember this.' Louise took it out and opened it up. 'Wasn't this like your life plan before Martin ruined everything?'

'Put it away,' Sam garbled as she swallowed the pills. 'It's nonsense.'

'Oh, come on.' Louise propped herself up and fanned the napkin out. 'This used to mean everything to you. I remember your thirtieth birthday speech when you were buzzing from scoring an interview with the chancellor and you raised a toast to completing Part A. '*If there's one thing I've learnt this decade, it's to never let anyone or anything stand in your way of success.*' Wasn't that what you said? I remember feeling quite inspired.'

Sam pulled the duvet up towards her head and groaned.

'I'm serious,' Louise said.

Sam flipped over and tried to grab the napkin, but Louise twisted the other way.

'Stop.' Sam tried to reach out for it again.

'Uh uh uh,' Louise said and bounced up to standing. 'This is your life plan, Samantha Elton.'

Sam scoffed and dropped back against the leather headboard. 'It doesn't mean anything anymore.'

'I'm not joking,' Louise said. She crossed her legs as she

sat in the armchair in the corner of the room. 'The last few years have been pretty shitty for you.'

'Thanks for the reminder.'

'This might help. Right. Part A,' Louise read slowly and deliberately, tracing each word with her hot pink fingernails. 'Age 21: Trainee TV journalist. Age 24: Political reporter. Age 27: Deputy Political Correspondent.' She looked up, eyebrows raised. 'Tick, tick, tick. And didn't you get political reporter at 23? I seem to remember it was just after we joined forces.'

'Just bin it.'

'Part B. Age 30: Political Correspondent. Age 34: Political Editor. Age 37: *You News* presenter. Between ages 34-40: Journalist of the Year award. I mean, you started this part well. What with *Real News* with Martin. Part C. Age 45: Own show. Ambitious but achievable.'

Sam bit her cheeks. She'd once loved that stupid napkin with its ridiculous career milestones. Ticking them off in her twenties had felt like she'd been winning somehow. Each new job took her closer towards the woman her awkward teenage self had dreamed of becoming: someone with enough money to not care about money and, more importantly, someone who was listened to, respected. She felt like she'd been edging towards some invisible finish line where she'd reach something unknown but inherently worthwhile, the pinnacle of success. Each more senior role was a diamond dangling out of reach. Only when she finally held it in her grasp could she feel satisfied or complete. And she did, for a couple of months – maybe even a year – until her mind would wander to what was next.

But moving to the new show had changed something in her. Leaving the hectic political bubble of policy pledges, by-elections and cabinet changes had left her able to hear a small voice in her brain asking whether she'd considered all she'd forgotten about along the way.

'Louise,' Sam urged, her voice low. 'Not now.'

Louise pretended to carefully reread the napkin, as if

searching for a hidden part. 'Hmm... I don't see anything about presenting vapid background filler with your sellout boyfriend against the advice of your long-suffering agent...'

Wake Up! had been pitched to Sam by Martin's agent after their initial contract with *You News* was up. It was a roster of inane C-list celebrity interviews, cooking shows, competitions and miscellanea, but it also offered a not insignificant amount of cash. Martin was ecstatic; Louise was incredulous. Sam assured her that it was a case of different genre, same career path, a temporary stint before political correspondency, but, three years later, she was still there.

'Look,' Louise sat forward, resting her elbows on her knees, 'you've been put through the wringer. This crappy show is making you famous, but it isn't making you happy. And now you've gone through all this?' She raised an exasperated hand to the ceiling. 'Maybe it's a sign? Telling you it's time to get your life back. It's time to get back to the plan.'

Sam drew in slow, steady breaths. 'No.'

'Really?'

Sam closed her eyes.

'I honestly think it will help.' Louise stood up. 'Look, you walked out of live filming today. If that's not a bloody call for help, I don't know what is. You're not yourself.' She perched on the bed, her face contorted with concern. 'Come on. You've dragged yourself through all this. And for what? Isn't this just Martin's thing? Let's be honest, you never really wanted kids.'

Sam clenched her jaw as she pushed back the covers and sat up, her heart surging into a heavy beat. Love and respect her as she did, she knew that Louise would never understand. She'd grown up in a household stuffed with siblings and aunts and uncles and cousins and noisy garden barbecues and squabbles over the remote. She might have an ordered adult life with daily workouts, carb-free meal plans and an immaculate new build with colour-coordinated candles, but she still visited her mum's south London madhouse for the post-church weekly Sunday lunches on the sitting room floor.

Sam had once gone along and almost had her roast potatoes slide off the plate as countless children tore in and out of furniture and adult legs. She had never had that type of life. She never used to think she wanted it. Spending hours locked in her room, trying to read over the din of her parents arguing in the kitchen and the later silent teenage TV dinners whilst her mother nursed bottles in bed had made her want to escape family ties. But that was then, not now.

'Give me that stupid napkin,' she said.

'Oh, come on.'

'Give it to me.' She tried to reach over and snatch it from Louise's hands.

Louise swept it away from her, like a toreador playing with a bull. 'No,' she protested. 'This is important.'

'Give me the damn napkin.' Sam lunged, tore it from Louise's grasp and threw it to the floor before launching her body back into a ball on the other side of the bed.

'Alright! Bloody hell. What's going on, woman?'

Sam clamped her mouth shut. There was a pause.

'Ok,' Louise said slowly and backed out towards the door. 'You're angry. It's fine. I'll sit in the kitchen. Shout if you need me.'

Sam continued to stare resolutely out the window, fixated on the afternoon air refracting above the grey pavement. She couldn't say anything in reply. Because now, after years of tightly held control, her cheeks were hot with tears.

CHAPTER 4

Louise was right. Kind of. For a long time she hadn't wanted kids, but things had changed.

It had all happened two years ago, after she'd found herself hyperventilating in the gynaecologist's office.

The doctor had leaned towards her. 'Mrs Elton, are you alright?' he said.

For the first time in a decade, she wasn't sure that she was.

But that wasn't what she replied. Instead, as she later found out from Martin, she managed to mutter 'Miss Elton,' before almost collapsing onto the carpet.

Because she'd been given some bad news. But it wasn't the bad news she'd expected.

Though loathe to admit it, Sam had always been a bit in awe of Martin. When she'd joined him on *Real News*, his reputation had been water tight. Confident and shrewd, he shredded the show's political guests before addressing the audience with buttery ease. Sam knew that she'd only been brought on as a token woman to keep the show appearing fresh, but she didn't mind; she was ready to do whatever it took to prove her worth to the producers. What she hadn't anticipated was the attention from Martin. Having such a titan of her professional world ask her out for a drink, and then dinner and then another felt like stepping through the looking glass. She'd liked him, of course, his smooth charisma made it hard not to, but her personal feelings were soon dwarfed by the force of their popularity in the media, something which only grew when they'd moved to *Wake Up!*.

However hard she worked as an individual, she knew that her presenting alone could never compare to their success as a couple. And it came not to matter anyway. They were generally happy, and, most importantly, what they had worked on screen. Neither was interested in marriage – too expensive, too much media attention – and he'd never mentioned a particular interest in kids. They'd had the baby talk in the early days, and he'd nodded along when she explained how it didn't fit into her plan. She'd been naïve enough to assume that was it.

But when he'd offhandedly asked whether they might drop contraception, she'd been too nervous to lose what they had by saying no. She stopped taking the pill, but also stopped initiating sex, something they barely found time for anyway. Coupled with her lack of attention to fertility windows, this meant she hardly expected to get pregnant. She was old and wise enough to know that the school sex-ed-induced fear of getting pregnant from a boy merely looking at you could hardly be further from the truth. Pregnancy in your thirties seemed to require ovulation sticks and thermometers and tracking apps, and she wasn't bothered with any of it.

So despite not having used contraception for almost a year, she and Martin weren't pregnant. She'd secretly hoped the idea might just dissolve into the ether, and when Martin suggested they go for fertility tests, she was more concerned that he wasn't letting go of the baby notion rather than with the results.

This meant she'd been completely and utterly knocked for six by what happened next. When they entered Mr Thomas' room, he'd broken the unexpected news: the reason they weren't pregnant wasn't their timing, but Sam's near total lack of eggs.

And rather than feel as she'd have expected – indifferent – she felt like her world had imploded.

Her problem, she realised, was that she never wanted a baby until she couldn't have one. It wasn't babies themselves that were the problem but the idea of being a mother.

Mothers – good mothers – were selfless. They woke up in the middle of the night to feed a crying mouth, they cooed and cuddled, tracked naps and teeth, compared cots and prams and car seats, and became interested in baby massage and breast pumps. Mothers took maternity leave then only returned part time. They had to find nurseries or nannies and leave meetings early to do pick up. And – from what Sam could tell – while mothers spent hours talking to other mothers about said cots and prams and breast pumps at coffee shops or swimming lessons or baby sensory classes, they lost control of their own life. And they certainly lost control of their career.

It wasn't a sacrifice she'd been prepared to make. Her own mother, who between moaning about how Sam had ruined her fledgling artistic prospects slurred expletives about her father's latest 'slut', had not exactly been inspiring.

And it was at her funeral, when Sam's teenage anger at the inevitable conclusion of the five year post-divorce vodka binge was still fresh, that she made herself a promise. She resolved, with knife-sharp certainty, never to lose her grip on her professional self. And it was at the reception to that funeral that she'd scribbled on a napkin her plan.

But then came the visit to Mr Thomas.

Something changed from that moment. She'd gone from not particularly wanting children to not having the choice available to her if she changed her mind. As she stepped out of his office and into the reception, a niggling thought started as to whether she *did* actually want a baby – just one – and a full-time nanny at home whilst she continued her professional drive. Being a mother might achieve the holy grail of what endless directors and producers had called 'softening her image.' *Less dragon lady, more wholesome-have-it-all*, Louise had once snorted in derision. Then on the journey home she had wondered whether she might just get an au pair and have the baby come with her on set, tucked behind the wall of cameras for quick kisses in filming breaks. Once they'd reached the entrance to the flat, she wondered whether she might actually want proper maternity leave after all, time spent in mother and baby groups, sling walks along the river and baby yoga classes with women who were content to ignore the turmoil of modern life and live besotted with their babbling offspring. And by the time she got into bed that night, the switch had flicked.

Months of *actually* trying went by. A general election passed, which she largely blinked and missed. Martin started to worry that it was taking their focus away from the show. He dropped a few comments about whether it actually might be worth them moving on, putting the prospect of a baby behind them.

But Sam was hooked. The whole idea had spilled through her being, like ink in water, until nothing else was visible. Every working day, every day off, every catch up with friends, every evening with Martin, every morning run, every Valentine's, Easter, Mother's Day, Halloween and Christmas took place against a backdrop of failure to get pregnant.

She had her 12th negative test, acupuncture, vitamins, stimulating pills, a 15th negative test, another blood test, more follicle scans, a fifth blood test, a 24th negative test. And, finally, IVF.

The media swirled around grumbles of a vote of no confidence. There was a new chancellor, a disastrous budget, a leader of the opposition biting at the bit. A political life which she was no longer a part of floated past, unnoticed.

And then, when she eventually felt like her mind and body had been peeled away from her skin and wrung out to dry, came blinking in amazement: a double pink line the week after their first transfer, any ambition for her own show with a bright, clean studio, needle sharp questions, and roster of powerful political figures evaporated into mist.

And now, as Sam wiped her eyes and reached down to pick up the napkin from the floor, it was only to rip it to shreds.

CHAPTER 5

As her fingers tore through the tissue, destroying decades of imagined life, Sam tried to pinpoint how the news could have been leaked.

Could someone have seen them going in and out of the clinic? But, if so, why no paparazzi? Where was the accompanying tabloid article detailing her 'fresh-faced, casual look' (aka 'death warmed up in a tracksuit with a food stain')?

And how had someone gotten hold of that photo? It was from Martin's sister Issa's wedding gallery. Unless…she shook her head. Surely not.

She sat back in the bed and closed her eyes, trying to remember the exact details from the event of the previous week. On Saturday, despite it possibly being the very last thing that she'd wanted to do during her post-transfer two week wait, Martin had pleaded with her to attend Issa's Baby Shower No.4.

She had been reluctant – to say the least. It was taking all her mental strength not to obsess over the tiny possibility of a baby inside of her, let alone cope with happily congratulating someone else. Plus she'd been due to spend the day with Louise to 'distract' her from the endless waiting with A Fun Day Out, and the shower only left them time for breakfast.

'Lord,' Louise rolled her eyes as she squeezed maple

syrup onto a waffle, 'didn't she just have the last one?'

Sam gave a curt nod. She didn't like to remember it.

For Baby Shower No.3, Issa had hired the rooftop pool area of a celebrity-soaked London members' club. The pool was edged by giant pink balloons and dotted with floating flower arrangements and shell-shaped inflatables. On these lounged Issa and various other pregnant friends in matching white bikinis that showed off their elegant bumps, primed for the many photos that Issa would post on her popular social media channels.

Sam had been a week away from her first IVF egg collection procedure. Her stomach and legs were purple from injection bruises, and she'd felt like she'd been punched in the ovaries. The entire afternoon had been a hellish nightmare of fizzy, pink mocktails and what Louise called jellyfish conversation, when you end up trapped in tentacles of comments and questions, each designed to sound sweet but deliver a separate sting. Issa herself had been a grand Portuguese man-of-war, introducing her to hordes of kaftan-covered mums with effortlessly tousled hair as *such* an impressive career woman, putting in *all* that hard work for herself instead of *flitting* away time on starting a family.

Sam had wanted to pierce Issa with a cocktail umbrella and scream that she'd been bloody trying to start a family for twelve awful months and that not everyone can be some fertile moon goddess who gets pregnant as soon as a man so much as looks at her vagina. But, with saint-like control, she didn't.

Instead she crunched on the ice from her drink and plastered her face with her best everything-is-totally-perfect smile, usually reserved for particularly awkward celebrity interviews. The worst had been when Martin had been given the wrong prep notes and mistook a recently highly decorated Olympian with a woman who was due to share tips on caring for houseplants. He'd kept pushing on whether to spray or feed from the bottom until the Olympian had walked out. As ever, Sam had kept smiling.

'What solipsistic nonsense has she dreamed up this time?' Louise said as she slurped her orange juice. 'Arriving on a cloud flown in by trained stalks?'

'Probably.' Sam felt queasy at the thought. 'I told Martin that I didn't fancy going and he looked at me like I'd just shot a puppy. Said she'd be devastated to not have me there.'

'Huh? Surely he knows that his sister treats you like a social pariah? I mean, no offence or anything.'

'Apparently not.' Sam closed her cutlery over her slimy half-eaten cold poached egg. She wasn't sure if she was just being paranoid after the transfer, but it smelt a little funny.

'Hang on.' Louise cocked an eyebrow. 'Let me get this right. Is this the same sister who blocked you from being in the family Christmas photo because your 'energy' was off? If not, fine. Otherwise I'm not buying it.'

'The very one. Apparently Issa might help me 'cope better' with my own pregnancy. That I might find her 'inspiring'.'

'Inspiring?' Louise barked. 'Piss off.'

Sam slid the invitation across the table.

'An intimate affair in our brand-new bucolic countryside home,' Louise read in her best plummy voice. She snorted. 'I hope they knew before they moved that the Cotswolds are more London suburb than peasants tending sheep. You can't go. It'll be like being trapped in a girls' boarding school where they only talk about how many horses they have and boys they'd like to snog. Except it'll be how many babies they have and new kitchens they'd like to put in.'

'I have to. Martin made me promise.'

'So fuck him. Simple.'

Sam scrunched her mouth. 'He and Issa are really close.'

'Ugh.' Louise mimed throwing up. 'Can you tell Keira I've got a pitch for a new show segment: *Help! My partner's family are arseholes.*'

'Perhaps I can pour her beautiful, wonderful, inspiring pregnant lady vibes into my body.'

Louise dropped her fork onto her plate in protest.

'Seriously though – maybe being around other pregnant people will be good for embryo implantation or something,' Sam said.

'I'm pretty sure that's *not* how things work.'

'Well I'll give anything a go.'

But, as she crossed her legs in the taxi from Charlbury station that afternoon and toyed with the scalloped edge of the invitation, she couldn't help wishing that her invite has been saved for one of Issa's south-west London mother friends instead.

The taxi had slowed down and veered onto a gravel drive. Sam looked out to see a colonnade of ancient oaks standing resplendent amidst a river of bluebells.

The car turned a corner, and its tires crunched against the golden pebbles. Thick greenery gave way to an enormous open field to the left and an avenue of coiffed topiary lollipop trees on the right. As they rounded one last curve, she had to stop herself from letting out a gasp - whether of shock or envy she wasn't sure. A huge Cotswold stone house had come into view, its layers of windows glittering in the early June sun and reflecting into rainbows on the windscreens of the tens of black Range Rovers and green Jeeps lining the drive. Issa had sighed to Martin on the phone that Clive, her lawyer partner husband, had found this near dilapidated *cottage* that needed *stacks* of work done to it, but it was at least *quite* charming in its own way and it really was almost *immoral* to keep the children in London now that Clive could work two days a week from home and they were keeping the Notting Hill house anyway so *thank goodness* she'd be able to pop up back to civilisation whenever she liked.

It wasn't that Sam herself wanted a country pile (London was and always would be home) but she'd flinched at the family life it represented. She and Martin lived in a converted warehouse flat overlooking a canal bordered by murals of graffiti and Australian coffee shops. It was sizeable but far from homely, done up to his taste in exposed brick, leather and industrial fittings since it had been his flat before they'd met. She'd never got round to buying her own place; before Martin, it had always made more sense to rent neat studio flats near Westminster. Their small size and soulless interiors paled in importance to her proximity to work.

The view in front of her now was less of an actual house and more of a Disneyfied representation of the English family countryside dream. A row of wellies lined the front of the building which looked out onto a lavender lined path leading up to a raised pond with a fountain in the middle of a freshly striped lawn. Beyond this lay a gently flowing stream and a stone wall separating a field of sheep. She'd seen it all before, of course, the outlook was the background to the many photos of Issa's almost white-haired flock of photogenic children plastered all over her social media feeds.

Birds chirruped out of a bright explosion of wisteria that framed the house's front door, which was held open by a young man in a linen shirt and chinos two sizes too tight, black hair tied in a top knot and thumbs tucked loosely into his belt loops. She recognised him as Tino, Issa's butler, though Issa would apparently rather die than refer to him as such; instead he was just Tino – 'such a great help' – as if he traipsed around carrying out Issa's every non-child-based whim (Noemi the nanny dealt with that field) as a favour rather than for his quite impressive salary.

'Signorina Elton,' Tino purred as the car came to a stop and he held out a hand to help her onto the drive. 'A pleasure,' he curled his lips slightly, 'as always.' He squeezed her hand and held her gaze. The first time Sam had met Tino she had been a little shocked at the intensity of his flirting and turned a stark shade of pink. After shaking herself out of the ridiculous idea that he'd fallen in love with her at first sight, she'd wondered if Issa had set him up to lure her into a compromising trap which would somehow end her relationship with Martin. But, with time, she'd realised that Tino treated every woman like an unspeakably delicious dessert and that it was probably why Issa had hired him in the first place. How Clive put up with it Sam would never know, but she supposed his presence kept Issa sweet.

'It's wonderful to have you here,' Tino drawled as he picked up a small cold towel from a silver tray on a table behind him. 'Please,' he pressed it to her, 'for your... refreshment.'

She smiled politely and dabbed her hands and neck. She had to hand it to Issa, having a man around who acted like he wanted to eat you for dessert no doubt added to the excitement of countryside life.

'Please now come with me to the back garden, Signorina Elton,' Tino added with a raised eyebrow. 'Signora Issa will join you there shortly.'

'Thank you,' she said quickly and glanced inside, relieved to be able to break his gaze. 'But don't worry, Tino.' She placed the towel on the tray and stepped over the threshold. 'I'll find my own way.'

Sam scurried through the flagstone hall, peeking into the offshoot rooms. Everything was already decorated in what Issa called her 'signature style', white and off-white walls and furniture, rustic wood, heavy metal lighting, an abundance of wicker, enormous candles and oversized vases filled with stylish plants, such as eucalyptus leaves, pampas grass or, what looked like to Sam, old sticks. She couldn't deny that, for all Issa's faults, how she kept a house looking like it had jumped straight out of Elle Decor when she had three children really was quite impressive. She hoped they had a room to themselves to cover in glitter, lurid toys and sticky handprints.

As she headed for the back of the house, the murmur of glossy women and acoustic guitar wafted towards her. On the side of a large living room, filled only with a white sofa and a gnarled piece of driftwood hanging from the ceiling, black metal bifold doors opened onto a patio at the top of a gentle hill, views of undulating fields spread out beneath. She noticed a young female guitarist strumming gently under a pergola on the corner of the crowd of women, each of whom were curled elegantly on sun loungers as young men circulated with trays of mocktails and untouched canapés.

Issa was nowhere to be seen, so Sam stood awkwardly in a corner as snippets of conversation danced in the mild air.

'Luna simply adores her prep school. But of course the fees are astronomical…'

'We're getting an architect in next week to talk through the new extension…'

'Umbria's booked for August, but we're going to sneak in a last-minute trip to Tamsin's villa.'

'Elliot always wanted a third, but I just don't think I can do the baby stage again.'

As with Issa's other parties, this was clearly not Sam's crowd.

It always amazed her just how many people Issa knew. She'd only ever worked for six months at an interior design firm ten years ago, so none of them were colleagues. Perhaps, Sam wondered, she had just invited every mum from her children's school, announcing it through the PTFA WhatsApp. Or maybe she'd just gone into every local organic deli supermarket and tossed an invite into each woven basket. Surely all Issa's social media followers weren't people she actually knew? Sam had struggled to scrape together a table-worth of friends for her last birthday. The early morning starts had made joining the few girlfriends she did have for evening drinks far from appealing. And, she couldn't kid herself, she'd made less and less effort as the fertility struggles wore on.

Having to listen to friends' endless conception advice on the need to just relax or put her legs up after sex or 'forget about it and it'll happen', she'd one day decided just to shut off. She no longer wanted to go through life listening to people who forgot that infertility is a medical diagnosis, rather than a state of mind, and so stopped opening up about her life. Apart from Louise, who was more like a vital limb than just a friend or colleague, the only non-work person she couldn't ignore was Issa. With Martin having lost his mother soon after starting at *Wake Up!* – one of the things that bonded the two of them in the early days – Sam couldn't bring herself to tell him that his remaining female relative, his beloved older sister, was a grade A pain in the arse.

'Sam, sweetie,' a voice called. Issa's best friend, Nina, swanned through the crowd in a silk pyjama-style suit and pointy black mules. She was so tall and thin that she simply glided through the mass of people like Moses parting the red sea. 'So clever of you to make it when you're no doubt so busy with work.'

Sam's stiff smile reflected in Nina's oversized tortoiseshell sunglasses. Martin and Nina had been 'a thing' in their teenage years, and Nina had a way of noting details to show just how well she knew him. Even after five years together, it still made Sam feel like a new addition to his life.

'And how's Marley?' Nina plucked a drink from a nearby waiter. 'I hear he's mind-numbingly bored by the recent segments on the show.'

That was tentacle one. Sam drew in a slow breath. She'd be the first to admit that she rolled her eyes at the more mundane (or insane) stories they covered – the ranking of laundry detergents, social media scam stories or people who believed they'd married aliens, dishwashers or trees. It wasn't exactly prime minister's questions. But her and Martin's camaraderie made it fun, and he spoke about the show as if it would run forever.

'I'm sure the items are just *thrust* upon you, and it must be *so* frustrating that there isn't anything more...,' Nina took a sip from her drink, 'interesting.'

That was tentacle two. Nina was one of Issa's few friends with an actual job in an actual office: fashion editor for *Dark White*, an achingly cool fashion magazine – the kind stuffed with double page spreads of models lying on the floor in head-to-toe black lycra or posing amidst rubble in couture tulle. Sam didn't imagine that the magazine actually sold many copies, but it gave Nina access to every launch party and fashion show in the country – not to mention licence to judge what should be deemed worthy of attention by those in the know.

Sam raised her chin. 'The thing is,' she tried to sound nonchalant, 'the show's audience is so large these days. We need mass appeal. And we have plenty of fresh and exciting segments.' Despite years of reducing powerful people to puddles, speaking with Nina made Sam feel about twelve years old. She tried to conceal her awkwardness by nabbing a chicken and bruschetta canapé, but it was too large to fit in her mouth in one. A spurt of tomato juice dribbled onto her top.

Nina curved her plump lips. 'I don't watch the show *myself*, but I did hear that you'd recently done a segment on a man who ate, I believe, an armchair? And, forgive me if I heard this incorrectly, on meeting Britain's best-looking cow?' She narrowed her eyes. 'Are these some of the *fresh and exciting* segments?'

Sam flushed. She couldn't exactly tell Nina about last week's meeting with a woman who gave advice on how to tidy your pantry. Nothing came to mind except... She cleared throat, 'There's something in the works called,' she swallowed, '*Help! My partner's family are arseholes.* People will call in to share their stories for a celebrity guest to give advice...,' she trailed off and looked to the floor. Nina's shoes really were pointy.

'Hah!' Nina barked. 'I like it. The brainchild of the new producer, hmm? Keira, is it? Martin mentioned she was bringing a different energy.'

Sam looked up. Was she? She hadn't paid much attention to Keira; things seemed to be ticking along as usual since she joined three months ago. It certainly wasn't something she and Martin had talked about. But, she had to admit, for the last few months they'd pretty much only talked about the IVF.

'Anyway, darling,' Nina disposed of her drink on a passing tray. 'It won't be for long. All change after the summer I hear. Younger direction and all that.' She gave a knowing look.

Sam tried not to look surprised. *All change? Younger direction?* The point of the contract renewal had been stability, continuation with what worked. She knew she wasn't hot on updating social media, leaving her pages to be managed by the show's assistant. Was this now a problem? Or had Nina meant her pregnancy? That would create a younger direction – about 55 years younger than their average watcher – but how could she know about that?

'Oh look, darling, Issa's finally here!' Nina said.

The guitarist broke into a breathy rendition of *Here Comes the Sun*, and Sam heard a collective gasp as the women started standing and pointing out across the fields.

She peered out, her eyes following Nina's finger. She blinked. It couldn't be. Rapidly moving towards them was a large blue and white hot air balloon containing Issa waving down like the Pope from his balcony. Sam couldn't help letting out a small laugh. If only Louise could be there to see it.

Murmurs of excitement spread through the dewy-eyed party as Issa glided closer towards what was now a stream of phones glistening in the sun, sharing her arrival live on tens of social media channels.

Sam bit her lip to save herself from scoffing.

As Issa started her descent to the field below the patio, the waiters marched in choreographed precision, breaking off into equally spaced rows to form a neat aisle. Issa dropped down, and they each lifted single stems of blue hydrangeas, forming a delicate floral arch up to the patio steps. Tino, Sam noticed, was there ready to help Issa make an elegant exit from the basket. The crowd of onlookers burst into applause as Issa floated barefoot under the arch towards them in a pale blue silk gown draped softly over her rounded belly like water. Clutching the front of the dress, with only a hint of blusher, no mascara on her white blonde eyelashes and her hair in a long fishtail plait, she looked like a mythological river nymph drifting through a wood in spring.

Sam felt the urge to vomit. As the crowd surged forwards

to where Issa was walking up the steps with both hands now cupping her stomach, she lurched into the house and rushed towards what looked like a kitchen where she retched into a white marble sink. Frowning, she stood clasping the side with her head flopped down. It was too early for morning sickness; she knew that egg had been dodgy.

Her reflection was visible in the mirrored backsplash. The bags under her eyes were a deep purple and her skin was tinged with grey. She'd been so desperate to have the IVF transfer, she hadn't considered how hard the wait afterwards might be.

She couldn't stay at the baby shower all day; Louise had been right. She'd show her face to Issa – let her know that she'd been there – and then slip out without anyone noticing.

Steeling herself, she headed back to the patio where Issa was standing at the top of the stairs and posing with her bump for photos. Sneaking behind a group of three women in near identical white puffed sleeve midi dresses, she hoped to catch Issa as soon as she entered the crowd. The women chattered and cooed about how fabulous the house was – even if the upkeep of the grounds would be a nightmare, how gorgeous the Cotswolds are – even if they're rather busy these days, and how stunningly happy Issa looked – even (the woman in the puffiest sleeved dress added in hushed tones) if the rumours were true. Sam twisted her head towards them, waiting for further explanation, but Issa chose that moment to glide towards them, silk dress pooling at her feet.

'Darlings,' she air kissed the trio, 'what a blessing to see you.' She put her hands into prayer position and smiled beatifically. Sam wasn't quick enough to suppress a small snort.

Issa swept over. 'How wonderful you could make it, Samantha.' She pulled her into a limp hug before standing with her hands on her shoulders, her face twisted into a near parody of concern. 'Are you,' she paused as if looking for the right word, '*okay*? Martin mentioned that you're very tense.'

She prodded some muscles near Sam's neck. 'Have you been working too hard? Not giving yourself time for,' she blinked, 'the *important* things in life?'

Sam flicked her eyes around the crowd. It wouldn't take much for someone to film without her seeing or even just take a quick snap and send it into the tabloids. Headline: 'Concerned sister-in-law stages intervention for burnt out *Wake Up!* star.'

'I'm fine.'

'Really? You don't look fine.'

Sam pursed her lips.

'I know that you and Martin work the same hours, but are you coping? It can be harder for women.' Issa looked around and dropped her voice to a whisper. 'Have you thought about the impact of stress on other *things*...?'

Sam ducked out of her grasp. 'Honestly. Never better.' She swallowed back the bile in her throat.

She had to get out of there. She wasn't exactly going to tell Issa that the past year had been like being smothered in gas, with nothing inside of her except a desire to be pregnant. How it was in every breath in and every breath out. How it felt like her life had revolved around her monthly cycle for so long – whether she was waiting to ovulate, ovulating, in the two-week wait or mourning another single line, that she felt detached from anything or anyone else. How she had been like a mad gambler in search of a hit, testing for days every month, spending hours interpreting indent lines under her phone light, wishing for something she couldn't see.

And she certainly wasn't going to explain how now that elusive line had finally appeared at five days post transfer – faint but unmistakable – with Martin acting like the baby was a sure deal, already asking whether they might sell a pregnancy reveal to a gossip magazine – that she wasn't only ecstatically happy, but terrified. How the prospect of so much riding on the next few days, with none of it in her control, was almost suffocating.

Issa shuffled towards her, her brow furrowed in an

exaggerated show of concern. 'But I *do* worry.' She took her hand and placed it on her belly. 'Don't you want this?' Her muted voice took on a slight edge. 'I'm sure Martin would love a family.'

The words darted through Sam like a barb. She snatched herself backwards, a surge of anger and nausea bolting through her stomach.

'Oh,' Issa raised her fingers to her cheeks. 'Silly me. Are you,' she paused and dropped her voice to a whisper, 'trying? *Don't worry*, I have a fantastic book of diet recommendations and my fabulous friend, Zor, who does pre-pregnancy hypnotherapy. She's here in fact. Let me just –' She craned her neck.

'No. Thank you, but no.'

'I think she's standing –'

Sam forcibly shook her head and put out a hand in front of her. Nausea sat high in her chest.

The women standing closest to them looked around at the whiff of commotion.

'Trust me. Tamara was dismissed as totally barren by her clinic and then she did five sessions with Zor and is having twins.'

'Issa,' Sam hissed. 'Drop it.'

Issa looked back at her and clasped her hands in front of her heart. 'Let me help. If you're having problems, it's probably due to stress.'

'No need. Congrats on the pregnancy.' Sam took a deep breath as she turned. She needed to leave.

Issa grabbed her arm again, her voice low and sharp. 'Don't you think Martin at least deserves for you to give it your best shot?'

Sam swung back round. Heart racing, cheeks flushed, mouth dry. Her best shot? Yes, he was the one who'd first brought it up and Martin did still vaguely want a family – in the way that most people think it sounds like a generally pleasant idea – but *she'd* been the one who'd sacrificed so much of her body, her emotions, her hormones, her time. She'd give up a limb to stay pregnant at this point. In the same way that her work had consumed her in her twenties, getting pregnant and staying pregnant was now all she felt she lived for. She opened her mouth to say as much when the surge of nausea billowed up her chest. She glanced left and right for a bin, a flowerpot – any appropriate vessel – but instead only managed to stumble forwards, hands on her knees, as her throat lurched, and she threw up over the glass of the bifold door.

There was an intake of breath from the trio of women, enthralled by the whiff of drama.

'Sorry,' Sam croaked, 'I'll help clean the –'

'Wait.' Issa put her hands on her hips, a smug half smile curving on her lips. 'You're not drunk.' She paused. 'Are you?'

Sam shook her head as she stood up and wiped her mouth.

Issa almost quivered in excitement. 'Are you...?'

Sam looked at her expressionless, focusing on keeping everything else down and suppressing the urge to run straight to the sink to wash herself in cold water.

'Oh my God!' Issa squealed. The crowd of women now gathered closer, desperate not to miss anything they could relay later. 'You are! Oh my God!'

'No,' Sam snapped, louder than she'd intended. 'It must be food poisoning.'

Her throat felt tight. It didn't feel like a good sign. Sickness couldn't be good for implantation.

'I understand if you want to keep things quiet. Though I'm surprised Martin didn't at least let *me* know.' Issa pouted.

'I had a bad egg for breakfast,' said Sam in a measured tone that hid her rising distress.

'Sure.' Issa winked.

'Seriously.'

'How many weeks? I was sick with Ottilie from around week six. Nothing major, no throwing up on people's houses.'

'I'm sorry. I'll clean it up. But, please, I'm not –'

'I did *suspect* you were looking a bit bigger, you know. Too early for a bump I'm guessing, but a bit of bloating?'

Sam looked around in frustration. There was only one way out of this. 'My taxi's due any moment. I need to get going.'

'You can't *leave*. I want to celebrate!' Issa stepped forwards to place both hands on Sam's stomach, but Sam jerked backwards, stepping through an opening in the bifold door.

'Have a nice day, Issa.'

'There's no need to hide it. I'm here for you.'

Hands clenched into tight, awkward fists, Sam walked straight forwards, not stopping as she passed the artistic twigs or neat layers of baby shower goody bags. It was too early to share any news. Far too early – not that she wanted Issa to be the first person who found out. And the food poisoning now felt horribly ominous. What if it dislodged things? Was that even possible? The thought made her want to cry.

Flustered, she walked straight out the front door without looking back, stopping only to dab her damp forehead with a towel from the tray Tino must have discarded, before pacing down the drive.

So now, a week later, as Sam tore into the last corners of tissue, she could only imagine what had been said as she had waited cross-armed and teeth gritted on the gravel for a taxi. Perhaps someone had overheard. Perhaps Issa had whispered 'Definitely pregnant' to a friend standing nearby. Or perhaps she had gathered in the crowd, including that woman who used society parties to gather insalubrious tabloid stories (usually invoking minor royals), and shouted out, 'Fantastic news, everyone, I'm *finally* going to be an auntie!'

She might never know. But what she did know was that right now – with the faded tests in the bathroom and the story swirling and growing online – it was the first time in her life that she truly felt like she couldn't cope.

CHAPTER 6

Martin was furious. He'd smoothed over Sam's outburst by saying to the camera that she was prepping for a surprise segment later, but then she hadn't come back – leaving his explanation hanging in the air like a cloud threatening to break. It had left him distracted during Graeme's salad segment and he'd dropped a lettuce on the floor before improvising boring questions to the reality star about the cookbook she was promoting rather than extracting any meaningful gossip. It hadn't been as bad as the Olympian plant saga – Keira assured him that most viewers probably wouldn't notice – but it wasn't the polished operation he took such pride in.

'How many times do I have to say?' he boomed as he threw open the bedroom door. 'You are not fit to be in work.'

Sam wiped away the tears she'd been letting fall as she'd been lying still in bed.

'You're not currently *capable* of live filming. It's *ridiculous* for you to be so stubborn. Insisting that you won't take any time off and then bloody walking out the set. Erin was terrified – thought she'd done something really wrong.'

Sam crossed her arms and stared straight ahead. She knew he wouldn't understand. Ultimately, the show would always come first for Martin – as it had once for her. It was why they'd always worked as a couple in the past. For him, a baby was supposed to be a nice side addition, not an interference in his professional life.

'For God's sake,' he sighed as he sat down next to her and pressed his temples. 'I should have told the producers myself that you couldn't cope with the show anymore. Took it on with me alone. Then we wouldn't be in this fucking mess.'

Sam's eyes flicked over to see Louise filling the doorway. With her neon oversized T-shirt tucked into leather trousers and be-ringed hands placed firmly on her hips, she was hard to miss.

'But you couldn't have done that, Martin,' Louise said. 'Because that would have been illegal. *You* don't determine Sam's contracts. I do.'

Martin rolled his eyes. 'Louise, what are you doing here? This is a private conversation. It doesn't involve you.'

'From where I'm standing, it sounds like you were discussing Sam's professional life, which very much *does* involve me.'

'Oh, piss off.' He batted a hand in her direction.

'No,' she smiled tightly. 'Thank you for the offer, but I don't think I will.'

'For God's sake,' he said as he stood, only just matching Louise's height in her square-toed heels. 'Leave us, will you? I'm here to talk to my girlfriend about her health.'

'And I'm here to look after my *client*, who has no intention of stepping back from her lucrative career.'

Martin clenched his jaw as he took a slow step forward. 'Look,' he said darkly. 'This isn't fucking working. She clearly can't work at the moment. We can't risk this happening on set again.'

'Oh, come off it,' Louise said, pointing a finger out in front of her. 'Sam isn't an amateur. She's not a *risk*. Today was a one off. She was never meant to be some meek housewife who waits at home with her screaming kids for her big shot presenter husband to return. Sam Elton was meant to be the country's most successful female political broadcaster.'

'Louise,' Sam said, but neither of them seemed to remember she was in the room.

'And,' Louise stepped even closer to Martin, 'you'll be pleased to know – she *won't* be working as your little sidekick on that bland daytime filler show anymore. Because I've found her a new role. Politics, current affairs – things she's actually interested in.' Louise turned towards Sam, her eyes flashing. 'It's *You News*. They're dead keen. Willing to match current salary. I was going to tell you earlier, but –'

Martin emitted a low, guttural growl and hit the wall with the side of his fist.

The noise landed between them all like a thrown dagger.

Louise caught Sam's eye as Martin quickly covered his face with his hand.

'Shit. Sorry.' He paced back and forth across the room and then sat back again on the bed. Louise crossed her arms and stepped forwards. 'You can't be serious, Sammy,' he added quietly. 'You cannot truly think that *I'm* the one who wanted all this? If we can have a kid, great. But I don't think you can cope with doing work and putting yourself through the treatment. It's messing you up. You need to choose. One or the other. You can't do both anymore. *I* can't have you doing both anymore.'

Sam's mouth went dry. It was true. She couldn't go on as she was. She could hardly find the thoughts – let alone the words – to explain her grief. She'd never had a bump, never had a baby kick, never seen any evidence of its existence other than those faint tests piled in the bathroom. It was a loss of something she'd never had, but it was such a loss. She'd put everything into the process, and she couldn't just try and carry on as if it hadn't happened.

Ever since they'd started trying – properly trying after the tests – she had started to imagine a new life in her head. Before Martin, before *WakeUp!*, things had always been so clear. She'd follow the plan. She'd thrive off ticking off those goals, edging her way to ultimate professional success. She'd show that a short, slightly dumpy woman from Croydon could rip politicians' heads off and serve their brains for breakfast.

But then – as she hit her early thirties – that imagined life started slowly to change. Her social media feeds morphed from round-the-clock news channels and friends posting about travelling and galleries to maternity shoots and babies gurgling in pumpkin farms and Santa grottos and sensory classes. It all looked so benign – so *boring* even. She'd blocked and deleted until the visit to Mr Thomas. A couple of years ago she would have slapped herself for being so ridiculous. But now the loss of these new imagined lives left her feeling entirely empty, like a bath with the water drained out.

So she was at a crossroads. There was still the glimmer of possibility of her newly imagined life. But it perhaps meant more pain, more punishment when it already hurt so much. Or there was the chance to take on a job she'd always thought she'd love. Perhaps Louise was right. It was the chance for her to build up Part B over again.

She clamped her eyes and mouth shut. She simply didn't know what to say.

'Come on,' Martin repeated in a low voice. 'First Nina tells me that you're pitching a segment for the show on why your boyfriend's family are arseholes and now this. What the hell's going on?'

'Ha,' Louise barked. 'Now that's really not what it sounds like.'

'Good,' Martin said, his voice louder again. 'Because it sounds like she's fucking lost it.'

He crossed to the other side of the room and sat down heavily in the armchair, his legs spread wide and hands clasped between his knees.

'Look.' He put his hands out in front of him. 'The producers can sign you off immediately. Erin can take your place in the short term, and we can re-launch as a one-man lead after the summer. There's really no need for you to put yourself through the stress of coming back. We can do another transfer. If that's what you want. Issa can set up a meeting with you and her nutritionist friend. You don't need to come back to work. We can do the show without you.'

Louise snorted. 'And what about her career? Sam, yes *do* leave that syrupy sweet of a show but come and join the serious stuff. Show the world what you can offer. You don't need kids to make you whole.'

Martin held up a palm to stop her. 'Jesus, woman. Can you just stop?'

Louise reared her head. 'Don't you 'woman' me–'

'Oh come on,' Martin scoffed. 'Sam can hardly breathe without you speaking over her.'

'And it seems she's only *allowed* to breathe when you give her permission.' Louise stood firmly in the middle of the room, her glinting fingers holding onto her hips.

A sharp blade of adrenaline pierced Sam's chest. The atmosphere turned so strained that she could almost taste it.

She sat up slightly. Both Martin and Louise turned straight to her. 'I… don't know if I can do another transfer right now,' she said, focusing on the floor.

'See.' Louise clicked her fingers. 'What did I tell you?'

'Shut up,' Martin snapped.

'But,' Sam hesitated, 'I don't know if I don't *want* to. In the future. And I don't know if I want to take on a new job.'

Martin released a breath like air escaping an inflatable mattress.

Sam closed her eyes. 'I don't know what I want. I think I need a break to find out.'

CHAPTER 7

Louise tapped on the door. 'Morning, gorgeous,' she whispered. 'Fancy breakfast?' She saw what Sam had seen in the mirror earlier: her gaunt face, pale and hollowed with dark circles under puffy washed-out eyes. 'Ok, I take back the gorgeous bit. You need to eat.'

Sam groaned. 'Where's Martin?'

Louise went to open the curtains. 'He left after you'd fallen asleep. He wanted to give you some space.'

Space? Sam wanted a bit of time to think about things, but she hadn't considered the prospect of him not being there as her soundboard.

'Why?'

'So you can have your break, of course. You can take a couple of days off – maybe even a week – before we get in contact with *You News* to get the ball rolling. No harm in them thinking you're considering other offers.'

'Where's he staying?'

'With Issa.'

The idea of Martin staying with Issa, listening to her advice and wining and dining with the likes of Nina hit Sam like a slap in the face. 'No.' She sat upright. 'He should be here.'

Louise handed her a dressing gown and they headed towards the kitchen. 'I actually think a bit of distance between the two of you is a good thing.'

Sam hadn't thought they'd needed distance. She'd imagined they'd have long evenings looking over options together, firstly working out who'd leaked the story before quashing it, and then planning together if/how/when they'd go about another transfer whilst weighing up the pros and cons of her taking the new job. There was a lot to decide, and she hadn't considered them not doing it together. The last thing she wanted was to spend lonely days and nights in the flat with only the awful online stories for company whilst Martin was infected with Issa's insidious vitriol about her inability to provide him with a family.

'I don't want him staying there.'

'Fine.' Louise opened a packet of bread. 'Come and stay at mine. He can stay here, and I can keep an eye on you. A couple of days apart will help you see things straight.'

Sam perched on one of the kitchen island bar stools and looked out at the blue summer sky beyond the bars of the window. Perhaps Louise was right: she needed Martin to stay in the flat, keeping things as normal until she was ready to re-enter their life. But she didn't just want to shack up at Louise's flat for the weekend. She needed actual, sustained time and space to think. 'I need more than just a couple of days.'

'No problem,' Louise said. 'Take a week. Take a fortnight. *You News* will wait for you. They're dead keen.'

Sam shook her head as the thought came to her. 'No. I want the summer off. A month.'

'A *month*?' Louise whipped round. 'What on earth for?'

Sam twisted a tea towel in her hands. 'To recalibrate. To work out what I want. To find my old self again.'

'You're not serious? You know what Martin said was total crap. You've gone through shit, but you're still you.'

'Am I?'

'*Yes*! Louise peeled slices of bacon from a packet into the pan. 'Look, if it's about the press reaction, I'll deal with it. Bloodsucking piranhas. I'll give them hell if anything pregnancy-related is published.'

'It's not the press.'

'Or the babies. Babies are bloody everywhere in London. You don't notice them until you notice them. You think you'd be safe in the city, but you're not.' Louise pointed round the room. 'It was like being on an assault course trying to dodge the pushchair terrorists in Battersea Park yesterday. Stay at mine and we won't need to see anyone apart from those I vet at the door. Anyone with a hint of a baby sling will be banned. We can even put up a screen in the garden so you don't see the neighbour's pregnant dog.'

Sam laid her hands out on the table in front of her. 'Lou, it's not just the press or the babies. And it's not trying to get away from Martin. I need a change of scene, somewhere completely different. Somewhere I can check out of life for a bit.' She got up and moved towards the window. She hadn't realised the truth of the words until she'd said them.

'You're kidding, right?'

'Why not? It's only one month,' Sam went to lay the table. 'Not six. People take long holidays all the time.'

'Not you. And not people who've got a top news broadcaster desperate to offer them a job and get rolling with meetings.'

'I need this, Lou. Whatever I choose next needs to be a proper decision, not something I fall into by default. And I need time to decide.'

'Fine!' Louise put her hands up and picked up a spatula. 'By completely different, you're sure you don't just mean a weekend spa break in the country? You're not exactly au fait with the world outside the M25.'

Sam crossed her arms.

'Right, right, ok.' Louise slipped the toast and bacon onto plates. 'I'll tell *You News* that you're taking time to fully prep between roles.'

'Lou, I'm not even sure I want the *You News* role. I'm serious: options are up in the air. Maybe I do want to do another transfer. Or maybe stay at *Wake Up!*'

Louise scoffed as she sat down. 'You would never have done the first transfer without Martin making you do those stupid tests. *You News* is your dream.'

'Was.'

'Excuse me?'

'It *was* my dream. Things have changed. I still want a baby. But I need to work out if I'm in the right headspace to actually try and have one. Work out if I can get on the IVF rollercoaster again.' Sam stared at the glistening bacon on her plate.

'So why not just do as Martin suggests? Quit work and lie in bed at home with your legs in the air for a year.'

'Because whatever I do I feel guilty: guilty for not having a family or guilty for not pushing my career. I need to turn life off for a bit. Go somewhere remote. Get some clarity.'

'Seriously?'

'Yes.'

Louise tapped at her phone. 'Well that can be arranged. Short term, of course. How remote? Surely not like no running water or electricity or decent restaurants remote? And what if there's an update on *You News* and they need you in for an emergency meeting? And you can't want to be somewhere too cold... or too hot? And I'm guessing no babies?'

'Ideally I wouldn't spend a month in the Arctic tundra in a child-centred resort with a ball pit.'

'Noted.' Louise scrolled through options. 'I'm not sure they have these filters on holiday booking websites... The Isle of Wight? Maybe too many retirees. You're not *quite* there yet...' She winked and took a bite of Sam's toast. 'Ooh. What about this cabin in the Lake District? Stylish kitchen and easy to jump on a train if you're needed back.'

'Too family friendly.'

'A bothy in the Outer Hebrides? Families don't drive that far.'

'Too cold.'

'A cottage in Cornwall?'

'Too busy.'

Louise clicked her tongue. 'Maybe we could stretch the you needing to travel the same day for emergency meetings thing. You can do Zoom. A ranch in Oklahoma?'

'Too hot.'

'An adults-only resort in the Maldives?'

'Zika.'

'Eh?'

'No travel to Zika hotspots if you're trying.'

'Jeez. Ok. A rainforest lodge in Costa Rica.'

'Zika.'

'Private island off Singapore.'

'Zika.'

'Shit.' Louise ran her hands over her neck and slumped back against her chair. 'Well, isn't this a bloody Herculean labour? It's glamping in North Wales, my spare room or nothing.'

Sam looked out the window at the cloudless blue. 'Maybe I could hire a camper van. Drive out to the middle of nowhere.'

'So you've had some additional driving lessons since that segment on testing electric cars when you went the wrong way round the roundabout and reversed into a ditch?'

'No. Your point?'

'Nothing.' Louise mimed a driver being run off the road, and Sam flicked a crumb at her across the table.

'Wait!' Louise scrambled again for her phone. 'Do you remember I told you about the hot guy I almost had a thing with in Thailand?'

'Which one? The guy with the lip piercing that looked like a mole?'

'No. The *hot* one. The one with the ponytail and surfboard. The one nothing *actually* happened with.'

'You said they all had ponytails and surfboards.'

'You know.' She lowered her voice. 'The one I *cried* about when I found out he had a girlfriend.'

'Oh. Hot taken guy. What's he got to do with anything?

He and his girlfriend have probably popped out loads of ponytailed surfing babies by now. Just like everybody else. And Thailand's a no go. Zika.'

Louise brought up a map. 'Not Thailand, for God's sake. Here.' She zoomed in. 'He'd worked for a summer on this crazy little island. I remember because I thought he was lying when he described it – it sounded completely bonkers. They speak English - it's in the channel. And there can't be many babies because hardly anyone bloody lives there.' She pressed the phone to Sam, who squinted at the tiny smudge of land.

'Sark. Never heard of it.'

'Exactly. And you can only get round by bicycle, horse and cart or tractor. No ditch reversing required.'

'Horse and cart? You can't be serious.' Sam flicked onto an information page. 'Bloody hell. Only 500 people.' Image after image showed green fields, bright blue water and deserted coves.

'Prepare to step back in time with a visit to Sark, an island which feels like an entire world away,' she read slowly from the site. 'With no cars or many of the trappings of the modern world, the island's unspoilt beauty is unparalleled in the British Isles. The world's first designated Dark Sky Island, it is with an overnight stay that you'll truly experience its enchanting magic. Come to witness the perfect clarity of the Milky Way glimmering in a cloudless sky and discover a different way of life.'

'That's it.' She looked up at Louise. 'It's perfect.'

Lousie organised the boat immediately, leaving Sam to mull over what to pack for four summer weeks on an island in the channel. It was still the British Isles rather than the Balearics, but the photos online showed such a bright sandy beach with turquoise water that it looked *almost* as tropical as Issa's social media reel from her Easter in Ibiza. Sam settled on a handful of cotton dresses, a pair of jeans and leggings, plimsolls, gold woven sandals, t-shirts and a denim jacket. The sun was shining brightly through the bay window of her bedroom and whatever else she needed she could surely buy there. And, as she'd pointed out to Louise, she could wear the same old thing every day as she didn't intend to meet anyone anyway. Anyone, that was, save Walter, the only person Louise could track down who offered chartered trips from England to the island and could leave the next afternoon. Then, at the last minute, she stuffed in her favourite silver lamé midi dress; the likelihood of her needing a dressy outfit was next to none, but she figured she should be prepared just in case.

'What sort of a name is Walter? I bet he's a proper fisherman,' laughed Louise as she confirmed the booking online. 'Flat cap, big white beard, over 60, smoking a pipe…'

'Don't be ridiculous.' Sam rolled her eyes. 'Real people live there, not walking stereotypes of ye olde yokels.'

Louise snorted. 'So says the woman whose recent countryside experience was to the deepest, darkest Cotswolds.'

'Hey! I'm not some snobby Londoner who doesn't understand what life's like for normal people. I grew up in Croydon, not Kensington, for goodness' sake. Plus, we have a massive regional audience.'

'An audience whose lives you are *completely* in touch with.' Louise poked her in the ribs and mockingly waved her arms around the flat with its bare lightbulbs hanging from the high warehouse ceiling and sharp glass furnishings against exposed brick walls.

'Watch it!' Sam screeched with a laugh as she poked Louise back. 'Or I'll banish you from my urban lair.'

She froze and brought a hand to her chest, bewildered by her own good humour. Just that morning, it felt like she might never laugh again. Like the part of her capable of warmth and excitement and joy had faded away with the tests.

But, she realised as she shook her head to clear her thoughts, the simple fact alone of having a plan of action was like opening a window on her mental fug. Rather than an afternoon writhing in musty sheets, her mind fixated on the stark emptiness of her body, she could now snap into the comforting busyness of having a bag to fill and a route to complete.

As she started packing her old wheelie suitcase, she thought about when she last holidayed abroad. Her most recent trip had been on a hen do to Barcelona over eighteen months ago. The bride-to-be, an old school friend, had gushingly revealed on the first night that she and her fiancé were accidentally but blissfully happily pregnant, and there was Sam with her most recent negative test discarded in the aparthotel bathroom bin. She burst into tears. Scrambling to give the hen an unusually tight hug, she just about managed to pass them off as tears of joy, but the next morning she claimed a dodgy tummy and spent the rest of the trip tucked away on the rooftop terrace researching diets to improve egg quality.

She blinked away the memory and focused on the task ahead: preparing luggage, saying goodbye to Martin, driving to the port, locating the vessel and settling in for the four-and-a-half-hour trip. When they'd pulled up outside the studio, Martin merely gave her a dry peck on the cheek and wished her luck, as if she was about to lead on a segment with a particularly unusual guest. But, she repeated to herself, it was ok. She needed this.

It was only when Louise swung into the parking space near Weymouth harbour and reached over to give Sam an enormous squeeze and press a little London bus keyring into her hand – to remind her of home and of the existence of motorised vehicles – that she'd felt the flutter of nerves and sadness like a tiny, trapped bird in her stomach.

CHAPTER 8

Everything was smaller than she'd expected. She'd imagined walls of cruise ships, like great floating beehives, fields of patchwork car parks, sprawling metal ferry terminals. But, instead, she peered out over the ice cream colour cottages, mint green painted railings and a tangle of fishing boats bobbing on the glinting water.

Checking the time on her phone, she balanced the coffee and muffin she'd bought on her bulging wheelie bag. She'd managed to keep light on the clothes packing but filled up the extra space with all the political autobiographies and social histories she'd bought over the past five years and never picked up from her shelf. Time for reading belonged to a different time, a past when she wasn't either at the studio or at home fervently scrolling through fertility forums, TTC social media pages or cycle tracking apps. She sat down onto the bench behind her, closed her eyes and rolled her shoulders. Her body was like a mug filled to the brim with grief. One false move, and all her emotions would spill over. But she could deal with a month away from home if it meant that she could live in that different time. And now, breathing in the fresh, salty air and hearing the soft squawks of seabirds circling in the cloudless blue sky above, she could almost believe she was there.

A buzz on her phone snapped her out of her reverie. It had to be Martin. A pulse of pleasure ran through her as she rummaged in her handbag. He would have just finished filming his first segment and no doubt was feeling the same pang of separation that she'd had in the car. It just hadn't felt right imagining him on the studio sofa alone. Sam imagined it being so empty, the atmosphere cold and thin without his usual warm banter and her mock-weary response. Though, she had to admit, that weariness had been less put on for effect and more her natural stance over the past few months. There was more than one occasion when Willa in make up had had to carefully add in drops and lotions to soothe her red eyes and puffy skin.

Her chest dropped. It was Louise.

Just getting petrol.

Remember to head to the jetty opposite the café in the pink building.

The boat's called Sybil.

Good luck babe xxx

She checked again that she was in the right place. Usually she'd tell Louise off for treating her like an incompetent teenage daughter, but today she appreciated it. Sam had been so tired and with her mind whipped with emotions that it was difficult to focus. She had half-heartedly kicked up a fuss when Louise had insisted on booking a private charter to avoid the crowds and stress of a London flight to the larger island of Guernsey and then a ferry to Sark from there, but now she knew she'd been right. This slow pace was exactly what she needed.

The water rippled as another small fishing boat approached. It must have seen better days, with its peeling, faded red paint, but the large round buoys on its side reflected the sun like glossy balloons. It was obviously too small to be her boat, so she took a sip of coffee and exhaled. She peered at the man at the helm. What a simple, easy life he must lead, out on the water in the sunshine, quiet save the murmuring of the waves – a world away from the bright lights, cameras and shouts of studio life.

She smiled smugly to herself. Clearly not all fishermen were the weather-beaten, Father Christmas types that Louise had imagined. This one wasn't wearing a flat cap but a woollen beanie and had a shadow of dark stubble framing a strong jaw, rather than a white beard. And, as she leaned closer, she noted that he was definitely at least a couple of decades off 60.

The man slowed the boat right down to a gentle chug and started to reverse. Sam sat back and took a bite of her muffin, stretching her legs out in the sun. Just as she was about to take another bite, she noticed something painted on the boat's side.

It was an S. She jerked upright. Followed by an Y. It couldn't be. *Sybil*. But this boat was bloody tiny. Surely it wasn't seaworthy enough to take her anywhere further than the neighbouring bay? A quick panic flushed through her, and she picked up her phone to call Louise. She couldn't be that far away. She could come and collect her. Take her to the airport. Or back to London. The man had moored the boat and was heading for the steps.

'Shit,' she hissed. She needed an excuse. She couldn't exactly say that she took one look at him and decided she did actually fancy a jet plane and a seatbelt after all. She'd just have to make something up. Say that she suddenly felt sick and couldn't possibly do the journey. God, she really probably would be sick in that creaky thing. Her hand went protectively to her stomach before she snapped it away with a snap of painful remembrance.

The man reached the top of the steps.

'Alright?' he said in a gruff voice, plunging his hands into his deep pockets. 'Sam Murphy?'

'Huh? Oh!' Sam blushed. 'Yes.' She'd forgotten that Louise had used her own surname for the booking on the off chance that Walter was a huge *Wake Up!* fan who'd sell the story of her clandestine post-chemical pregnancy escape to some national rags. Glancing at his heavy boots and weathered skin, this now seemed unlikely.

'Urm, Walter, is it?' She said in a small voice, still clutching her half-eaten muffin in one hand and her phone in the other. Now was the moment; she had to say she wouldn't be coming.

'Call me Walt, and I'd be careful with food here if I were you.' He gave a brisk nod to motion above her head.

'Excuse me?' Sam squinted as she looked up into the sunshine, but it was too late.

A pair of hands grabbed her hair, and a great white shape swooped down over her face. She screeched, blinded by white hot terror. Walt must have pulled a bag over her head. Squeezing her eyes shut and screaming, she kicked out her arms and legs in a wild frenzy. 'Get off! I'll scream! I'll bite!' She bared her teeth and opened her eyes wide ready to face her attacker.

Walt stood in the same spot, hands still sunk into his pockets and head cocked to the side.

Sam blinked. He'd moved back so quickly. Where had the bag gone?

'Sam?'

'No!' She shouted, standing and putting one arm out in front of her as a barrier and holding up her phone in the other. 'Don't touch me. I'm calling the police.'

'Urm, that was –'

'Don't make things worse.' She shook back tears and shakily dialled 999. 'I'll scream!'

'Hang on. Just listen a minute.'

Sam remembered a segment they'd hosted on the show on repelling attackers in the street. The woman had said that you should bark like a dog because they'd think you were crazy and leave you alone. She held the phone to her ear as it rang, flapped the other arm and barked as loudly as she could.

Walt baulked then lunged forwards, pinning her arms to her side as the phone clattered to the floor. Sam kept barking as she tried to struggle free, but she was like a rag doll in his grip. He held her firmly until she finally gave up and looked straight into his eyes. She took in each detail of his heavy brow, tanned skin, thick eyelashes and bright green eyes flecked with gold, the same colour as the water. If she managed to escape alive, she'd at least be able to give a detailed description of him. She scoured her mind for a way to escape and moved her tongue around to gather saliva before spitting clean onto his forehead.

Walt crumpled his features together without loosening his hold as the globule slid towards his nose.

'Delightful. Now listen.'

Sam stared back resolute. The woman on the segment had stressed that you mustn't show any fear. You should stand strong and show that you too would fight.

'That wasn't me. A seagull stole your muffin.'

She blinked. 'What?'

Walt held her gaze, hands still firmly holding her like she was a horse ready to bolt. 'A seagull stole your muffin. It landed on your head and reached down. Look, you don't have it anymore.'

She glanced across the floor. All she could see was her phone, which didn't look in the best condition, and her suitcase. The coffee balancing on top had fallen and spilt across the cobbles.

Crap.

She opened her mouth to speak but wasn't sure what to say.

Walt loosened his grip. 'No more barking?' he asked warily. 'Or kicking or screaming or threatening to call the police?'

She nodded numbly and sat down, a flash of embarrassment thrumming through her. 'Urgh,' she mumbled. 'I'm sorry. Are you ok? I didn't mean... I thought...' She covered her face with her hands.

He wiped his forehead. 'Well, I think you might have a bigger problem.'

She looked forwards into the glittering water. 'I do. I know I do. It's been a really bad time. I'm going through a lot. I know it's no excuse. I probably seem like I've completely lost it.'

'No, urm.' He cleared his throat. 'Your hair. The seagull...'

Sam ran a hand over her head and let out a cry of disgust as she looked at her palm, now smothered in warm, white dropping.

'Could be worse.' Walt said as he passed Sam the hosepipe of running water. 'Bird crapping on you's good luck. Could have done with it myself.'

He brushed past her, his large body swiftly moving round the boat tying and untying knots. His thick arms gleamed in the sun like polished wood.

Sam shivered as she ran the icy water through her sticky hair before squeezing out the cold ends. The IVF had failed, the entire world thought she was pregnant, she'd walked out on live filming, was potentially going to turn down her dream job, her phone was smashed and wouldn't turn on, her suitcase was being stored underneath a pile of lobster pots and now she had no way out of traversing the channel in a barnacled bath tub with a total stranger she'd just spat at in the face. She'd embarrassed herself in the last half hour almost more than in an entire 14-year career on national television, and she simply wanted to slip between the cracks of the pontoon and never see the man in front of her again. *Could* it be worse?

'You'll be needing these.' Walt took back the hosepipe, heaved himself on board and pointed to a blue jumper and a heavy yellow anorak on the outside deck.

He held out a large, calloused hand to help her to step onto the boat, and Sam reluctantly took it before tiptoeing in her sandals over the piles of rope and perching within a ray of sun on a bench. The clothes looked enormous and emanated a faint but unmistakable smell of fish. She pulled her denim jacket closer around her floral tea dress. 'I'll be fine.'

He muttered something under his breath.

'What?' She pursed her lips, irritation mixing with her anxiety.

He hummed. 'Nothing.'

'What did you say?' She put her hands on her hips.

Walt passed an eye over her and raised an eyebrow. 'I said that you're a stubborn thing.'

She looked straight back at him. 'I am. Yes.'

'Well,' he sighed, 'you'll freeze a finger off but suit yourself.' He nodded towards a pile of items in the corner. 'Life jacket's mandatory.'

Rather than being designed as a vest, like those she and Martin had worn on a segment kayaking in the Thames, these life jackets seemed to have a bizarre number of straps, buckles and arm holes. Sam tried one hole over her head but that left several straps flapping at her side. She then tried an arm through one hole and a head through another but that left a hole in the wrong place for another arm.

'Stupid thing,' she cursed under her breath.

'Alright there?' Walt stood in front of her, arms crossed.

'Never better,' she huffed as she tried two holes through two arms but still with another hole spare. 'This life jacket…' She untangled both arms, 'is broken.' She freed herself and dropped it to the floor in a heavy clunk.

Walt picked it up, dusted it down and inspected it. 'Not broken. Can I help you, or will you start meowing or something?'

She raised her chin in the hope that he couldn't see her blushing in the sunlight. 'Please do.'

'Only if you wear the other stuff.'

What was with this man treating her like an ignorant six-year-old? Yes, she might have made a stupid mistake, but she was capable of judging whether or not she wanted to wear a stinking anorak for several hours. She'd reported more than once on local apathy towards tourists in British coastal towns – perhaps he saw her as an obnoxious Londoner come to make problems with housing supply or the like. This whole saga might just be some ritual humiliation of visitors stupid enough to hire a private charter. Or he could just be a plain old prick.

'Trust me. I'll be fine without.'

'Trust *me*,' he replied. 'You won't.' He picked up the jumper and coat and held them out to her. 'Ever done this journey before?'

'No.' She narrowed her eyes. 'Your point?'

'Just take my word for it.'

She sighed. If this was going to turn into a battle of wills, she couldn't be bothered to fight. Not today.

'Fine,' she scoffed and soon had her hands on her hips standing in the scratchy woollen jumper with a high neck and heavy yellow anorak with Walt tugging the life jacket over her arms just like, as he pointed out, you put on a jacket.

'And all these?' She dangled the loose straps.

He put out a hand towards her and then immediately pulled it back. 'May I?'

'It's not like I have any dignity left.'

She closed her eyes as he secured a strap over her chest.

Other than their limp goodbye kiss, she and Martin hadn't been physically close for months. After two years of perfunctory sex, adhered to against the strict schedule of her ovulation calendar, Sam couldn't deny a sense of relief when he hadn't made a move to touch her since the transfer. The idea of someone handling her body after all the poking and prodding of injections and speculums made her squirm.

But now, even through the layers of fishy outerwear, the warmth of Walt's body radiated against her face as she breathed him in, a heady mix of petrol, sea salt and something sweet, and the dark hairs on his arms almost tickled her neck.

The boat nudged against the pontoon, jolting her back to her senses. What was wrong with her? He wasn't even attractive – well, maybe to some, but the brooding, leathery skinned, bearded hermit type wasn't really her thing. Comparing him and Martin was like comparing a Ferrari to a mud splattered off-road Jeep. And why should she be comparing him to Martin anyway? Ugh. She flicked open her eyes and stood backwards. The hormones must still be messing with her brain. She clearly wasn't herself.

'All good,' she said, louder than she'd intended.

Walt stepped backwards and sheepishly pointed at her groin.

Blood drained from her upper body and a lump rose in her throat. This couldn't be happening. Yes, she'd sniffed him a bit when he was standing close to her, but that didn't mean anything. It certainly wasn't an invitation.

He chewed his lip. 'The other strap…'

'*Excuse* me?' She wrapped her arms over her pounding heart, praying for Louise to make a sudden U-turn down the motorway.

'You need to clip it,' he nodded. 'Between your legs.'

She steadied herself against the bench and closed her eyes in exasperation. Jesus. She was like a fox with its hairs on end, constantly prickling and ready to pounce. She secured the strap and nodded, pretending to be engrossed in the harbour wall behind her to avoid Walt seeing her now cherry red cheeks.

* * *

Four and a half hours in a plane gets you to North Africa. There might be a few bumps along the way as you pass over the Atlas Mountains, but the flight's probably long enough to at least get a free drink, watch a film and have a kip. Four hours on a fishing vessel in the channel is, Sam swore to herself, pretty bloody different.

Endless dark, menacing waves rolled heavily around them; the bright blue sky was now smothered by thick cloud. She begrudgingly sunk further into her anorak, hiding under its hood from the spray that flicked into the open-backed cabin as Walt stood firm at the helm, only speaking to her to point out the grey outline of the French coast and the jagged rocks of another island.

It was the only time in the past few days that she hadn't mourned not being pregnant. Staring fixedly at the horizon, she couldn't imagine combining the current churning of her stomach with any nausea. But, she scoffed to her inner voice, she wouldn't be in this God-forsaken situation if she *was* still pregnant. She'd be giggling with Martin as he sampled ciders as part of the *Wake Up!* annual cider competition, smugly declining any alcohol as he decided which scrumpy warranted a prize from their sponsor, not staring past frothing black water with a man she'd rather not see again as her only company.

Just when the moment came that she really did think she might throw up and was deciding whether to shout for a bucket or risk splattering over the side, Walt slowed the boat down and pointed into the distance. It was close to nine o'clock and the sun, hidden in cloud, had already dropped off the horizon, leaving them surrounded by a cold, darkening sky.

The water calmed and Sam walked out across the deck of the boat, a gentle breeze circling within her still slightly damp hair. She looked out. Half concealed in sea mist, like a miniature mystery island that they might scramble around in *The Famous Five,* was Sark.

She held her breath and leaned over the side, hungry for details of her new home. It was small – tiny, in fact. The entire width of the island fitted into her vision. It couldn't be much bigger than Battersea Park. As they came closer, she scanned the headland for signs of houses or people, but it was entirely flanked by looming brown cliffs tipped with empty green fields below the muted white sunset. No one.

Remote, she gulped. She'd got what she'd asked for.

As they approached, a thick gloam fell onto the island like a blanket, and soon there was little light left save that of a vehicle light flashing on the harbour wall.

'That's Jack with the luggage tractor.' Walt murmured as they chugged into the sparse corner, empty apart from three other boats lashed to faded buoys. He pointed to the steps where he'd drop her off. The tide was in and there was only a narrow strip of granite steps between the dark sea and the tarmac.

The air was silent, and mist floated phantom-like down towards the now eerily still water.

Walt manoeuvred the boat next to the wall, tying its front to a peeling metal ring and keeping the back in close by holding onto a tyre suspended from the path above. He noted that the bird crap luck must have worked because the now calm high water meant Sam didn't have far to jump from the boat to the shore, but wings of nerves beat violently in her stomach.

Heart in her mouth, she leapt onto the damp steps. Walt threw over her suitcase as if it was now filled with air, something quickly disproved by Sam's huffs and groans as she lugged it up the steps towards the tractor.

She looked down to wave goodbye. After seagull-gate, a mildly amicable parting at least made the chance of him spreading the story of a morning TV-presenter barking incessantly in his face somewhat less likely. But he had already gone, the boat swallowed by the night.

CHAPTER 9

Now in his sixties and having been ferrying things round the island on the tractor since he was 12, Jack Le Page was used to collecting strange cargo from the harbour. But when Walt had asked for a visitor collection, he'd anticipated the usual family group, rucksacks and tent in hand for a weekend camping or possibly some French sailors coming in off their boat. What he hadn't anticipated was a wind-swept single woman in her mid-thirties who vaguely reminded him of someone off the telly and with sharp eyebrows and a serious glare more suited to London boardrooms than cold seas and muddy fields. He clicked his tongue at her flimsy sandals, glinting in the glow of the headlights. Still, he noticed, at least she had a sensible coat and, he stroked his white beard in approval, the same woollen Guernsey jumper that he himself had snugly covering his large belly. It was nice to see a tourist who'd clearly done a bit of research into island life.

'Alright, love?' He jumped down from the tractor cabin – not as nimbly as back in the day but with a sprightly step for a man of his age and, as his neighbour, Judith, liked to remind him, his weight. 'I'll get your bag and you clamber on in. Normally we've got the toast rack trailer running up and down the hill, but it's just me at this time of night.'

He was surprised to find his warm smile met with the woman's warily crossed arms.

'I'm fine,' she said. 'I can walk.' In truth, Sam was starting to feel slightly dizzy and had an empty feeling in the pit of her stomach. But, after the day she'd had, she was determined to prove to herself that she was still that confident, able woman who'd been lost for a while.

Jack narrowed his eyes and nodded towards the shadowy darkness of a tunnel behind the tractor. 'You're sure? That tunnel leads to a fair steep hill on the other side. An' then you've got quite a lot of bumpy paths to navigate in them fancy shoes.' Sam crossed one foot behind the other. 'An' no streetlights on the island. We're a dark sky island. Or so people call us.' He chuckled to himself, his cheeks rounding above his beard.

She sighed inwardly and glanced around. It *was* getting dark, and the suitcase did seem heavier than she'd anticipated. This seemed odd at first, given how little she'd packed, until she remembered her hoard of untouched political tomes tucked neatly next to her wash bag, each at least three inches thick. 'Fine,' she exhaled. 'Where do I get in?'

Jack guided her into the open trailer, clunking the door shut behind her. As she folded herself into the corner, leaning against her suitcase, she figured that it was a least a new – possibly *recalibrating* – experience, one that Martin would never imagine for her. And it was certainly different to catching an Uber.

But this glimmer of optimism soon deflated as the trailer hit every hole and rock in the un-tarmacked road. Too bumped around to focus on anything in the gloom, all she could make out of the town was a few outlines of houses and bicycles. She tried and failed to remember what her new accommodation was supposed to look like; the rental company didn't have a website beyond a social media listing, so Louise had booked a place over the phone.

The tractor soon rumbled past any signs of life, the dusty roads edged by acre after acre of black hedges. Sam chastised herself for thinking that she didn't need a lift. She'd never have made it through these narrow paths that twisted and turned, serpent-like, through the darkness. A slice of wind shook the trailer as it clattered round a corner, its creaking body rolling like an unsteady ship. The air was now clammy cold, and she huddled into the folds of the raincoat, pulling the thick arms of the jumper over her numb fingers. She tried to peer out across the island, but any view was hidden behind the veil of night, and instead she knocked her head against the metal wire as the wheels of the trailer sunk awkwardly into ruts on the road.

Just as she was considering how to get Jack's attention to find out how much more she'd have to endure, they lurched forwards onto a field, the tractor and trailer staggering to an abrupt stop.

He swung down onto the grass and came round to let her out.

'Alright?' He smiled, his breath condensing in the crisp air. 'Enjoy your local massage?'

Sam groaned, clicking out her back as she stood on the wet grass. She looked around at the empty field. 'Where are we?'

He waved a large hand out in front of him, like a conjuror revealing a trick. 'This is it.'

She blinked. What was *it*? There was nothing there.

He heaved her bag down into a patch of dry mud. 'I don't like to be rude, but you'll have to walk from here, I'm afraid. I'd go further, but last time I got stuck. Took bloody ages to reverse. Not exactly an even path, see. Landlord should sort it out really. Not that anyone's stayed here for years. Bit different to what you're used to, eh?' He chuckled again and nudged her bag towards her.

Sam flinched. She had so many questions to ask. Who was there to let her into the cottage? What time did the island supermarket open? Did the island *have* a supermarket? Could she drink the tap water? What was the Wifi code? Most importantly, she peered into the black mist, where exactly was the house?

But, as if in anticipation, Jack stepped back from the power of an enormous yawn, rubbing his hand over his stomach. 'Conked, I am. Been up since the crack of dawn ferrying all sorts ready for Sunday. I'll be off. See you then.' He nodded and gave a small wave and swung back over the wheel of the tractor before Sam could make a sound from her open mouth. 'Cheerie, love,' he called, and the brawl of the engine dispersed to a gentle hum as the vehicle chugged into the empty sky.

She looked round blankly. London didn't know the dark. Not really. Martin had installed heavy black out blinds to shut out the incessantly winking lights of cars and flats and bars and the great lanterns of office blocks. He'd even been known to use the silk eye mask that Issa had given Sam one Christmas and that she had never worn. She'd never needed it herself; her childhood bedroom window had been watched over by a trusty streetlight, and now she hated the idea of losing sight of her surroundings. Nothing quite matched the claustrophobia she'd once felt on a weekend country trip, when she'd laid unsleeping in bed the first night, dangling her hand, unseen, in front of her face.

And now the suffocating night hung around her like a black bag over her head. She took a sharp intake of breath.

There was nothing and no one save the cold, clean air. She fished in the enormous pockets of the anorak for her phone before realising, with a drop of her stomach, two things: firstly, it was still Walter's bloody jumper and anorak and she would have to get them back to him; and secondly, her phone was, of course, smashed to smithereens in her back pocket, leaving her without means of contacting anyone and, more pressingly, without a torch.

But as the panic rose in her throat, her eyes slowly adapted to the cracks of moonlight that brightened the clouds. Her awareness clocked a small house on the other side of the field, and she did her best to stumble towards it. As she dragged her suitcase closer, she realised that it was not the house and garden she had, without consciously admitting it, imagined. It was not a neatly paved quaint front path, flanked with turf on either side, mowed to a soft carpet. Her eyes could now see that this approach was open and lumpy underfoot and pulling her suitcase over it felt like guiding an elephant over moguls. As she neared the building, to the right was a tangled mass of trees, whose branches grasped and intermingled with one another in a solid mass, shivering and creaking in the gentle wind but with no light penetrating the thickly entwined leaves. To the left was an old wall covered with damp green moss, and, beyond this, the green field curved downwards into what she assumed was the silent sea, as if dropping towards the end of the world.

The moonlight pierced through a patch of sky, illuminating a small granite cottage with a thatched roof. There was no cottage garden to be seen, no spray of flowers or spread of wisteria; instead the dry, uneven sparse grass surrounded the house, which itself appeared squat and bare, with simply a small, plain door between two short windows and the roof ragged and unkempt. It was, Sam huffed to herself as she blindly pressed her hands over the door, hoping for a key or handle, less singing animals in a fairytale and more creepy Brothers Grimm.

She yelped as the door's unlocked handle gave way and she and her suitcase fell forwards into a matchstick-thin wooden porch opening onto a thinly furnished single room.

The air inside was damp with a sharp breeze piercing through an unidentifiable hole. It certainly wasn't the countryside Sam had experienced in Issa's world of SUVs, designer wellies and flirty butlers, and, drawing herself up at the threshold, she marvelled at how shut off it was from her studio life. She might as well have landed on a different planet.

She felt along the uneven stone walls until she found a light switch, revealing a small kitchen to one side and a large hearth on the other facing a small brown sofa. The hearth was almost the height and width of the room and – she wished she could send Louise a jokey photo to compare to her and Martin's flat – made of exposed bricks framing an enormous black metal wood burner, as round and dark as a witch's cauldron. The kitchen was thin white laminate with a stained ceramic sink. She noticed with some alarm that there was no dishwasher or washing machine, but, she reasoned to herself, what had she expected? This was remote simplicity. She'd wash her clothes in the local launderette. If there was one. Or do everything by hand in a bucket. It would be just like the times she and Martin camped at festivals. Except that they would go glamping, not camping. And he had insisted that their tent really *was* glamorous, at a minimum boasting a double bed, electricity and a separate shower room with hot water. She traced a long crack in a kitchen cabinet and noticed that it forked round to a bowl collecting water from a drip in the ceiling. The glamping had definitely been more glamorous.

But she'd be fine. She gulped back another wave of nerves as she shrugged off the anorak to hang on the sole hook by the door. This was what she'd wanted, wasn't it?

A sharp blast of wind rushed through the house, pushing the front door shut with a slam. Searching for the open window, she crept up the small staircase towards the top floor. To her left was a grimy bathroom with a '70s avocado suite and to her right was a bedroom – her bedroom – complete with a queen-sized bed with a metal frame and a window left slightly open on the hook.

She tugged the window shut, taking one last breath of the cool fresh air. Tiredness suddenly seeped through her body and her legs sunk heavily onto the bed behind her. The soft mattress creaked as if in greeting and she lay back, burying into the thick, feather duvet and pillow. 'Hello,' she muttered, 'it's nice to meet you. You're very comfy.'

'Christ,' she thought to herself. 'I'm talking to the furniture. I really have lost it.'

But as she kicked off her shoes, took her phone out her

pocket and closed her eyes, she no longer cared. She was just tired. It was as if her body was trapped beneath a weighted blanket of all the emotional exhaustion of the past few days and weeks. Of the loss of her plan for life as she knew it: her boyfriend, her job, her hoped-for baby. She put a hand to her stomach. She had never before felt so empty, so alone. If talking to her bed meant some company, then who was her inner critic to judge? And so she pulled the duvet round her still clothed body and allowed herself to sink into its folds, the tiredness taking over, dragging her into a deep and dreamless sleep.

CHAPTER 10

A seven-year routine of 5am starts doesn't break easily, and Sam's eyes flicked open on cue. She turned to reach out for Martin, but the other side of the bed was empty – cold. She sat bolt upright. Where was she? The realisation seeped through her clouded brain, and she slid back under the cover, closing her eyes against the still dark and quiet morning. She had nowhere to be and no one to see, no rushing to rustle up her and Martin's morning smoothie, no hour with Willa in hair and make up, no run through of the day's schedule with Keira.

She lay still for about an hour, just making out the silhouette of a spider weaving a web on the ceiling. The lack of noise was unnerving. Her and Martin's London flat was off the main drag, but even in the middle of the night you could never quite escape the drone of traffic, sirens and flight paths. Now she felt smothered by the heavy, unbreaking silence.

But then she heard something. She froze. Her heart leapt into action. There it was again: a rattle, a clang. The front door falling open. Shit. Her pulse redoubled. Someone had broken in. Bloody Jack or Walter had told their dodgy mates that she was here alone in a house with a door that didn't lock. Someone had come to steal all her possessions, or attack her, or take photos of her snoring to sell to the press, or… There was silence. She lay still, forcing herself to breathe before shuffling through the expanse of sheets to the other side of the bed where she could see out the small window. The handle on the front door was so flimsy it had probably swung open in the wind.

The smashed screen of her phone glinted in the dull morning moonlight, a reminder that she couldn't even call the police if she wanted to. Did 999 even work here? Did the island even *have* police? Looking out the window, there was only the static blackness of the field. She held still, ears cocked like a cat. Nothing. All silence. Breathe.

Her mind must be playing tricks on her – and not for the first time in the past 24 hours, she sighed. She pulled the duvet closer and huddled into the pillow. Her stomach rumbled, and she realised how hungry she was, wishing she did have her morning smoothie after all and cursing the snack-stealing seagull.

This time there was a loud bang, accompanied by the click of footsteps on the stone floor. A sick feeling rose in her chest. Whenever there was a clunk in the night in London, she'd prod Martin to go and take a look, and he'd return bleary eyed and shaking his head, declaring them safe. But now she had to face whatever it was on her own. She fought the urge to hide and scoured the room for a weapon. Whoever it was might have a knife or a cricket bat or something. Or – her stomach dropped – there must be farmers on the island. Didn't farmers have guns?

But then there came another noise different to the others, more like a squeak or high bleat. She took a breath. A weapon-wielding farmer was unlikely to bleat at her – unless he'd brought along a sheep.

She grabbed her phone on instinct, steeled herself and tiptoed towards the staircase, gently padding down towards the kitchen. With every step she came closer to a kind of whimpering noise. Oh God. Maybe someone else had been attacked and was finding shelter in the cottage. Maybe the islanders were scouring the fields for non-natives to kill and put their heads on sticks.

Another cry echoed across the granite walls. So lonesome and desolate, it pierced her with a great longing for it to be over. She turned the corner of the staircase and reached round for the light switch.

'He...Hello?' The word came out as whisper through her quivering lips. She glanced round but, save for the kitchen, sofa and dark, looming hearth, it was empty. As she blinked in the bright light, she felt more in control of her fear, and it occurred to her that it was more likely that the noise might be from a lost pet or bird. She'd once had a call-in on the show from a woman who hadn't noticed a squirrel living in her armchair for a week. Maybe it was a badger or another bloody seagull. Or maybe it was a mystical wolf... She gave her head a sharp shake.

She really hoped it wasn't a mystical wolf. It might bite her, and she doubted there was a proper hospital on the island. She dug her nails into her palm and told herself to stop being such an idiot.

She peered into the corners of the hearth, behind the large black wood burner, coughing from the musty dampness of a deserted room. The sleeve of her jumper brushed the top of it, and she sneezed as her head was consumed in dust. Another high yelp pierced the air, accompanied by a sort of snuffling and shuffling.

'Shh...shh,' she stammered, looking warily around her and not quite sure whether she was talking to herself or the mystery beast. 'It's ok.'

The door to the porch jangled, and she held her breath as she tiptoed over and gently pulled it towards her.

'Oh!' She almost jumped backwards as she took in her findings. 'Hello. I didn't expect to see you here.'

Nestled in the corner between her suitcase and the open front door, with long, pulled-back velvet ears and a tangle of folded legs was a tiny horse. Sam slowly knelt down next to it, and it turned its muzzle towards her. As she carefully lifted a hand to its soft grey and white fur, it squealed out with an ear-splitting screech. 'It's ok, it's ok,' she repeated, carefully stroking its trembling back. 'I'm here now.' As the foal's long fuzzy ears flicked forwards, brushing her nose, she realised – wanting to slap her forehead – that of course it wasn't a horse. It was a donkey. A very small and very scared young donkey. It was a funny looking thing, with white flecks in its grey fur and a white fringe of hair on its forehead hanging over its eyes like an awkward teenager.

Sam looked up at the thin front door swinging on its hinges. It wouldn't have taken much effort for a donkey to push it open. The noise must have come from it clattering against the wall. She looked around the porch and noticed a large hole and some teeth marks in her left sandal.

The donkey stared up at her with its large black eyes, too innocent to reprimand. Sam couldn't remember actually seeing a donkey in real life before so didn't exactly have much to compare it to, but it certainly seemed like a very small donkey, not the sort of animal which could carry Biblical figures across the desert or take plump children for rides on the beach.

'Are you lost, little one?' The donkey repositioned its front legs and nuzzled its head on the floor next to her leg. She looked out beyond the door. Wisps of sapphire clouds split open to reveal the newly rising sun, bathing the field in front of the house in a copper haze. A soft wind whispered through the grass and curled into the porch to shake the loose strands of her hair as if in a morning greeting.

The donkey snuffled slightly and sighed, and she could feel its heart calming to a gentle beat.

'Or were you just alone,' Sam looked down and gently ran a hand over the foal's ear, 'hoping for company?'

She sat back against the wall of the porch, becoming aware of a waterfall of morning birdsong pouring through the air outside. As the donkey's snuffle turned to a muffled snore, she decided to just let time slip away and enjoy the moment.

But as the minutes wore on, her eyes darted through the house, and she noticed even more of the flaws that had been concealed under the sheeting of night. The sofa wasn't only a depressing colour, but it was holed and fraying. The windows were dirty outside. The floor was uneven and home to several colonies of ants marching towards the kitchen.

What had she done? Living alone in a leaking ruin in the middle of a field wasn't going to make her feel better. How could it? Not telling Martin that of course she would be back with him in work in the morning was a ridiculous mistake. Now she had less than what she'd been lacking before. She didn't want a month to recuperate without her boyfriend or career or home or prospect of a miracle conception on the off chance that she did ovulate this month. Or, failing that, her period should come back in three weeks and then they could get ready for another transfer. Being marooned on some silly little island just delayed things more. Her phone was probably littered with desperate messages from Martin begging her to come back.

Surely she could just slip right back into her old self – the one from three years ago? The kind of woman who could entertain the nation with wry wit, skewer the political classes and hum cheerily as she and Martin skipped out the studio doors twelve hours after entering to join friends by the river for an Aperol Spritz. Not the kind of woman who tracked her daily bowel movements and discharge on three separate apps and who'd once cried in a supermarket when a pregnant woman walked in front of her trolley.

It was fine. That person *had* once been her. It couldn't be that hard.

Plus she'd never managed to ask Martin about the changes and *younger direction* that Nina had mentioned. What if Keira was planning whole new segments that she wouldn't get a say on?

A rooster crowed in the distance as it was let out its coop, and Sam felt the ground loosen beneath her like the unravelling of a woollen jumper. She couldn't stay here. It had been a stupid mistake driven by her knotted hormones. What she needed was to get her phone fixed and contact Louise to get her back as soon as possible.

She headed upstairs to change and sort out her bird's nest of hair, but any attempts at beautifying were interrupted by the donkey's loud groaning yawn.

'Ok, sleepy head,' she called back down. 'We'll get you home.'

In all of Sam's professional life, she'd never needed to move a farm animal, and she wasn't sure she was up to it now. Thankfully, she had an enormous stroke of luck as the donkey chose to follow her without prompting as she crossed the field towards the neighbouring house. She hadn't quite considered an alternative plan if it had stayed slumped in the porch.

Marching through the field, the dew-wet blades of grass twinkling in a diamond dust and bees blowing like sequins through the golden air, she couldn't help admiring the beauty of the island. But, she repeated to herself, she would leave as soon as she could. She had a life to tend to.

They reached a clump of trees, under which morning shadows cast echoing shapes and where the grass sloped sharply downwards towards the other house. Unlike her melancholy cottage, with its mournful face of two windows and a door peering out from slabs of grey granite, this white-painted building glowed in the sunlight, its front festooned with jasmine whose riot of tiny white flowers glistened like stars. To one side of the house was a bright little garden full of roses, lavender, cabbages and fruit bushes and to the other was a patch of lush field ringed by thin wire and, plain to see, an open gate.

'Ah ha,' Sam ran a hand through the donkey's mane as it trotted merrily beside her. 'Eyes on the scene of the escape.'

She was surprised that no one had noticed. Whoever lived here, she sniffed, was either unwell, absent or a terrible owner of donkeys. Despite not being *entirely* sure what owning a donkey foal entailed, she could say with confidence that it didn't involve letting them trot out into to the big, wide world unattended.

Not without difficulty, she ushered the donkey under the awning over the cottage's front door where it took a large bite out of a yellow rose. She sounded a clean, crisp rap with a black knocker and counted the seconds to distract herself from her wriggling nerves. It was silly, really, she told herself sharply.

1,2,3…

She had nothing to worry about. She'd simply hand back the donkey, point out that the gate was open and advise that it remains shut in the future.

4,5,6…

Or maybe scrap the advice. It might be an old, experienced farmer who thought she was some prissy city know it all.

7,8,9…

But they *had* let a donkey run loose…

10,11,12…

But they might recognise her from the show. She should be nice. Just in case.

13,14,15…

Actually that was nonsense. She wasn't Beyoncé; no one on the island probably watched *Wake Up!* No doubt they spent their mornings out feeding livestock or having brisk sea swims or simply didn't have TVs.

16,17,18…

Maybe no one was in.

19,20,21…

Or maybe the person who lived here had died days or weeks ago. Maybe they were upstairs rotting and waiting for her to barge in and find her like in a news item they'd had on the show about a woman who'd been dead in her flat for two years before anyone noticed. Sam had shivered at the thought.

22,23,24…

At least she had Martin. And Louise. Sometimes it felt like all the good in her life was in the shadow of her lack of a baby, of what she didn't have. Like she'd been cut open and had everything removed inside except want for a child. But she did have a wonderful best friend/agent who'd tease her mercilessly but would chop her right arm off for her. And Martin... He wouldn't give up on her, not now that she was returning to slot back into her old self.

25, 26...

'Trevor D!'

The door was filled with a large older woman in a bobbly pink dressing gown, tangled grey hair tousled in spikes around her plump face. Cradled in her arms, like a fat, spoilt baby, was an enormous white cat with sharp yellow eyes, which stared distastefully at both Sam and the donkey like they came from a particularly foul-smelling bin.

'Oh, Trevor D,' the woman cooed. She bent down to kiss the donkey on the forehead, the cat crawling up to cling to her shoulder. 'Where have you been, you silly sausage? Did you jump over the fence again?' She ruffled the hair over the donkey's eyes, but it lunged backwards from a strong sweep of the cat's tail.

Sam cleared her throat. 'The gate is open. I think he just walked straight out.'

The woman straightened up to look at her, the cat repositioning itself again in her arms. 'Deary, me.' She shook her head. 'What you must think! I've just got so much on my plate these days. Poor Trevor D – he's named after my husband, Trevor, who passed last year. So he's Trevor D, Trevor Donkey. But he's been no end of trouble.' The cat gave a loud thin cry as if in agreement.

'He was fine. Honestly.' Sam looked back to find Trevor D merrily tugging at a cabbage in the ground.

'Bless him,' the woman sighed. 'His mother didn't take to him when he was born, so we were hoping to bond him with a new mother here, but she didn't take neither. I was hoping to send him to Guernsey where there's a few jennys might what take him on, but it's a bit late now he's two months old.' She stroked the cat's head, flattening his ears as it stared at Sam with a look of pure loathing.

'God knows what will happen. My grandson usually helps out, but he's so busy with work and little Daniel, poor mite, and I can't cope, see. What with Daniel here in the afternoons and Jeremy, of course. I'm sure I didn't leave that gate open.' She sighed heavily. 'But maybe I did. I forget.' She raised her eyebrows before kissing the cat on the forehead who only glowered in response.

Sam plunged her hands into her pocket. She wasn't quite sure of island etiquette. Was this much talking to strangers normal?

The woman looked at her as if for the first time. 'Say, I've just blabbed away, and you don't even know who I am.' She gave a thick, gurgling laugh and squeezed Sam on the arm. 'Judith. Lived here all my life, so anything you need just ask. You on holiday, love?'

Sam hesitated. 'Sort of. I've rented that cottage for a month.' She pointed over her shoulder. 'But I'm not -'

'Never! That falling down thing? But no one's even been in it for years! Is it safe?'

Sam crumpled her forehead. If she'd had any qualms about leaving, they'd now been fully brushed away. 'I hope so. I'd actually be really grateful if I could use your computer or mobile? I dropped mine yesterday.' She went to take out the smashed pile from her pocket as proof.

But as she finished her sentence, the cat reached down to swipe at Trevor D, who reared up and let out a rip-roaring neigh.

'Jeremy!' Judith squealed. 'That's naughty! What's poor Trevor D ever done to you?' But then she gave the smug-looking cat another kiss on the forehead.

'Say,' she looked again at Sam, a glint in her pale blue eyes, 'you wouldn't mind helping look after him, would you?

Do some of his feeds? It would be ever such a help. Daniel loves doing it, but he's getting very interested in putting his hands in the slop, and I don't think Jeremy likes the smell.'

Sam shook her head, and before she could give an explanation Judith smiled wistfully and raised her eyebrows. 'Never mind! You just never know. Trevor always used to say – 'You've got a tongue in your head, Judith. If you need help, just use it.' What was it you were asking?'

Sam took a deep breath. This was all taking a lot longer than she'd thought. 'Could I borrow your phone or computer quickly?'

'Landline alright?' Judith wrinkled her nose. 'Don't do new-fangled modern technology.'

Sam had to consciously stop her jaw from dropping open. She apparently hadn't only travelled across the channel, but into the 19th century. But then her surprise turned to frustration as she realised that she didn't know either Louise or Martin's number. She'd never needed to memorise them. The only number she could remember was her childhood family landline in the Croydon house she'd sold straight after the funeral.

'Don't have use for it, see,' Judith hoicked Jeremy higher towards her chest and placed a hand on Trevor D's head. 'Too much to keep me busy here. Try up on the high street, the Avenue. Plenty up there do surfing online.' She wiggled her fingers on the last two words as if explaining witchcraft.

Sam thanked her and ran a hand along Trevor D's back as he trotted towards the door and turned to look up at her with his wide dark eyes, nervous under the looming shadow of Jeremy's tail. 'Good luck with both of them. And sorry I couldn't help.'

She turned on her heel and stormed up the hill towards the road, keen not to waste another minute.

CHAPTER 11

Sam rarely went shopping these days. Clothes were largely provided for her at work, and she'd hardly bought anything new for herself for years. What she'd wanted was to be buying maternity clothes or one of those coats which covered your baby on your chest. Buying a slim dress or a slinky top was like admitting defeat, preparing herself for a future she didn't want to live in anymore. This meant that – bar the shops on the road next to the IVF clinic – she hadn't been to a 'standard' high street for a while. But despite her limited reference points, she still baulked as she turned onto the Avenue. She hadn't exactly expected the shopping area to be big, but she hadn't expected it to be quite so small. Dotted along a straight dirt track were a couple of bungalows of restaurants, a bike shop, a food shop, a souvenir shop and a jewellery shop. That was it. And now, at 8am in the morning, they were all closed.

She peered through each window, searching for signs of somewhere to fix her phone, but there was little beyond tins of food, buckets and spades, and Sark-branded soft toys. The buildings themselves were a higgledy-piggledy mix of exposed stone, painted fronts and metal sheeting. The main sign of life was the layers of glossy basket-fronted bicycles lining the front forecourt of the shop on the other side of the road, and it was next to this that she spotted the sign for Sark Shipping.

She dropped her shoulders in relief as she read the schedule of multiple daily ferries, with the soonest one getting her to Guernsey before midday, leaving plenty of time to fix her phone and catch an afternoon flight. She now had three hours to gather her things, buy a ticket and make her way down the hill and, given that the office didn't open for another hour, she decided to take a scenic route back to the cottage. At least she might find somewhere to have breakfast.

With no map to follow, she turned off the road towards a church, passing a golden post box and a series of pastel painted clapboard houses along the way. The track led her past a small graveyard and a house with a tractor in the drive. It was only when she saw the sign reading 'Sark Medical Centre' that she realised, not without alarm, that this was the doctor's surgery and the tractor the ambulance. With a deep breath and a reminder that she was leaving, she walked sharply onwards towards a quite beautiful straight track shaded on both sides by long rows of trees. The track brought her past an orchard, a dairy and a school before she turned through a stone arch into an area with a restaurant in a granite cottage surrounded by a white picket fence. Behind it was a middle-aged woman, hurriedly pulling up a canopy of white parasols.

Sam smiled as she caught her eye and gave a friendly wave.

The woman glowered back, her lips twisted into a tight shape resembling a cat's bottom. 'If you're looking for a table, we're full.'

'Oh.' Sam took a step back. 'No, I –' She didn't have a reason for walking through the arch other than general curiosity, something her usually highly structured life didn't have time to indulge. Her stomach growled again. Breakfast in the cafe would have been ideal.

'Or are you after the garden?'

Sam looked around to see a wooden shed and sign pointing to La Seigneurie gardens. She nodded.

The woman hoisted up the last parasol. 'It's closed.'

'Ah.' Sam swung her fist, feigning disappointment and turned back towards the arch.

'But s'pose I can take ticket payment and you let yourself in. Might as well reduce queues for later. It's £8.'

Sam peered down the path towards the garden. It looked empty and peaceful. It was hard to imagine throngs of people jostling to get in. 'Thank you.' She fumbled for the £10 note she kept tucked behind her phone case. 'That's very kind. Keep the change.'

The woman looked at Sam as if she'd announced her purchase of a fleet of Lamborghinis.

Through the small wooden gate and along a path flanked with grass, Sam was faced with what looked like a mediaeval chapel hidden behind a spray of magenta hydrangeas and a large manor house. Beyond this was a wall with an arch, opening into row upon row of beds exploding with blooms.

Every inch was thick with flowers, small grasses and neatly pruned hedges dotted between a profusion of brilliant colour, like a diamond catching the sun. To the left of the arch was a jewel-like greenhouse and square lily pond edged by four columns of hedge. Ahead of her, the narrow path led under the shaded arms of waxy-leafed trees and wooden trellising entwined with sun-drenched roses towards parallel lines of daisies and lavender. She walked past two wisteria-adorned pergolas and a series of pink rose bushes arranged around a sundial towards a box-hedge maze.

As she ran her hand along the tightly packed leaves and turned into a dark corner and then another, a forgotten memory rose to the surface of her consciousness: her visit to the maze at Longleat as a child and losing her mother only to see her standing in the castle in the middle, seemingly unaware that Sam wasn't with her. She remembered running, crying, panicking, finding only twisting tracks of high walls, never getting any closer, other children laughing and shouting at her to go the other way.

She breathed in sharply. This maze was small, tiny really. The hedges ran higher than her gaze, but it could only be five or six metres across. A different path led her closer to the red flag flying in the middle, which fluttered gently in the breeze. A dead end; she turned the other way. She jumped up to look for a route, but something else caught her eye. The back of a head. She froze. Had someone been there the whole time? There was no sound other than the overlapping birdsong, an orchestra of miniature bells.

She jumped again; the head had turned. As she marched towards the entrance, the path turned off the other way, bringing her closer to the flag. There was the crunch of footsteps ahead. She turned another corner and yelped, falling back into the hedge in surprise.

Standing in front of her was a man in chinos and a linen shirt with a camera round his neck. Sam quickly covered her face in anticipation of an awful paparazzi shot, but instead he held out a hand towards her. 'Need some help?' he said, his thin lips curved into a sideways smile.

'Are you...?' She pointed at the camera. The last thing she needed was a story published about her escape.

'Of you?' He cocked a sharp eyebrow. 'Of course not. Just shooting the garden for our website.'

'Oh.' Sam's cheeks flushed. 'Phew. Sorry.' She let him help her up and brushed herself down. 'Thanks. I didn't know anyone was here. I thought the garden was closed.'

The man gave a deep laugh. He looked at her with wide blue eyes and the playful, mock-reprimanding quality of his gaze sent a prickle down her backbone. 'I could say the same thing. Snuck in for free, did you?'

'No!' She blushed, flustered again. 'I paid the lady at the restaurant.' She brushed a twig from her shoulder.

'Trust Mrs Pedvin. Never misses a chance to pocket a sale. How much did she charge you?'

'£8.'

'Ouf.' The man blew out his cheeks. 'Sneaky bit of tourist

tax there.'

Sam checked her watch and nodded over his shoulder. 'I think that's the way out?' she asked.

He smirked and ran his hand through his loose blonde curls. 'I'll show you.' He sidestepped past her and turned expertly through each turn until they were back in the bright sunshine of the garden, and he put on a pair of sunglasses from his pocket. 'Easy when you know how. Caspar by the way.' He leaned forwards, looking her straight in the eye and offering his hand.

Sam had met men like Caspar before, cavernous voice, floppy haircut and confident gaze. Issa's husband, Clive, was a prime example. She had interviewed heaps of them, burrowing into glib explanations until their coloured socks squirmed in their suede brogues. Caspar certainly wasn't the type she'd expected to meet outside Westminster or the Home Counties, and nor had she wanted to.

'Sam.'

He squeezed her hand and smiled.

She thanked him in a clipped tone and turned onto the path towards the sundial.

'What do you think?' Caspar asked before she could move. 'Not bad, huh?'

He motioned towards a bed of bee-loud lavender, behind which a red butterfly flitted into pride of foxgloves. The question seemed almost absurd.

'The garden? Of course. It's beautiful.' High up, a kestrel descended into her sight, swooping past the resplendent white and pink magnolia. She took a deep breath of the sweet air. 'It's quaint and cottage-like but with an edge of the wild, as if the plants are ready to pour out of their borders and smother the island. I love it.' She paused, watching the kestrel spiralling back up into the endless blue sky before she snapped back to herself. What was it with this place and people wanting to chat? And how did she manage to get sucked into it? She nodded politely and stepped resolutely forwards.

'You're absolutely right.' Caspar said slowly, putting his hands on his hips. 'Never managed to put my finger on it before. But that's totally it. Banged the nail on the head. In fact, there's something...' He paused. 'How long you here for?'

Sam sighed to herself as she turned. She'd lost track of the minutes slipping by and now she really needed to get going.

'Leaving this morning. Just need to buy my ticket.'

'Doubt it.'

She frowned.

'Ferry's out of service today then sold out until Sunday.'

A sinking feeling dragged through her stomach.

'That bloody racing event is clogging everything up for the weekend. Total madness.'

'Racing?'

'Just another local piss up. This should be the last year of it, thank God.'

Sam hid her face in her hands. She was overreacting, she knew, but she didn't want to spend three more days phone and internet-less in a rundown granite shack with only a donkey and a batty old dear for company. She wanted to get back to London. To Martin. To work. To the possibility of their next fertility step.

Every new, small problem didn't feel like a small problem anymore. Instead it felt like the expansion of her black hole of grief, like pulling a Jenga piece from an already skeletal tower.

She squeezed her lips to stop them from wobbling and gave a small nod. 'Thank you for letting me know.' She took a firm step forward and headed for the garden entrance. Familiar hot tears dribbled down her cheeks, but she didn't bother to wipe them away. Stoicism seemed pointless now. There was nothing left to hold her together.

With her vision blurred, her view of the garden ran like watercolour, the delicate flower beds now green and pink splodges against the glittering fountain and greenhouse, gleaming silver under the high sun.

All she could focus on was putting one step in front of the other, storming forwards into a life she no longer recognised as her own.

'Ow!' A piece of gravel lodged between her foot and sandal. She hopped then stumbled, unable to see anything to break her fall.

'Got you!' Two strong hands grabbed her arms.

She blinked back the tears and turned to see Caspar.

'Ok?'

'Yes, I...' She leaned on him to shake out the gravel from her foot. The garden sharpened back into view. 'Sorry, I didn't mean to be so dramatic. It's been a rough time.'

'Need to get back, do you?'

She nodded.

'It's no problem. My rib's out today, but I can take you in the morning.'

'Your *rib*?'

'Rigid inflatable boat.' He grinned. 'Don't worry. It's less dinghy, more James Bond. We'll speed over to Guernsey in half an hour.'

Sam bit her thumbnail. Was that safe? She didn't even know who this man was. The sunshine glinted off his sunglasses and another butterfly passed between them. But this was *Sark*, not London. How dangerous could he be?

She nodded quickly. 'Yes, thank you.'

'No biggie.' He pushed his sunglasses onto his head and looked at her again with those dancing blue eyes. 'I just want one small favour in return.'

She crossed her arms. Here it was. He'd want some pictures to sell. *Photographing the garden, my arse*, she said to herself. 'Like what?'

'Nothing weird,' he snorted. 'I just need,' he clicked his finger as he searched for the right words, 'an opinion. A design opinion.

'A *design* opinion?'

'I'm renovating a house, and I doubt a new piece of furniture has entered another house here in the last decade. I need an eye cast over by someone who has at least some sense of aesthetics and has been within sniffing distance of some decent modern interiors in the past year. You're from London, yes?'

She nodded. Was it that obvious?

'Well that makes you highly qualified for the job compared to the rest of the population here. Look, it's five mins down the road. It would be a great help. No funny business, I promise. And I just whipped up some croissants.'

She bit her cheeks. Croissants. Manna from heaven. Accompanying a stranger to evaluate his interiors was far, far out of her comfort zone. But if she wanted to get off the island tomorrow – and not to starve in the meantime – she wasn't sure what choice she had.

❉ ❉ ❉

Caspar's house was one the loveliest buildings Sam had ever seen.

A few minutes on the dirt track running past Mrs Pedvin's restaurant, they had turned onto a path that curled up a lushly planted hill. Tucked within a frame of trees and a magnificent white magnolia, a sprawling manor came into view.

It was sizeable but not intimidatingly so, more homely than formidably grand. A wide veranda ran along its middle, held up by two large bay windows overlooking a pristine lawn and fountain.

'I inherited it from my uncle,' Caspar declared as they crunched on the gravel towards the large door. 'It was a total wreck. Years of no upkeep. But we're getting there.' He ran a hand through his hair as he twisted his key in the lock, opening the door to reveal a sage green painted hall with a round stone table adored with an enormous glass vase of dried hydrangeas.

Sam bit her cheek as she looked down at her sandal clad feet, terracotta orange from the dust of the road, against the gleaming parquet floor. 'Shoes off?'

'Don't bother. There's a constant stream of builders and delivery men round here. It's filthy. There'll be a big clean before the promo shots later in the week, but no point worrying about it before then.'

'Promo shots?' Her stomach jolted. *Had* he recognised her? She pushed the thought away. How many times would she need to remind herself that she wasn't Beyoncé? Probably no one here would know the first thing about her.

'Sorry,' Caspar shouted over his shoulder as he walked through into the front room, throwing back the heavy curtains and opening a door to reveal a glistening turquoise swimming pool and long garden flanked by high trees. 'I've been in this bloody island bubble all summer; I forget other people don't know our news.'

He turned to face her, his body dark against the brightness flooding in from the window. 'It's going to be a hotel. Total luxury. World class. Unlike anything these islands have seen before. I've got huge plans for the place.'

Sam edged forwards out of the hall, taking in the pale, wooden furniture set against the marble fireplace and panelled walls. Compared to the rickety high street, it was like stepping into a design museum.

She reached down to run her hand through a faux fur rug. 'And the people of Sark are ready for total luxury?'

'They will be when they see how many jobs this place brings.'

'So you'll be hiring local people?'

'Sure.' He marched back towards the hall, the basket of freshly baked croissants in his hand. 'Try one. They'll be delivered to each room every morning.'

Sam had to stop herself from taking three.

'Good, huh?' Caspar smiled. Sam thought he might even have winked, but she was too preoccupied with trying to politely eat the pastry flakes that had ended up all over her fingers to care.

'Now for the tour.'

She coughed, brushing down the top of her dress before glancing guiltitly at the crumbs on the floor. 'What about this design dilemma?'

'Well you can't do that until you've got a feel for the place. Let's start upstairs.'

Sam hesitated. Was she mad – following a total stranger up to a floor of bedrooms? Back in the city, there was absolutely no chance she'd put herself in such a position. But things seemed different here – safer. Besides, if he had been trying any funny business, he likely wouldn't have spent quite so long detailing his choice of finish for the hall tiles. And, she reminded herself, Caspar was currently her surest bet on a speedy trip back home. She certainly wasn't going to be pleading with Walter for a lift.

The twelve bedrooms were beautiful, each bedecked in pale greens and greys with angular four-poster beds, deep-seated sofas and sumptuous marble bathrooms with roll-top baths. The two largest rooms were positioned in the middle of the house and had ceiling to floor windows which opened onto balconies with sun beds and hot tubs. It reminded Sam of a country hotel that Martin had once taken her to. She'd imagined they'd spend the weekend wrapped in each other's bodies and high cotton count sheets. Instead they'd planned a new segment together on whether golf courses were taking up too much countryside space.

Downstairs, Caspar led her through the library, two dining rooms and cinema room and pointed out the barn on the other side of the drive which was being converted into an indoor pool and spa. He talked about it all quickly and with passion, pointing out the top-quality taps, expensive wood and Italian furniture. He knocked on walls, showing her where they'd made rooms bigger, flicked light switches to showcase the intended mood and waxed lyrical about the sleek, newly polished staircase and balustrade.

Sam had smiled politely but with increasing bemusement. He was treating her like a top hotel critic, rather than a stranger he'd met in a maze.

'Well you've done a fantastic job,' she said as they stepped back into the hall. 'I really can't see what I can help you with. What time shall I be at the harbour tomorrow?'

'Wait,' he said, looking sheepish. 'There's one more room. And it's the one I need the advice on. Please.' He pushed his hands into his back pockets, his easy charisma momentarily slipping away.

She looked up to see a pendant light made of complex, intertwining circles of LED and brushed gold, like a tangled ribbon thrown into the sky. 'I'm not sure you need my help.'

Caspar scrunched his lips, as if debating how much to give away. 'I'm not a design guy.'

'Right.' Sam pointed a finger round the room. 'So your interior designer's quit and you've picked up a random stranger to help finish the job?'

'Something like that.'

'Really?'

'Yes.'

'Bullshit.'

'It's the truth.'

'I'm not buying it.'

Her heart quickened. Interrogation was what she was made for. She'd forgotten its flickering thrill.

Caspar sighed and turned to lean against the stone table. 'I project managed it all, but my girlfriend – now ex-girlfriend – planned the interiors. She never got round to doing the bar. Things...' he paused, 'ended before then. I bloody left it for ages but with the barn almost finished we're nearly ready to go, so I figured I'd better get on with it. The guys spent the past week painting it and shifting round furniture. We finished late yesterday. I tossed and turned all night wondering if I'd done the right thing. Figured I'd take an early walk, clear my head, see it fresh – try and imagine stepping into it as a glamorous, London-based weekender who's used to quality and has a discerning eye. And then,' he looked up at her from beneath his floppy hair, 'I found you.'

'And I'm a fussy, glamorous Londoner am I?'

'Are you not?' he looked at her as if posing a challenge.

She crossed her arms and tried not to smile as she pulled her old denim jacket across the thin tea dress. 'I'm a Londoner, but that's about it.'

'I wouldn't say that.'

She flushed before immediately steeling herself. *Did* he recognise her? Surely he'd have said by now. Perhaps he was just layering on the charm. She knew his type, the kind of man who'd drip praise over you like custard onto a cake to get what they wanted. Well, whatever he thought he was getting, she was only here for her own end of the deal: to get onto that boat.

She cleared her throat. 'Be warned that the peak of my decorating experience is choosing whether to get a cream or chrome coloured kitchen toaster.'

'Chrome, I hope.'

'Of course.'

'Thank goodness.' He sighed in mock relief and ushered her through to a door in the back corner of the house where he paused before pressing down on the handle. 'If you hate it, just tell me. I want a genuine opinion, not empty flattery. Your rib trip depends on it.'

Sam held up her palms. 'Warts and all.'

He pushed open the door to reveal a room quite different from the rest of the house and thick with the smell of fresh paint. Pairs of dark, velvet armchairs lined walls such a deep blue they were almost black. Facing the door was a carved wooden bar, behind which hung three polished brass porthole mirrors. Sam stepped inside and turned around, noticing the stars painted on the navy ceiling and a series of etchings on the back wall which, as she looked closer, she realised were antique maps.

Caspar switched on the little lamps on each side table and tugged the velvet curtains closed. She sunk into one of the armchairs.

'So...?' he perched on the seat opposite her. 'What do you think?'

She looked round. This dark, quiet space was exactly what she needed; it felt like being cocooned in the belly of a great ship, safe from the problems of the shore. 'I like it.'

'Honestly?'

'Honestly.'

'It's not too dark? Too old fashioned? Too different from the rest of the house?'

'I'm not sure what a glamorous weekender with a discerning eye would make of it, but I think it's perfect.' She frowned slightly, hoping she hadn't sounded flirtatious.

'If you think so, that's good enough for me,' Caspar said in low voice. She'd clearly failed.

He held her gaze until his phone vibrated in his pocket, and he took it out to answer a message.

Sam cursed inwardly. This was not the sort of scenario she needed to be in right now. All she needed was to focus on sorting out logistics for getting on that rib. She stood and looked at the largest map, reading the place names to sooth the raised beat of her heart. She rounded her mouth over the French words – La Ville Roussel, La Grand Greve, Brecqhou, Point du Nez. She kept reading mindlessly until she reached the tail at the bottom of the island, an outcrop called 'Little Sark'.

Had Caspar been looking at her like *that* or had she imagined it? After the life jacket incident yesterday, she couldn't trust her judgement. It was so long since she'd been flirted with. Any new man she met was either through work when she was with Martin or was one of Martin's friends. Sam hadn't been conventionally pretty at school – short, prone to blushing, no boobs to speak of and with a nose her mother had always hoped she'd 'have sorted' – and she'd grown up gaining respect from the boys as a sparring partner, a source of quick-witted banter with a lightning fast tongue. It was only when she'd later reluctantly given in to the fact that a television career for a woman still demanded regular blow dries, painful heels and push-up bras that men started addressing her in a different way. Men, that was, including Martin.

The reality of being in a stranger's house suddenly made her feel nervous. What had she been thinking? Yes, he was charming and good looking, but – from a quaint little place or not – Caspar could be anyone. He could pick up a new woman and use his corny lines every week.

She almost shuddered as he stood next to her, his shirt touching her jacket as he put his phone back in his pocket. 'That map's about the only thing left in the house from my uncle's days.'

A phone. Sam could finally contact Martin. He'd be worried sick. She could look up the studio's number online, and they'd put him through.

'Any chance I could borrow your mobile? Mine broke yesterday.' She hesitated. 'My boyfriend will be worried about me.'

'Oh, right. Of course.' Caspar passed it to her. 'Whatever you need.'

She gave a tight smile and slipped out into the corridor as she searched for the studio number. Once she dialled through, she was passed round a couple of secretaries who asked code words to check that she really was who she said she was before she was eventually transferred to Martin.

'It's me!' Sam said. 'I'm all ok!' She could hear the rush of the studio in the background and longed to be back in its midst.

'Who's me?' It wasn't Martin's voice, but a woman.
'Who's that?'
'Who's *that*?'

'Sam, of course.'

'Oh. It's Keira.'

Sam let out a breath she hadn't realised she'd been holding.

'Keira! Everything ok? I'll be back the day after tomorrow. Is Martin there?'

'Aren't you supposed to be ill? Martin said you'd be off all summer.'

Sam stole into the opposite room to avoid being overheard. It looked like Caspar's office. She took a cursory glance at a letter on desk addressed to Caspar Rowe – well at least he was who he claimed to be.

'I am. Well was. I'm recovering. But I'm coming back on Monday. I'm much better.'

'That's not what Martin…'

'I know, I know. He's been so worried about me. But I'm better. Fine. Ready to get back on the show. Could I speak to him? I need to let him know I'll be back tomorrow.'

'Why didn't you call him yourself?'

Sam bristled. 'Slight issue with my mobile,' she said as brightly as she could muster. 'Could you just put him on?'

'I'm not sure he's available.'

'He'll be waiting to hear from me.'

Sam checked her watch. It was almost twelve. Martin should have just wrapped up morning filming.

'I'll check,' Keira said before returning a moment later. 'He's not available. Sorry. Feel better soon, but don't rush to come back. We've replanned the summer content without you.'

Bile rose in Sam's throat. 'Just tell him it's me, will you?'

'Now's not a good time.'

'He's not heard from me in over 24 hours and has no idea where I am. Now *is* a good time.'

'I can leave a message?'

'Just put me through, Keira, for goodness' sake.'

'He's busy.'

Sam leant against the wall. 'Fine. *Fine*. But please tell him that I'm coming home tomorrow. And ask him to call me back on this number in the next hour, ok?'

'Ok.'

'Make sure it's within the hour.'

'Sure.'

'Good.' Sam shut down the call and frowned. She figured there must be a reasonable explanation for why Martin couldn't take the call. She just wasn't sure what it could be.

CHAPTER 12

'Everything alright?' Caspar stood as she entered the room.

Sam mustered a non-committal mumble.

'Is that a yes?'

She slumped in a chair, the phone held close to her chest. 'Things are just in a funny place at the moment.'

He crossed his arms and nodded as if waiting for an explanation.

'It's too...' she looked up again at the star-studded ceiling, 'complicated to go into.'

'No problem. No need to tell me anything. I'm no good with relationship stuff anyway. I mean, I'm assuming it *is* relationship stuff? You've not run away to Sark to escape the clutches of the mafia or anything like that?'

'No,' she laughed. 'It's...' she thought about the past few weeks. 'It's relationship stuff. Sort of.'

'And it's why you've ended up in Sark on your own but desperate to leave?'

She rubbed her temple with her hand. 'I guess.' She looked down at the phone, wishing for it to ring. 'Do you mind if I stay for a bit? I'm due to be getting a call back within the hour. I'll be out of your hair straight after. It's from my boyfriend,' she added after a pause. 'He was busy with work.'

Caspar walked behind the bar and picked up a bottle of

gin.

'Not an issue. Fancy a drink? Martini? It's past midday so it's officially allowed. Feels like a good moment to christen the bar.'

She batted a hand away. 'Not for me. You can get on with your morning. I'll just wait here if that's ok?' She couldn't remember the last time she'd had alcohol. For years she'd drunk a couple of glasses of wine in the run up to ovulation and then went sober for the two-week wait to find out if she'd conceived. Every time her period came, Martin would join her that evening for a commiserative glass of Rioja. For the first few months they used it as a little celebration of everything that she could still do for two more weeks – drink, eat sushi and soft cheese – but soon it became a numbing mechanism, something to help her through the pain of the knowledge that it had been yet another failed month. But when the IVF started, she'd given up alcohol entirely, along with caffeine and fast food, replacing both with herbal tea and copious prenatal vitamins.

But now, she realised with a pang, there was nothing stopping her. There was no chance of her being pregnant. 'Actually, why not?'

'How do you like it? Dry, wet or dirty?'

Despite herself, Sam blushed.

'Don't worry. I'll make it my special way.' He turned and started picking out different bottles from a cabinet behind the bar. 'So how long have you been on the island?' He called over his shoulder.

'Just since last night.'

'That all? So you've hardly seen it?'

'How much is there to see?'

'Touché.' Caspar turned round as he mixed the cocktail shaker, the muscles in his arms tensing under his shirt. She slid up onto a stool.

'Cheers.' He poured the liquid out into two iced glasses and passed her one. 'To the new bar.'

'To the new bar.' She took a large gulp, and tried and failed to conceal her spluttering.

'Bloody hell,' she coughed. 'You've got a palate like a fireman's glove. Is that pure gin?'

'Pretty much.'

'No more for me.'

'Go on.' Caspar smiled as he knocked his own back. 'It sounds like you need it.'

She rolled her eyes and checked the phone again. Nothing. 'Fine.' She drained it in one before clamping a hand over her mouth to keep it from coming up again.

'Attagirl!'

'Christ!'

'You like it?'

'It's like drinking petrol!'

'Ah!' Caspar smacked the bar playfully. 'You'll get used to it.'

Sam cleared her throat and looked out the window to see the newly arrived group of builders carrying wood into the barn. She peered more closely. One of them looked familiar. A man with dark stubble, wide shoulders and thick arms. How did she know him? He turned and caught her eye. Walter. She stumbled forwards, the chair slipping back behind her.

'Woah!' Caspar ran round to grab her. 'Easy, tiger.'

'Sorry.' Sam flushed. 'I'm fine.' She dodged out the view of the window. 'Is one of your builders called Walter?'

'Probably.'

'Oh. I just... I thought he was a fisherman.'

'They all do about six jobs each here. No proper economy to support anything full time.' He fanned his arm around the building. 'The Rowe will change all that, of course.'

She smiled politely and there was a brief awkward pause before both spoke at the same time:

'Look, they don't need me here today.'

'I'd better be getting back.'

They laughed. Caspar pushed his curls out of his eyes.

'No need to wait for the phone call?'

'Oh, yes. Right. Do you mind? I didn't think he'd be long. I can just wait here.'

'Not at all. But at least let me give you a tour. You can't come to the island and not even see it. Come on. Ever been on an electric bike?'

'I'm not sure...'

Having a martini was one thing, getting on a bike was quite another. She had hardly exercised properly in years. There'd been stretching and gentle yoga, but no overheating, no sudden movements. There'd been a time when she'd run to work every day, loving the rush of pounding across London Bridge to the studio, parliament on one side, the Eye on the other. But, like so many things, it had slipped away.

'Trust me. You'll be fine.'

Sam shook her now slightly dizzy head, but, as she did so, she saw the builders reappear in a different window. Walter turned to pick up a hammer. She slunk back against the wall, trying to conceal herself by the curtain. Her limbs felt light and her tongue loose.

'You know what, sure. Let's get out of here.'

'Great.' Caspar gestured for her to follow him into the hall. 'You'll love it. It's like flying.'

Soon Sam found herself whizzing down the hill, teeth chattering and knuckles white.

Caspar whipped past her and swung round the corner, cycling to the end of the road and back as she trailed behind.

'Get that throttle on!' he called. He pointed at a café in what looked like someone's back garden. 'I'll grab some sandwiches and catch you up. Just cycle straight. You can't go wrong.'

She didn't dare turn to look at him so stared resolutely forward, amazed at the curious sensation of floating with such little effort on her part. In her peripheral vision she noticed hedge upon hedge and a patchwork of fields and cows and sheep, and she couldn't help mildly panicking that this straight path she was on seemed to lead directly to the edge of a cliff.

Just as she really thought the road might end at any moment, Caspar sped up next to her, a cloud of dust in his wake. 'Left,' he shouted, 'to the monument.'

She followed him down a bumpy, narrow footpath, lined on both sides with the last of the year's bright yellow gorse, perfuming the air with its coconut smell. As she rattled round the corner, she found him standing at the foot of a large granite obelisk.

'Top five best view. Right here.'

She laid her bike down and Caspar helped her up onto the foot of the monument, in front of which was a wide, glittering expanse of sea framed by green, rocky islands.

'Top five on the island or in the world?' she asked.

'The world, of course.'

Holding onto the railing in front of her, she took it all in. London was her city, and she loved its quirky skyline of oddly shaped skyscrapers against centuries-old buildings, but one thing it didn't offer was space. Here she looked out onto a vast, seemingly untouched landscape, inhabited only by the wind and waves beneath.

'Isn't it fantastic?' He moved next to her and pointed to the island furthest away. 'The larger one is Guernsey. That small one to the right is Jethou and the one next to it with the long, white beach is Herm. Right in front of us is Breqhou and to the left is Little Sark.'

'Quite the metropolis.'

'You could say so.'

The air was fresh and salt tinged. Sam breathed it in and listened to the waves sloshing round the rocks below.

She slunk down and swung her legs over the lip of the monument floor. Caspar joined her and pulled out a crab sandwich from his rucksack. 'You can't leave without having one of these. Only thing worth eating on the island. They'll be on our lunch menu. With a few extras to tart them up, of course.'

She noticed the phone in the bag. 'No one's called?'

'Negative.'

She bit her lip. What was going on? It was over an hour now. Maybe Keira hadn't passed on the message. But why wouldn't she? Sam back on the show with Martin was what they all wanted, wasn't it? The show needed them together to work. Surely – of all people – the producer would know that.

Caspar ate his sandwich in two bites, licking the mayonnaise from his fingers. 'So what's this boyfriend done that's made you run away here? And then what's he done to make you run back?'

'I haven't run away,' she garbled between mouthfuls. The sandwich was delicious; rich and fresh with a squeeze of lemon.

He curled his lips.

'I haven't!'

She shielded her face from the sun, looking straight out into the glass-like blue green water.

'Well maybe.' She swallowed. 'I think I needed to run away to know why I needed to run back. If that makes sense.'

'I get it. Like me with the island.'

'Really?'

'I came here a lot as a child. Holidays. Boating. But then London called. I worked in the city.

She smiled.

'What?'

'I knew it. You have that air.'

'What air?'

She ran her hand through her hair. 'Ya. Ya. Fantastic. When's the deal going through?'

'I do not have that *air*!'

She raised her eyebrows.

'Fine! Do you want to hear or not?'

'Go on.'

'Good. Well. When my uncle died last year, I finally came

back. And I realised what I'd been missing. The opportunities here are fantastic. I mean look at this place.'

She looked carefully again at the view, noticing the caves carved into the cliff faces and the carpet-thick coverage of bracken, glistening beneath the now risen sun.

'And when I saw the house again – with adult eyes – I saw its potential. I brought my girlfriend over. We did it all up over the winter – well, almost all. But she decided island life wasn't for her. And I get it, I do. They're small minded here - you're cut off from everything. No shops. No takeaway apps. No spas. Nothing. And she was a bit of a party girl. It was feudal until only a few years ago, can you believe? And there's still nonsense like Christmas tractor runs and lawnmower hill climbs and local princess pageants. But it's changing.'

Sam thought it all sounded like good, clean fun. 'Why?'

'Lawnmower hill climbs don't pay bills. Who's going to pay for basic services? No tax. No proper government – just a couple of busy bodies with bees in their bonnets over minor issues. No proper leadership.'

'And the hotel's going to solve all that?'

'Totally. It'll put Sark on the map as *the* luxury destination in the British Isles. The island's crying out for it. Even if the locals don't realise it yet.'

The phone suddenly rang, and she stood to attention. Caspar put out a hand, 'Sorry, it's my guys back at the house.'

He walked towards the footpath, hand on his hip as he took the call.

Bells tinkled in the distance, and she looked round to see the cows in the nearby field lying down or heading under the trees. In front of her, the other islands faded into mist as a blue grey cloud brewed over the sea.

She looked at the monument behind her and noticed an inscription. It was a bleak story, telling the sorrow of a family after a boat wreck. She scanned the middle section and was about to turn when the last section struck her. 'Caution and Warning' was engraved in capital letters and below were the words of a psalm: 'Thy way is in the sea and thy path in great waters and thy footsteps are not known.' She spoke the words over again to herself. Though she wasn't entirely sure what they meant, they felt apt somehow. Never before had she felt so much like a rudderless boat in the ocean.

'I need to get back,' Caspar called from behind her. 'Join me later? Dinner? I can rustle up one of our new dishes.'

She looked down at the water which was starting to churn white with roller waves. Martin hadn't called. It really wasn't what she'd expected. She'd have to try him again in the morning. And was Caspar just being friendly? She couldn't tell anymore. 'No. No, thank you. I shouldn't. What time shall I be at the harbour?'

'Well,' he nodded up to the now blackening sky, 'weather dependent… nine? Look, come for dinner later. Nothing awkward. I'm not asking you on a date or anything. It's just the weather's crap, and you're not going to want to trudge round the island to any of the sorry excuses for restaurants. Trust me. Nothing formal – come for seven.'

She looked out again to the churning waves below the cliff edge as the first fat raindrops began to fall. She sighed inwardly. At least if she went back in the evening she'd know if Martin had rung her back. 'Ok,' she said. 'Will do.'

❋ ❋ ❋

Sam caught sight of her reflection in a window as she approached Caspar's door. Her hair was mildly less electrocuted mad scientist, despite her curling tongs not working, but, with her tea dress still damp from the earlier rain, she only either had jeans and T-shirts or her silver lamé dress to change into. She'd gone for jeans and T-shirt of course, very keen *not* to give the wrong impression, but felt scruffy approaching the grand house with its gleaming door. She went to knock, but it pressed open on her touch, and she stepped tentatively onto the stone floor.

'Caspar?'

Soft jazz notes danced in the air, and she followed their trail towards the kitchen where he stood chopping behind the oven in the middle of the gleaming metal units, his back towards her and his hips twirling in time to the music. She tried and failed to swallow a laugh.

'Hey!' He turned, putting down a knife. 'You made it.'

'And just in time for the dance show.' She slipped past the door, her fingers twisting behind her back with unexpected nerves. It was silly, she told herself. Dinner didn't mean anything. *She* wouldn't mind if Martin went out for dinner with a woman. Her throat tightened. God, she really hoped he wasn't out for dinner with Nina. 'Any call back for me?'

'No,' Caspar said and turned to take out a different knife.

It was like a stone had been dropped in her stomach. What *was* going on? In a way it could be quite cute turning up as a surprise tomorrow, but she'd prefer to let Martin know.

Caspar turned up the music on his phone. 'You like a bit of Bossa nova?'

'Sure.' She gave an awkward laugh. 'What's that?'

'What's that?' He threw up his hands in mock shock. 'What's that? You, my friend, are in for a treat. Bossa nova is samba. I first heard it in Brazil on my gap year. It's the best.' He rolled his shoulders in time to the gently knocking beat. 'We're going to have it playing in reception rooms. Live band on the weekend. Sexy, exotic vibes.' He turned back to the chopping board. 'You'd love it.'

She snorted and leant against the unit behind her. 'And how do you know that?' The question came out far more coquettish than she'd intended.

Caspar headed towards the hob, a board covered in a mound of small, red vegetables in his hands. 'I always know what people want.'

She squeezed her thumbs, desperately hoping that the blood would drain from her flushing cheeks. 'Is that red pepper?'

'Chilli.'

'*Chilli?*' Sam didn't so much cook as occasionally heat things up in the microwave, but she'd watched enough chef masterclasses on *Wake Up!* to know that was a huge pile for two people.

'I'm treating you to my famous chicken. Better than anything you'll get in these bland islands. You ok with a bit of heat?'

'Yes,' she lied. 'Of course.' This didn't seem like the best time to mention that her favourite food was Cornish pasties from a London Bridge station kiosk.

The contents of the board slid into a hot pan which spat and shivered. Sam spluttered as the spice-laced steam hit her throat. Caspar laughed and shook the handle of the pan. 'Head out to the terrace. I won't be long.'

She stumbled towards the back door, eyes and nose streaming like a soldier in gas. Her throat fizzled and she coughed, gulping in the crisp evening air. How did she manage to fail in every social situation these days? On her first proper date with Martin she'd been on fire. Wearing a bandage dress, leather jacket and rock-stud heels, she'd quipped, laughed, questioned, matched every one of his sharp comments. He'd gaped at her like she was the coolest girl in the city.

Now she perched on the edge of a sun lounger and dabbed her damp eyes, trying not to smudge her mascara but knowing she looked a state. Not that it mattered, she repeated to herself. Caspar Rowe wasn't someone she needed to impress.

She sighed and leant back. None of it mattered really. That was why she was there: to step outside her life. And with only one more night away, she might as well make the most of it.

Her thoughts were interrupted by the click of the door and a trickle of languid guitar strings.

'Martini or margarita?'

Caspar moved into her line of sight, a cocktail glass in his hand.

She pushed herself up onto her elbows. 'Absolutely not. I'm never having a martini again.'

He snapped his finger. 'I knew you'd say that. So here's your margarita.'

'I'm not sure –'

'No excuses.' He pressed the cold glass into her hand. 'You're going to love this one. Trust me.'

'You seem very sure about my preferences.'

'Lucky I'm going to be a hotelier then. As I said, I know what people want.'

She laughed, but as he went inside to serve up and she drained the crisp, sour liquid, she wondered whether he might be right. Her slightly fuzzy head, the mint clean air, the soft music on the breeze; a glimmer of something – not happiness, she was far from ready for that, but something like not *un*happiness – seeped into her veins like water in paint.

'Madam,' Caspar called from the kitchen. 'Your dinner awaits.'

He ushered her into the restaurant on the other side of the hall. It was an absurdly big room for just the two of them, with ceiling to floor windows covered by long white drapes and enormous metal bauble lights hanging over a sienna orange banquette spanning almost the length of the room. He had set them up a round table in the corner in front of a large mirror.

Sam was tipsy now and could say out loud what she hadn't wanted to admit before. 'You know I have a boyfriend. This looks suspiciously like a date. You were very clear –'

'Not a date,' Caspar interrupted as he pulled out a chair for her and took a match from his pocket to light the candle. 'Research.' He pointed at the mirror. 'You see, this is where I'm going to sit to watch the customers. Track their reactions to the service and the menu and the food. But for now you're my only guest. And your payment is that you must tell me what you think.'

Sam smiled as she unravelled her napkin. 'It's very nice. Fancy.'

'Nice?' He wrinkled his nose as he checked the label on a bottle of wine. 'Fancy? It's not a supermarket cake. That all you got?'

'Well, I don't know,' she laughed, sitting on her hands. 'It's sleek. Modern. Sort of scandi meets Art Deco. Ikea meets Claridge's. Is that any better?'

He let out a deep throaty laugh. 'Fine as long as you don't mention flat pack furniture in here. Everything is –'

'Custom made?'

'And don't you know it.' He gave a wry smile. 'Wine?'

She went to shake her head, but then figured she'd be back on the egg transfer no-booze train by tomorrow. She shrugged in agreement, and Caspar met her gaze before he squeezed out the cork on the bottle, sniffed it and poured them both large glasses.

'But now,' he clapped his hands together, 'the main event.'

She ran her fingers over each other. She couldn't deny that she was enjoying herself. Of course she'd so much rather be snuggled at home with Martin, his hand on her growing belly, but she wasn't. She was here. So she might as well make the most of it.

Caspar strode back and forth from the kitchen, both plates balanced on his long fingers.

He slid a dish under her nose. 'Once you try this, you'll never want to go near flaccid fish and chips or whatever other lifeless crap the sorry excuses for restaurants serve here ever again.'

Her mouth was suddenly dry. She hadn't been near chicken since that fateful vomiting at Issa's. But this would be fine, she steeled herself. It *looked* good. A few more chillis than she'd usually go for, but... She pierced a mouthful with her hammered gold fork. Fine.

She chewed, swallowed and smiled. Absolutely fine. Decent, in fact. Casper wasn't lying when he said he could cook. She went to take another mouthful. Her lips started to tingle.

'It's got a nice little kick.' She nodded slowly. 'Comes through in the aftertaste.'

'Great news. Because a couple of mates have complained that it's too hot. Ridiculous, right? I want the restaurant to serve food that actually has flavour. Not some depressing excuse for a burger in a defrosted bap.'

She tried to subtly wipe her running nose. Beads of sweat started to form at her hairline.

'I'm thinking sea bass ceviche, caramelised lamb wrack, garlic black tiger prawns, sticky beef short rib, wagyu empanadas.' He waved his fork in the air like a conductor.

A cough escaped her throat.

'Big flavours. Fantastic ingredients. That farm to table nonsense is over. This'll be bold, international luxury. I'm keen on getting an open fire so the chefs can sear meat over raw flames.'

She smiled stiffly and drained her water glass, holding the last gulp in her mouth like a puffer fish.

Now everything was burning – her lips, her cheeks, her tongue. Sweat dribbled down her neck and along her forehead. She tried to quickly fan herself.

'Everything alright?' Caspar asked, tucking into another large forkful.

'Mmhmm.' She wiped her eyes with her napkin.

He leaned forward as he took another bite. 'It's ok if you can't handle the spice.' The corner of his mouth curled upwards. 'Not everyone can.'

'I'm good,' she managed to whisper. 'It's,' she cleared her throat, 'nice.' She took a large gulp of wine and blinked back the tears as the acidity hit her throat.

As she went to cut off another piece, the plate of food suddenly appeared enormous. How could she eat another mouthful, let alone anywhere near a half socially acceptable amount? She tried to carefully scrape off every last spot of chilli from a corner of chicken.

'You're not a fan of the sauce?'

'Oh,' she smiled, 'no, the sauce is delicious. I, just, you know...' she forked another mouthful. 'Best 'till last.'

'Glad to hear it.' He took a sip of wine. 'What do you make of the lighting? Too dark? Too light? Too yellow?'

She placed the chilli-free morsel of chicken into her mouth and tried to chew it as gently as possible. If she could avoid letting any of the flavour out, she figured, then she might be able to swallow with it barely touching a taste bud.

It didn't work. As soon as the fork brushed her lips, it was like eating fire. Her nose ran onto her top lip and sweat ran across her temple. She took another large swig of wine.

'You're sure you're ok with it? I can try to mix it with a dollop of yoghurt.'

'Don't worry,' she tried to say, though it came out like the wheezing splutter of an old smoker.

'Are you sure? You're sweating.' Caspar scanned her face. 'Like a lot.' He reached over to touch her forehead. 'And you're burning up.'

She flinched at his touch and was suddenly consumed by unease. Her being here on her own was ridiculously inappropriate. Martin probably hadn't been able to pick up because he was really busy with work, trying hard to sort everything out with her being away. And here she was – laughing and joking over dinner.

'Actually,' she croaked. 'I think I am unwell. I'd better get back.' She pushed back her chair.

'Wait,' Caspar walked round the table and put a hand on her back, 'let's get you upstairs. You can stay in one of the suites.'

She so wanted to take him up on the offer – to luxuriate in one of those enormous, roll-top baths and curl up in a four-poster bed's soft sheets. But something held her back. Staying the night at the house of a man she'd only just met – even if it was, technically, a hotel – was far from ok. Martin would be furious.

She took a step backwards. 'No, really. I'll see you at the harbour in the morning. Thank you for everything.'

And with a curt nod, she turned and paced out of the hotel and along the ink black road.

CHAPTER 13

As Sam approached the edge of the field, she looked across at the grey cottage, now only half visible in the mist and rain. Her feet and clothes were soon soaked from the wet grass and air as she stormed, head down, towards the door.

The cottage wasn't much warmer inside than out, and she ran into the kitchen to boil water for tea, trailing a path of pools on the stone floor from her dripping jeans and hair. The switch flicked stubbornly back into place. She pressed it again. The same happened. She swore and went to the sink to run hot water – at least she could pretend it was a cup of tea – but it ran cold. She banged her fist against the plastic worktop and ran upstairs to the bathroom, turning on the corridor light on her way. Nothing. She tried the bathroom light. It didn't work. She shouted out, stamping her heel on the peeling, linoleum floor before sinking down onto the toilet seat, head in hands. Stupid cottage, stupid island with stupid power cuts. Caspar was right: things were a mess and needed fixing. They clearly did need a business like The Rowe to come and improve things.

Growling in frustration, she got up to see if she could at least build a fire to dry herself out downstairs. A grim reflection caught her eye in the dirty mirror. Her damp hair fell limply around her pale skin and old mascara was smudged under her tired eyes. She rubbed it away, mortified that Caspar had seen her like that before telling herself off for caring: she'd never see him again after tomorrow, so why should it matter?

Peeling off her sodden jacket, she realised that she desperately wanted a hot shower. The wind rattled against the small window, and she looked out to see the rain subsiding into drizzle. But across the field towards the bottom of the valley, she saw lights from what must be Judith's farm.

'Huh,' she muttered. Judith must have a generator. And therefore she'd have heat. And warm water. And cups of tea. And Sam *had* returned her donkey to her earlier, so she *did* technically owe her a favour. She was also still a little bit tipsy, so the idea of running across a field to ask her neighbour for a shower didn't seem quite as mad as she might normally have found it.

She stripped off her wet clothes in favour of dry leggings and a jumper and headed quickly out for the field, grabbing Walter's tent-like coat before she pulled the fragile front door frame behind her.

Judith was strangely pleased to see her.

'Wonderful! I knew you'd change your mind!' She ushered Sam into a busy hallway clogged with pile upon pile of coats, towels, boots and umbrellas. 'I'll get my anorak – foul weather for summer – and show you how to do it first time round.'

Sam was about to protest when Judith reached up a frail hand to her shoulder. 'Bless you. I knew you'd want to help. I can always tell a good egg.' She moved to poke her head into a room opposite the staircase. 'We won't be long, Jeremy. No crying. Mummy will be back soon. I've got to show this nice lady how to feed Trevor D.'

Sam sunk her hands into her deep pockets. She really didn't have the heart to say otherwise.

'Right, my love.' Judith stepped forwards, swamped by a huge yellow raincoat. 'Let's be quick as Jeremy'll be missing his cuddles.'

'I didn't come to...' Sam hesitated. Judith looked up at

her with large, warm eyes.

'I didn't come *home* to electricity today. Any chance of a shower when we're back?'

Judith tutted. 'That house is left to wrack and ruin. That landlord who owns it's no good. No good at all. Don't worry, my love. Shower until your heart's delight, and I'll ring my grandson to come and sort you out. He's a handyman, see.'

Sam's shoulders relaxed from tension she hadn't realised she was holding. But before she'd had time to thank Judith, she was out the front door and heading over to the enclosed field.

'Poor, Trevor D,' Judith called as they walked towards the shed at the other end. 'He'll be huddled in there, scared as anything.'

And that was where they found him. Tucked into the corner in a pile of hay, his legs tightly folded underneath him and ears pulled tightly backwards.

'Hello, my love.' Judith ruffled the fuzz of hair on his forehead. 'You don't like rain, do you, silly sausage? It's alright now. Almost gone. And your new friend's here to feed you.' She turned round to smile at Sam who tried to both look enthusiastic and conceal a hiccup.

'The formula's in the little room next door. You just put it in the bucket with some water. Fill it up to the line. You're ever such a help. Daniel just can't keep his little fingers to himself these days. Wants to put everything in his mouth – including donkey feed. And if I bend down to give him it, there's no guarantee I can get back up again.'

Sam brought the formula into the room and sat carefully next to Trevor D as he lapped it up, his entire face covered by the bucket.

'Go on,' coaxed Judith. 'You've worn yourself out trundling up and down the field to poor Sam's house. Silly thing. I *am* sorry about that.' She looked up to meet Sam's eye. 'Must have given you a real shock.'

Sam laughed and agreed.

'And you're staying there all on your own? No one with

you?'

Trevor made a loud snorting noise as he snuffled up the milk.

'On my own. But I'm going back tomorrow. To London. Leaving early. Some personal stuff to work out.'

'Right. Of course. You said. Lovely that you wanted to help me out this evening at least.'

Sam flushed in her white lie.

'If you don't mind me prying, is anyone waiting for you back in London?' Judith said the name of the city as if it were one of Pluto's moons.

Sam ran a hand over one of Trevor D's velvet ears. 'My boyfriend. I'll be back to see him tomorrow.'

'He didn't fancy the trip?'

'No,' Sam said, straightening her neck. 'He...' She wasn't sure what to say. 'It's complicated.'

'Right. I understand. Well, not that things were complicated with Trevor and me. Childhood sweethearts. Married at 19, together over fifty years without an unkind word. I don't half miss him.' She gave Trevor D a scratch on the forehead as he lifted his nose.

'Sorry for your loss,' Sam replied, immediately regretting the phrase's shallow tokenism.

'Oh no, my dear. All that time with Trevor. I was lucky. It was simple: we loved each other. None of this nonsense young people go through these days. I can't tell you my granddaughter's palaver. Poor love.'

Sam mumbled something nondescript in reply as she went to clean the bucket, keen to close the door on discussions of her love life. Not that Judith would probably even know how to sell a story to a tabloid if she wanted to.

The women stepped out into the early evening sky where the rain had been replaced by a thick layer of mist, which lay low over the valley like the gassy surface of a distant planet.

Neither spoke until Judith turned after closing the gate.

'Don't mind my prattling. As long as you love him and he loves you, then you'll get over anything. Your partner should be like your home; it might have a leaky tap or a messy room or sticking door, but it's where you feel you belong.'

A reminder of Martin's lack of a call sliced through Sam's stomach. Tomorrow, she told herself, would be different. He'd be so pleased that she'd decided to come home.

* * *

Sam returned to her cottage freshly showered, fed and having had two hot mugs of tea. Judith had called her grandson over to fix the electricity, and he was due to arrive any minute.

After hours of Judith's nattering about the various summer events and her sadness that they might not happen again – though Sam had been too distracted by thoughts of Martin's lack of contact to work out quite why – the misty sky had turned from white to a deep navy, the light of the moon muffled by thick cloud. Judith had given Sam a pile of candles, and she lit them around the cottage, basking the rooms in a sepia glow. It was, Sam had to admit, rather cosy, and the soft light did blur out some of the dirt and rough edges.

It wasn't long before she saw the beam of a torch streaking white stripes across the fields, followed by a sharp knock, loud clatter and even louder swearing.

'Careful!' She ran for the porch, 'the door doesn't...'

But as the doubled over figure righted itself and stood back up to its full height, she recognised who it was.

'Walter. What are you doing here?'

'Should probably be asking you the same question.' He bent down to rub his knee. 'This place isn't safe enough to use as a barn, let alone a holiday cottage. And, please, it's Walt.'

'Well here I am. And someone's about to come over to make me an awful lot more comfortable.'

'Is that right?' His lip raised into a half smile. 'And who

might that be?'

'Someone my neighbour knows. If you don't mind, he'll be here any second.' She nodded at the front door.

'Well if my help's not wanted.' He bent to pick up the toolbox that Sam hadn't noticed by his feet.

'Judith called *you*?'

'I tend to call her Nan.'

'Huh. Exactly how many jobs do you have?'

'A few. Small island. We all share the load. Life's a bit different here to London.'

'Obviously.' She fanned a hand around the candlelit room before immediately cringing at how much she sounded like a sulky teenager.

'So do you want the electricity fixed? I'll get on with it or get home. The babysitter clocks off soon.'

Sam paused. She really hadn't wanted to see Walter again. Granted the spitting incident had been her mistake, but she wanted now to forget about it – not have her victim pop up in every corner like a human Whac-a-Mole. That was the beauty of London: it was so easy to avoid people. It was how she'd managed to slip quietly through the net of her social groups – making excuses for various events until she stopped getting asked along and resting peacefully in the knowledge that she wouldn't bump into any acquaintances in her day-to-day existence.

She scanned the room. It did look nice now, but she wouldn't be able to light all the candles at once if she heard another bump in the night. But the last thing she wanted was Walt swooping in to save the day whilst she loitered in the corner like some damsel in distress. But it really was bloody dark. What had Jack called it? A dark sky island. Great.

She shifted her weight to the other foot. 'That would be useful.' She faltered. 'Thank you.'

He slipped off his jacket and boots and swung his toolbox past her before heading straight for a cupboard in the kitchen which opened to reveal a fuse box.

She followed him across the room. 'You found that quickly.'

'What appliances did you use this morning?'

'Nothing.'

He turned to her. She could see him frowning in the flicker of light. 'You're sure?'

'*Yes*.' She glared back. 'I'm sure.'

He flashed his torch around the ground floor, inspecting each of the plugs, before heading upstairs.

'I haven't touched anything.' She followed him. 'I've barely been in the house.'

His torchlight illuminated her pile of underwear on the floor.

'Is this really necessary? She tried to push it behind the suitcase with her foot as he scoured the rest of the room. 'I left with it working and came back to it broken. Nothing has been plugged in. I imagine it's a problem with the mains on the island. Do the cables run properly into the house? Should they be checked?'

'So this isn't yours?' He held her curling wand out at arm's length as if he'd discovered a murder weapon. 'Because it looks like it might have tripped the switch.'

She snatched the wand from him. 'It hasn't.'

He raised an eyebrow.

'I didn't even get a chance to use it because it wasn't working.' Sam realised her mistake as the words came out her mouth. She bit her lip, waiting for a snide comment on city dweller ignorance.

Instead he strode back downstairs.

She perched on the end of the bed, clutching the wand to her chest.

'It's an old system.' Walt emerged again, only his strong profile visible in the darkness. 'So don't try to use any more fancy hair appliances. You'll blow another fuse.'

'I won't,' she said. The words came out harsher than she'd meant them to. 'I'm leaving in the morning.'

He looked back over his broad shoulder from where he was crouched by the plug, his forehead creased. 'Tomorrow? I thought I was due to take you back at the end of the summer?'

'I changed my mind.'

He shrugged and turned again to the wall. Sam stuffed both the curling wand and underwear pile back in her suitcase and shut the lid. Both she and Walt stood at the same time, their arms brushing as they did so. As she flinched and shuffled backwards, she noticed that his hair almost touched the beams of the ceiling.

'Fixed?'

'Almost.'

'Good.'

They paused. Walt tucked his screwdriver into his pocket. 'I know this place well.'

'Really?'

'Tried to buy it last year.'

'I thought you said it wasn't safe?'

'It's not.' He glanced up. 'The roof's shot and the floor's damp.' He tapped the beam above him. 'Thought I'd get it cheap and fix it up. Would be good to be closer to Nan.'

Sam scoffed. 'You can't exactly be that far away.'

'You try crossing La Coupée on a January night in a high wind because your nan can't work the TV remote and tell me it's not far.'

'Where?'

'The causeway.' He paused as if that would make perfect sense. 'To Little Sark.'

'Oh.'

Walt tapped the beam again, his arms flashing bronze in the light. 'Anyway.' He sighed. 'Owner wouldn't budge. Apparently it's some English idiot who's still flogging it out for holiday rentals even though the roof might cave in at any minute. Though I think you've been the only person stupid enough to actually take it on.'

'I am?' Sam stepped backwards and stumbled over her

suitcase. She yelped. He grabbed her arms and pulled her up, his hands hot against her cold skin.

'Steady. Let's get those lights on.'

She followed his large form down to the kitchen where he flicked back the switches.

They blinked under the harsh strip light as it exposed the room, replacing the softness of the candles with stark, laboratory white.

'There.' Walt nodded and headed for the door. 'You'll just need to wait a bit for the hot water to kick in.' He tugged on the muddied boots, knotted his laces and took his jacket from the hook. Sam pointed to the coat and jumper he'd leant her yesterday. 'I'll be back to get those tomorrow. My bike's full.'

He pushed open the door, letting in a fresh blast of damp air. 'Right then.' He briefly met her gaze. 'Good luck.'

But as the door clattered shut behind him, Sam stuck her foot out to open it. Perhaps he wasn't so bad. And this might be her last chance to avoid him selling a story if he ever happened to recognise who she was.

'Wait!'

He turned, still frowning, and she suddenly felt like a little child, not quite sure what to say.

'Yes?'

'Look,' she twisted her fingers behind her back, 'about the whole barking thing. And,' she cringed, 'the spitting…'

There was a long pause, and she waited for the ground to give way so she could be swallowed whole by her shame.

'Mistakes happen.' He gave a curt nod then turned and disappeared into the night.

CHAPTER 14

Hopes for a bright, clear morning and calm sea were dashed before Sam had even opened her eyes. Wind howled through the rafters and whistled through cracks in the windows. Once she'd persuaded herself out of the bed covers, she looked out to see the surrounding fields shrouded in a thick mist.

She clasped her forehead. How had she ever thought she'd want to stay for an entire month? Being trapped there for two days was a day too long.

As she trudged downstairs to put the kettle on, she found a note that had been slipped under the front door. She hadn't expected post, but at least it was less surprising than a donkey.

'Sorry, Sam,' it read in bold, sloping handwriting. 'No go in this weather. Due to clear midday. Meet me at the harbour 1pm. Caspar.'

She slunk onto the sofa. One more morning. She tucked her feet up underneath her and looked around the tatty room. What did people do when they wanted to relax without a phone? Any recent downtime she'd had she'd spent scrolling mindlessly through fertility posts, desperate as an addict for the latest success story to prove to herself things would work out. Perhaps she should do yoga. Or mediate. Then she remembered her library of political books in her suitcase and went upstairs to fish one out, slumping back on the bed with one in hand.

But, try as she might to concentrate on *Democracy and Debate in the Digital Age*, the words kept blurring into one and the sentences fell through her mind like sugar in a sieve. Sighing, she chucked it back in her suitcase and changed again into her jumper and leggings. It might be windy and misty, but she'd feed Trevor D one last time and go for a walk. If she was leaving the island today, she could at least see a bit more of it first.

Having nuzzled Trevor D and narrowly missed spilling his slop down her front, she headed past Judith's house towards the sea below. The dirt road running by the field soon split off into a path, and she walked resolutely forwards, heading towards the cliff. Soon enough, she was met with the steep, bracken-lined edge, under which the wild waves crashed into whipped curls of foam. The mist hung thick over the water, and it was hard to tell where the sea ended and the sky began. Shuffling along the wind-lashed path, she held onto branches and grass as she went, following the curve of the land above the bays and coves below. She pulled her denim jacket round her and wished she'd brought Walt's monstrosity of a coat with her. But, she figured, at least he might come and collect it whilst she wasn't there. Save her from having to face him again.

That stupid curling tong. She kicked at a rock on the path. There was no reason to have brought it with her; any hairstyle wouldn't last five minutes in the island's damp and wind-swept air. And there'd been something about Walt's swaggering about the cottage that had made her feel particularly inept. He'd probably gone home and had a good laugh with his wife about the ignorant tourist.

She furrowed her brow until she realised that the mist had lifted, revealing black clouds interspersed with sunlight and the waves calmed to a flat field of sea. The path eventually ended in a field next to a strange walkway connecting the island to another even smaller body of land. She stepped down onto the path, clutching onto the railings which kept her from the sheer drops on either side. As she peered over for a better look, the sun broke through, and the silver water glistened when it rippled over the rocks. It was, she had to admit to herself, really quite beautiful.

This must be **La** Coupée, she realised, the causeway. And the land on the other side must be Little Sark. It certainly suited its name; there wasn't a single building visible from where she was standing. She couldn't help wondering what had kept someone like Walt living there into his adult life. It had to be a love of nature or hatred of humans. Probably the latter. He was likely one of those weird, bitter isolationist types who thought people from the other local islands counted as foreign. She wondered what his wife – or girlfriend – was like.

She turned to head up the road on the hill back towards the cottage, leaning into each thigh as she went. Her body just wasn't as fit as it had once been. Expecting to get pregnant each month, she'd lost the will to keep active, even if it had meant Erin musing out loud about how the designer samples fell much better on gently sculpted muscle tone.

Field after field passed next to her, with one of them resembling the area being used for the racing she'd heard about, with piles of hay bales, sound equipment and tents. She'd never been particularly into racing but had once enjoyed dressing up in a chic hat for Ascot and not caring how much money she lost after Louise bought her four glasses of champagne.

Her chest tight and breathing laboured, she was relieved when the layers of thick hedges and fields gave way to granite houses, churches and tiny food shops where the unpackaged produce was laid out next to paper bags. And then, finally, a café. She figured it might not serve her usual double shot flat white, but it looked decent-ish. Rustic in what would be a purposeful way in east London, but here was probably a lack of a recent lick of paint.

She paid for a watery coffee from a gum-chewing teenage waitress and tucked herself into the corner of the room. It was only once she'd sat down that she noticed the television on the wall and on it, she blinked in surprise, was *Wake Up!*

'Espadrilles are seriously hot right now,' Erin pouted at the camera. 'My personal favourite is a cap toe ribbon lace wedge, as seen on the gorgeous Demi here.'

A po-faced model paraded into the studio before rooting herself, wide legged, next to Erin, who cooed in approval.

'That ribbon tie is fabulous for elongating the leg. Plus,' Erin widened her eyes, 'it's *such* a versatile shoe. Ideal for weddings, work or even a holiday romantic stroll through cobbled streets.'

'They look fantastic.' A smiling Martin emerged onto the screen. 'Are they all from our sponsor retailer?'

'Absolutely.'

Sam stared, fixated. She hardly ever watched the show but to see it now running without her was like returning home to find the rooms empty. Had it really been so easy just to continue as if nothing had happened? She'd expected Martin to look exhausted, chiselled face wan and lined, swept back hair hanging limply round his forehead and brown eyes tinged with red, hinting at how he'd been up all night worrying. Instead, he looked neat and composed in his usual workday outfit of suit trousers, crisp shirt and not a hair out of place.

She leant forward, trying to breathe her beating heart to calm. On set it was typically uncomfortably hot under the lights, with last minute cue cards and Willa sprinting in to touch up foundation in the breaks, but seeing it on screen it looked slick, effortless. As she watched Martin saunter over to the sofa, he seemed to be gently chuckling at something he'd said, not a care in the world.

'And,' he crossed his legs, arm splayed out behind him, 'in case you missed this morning's big announcement, I'm excited to repeat that for you.'

Her hand wobbled as she put down the mug and liquid splashed over the side. She felt like someone had grabbed her throat. What big announcement? Was this Nina's 'younger direction'?

'*Wake Up!* is evolving. With Sam having left us, I am proud to announce that we have now relaunched as *Martin Makes Mornings*, helping to get you energised and eager for the day.' He flashed a bright white smile and, Sam jolted, a wink.

She sat up. Hot liquid dribbled onto her hand, but she barely registered it. Her heart pounded.

This couldn't be real. *Martin Makes Mornings?* She blinked and shook her head, but the same image flashed up when she looked back at the screen. *Martin Makes Mornings?* She repeated the words to herself. Yes, it was a crap name but, more importantly, she hadn't agreed to quit the show. She was still in contract until the end of the year. They couldn't just write her out in the space of 48 hours. Could they? And after five years all she'd got was a two second mention before making room for a Martin ego-fest? She hadn't exactly expected a state funeral but figured there'd be something more solid. At least a cake.

She couldn't believe he hadn't warned her. What a shit. Frustration blasted through her. Frustration with Martin. But also frustration with Keira. With Willa and Erin and with everyone who worked in the studio and knew and let her bob around on this ridiculous island whilst her job was swept from under her feet. She was frustrated with the morning television industry and lawyers who found holes in contracts and fake smiles and smugness.

She thought about storming out. About getting the phone off Caspar and calling and calling Martin until she was put through and could make clear just how far her respect for him had fallen.

It took a moment for her to register exactly how she felt towards him. She felt anger, bitter as grass, rising in her throat.

But the real feeling was betrayal. It felt like he had sized up her plan to take a break, to make an informed and rational decision about her future, and pissed all over it.

The show went to adverts, and she slumped, numb with shock, back against the wooden chair. No wonder Keira hadn't wanted him to speak to her. Probably thought Martin would tell her what had happened, and Sam would rush back to London and storm the set, asserting her right to be in the role she was contractually employed to do. Maybe she still would.

She was seething, but underneath the initial fire of adrenaline was a niggling anxiety. What, a small voice in her brain piped up, would rushing on set actually achieve? The announcement had already been made; the production team were unlikely to change it in the morning just because she'd walked in.

'Shit,' she muttered and stomped her foot under the table. Keira was clearly hard-nosed but in a position Sam could understand: new, young, a woman needing to prove herself in a savage industry and therefore willing to cut the absent co-star to launch with something fresh. It was a dick move, but she got it, particularly given that the two women hardly knew each other personally. But Martin. Not only her co-star, but boyfriend and would-be father of her child. *Martin*. She shook her head. Bastard. Completely.

'Welcome back,' Martin gave a small wave, 'to *Martin Makes Mornings*. Now,' the camera panned out to reveal him sitting next to a neat woman in thick rimmed glasses, 'I'm here with the lovely Dr Carolina Lopez who is going to talk us through simple steps to improve gut health. Because, Doctor, we shouldn't leave it all down to,' he smirked, 'gut feeling. Is that right?'

'Fuck'. Sam beat her fist on the table. What an *arsehole*. She managed to catch the mug before it spilt again.

'Everything alright?' The waitress appeared. 'Is the coffee ok? I didn't actually have filter so it's instant.'

Sam squeezed her lips. 'Fine. It's just. Something silly.'

She flapped her hand. 'Something annoyed me on the TV show.'

'I get it,' the waitress stated, deadpan. 'I was pretty surprised when I found out that stuff about Sam – the other presenter.'

There was a pause. Sam tilted her head. The waitress chewed her gum with an open mouth.

'What stuff?'

'You know – Sam Elton? The woman who usually presents it with him? She's Martin's girlfriend – well *was* I guess. Walked out of live filming a few days ago and just left the show. Turns out she's an impossible diva who was always starting massive arguments and traumatising the other women on set. Someone who worked there leaked it. I wouldn't usually care but,' she nodded towards the TV screen, 'it's always on during my shifts and, you know, Martin seems nice. Seems sad for him.' She shrugged and went to wipe the table behind her.

Sam felt sick. Someone had leaked *what*? Her hands dampened. She couldn't speak. Couldn't think. She stood up slowly, focusing carefully on every move as she placed one foot in front of the other.

'Hey,' the waitress called as Sam was about to cross the threshold. 'You actually kind of look like her. She's probably a bit younger – no offence. Don't worry. It's not an insult; she is pretty. Just clearly also a bitch.'

❊ ❊ ❊

'Sam,' Caspar smiled as he opened his door, 'great to see you.' He leant in to kiss her on the cheek. She didn't move. 'We're not due to leave for another couple of hours. But the weather's cleared already. We could go earlier. Is that why you're here?' He clocked her wan cheeks and fidgeting fingers. 'Is everything ok?'

'Yes.' She bit her lip. 'No. I mean… Can I use your phone again? It's sort of an emergency.'

'Oh right. Shit. Of course.' He ushered her into the hallway. 'Come in. Here.' He handed her his phone and guided her towards the living room. 'Take as long as you need.'

'Thanks.' Standing by a dark, wooden table by the window, she reached for a The Rowe branded pen and notepad. She took a deep breath and called, starting to doodle a series of tight black squares as the dial sounded. It was midday; the show would have just finished. She was transferred straight through to Martin.

'Hello –'

'What the hell is going on?'

She could almost feel him squirm. 'Sam? Is that you?'

'At what point did you just decide to write me out?' She tried to keep her voice level as she coloured in alternate squares to make a checkerboard. '*Martin Makes Mornings*?'

'Babe! All ok? Louise mentioned she'd been struggling to get hold of you.'

'What's happening with *WakeUp!*?'

'Getting back to your old self?'

'I asked you what is going on.'

'How's things on the island?'

Sam had to breathe deeply to stop herself from shouting. What she wanted from Martin was a grovelling apology and an explanation of how he'd been forced down a road he completely disagreed with, not limp evasion that smacked of his complicity in cutting her out.

'Are you talking shop? I thought you weren't meant to be watching the show. It's not great for your switching off.'

'Just answer the question.'

There was a pause. 'Surely you understand, Sammy?'

'Enlighten me.'

'It's for your own good.'

'My own *good*?'

'Because you're stressed, sweetheart. It's not what you need. It's great that you're taking a month off. Really great. But it's not enough. I don't think you *can* work right now.'

'Bullshit.'

'Has Louise put you up to this? Isn't this what you wanted?'

'Whatever I want, Martin, should be on *my* terms.'

'But Issa said –'

'Don't talk to me about Issa.'

'What's wrong with Issa?'

'Just stick to the point.'

'We're looking out for you, babe. There's no need to martyr yourself. Louise seems to be obsessed with pushing you like a cart horse. I know she's your agent, but still. You need time to recuperate. Isn't that why you've gone on holiday for an entire month? Have I misunderstood something?'

'Yes.' She scribbled in the other squares to entirely blacken the page. 'You very much *have* misunderstood something. I'm still under contract for God's sake. I could sue!'

'Oh, come on, sweetheart.' His voice stiffened. 'You knew you weren't going to return to the show. Walking out on set and taking off a whole month. It's as good as quitting.'

'But I haven't quit, Martin. I still want that job.'

'Really?'

'*Really.*' She paused, holding up the pen. 'Well, I want the option.'

He snorted. 'See what I mean. You're not returning to *Wake Up!* We just sped up the process. A process focused on *you*. Allowing you to be relaxed and happy and healthy enough to have a baby.'

'We?' Sam's left hand started to shake. The prospect of the team having met without her to discuss her post-IVF career made her feel ill. It wasn't their decision.

'Keira and I have been planning *Martin Makes Morning* ever since she took over. Look,' he sighed, 'she even leaked that article about the IVF, so it didn't take viewers by surprise.

It was due when you went on maternity. We just brought it forward. No big deal.'

Sam felt winded. 'Keira leaked that story?'

'Only to help things. You know, we thought it might be good to plant the seed of an idea.'

The pen tore through the page. Sam tried to control her breathing. '*We?*'

'Me and Keira.'

'Right,' she took a step backwards, 'and where was I in this decision to announce our pregnancy to the world two weeks after I'd had IVF?'

'Babe,' he made a near whine that made her flinch, 'you were stressed. I figured I'd take care of it. When you had a positive test, I didn't think it would… you know. Stop being positive.'

Sam tried to focus on the lines of an abstract painting on the opposite wall, tracing each squiggle in her mind to stop her from screaming.

'And what about me being some Miranda Priestly bitch, terrorising other women? Was that info from Keira, too?'

'Of course not. I don't think so. I mean probably not. You're not always the most *approachable* of people on set, honey. Always so focused. It was probably some intimidated junior intern.'

'Well, I'm sorry for being so *focused*. How awful for everyone. And what about this younger direction?' Her voice came out thinner and sharper than she'd expected. 'Are you being replaced as well?'

He laughed, as if the prospect was an inconceivable joke. 'Replaced? Of course not. It's my show now. You know how it is. Women over thirty are better suited to an older female audience; men are more universal. They'll probably up Erin's role, get some other young, diverse women on for segments. Nothing personal.'

Sam's throat twisted in disgust. She didn't have the words.

'It's actually great news,' he continued, buoyed by her lack of complaint. 'I get to be at work. You get to be at home. Everyone's happy. They've also upped my salary, so it won't be like we're on a single income. It's ideal. So tell me about the island. Is it hotter, colder?'

'Martin,' she blurted, pressing her temples.

'Are the locals all crazy? No teeth and illiterate?'

'Martin.'

'Have people recognised you? Or do people not have televisions?'

'*Martin.*'

'Alright, Sammy. What?'

Her head had started to swim. 'You're not listening to me.'

'I am.'

'No,' she took a deep breath and steadied herself against a marble fireplace. 'You're not. If I want to leave the show, it's under *my* terms and in *my* time and *I'm* the one who communicates that message. And I'm certainly not ending my time at *Wake Up!* with everyone thinking that I've had some hormone-induced hissy fit and walked out. I'm coming back next week, rejoining the show and showing everyone that I'm a professional.'

Martin's voice took on a sharper edge. 'So this is what it's all about.'

'What is?'

'Caring about how you look.'

'It is not.'

'Of course it is. You don't want to return to work. Not really. You know as well as I do that it's not the right choice.'

'No–'

'Don't lie to yourself, Sam. The old style *Wake Up!* is over. Stay there. Come back in a month, and then we'll go for a meeting about doing another transfer.'

'I'm coming back tomorrow.'

'That's not a good idea.'

'I'm going to get things back to normal.'

'Don't.'

The finality of the word caught Sam by surprise. She'd figured Martin might make polite noises about her staying in Sark if she really wanted to, but, inside, be desperate to have her back. She hasn't anticipated this.

She could hear the clamour of voices in the studio on the other line. She'd been utterly disposable – wiped out overnight by a new name and one explanatory line.

She held her head in her hands. Was he right? She didn't know. She certainly did have a fan base – Comms were constantly assessing online popularity polls and presenting evidence of public opinion in cold, unarguable numbers. But if she returned now she'd face a barrage of questions on why she'd walked out and whether she really *was* pregnant and when and, most painfully, why she wasn't anymore... The cold shiver of realisation ran through her. She couldn't deal with it. Not now. Not when it was so raw.

She cleared her throat, dizzy with shame at just letting things go without a fight. She put the pen back on the side and scrunched up the piece of paper.

'Fine. I'll do a few more days.'

'Do the month, baby. Take the time.'

'Maybe a couple of weeks.'

'Good decision.' He paused. '*Are* you alright? Staying somewhere comfortable?'

She thought about the damp, draughty cottage. 'It's not the best. But...' she looked at the glossy room around her. 'I have some other options.'

'Well make sure you take up on one of those. I don't want my princess coming back cold, grumpy and miserable.'

She bit her thumbnail. It wasn't how she'd expected the conversation to go. Nothing seemed to be in her control. 'See you –' But the phone was already dead.

She sat back and crossed her legs and arms, her mind awash with conflicting ideas.

'All ok?' Caspar poked his head round the door. 'Don't worry. I haven't been snooping.'

'It's fine.' Sam held up a palm. 'Things are just… I don't know. The circumstances have changed.' She looked out of the window to see a sparrow drinking from the pool.

Caspar sat on the opposite sofa and rested his hands on his knees. 'Anything I can help with?'

'No,' she grimaced. 'And I won't need the boat trip today. After all that. Sorry for wasting your time.'

'No problem. I still need to head off island for a couple of nights for some meetings, so no skin off my nose.'

'Good.' A thought came to her. If she did need to stay on the godforsaken island, then she might as well make herself comfortable. 'Actually, and I hate to ask for another favour, Caspar, but, if you are going to be away, can I take you up on that offer of a room?'

CHAPTER 15

Sam almost forgot where she was when she woke up the next morning. The soft sheets, the feather pillows, the view out over to the sea. She exhaled and stretched out her limbs, hardly reaching the end of the enormous bed. Everything was just what she needed.

Everything, that was, until she turned on her side and saw the TV in the corner. She'd vaguely noticed it the night before, but it had slipped her mind as she'd finally been able to string some sentences of her book together. But now it sat there like a dark, menacing door to another world. If she turned it on, she could watch Martin, cringe at his corny jokes and shout at the screen about how little differences there were to the format of the new show and what total, utter horseshit it was that she was too old whilst he had *universal* fucking *appeal*.

No. She turned onto her other side. She wouldn't torment herself. Today was the day of the races that everyone had been arriving on the island for. She'd get herself glammed up and go along and distract herself. No to watching Martin or running over their conversation from yesterday; yes to champagne as everyone pretends to care about horses but is more concerned with what outfits people are wearing.

She padded into the marble bathroom and looked closer into the mirror, tilting her chin upwards slightly. Surely her wrinkles couldn't have deepened so much overnight. She rubbed the skin between her nose with her fingers, trying to massage away the two grooves. She didn't *remember* looking like this before bed. Maybe it was just the light – she was usually up before dawn and got ready in Martin's somewhat dingy, windowless bathroom. She could have been this wrinkly for years. Or maybe it was just part of a package: wrinkles, memory loss. Maybe she really was old now; the IVF injections had certainly made her feel about 85. She'd be booking herself onto a senior citizens cruise next.

Sighing, she snapped open her concealer, hoping to fill in the cracks of her face. The effect was less dewy goddess and more Victorian death mask.

But once she'd swept on a slash of red lipstick, squeezed into her heels and silver lamé midi dress and tucked a twenty-pound note in her bra strap (and if she half closed her eyes and stepped backwards slightly), she at least resembled a version of her normal self. The only concern now was whether she'd be let in without a hat; she knew that race days could be very strict.

Her dress was tighter round her calves than she'd remembered, and she had to shuffle along the gravel paths with geisha-like steps, politely smiling at the rowdy groups who strode or cycled past her. Given the amount of people in denim shorts and hoodies, she assumed there was a neighbouring event – no doubt a scarecrow festival or chicken catching competition or the like.

But as she rounded the corner into what was signposted as the race entrance, she was surprised to find crowds of families, the parents in jeans and t-shirts surrounded by a maelstrom of scruffy toddlers and dogs.

'LOOK, MUMMY.' A little girl in yellow dungarees holding a toy monkey pointed up at her. 'That lady is wearing TIN FOIL!'

'Olive!' A woman in a striped jumpsuit with a chubby baby on her hip tugged her back. 'Do not be rude!' She looked up at Sam and smiled apologetically. 'Kids, heh? I am sorry. Your dress is lovely.' She had a slight accent which was difficult to place – Scandinavian or German or Dutch.

Sam's breath tightened. She knew she was being ridiculous, but she couldn't bear to be around mothers parading around with their children, proudly swanning around with everything she didn't have. Every time she chatted to people with kids it felt like engaging with someone who'd managed to gain membership to a club that wouldn't accept her. It made her feel ignorant and teenage-like – as if her own life paled in comparison to the important, actual adults in the room.

'It's ok,' she said tightly. 'I think I'm in the wrong place.'

She peered over the people to the field behind them. There was bunting and beer tents and hay bales and crowds, but nothing that resembled a horse.

'You are not here for the sheep racing? It is great fun.'

'*Sheep* racing?'

'YES!' shouted Olive as she ran between the woman's legs. 'They run and run and run with teddies on them and Daddy gets CROSS because he always loses but my sheep always comes FIRST. Last year I won THREE POUNDS.'

The woman laughed. 'It is true. Fortunes can be made.'

'Ah,' Sam said and twisted one ankle behind the other, a knot of shame pulling in her stomach. Of course it would be bloody *sheep* racing. And of course no one on the island would be wearing heels and slinky dresses. Let alone a hat. 'Well. I misunderstood. Thank you.' She nodded sharply and turned to leave.

'Wait.' The woman reached a hand out to her arm.

Sam flinched.

'Sorry, I did not...' The woman hesitated. 'You will love it. Everyone does. You are a bit,' she wobbled her head slightly, 'smart. It is Sark, you know, not... what is that posh one in Britain?'

'Ascot?' Sam offered.

'Ascot!' The woman laughed and slapped her palm to her forehead. 'Sorry. Baby brain.'

Sam crossed her arms.

'Look, those heels and grass is no good, but I have a spare pair of flip flops. You are welcome to borrow them.'

'I...' Sam faltered. The woman, the baby and Olive all looked up at her with the same wide, expectant eyes. 'I don't...'

'You will have the BEST time.' Olive jumped on the spot. 'It is my FAVOURITE.'

Sam looked back at the empty gravel road behind her and the bustling field over the woman's shoulder. She *had* wanted to keep herself distracted. Any more time back at Caspar's house and she'd just be tempted to binge watch all of this week's episodes of the show.

'Ok.' She nodded slowly. 'I'll stay for a bit.'

'HOORAY,' Olive squealed and held her monkey in the air. 'Tin foil lady is coming!'

The woman grimaced. 'Sorry. She can be a handful. Here,' she leant down and pulled the flip flops out of a buggy laden with all manner of toys, creams and muslins, 'just leave them by the gate when you have finished.'

'Really?' Sam frowned. 'Won't someone take them?'

'No!' The woman laughed. 'As I said, it is Sark, not Ascot!'

'Thank you.' Sam gave a small smile. 'I appreciate it.'

'No problem. Olive can be persuasive...' The woman looked around at her feet. 'Olive?'

They both peered into the field where a small, yellow figure was tearing towards a group of sheep.

'Shit. I better go after her,' the woman muttered, placing the baby into the buggy as it started to whimper. 'It's ok. It's ok,' she cooed. The whimper loudened to a wail, and Sam could see the woman close her eyes for a moment and take a deep breath before continuing in a sing-song voice, 'No more crying, sweetheart. We have just lost Olive again, but we will find her, won't we?'

She glanced back at Sam. 'Sorry,' she grimaced. 'Life is

chaos with these two. Wonderful, but chaos. Enjoy the day.'

'Thank you.' Sam nodded. 'You, too.' But the woman had already started charging off into the crowd, steering the buggy over the uneven grass like a tank.

Sam padded gently into the field, clutching her heels close to her chest. Given that she'd hardly seen anyone out and about, there was a huge amount of people; it must have been close to the entire population of the island. The grass around her was peppered with groups drinking beer and Pimms and face-painted children scattered in all directions, running between a tombola on one side of the field and a betting stand on the other. She meandered past a queue snaking out of a food and drink tent, around which swirled the sizzling spit of the fat of cheap burgers and hot dogs, and she wandered towards the crowd forming around a fenced off area where hay bales were set out in ordered rows.

'Great God alive,' a deep voice suddenly boomed behind her. 'No one told us we'd be having a celebrity guest.'

Her heart dropped. The last thing she needed was to be recognised. All she'd wanted to have a nice time, keep herself busy and not think about Martin or work. Was it really too much to hope for? She turned, a practised smile plastered on her face.

She was met with a man in a deep bow taking off a flat cap.

She cleared her throat as the man straightened up, a wide grin visible behind his thick, white beard.

Sam frowned. He looked familiar.

'You scrub up well, don't you, love?' He laughed, putting back on his cap. 'If I knew you were such glamorous cargo, I'd have allowed you to ride in the front of the tractor. You realise the Miss Sark competition's not for a couple of weeks?'

She breathed out in relief. It was Jack, the man who'd given her a lift to the cottage, not some avid fan.

She grimaced. 'I didn't quite get the dress code.'

'No bother, love. You look grand. All alright in that

ramshackle shed you're staying in? Met that lovely lady on the farm next door yet?'

But before she had time to answer she was interrupted by a tinny voice on a tannoy, announcing the first of the day's races.

'We better get going,' Jack said. 'Got your bet in?'

She shook her head.

'What?' he raised his eyebrows. 'No fun without something to lose.' He winked. 'Or win.' He dropped a slip into one of her heels. 'Here. That's a fiver on red.'

And with that he darted off into the crowd before she had a chance to protest.

Sam tried to follow him, but the group was now a great chattering mass of excitement, and all she could do was to squeeze into the last empty slot by the fence. As she leant over, she could see the pen of sheep at the other end, each with a cuddly toy rider strapped on top. The one with the red rabbit, she noticed, was happily standing facing the wrong direction, oblivious to the task in hand.

'Good afternoon, ladies and gentlemen,' the voice of the tannoy projected out. Sam looked round to see a ruddy-faced man in a rather-too-small striped waistcoat holding up a microphone. 'The time has finally come.'

A ripple of anticipation washed through the arena and camera phones were positioned at the ready.

'This is the first of our five heats today, all building up to the much revered Sark Trust Cup, raising money for a cause close to all our hearts.'

A few whoops and whistles punctured the air.

'I know that many of you have staked livelihoods, reputations, hopes and dreams on these races,' he continued.

Sam rolled her eyes to herself. Surely that was a bit much?

'And I won't make you wait any longer for the excitement to begin. Sheep,' he paused, 'on your marks.'

Someone moved to hold the gate of the pen ready.

'Get set.'

'Go on, Gloria,' shouted a passionate voice in the crowd.

'You can do it, Cream Puff!' called another.

'Quiet, please.'

The commentator waited until a loaded silence descended.

'Go!'

After a moment of gormless confusion, the sheep were off, bouncing towards the first hay bale hurdle with the various teddies and bunnies wobbling on their backs.

The crowd whooped and cheered as the sheep cleared the first jump, the yellow rider tearing doggedly ahead.

'An impressive start for Baaabara in blue,' the voice rang over the tannoy. 'Followed by Cream Puff in yellow at her heels.'

The crowd surged forwards, and Sam had to crane her neck to see.

'Mint Sauce in green is holding up the rear followed by Crumpet in red, Wooly Mammoth in purple and Obi Wool Kenobi in black as they approach the second jump. Cream Puff pulls ahead.'

'Go on, Baaabara!' A voice cried. 'Don't let her have it!'

'Come on, Crumpet,' Sam found herself muttering through gritted teeth.

The sheep all cleared the second and third jumps, clumping together slightly as they did so.

'Come on,' Sam repeated under her breath. 'You can do it.'

'Baaabara drops back as Cream Puff makes impressive headway. Crumpet widens the gap with the rest of the group.'

The sheep approached the fourth jump. Mint Sauce and Baaabara relaxed into a gentle trot.

'Cream Puff and Crumpet battle to win.'

The air was alive with shouts of encouragement and the fence wobbled with the weight of tens of bodies.

The two sheep were neck and neck at the final jump.

'You can do it, Crumpet!' Sam found herself joining in with the crowd's shouting. 'RUN!'

'And Cream Puff in yellow surges forward at an incredible pace to take the win!' the announcer declared. 'And what a fantastic performance that was for our reigning island champion.'

There was a crack of applause as the other sheep bobbed past, with Mint Sauce happily trotting by in last place.

The next race was announced for in twenty minutes, and the crowd started to disperse, with a merry group bearing winning slips bouncing towards the betting stand.

Sam took a deep breath out. She hadn't been aware of how fast her heart had been racing and told herself off for getting so wound up over some sheep. The sun was now higher in the sky, and her dress itched against her hot skin. She'd given it a go and seen a race, but that was probably enough now. With the rest of the island here, she could enjoy a quiet walk or sit on a silent beach.

'TIN FOIL LADY!'

Sam looked down to find Olive tearing towards her, her yellow dungarees now smeared brown and green from grass and mud.

'I WON!' Olive punched the air. 'Cream Puff was MY sheep!'

'Congratulations! How much do you get?' Sam flushed as the words left her mouth. It probably wasn't appropriate to ask an under five about betting.

'We are about to find out.' A soft voice emerged from behind her as the flip-flop woman approached, negotiating her buggy over the lumpy field.

Olive looked up at Sam, her face dark with suspicion. 'Did YOU win?'

'I'm afraid not.' Sam nervously returned the woman's smile. 'Is it ok?' She lowered her voice, 'to talk to her about *gambling*?'

The woman looked at her like she'd just stepped straight

off a spaceship. 'Gambling?' She laughed in bemusement. 'Of course. Olive has been betting 20ps on sheep and chickens and lawn mowers since she could talk.' The woman leant down to the buggy as the baby started to whimper. 'Remember,' she said over her shoulder. 'This is Sark. Things are different here.' She straightened up with the baby on her hip as its cry strengthened. 'I am Nixie, by the way.'

'RED!' Olive shouted, pointing a stubby finger at the slip tucked into Sam's shoe. 'Second place. Not me. I WON.'

Sam went to crumple up the slip, but Nixie put her hand on her arm. 'Wait. You will still get something for second place.'

The baby's cry suddenly became foghorn like, and Nixie paced in a circle, jiggling it on her hip.

'I want to get my money!' Olive jumped in front of her mother's path.

'In a minute, please, Olly.' Nixie stepped around her. 'I think Ash needs a feed.'

'I want my money NOW!' Sam inadvertently jumped as Olive's shout matched the strength of the baby's scream.

'Wait, please.' Nixie ran a hand through her hair. 'Just one minute.'

Olive stamped her jelly-shoed foot and gave a quite an impressive pout. 'NOW!'

'I'll take her.' Sam found herself saying. 'I'll cash in my own at the same time.'

'Would you?' Nixie grimaced. 'I hate to put Olive on anyone when she's like this, but...'

'It's fine.' Sam smiled. 'I owe you a favour. It's nothing. Come on, Olive.' But, as she looked down, the dungareed figure was already charging over to the other side of the field, leaving Sam waddling in her tight dress in her wake.

* * *

'NOT FAIR!' Olive knitted her arms across her chest. 'I win £2 but you win £10. My sheep won. You got second. NOT FAIR!' She pushed her lips into a pout and Sam had a horrible feeling that the red cheeks and eyes squeezed shut indicated tears.

She started to slowly and gently explain that, proportionately, Olive had *actually* won more, her original bet being 20p compared to Jack's £5, but the message didn't seem to be getting through.

'BUT I AM THE WINNER!' Olive stomped both feet.

'Yes,' Sam tried to smile agreeably. 'You are. You did very well, but due to the size of the initial bets…'

Olive's bottom lip started to wobble.

Sam looked desperately round for Nixie but couldn't see her in the growing crowd.

'£2 is an excellent prize,' she added. 'Really fantastic.'

A strange noise emerged from the small child like the stuttering of an unhealthy moped engine.

Sam bit her cheek. She had to do something before there was a scene. 'Are you going to bet on the final race, Olive? Who will you put your £2 on? Cream Puff again?'

The engine stuttering morphed unmistakably into the opening notes of a full-throated scream.

'Or we could put our money together? *£12* on Cream Puff? You could win,' she scanned the blackboard of odds, '£20 in total.'

The noise stopped. Olive cocked a damp eye in Sam's direction. '£20? All for Olive?'

'Well, yes.' Sam *had* thought they might split the winnings, but she'd happily give up her share to keep the peace. She grimaced, realising she'd just bribed a small child with cash.

'£12 on MINT SAUCE!' Olive punched an arm into the air.

'*Mint Sauce*?' The shock dissolved Sam's ethical debate. 'You can't be serious. She was *rubbish*. Hardly made it across the finish line in the last race. Isn't Cream Puff a safer bet? Or

Crumpet at least?'

Olive wrinkled her nose and released a threatening rev of displeasure.

'Mint Sauce it is! I mean, it's *seriously* unlikely, but with the current odds, a Mint Sauce win would get us...' Sam read the blackboard again, 'Bloody hell. 252 quid!'

Olive's eyes narrowed. 'More than £2?'

'Just a bit. In fact,' Sam slipped the £20 note out from her bra strap, 'let's go the whole hog. Go mad.' Her heart leapt slightly as her cheeks flushed in excitement. She couldn't remember when she'd last felt so giddy.

'Go MAD!' Olive threw her hands up in the air. 'I'm going to tell my friend Daniel that I will WIN!'

'Well,' Sam frowned, but by the time she thought of a gentle response to temper expectations, Olive had already run back into the middle of the field.

Sam tucked the four green slips against her strap. She knew it was ridiculously unlikely, but she was getting carried away with Olive's enthusiasm. Just the possibility of such a win felt like carrying a ball of sunshine in her pocket.

'Thank you!' Sam heard Nixie's voice and turned to see her approaching with two glasses of Pimm's. 'Please, take one. Even five minutes with Olive can be exhausting. But she seems very happy with her win today, so hopefully there will be no battle to take her home later.'

Sam ran her thumb over her fingernails. 'The thing is,' the thrill of the bet dissipating into embarrassed realisation, 'she really *wasn't* happy with her win, so I offered her my bet on another race. I'm so sorry. I really shouldn't have offered money to a child, particularly one I don't even know, and without your permission –'

'It is fine,' Nixie laughed, pressing the glass into Sam's hand. 'Honestly. Not a problem. Thank you for taking her. I managed to give Ash to Leo. And I am not supposed to be drinking much whilst breastfeeding, but...' she looked off into the crowd where Olive was trying to get a smaller boy to climb a hay-bale, 'I need a little break. *Prost!*' She clinked their glasses.

Sam tilted her head. 'What was that?'

Nixie let out a laugh much deeper and louder than Sam had expected from her dainty frame. 'Prost!' she repeated. 'Cheers! There are so many of us Germans on the island now I almost forget!'

'Oh. I hadn't noticed.' Sam took a sip of Pimms and inadvertently swallowed half a strawberry. 'Why?'

Nixie shook her head. 'You will have to speak to my husband for specifics. Leo... he is amazing, but... how do I put this? He gets funny about things. Hates big government, intervention... and when he saw this other German guy on a little island trying to encourage people to move with their tech businesses, he was sold. Limited bureaucracy, low taxes, everything safe, a life of fun and freedom.'

'Really?' Sam looked around at the crowd. It looked more like a county fair in rural Wales than somewhere you'd find annual attendees of Davos.

'We are about a hundred now. And counting – with the kids.'

'And the population's growing?'

'Quite a bit.'

'But isn't the island struggling financially?'

'Not really. Things could be better, sure, but it is not like some people claim.'

'Who?'

'Ooof.' Nixie smiled good-naturedly. 'It is like being interviewed for the BBC.'

'Sorry,' Sam said. 'Bad habit.'

'Anyway.' Nixie batted a hand away. 'I am no good at politics. Tell me about you. This is your first time on the island?'

'That obvious?' Sam reached down to lay her heels on the grass. 'I'm here for a couple of weeks I guess.'

'Wow. A long time. How come?'

Sam looked round at the woolly clouds of sheep, cooler

bags, plastic cups of cider and parents applying sunscreen to wriggling limbs. It was a different world to the hours spent sobbing in toilets over a stubborn single line on tests, the prospect of painful press headlines, Martin writing her out of her career. 'Urm.' She looked down into her drink.

'It is ok.' Nixie reached over and squeezed her shoulder. 'You don't have to say. Life can be complicated.'

Sam looked up for a moment, the sky filling her vision like a screen of blue honey. 'Can I ask one more question?'

'Fire away!'

'Do you like it here?'

'Of course!' Nixie laughed, as if the question itself was ridiculous. 'It is perfect for the kids. So quiet, so safe. A proper community – nothing like a big city like Berlin. Olive can be so wild. I cannot imagine trying to rush around doing chores, trying to stop her running into traffic. My parents come to stay for one month a year. I am very lucky.'

'But what about you? Do *you* like it? I'm sorry if I'm being intrusive. I'm just curious. Trying to imagine an actual life outside of London and work and a supermarket on every corner.'

Nixie knocked back the rest of her drink. 'I used to be head of marketing at a big firm, and now I volunteer at an island school doing art lessons once a week.' She raised an eyebrow then laughed again and shook back her blonde curls. 'But now I have my children. And they are happy and safe. Kids change everything.'

'MUMMY!' As if on cue, Olive charged into Nixie's legs, sending her almost toppling backwards into the betting stand.

'It's the big race. Come watch. I am going to WIN!'

Sam's heart jolted as she felt for the slips against her skin. She'd almost forgotten.

They rushed over to the thickening crowd surrounding the largest pen, jostling through to the front where Leo had used the buggy to save them some space. Nixie introduced Sam, and the group of them pressed up against the metal barrier, the hum of bodies widening behind them.

'Olive put the money on Mint Sauce,' Sam tried to whisper – which wasn't very quiet given the rising noise of the crowd. 'You might need to prepare her not to win.'

'Ha,' Leo snorted. 'Trust my little girl. It will be a good life lesson.'

'She spends a lot of time talking with the farmers, you know.' Nixie shrugged. She might know something we do not.'

'Ladies and gentlemen. Boys and girls.'

A momentary quiet fell as the voice boomed over the Tannoy.

'It's the moment we've all been waiting for.'

CHAPTER 16

Sam woke to bright, white sunshine pouring in through the open window.

'Ughh,' she mumbled, rubbing her eyes. Why weren't the blinds closed? She noticed her fingers smudged with black. And why was she wearing mascara? Since joining *WakeUp!* and suffering Willa's endless lectures on four-hundred-step skin care routines, she never went to bed without at least taking her makeup off.

Yawning, she tried to turn onto her back but found her calves were strangely bound together. She looked down to find she was still in her silver lamé dress, her heels in a pile by the bed on top of some mud-clad flip flops.

Her stomach dropped. Why hadn't she changed? Where was she?

She glanced round the room. The bed was an enormous modern four-poster with a faux fur rug with a deep-set, grey velvet sofa at its foot, overlooking a fireplace. To her right was an open window, its linen curtains fluttering in the morning breeze, and, to her left, glass doors opening onto a large patio with a hot tub looking out over the sea. It was the Rowe. She smiled in relief.

She sat up but groaned as she did so, her head suddenly swimming and nausea rising in her chest. *That* was why she was in bed fully clothed. But she didn't remember drinking much...There was the Pimm's with Nixie. Was that it? She pulled the duvet up closer and closed her eyes, forcing herself to remember.

Pimm's with Nixie, and then...

She snapped her eyes open. That sheep! Olive's sheep... what was it called? Redcurrant Jelly...? Coriander...? Mint Sauce! Mint Sauce had won! Over £400!

It all rushed back to her. The shouting in the race, Cream Puff getting distracted by some grass, Mint Sauce pulling ahead, the cheering, the whooping, Olive helping attach the little purple rosette, Leo proudly presenting her with £25 and whispering to Sam to keep the rest. Sam putting it behind the bar in the beer tent for free drinks all round, clinking plastic cups of warm white wine, downing a bottle of cider, feeling the cool can of a G&T.

She groaned. Surely that was it? Another memory flickered behind her eyes. God.

There was a rock classics cover band and singing and air guitar and... she cowered into the covers. Shots. She distinctly remembered the sharp acid of tequila then her terrible dancing and... shit. Had she actually *cried* at one point? She remembered standing in the middle of a crowd, throwing her hands in the air to *Bohemian Rhapsody* and letting tears fall down her face as she screeched out that 'Nothing really matters to meeeee!'

Christ. She slipped fully under the duvet, a wave of shame swelling in her chest. That was not her normal behaviour.

She must have stumbled back to the hotel in the dark and collapsed into bed. Everything was foggy after the crying episode. Ugh. The last time she'd been drunk like that was when she was a stroppy teenager, stealing her mum's bottles of vodka to swig with friends in the park. She couldn't even remember how to deal with a hangover.

The layers of duvet and fur rug suddenly felt hot and clammy, and she threw them off and forced herself up and out onto the balcony, taking greedy breaths of fresh, clean air. She checked her watch: just past eight. A lie in. Leaning on the glass barrier, she looked out to the green cliffs and denim blue sea in the distance. That was it. She'd get up and out and feed Trevor D.

※ ※ ※

Judith saw Sam coming down the hill and thrust her a mug of tea upon arrival into the shed. 'Morning, love. Thought I'd say hello. See whether you're…' she paused and crinkled her nose, 'feeling alright?'

Sam made an ambiguous grumble as she knelt down to stroke Trevor D's velvet ears. 'Been better.'

'Try a sea swim. Dixcart bay's just down the hill.'

Sam almost recoiled at the thought. Growing up with a local leisure centre of dubious cleanliness as her nearest body of water, she'd never been much of a swimming person beyond brief holiday dips – and she'd certainly not taken to the modern fad for freezing plunges amidst the duck poo of London's ponds.

'I'll be alright.'

'Does wonders to clear your head. My Trevor used to swear by it.'

'Honestly, I'll be –.'

She'd been about to say 'fine', but the word was swallowed in the wave of a hangover-induced hot flush. Judith gave a knowing nod as Sam wiped her damp forehead. There was no way around it: she did not feel good. Thank goodness Caspar hadn't been there to witness the debacle. Not that it mattered what he thought, of course.

'I don't have a swimsuit. Or a beach towel,' Sam said. 'I'll just go back and take a shower.'

'Don't be silly,' Judith tutted. 'You're fine in your undies. As long as it's not one of those g-string whatsits.' She raised an eyebrow.

Sam quickly shook her head. With her and Martin's sex life out the window, she almost exclusively wore thick black granny pants and a no-underwire bra. The idea of contorting herself into a pokey lacy thing with matching stringy knickers felt as unlikely as her dressing up as a clown.

'And I'll get you a towel back at the house,' Judith nodded.

Sam thanked her and the two women gathered Trevor D's feed in comfortable silence. As they sat back down again, the grateful donkey munching in front of them, Sam plucked up the courage to ask the question that had been niggling her since she'd woken up. 'Be honest, Judith.' She twirled a nervous finger around Trevor D's mane. 'How much of an idiot of myself did I make?'

Judith laughed. 'No one's got an issue with anyone getting merry here. But I do blame Jack. I told him you didn't need any more after you'd tried to climb up on stage during that chant, but he handed you another when you really didn't need one –'

Sam groaned and buried her face in Trevor D's fur.

'The man's a liability. Always has been. Trevor's best friend he was, but I never liked him. Too wild by half.'

'I tried to get up on stage?'

'You didn't *quite* manage it. That dress was too tight for you to get a leg up, so Walter helped you off.'

'Walt?' Sam groaned. What was it with that man emerging at her lowest moments?

'Don't worry, love. Most people were completely pie-eyed. It'll be far worse at the festival at the end of the month.'

'I won't be going.'

Judith put her hands on her hips. 'Say, is the electricity off again in the cottage? I didn't see any lights last night.'

Sam stood and busied herself with the food mixture, squeezing her lips tight to try not to gag at the smell. She was acutely aware that Judith was a woman who didn't even have wifi. She highly doubted that she'd appreciate the 'bold, international luxury' of the hotel.

'I'm staying at The Rowe for a few days,' she garbled. 'More reliable hot water.'

'The what?'

'Caspar Rowe's new hotel?'

'Oh.' Judith pushed her shoulders back. 'Right.'

'It's looking good. Really stylish.' Sam immediately regretted her choice of words. She couldn't imagine Judith wanting to step into a room with a brushed chrome ribbon light feature or velvet banquettes. The Rowe was like an island within an island, a slice of London luxury floating in a hay bales and bunting-filled sea. 'It'll be great for tourism when it opens.'

'Mm.' Judith gave an unconvincing smile. 'Now, you'd better get going whilst the tide's right. The sea won't swim itself.'

* * *

The walk down to the bay was longer but more beautiful than Sam had expected. A gravel path twisted down through a lush valley, flanked on either side by sycamores entwined with ivy set above a thick carpet of ferns. A flickering stream ran next to the path until branches gave way to bracken-thick cliffs and a wide vista over the glistening sea. As she stepped down onto the steps to the beach, she could only see a handful of people, each turned gratefully towards the morning sun. The sand was intermixed with small pebbles, and the water drew gently back over the shingle.

She passed a pony-tailed man as he picked up his bag whilst she looked for a good spot to drop her towel.

'You going for a dip?' He caught her eye.

Sam hesitated. Did she know him? Did he recognise her? Or had he remembered her from her antics last night and now thought it was hilarious that she obviously needed help for her hangover? She really hoped not.

'I might,' she said.

'It's beautiful. Fresh.'

She tried to nod politely and hurried further down towards the shoreline. She slipped off her shoes, dropped Judith's towel on a rock and dipped her toes in before immediately lifting them out. It was less what she'd call fresh and more like a freezer.

But the water glittered in the sunlight and, down in the shallows, it lightened to a bright turquoise. She was pleasantly surprised by its clarity – less duck faeces-filled pond, more Mediterranean. It was like newly blown glass. Very, *very* cold newly blown glass, but she hoped it might clear her crushing headache.

She stripped to her underwear and walked in up to her knees, letting the cold tickle the thin skin on the back of her legs. Looking out, she couldn't see a single other person. Save a handful of buoys, she was alone. She breathed out and raked her fingers along the surface, watching the ripples disappear in the distance. It had been so long since she'd been in the sea, it felt almost overwhelming in its size and deep emptiness, worlds away from when she'd been looking down at the busy Thames.

She walked deeper, shivering and wincing at her dampened pants and stomach and chest and... she gasped as she launched forwards. She was in. For a moment her body felt stiff in shock as she held her breath, and wisps of pain shot through her hands and feet. She kept kicking, counting her breaths until the iciness thawed to refreshing cold, and she powered away from the shore until she reached deeper water. Turning inland, her arms outstretched as her body stood upright, she took in the view. Curves of green cliff folded over one another, tapering into the patchwork of sand and shingle below.

She lay back into a star float, her hangover fog dissolving

into the crisp water. It was just what she needed, she thought as she bobbed weightlessly on the surface, looking up at the cloudless sky. Maybe she *could* become one of those cold-water connected-to-nature swimming people in a fleece-lined coat and gloves, huddling the group like a penguin in a waddle as they collectively headed towards the Serpentine or Hampstead ponds. It would certainly make a good segment for the show.

Her chest tightened as she remembered Martin's shining grin during his *Martin Makes Mornings* nonsense announcement, and she kicked upright again and squeezed out her hair.

It was then that she realised that a shape in the distance was moving towards her. That was odd. Her heart fluttered as she kicked towards the shore. She glanced back over her shoulder. It was definitely heading in her direction.

She scrambled forwards to where she could just about stand and peered closer. Sighing in relief, she realised it wasn't some strange phantom but a person paddle boarding with a small child sitting in front of them and an oar bobbing rhythmically in and out of the water. As she leant back again, she let her feet rise to the surface. Her limbs no longer shivered, and her groggy headache had been replaced by a soothing numbness.

The paddle boarding figure approached to her left, and she looked over in her peripheral vision as he floated over. He approached the shallows and unzipped his wetsuit, stripping it back over his broad arms and shoulders before bending down to reach the child on the front of the board.

As the board came closer, she realised it wasn't quite a child but a baby. A toddler at most. Happily babbling away perched on the front in its own miniature wetsuit and life jacket. She looked again and could see it was a little boy – no more than about one – with soft blonde hair and a gummy grin. Wasn't that dangerous? Could he swim? But then she thought about Nixie's laughing comments on the sheep bets. *This is Sark.* It was probably a local tradition to throw six-week-old babies in the sea and watch them swim.

The boy looked up at the man and smiled. Something dropped in Sam's stomach. He was adorable. The familiar, niggling thought rang through her brain: there was still a chance that she might have a little boy or girl of her own. A small chance. She flinched. A very small chance.

Pushing the thought away, she looked up at the man. Walt. *Again*? She dropped her legs, hoping to hide, but lost her balance and slipped beneath the water. She spluttered and snorted as she surfaced, her arms flailing as she tried to regain her footing on a large rock.

'Sam? Everything alright?' he said.

'Fine,' she managed between coughs.

'Do you need help?'

'No.' She tried to hide her face as seawater dribbled out her nose. 'I'm good.'

'Really?'

'Yep!'

He didn't look convinced. Sam mustered an 'I'm totally competent' smile before remembering she was swimming in her underwear and wrapped her arms over her bra.

'Ok,' Walt said slowly before picking the boy up and wading them to shore.

He must be Daniel, Sam figured. She watched him as he looked down at the water, his chubby arms and legs tucked into Walt's torso. Despite the difference in hair colour, she could see their similarities: both had wide, dark eyes and serious, pensive expressions. Walt hoicked Daniel closer to him as he pulled the board onto the sand and gave him a kiss on the forehead.

'Well done, buddy,' he said. 'Good job.' Daniel gurgled in return and buried his head into Walt's armpit.

Sam felt something twist her heart. She could only imagine how it must feel for a child to cling so closely, for you to be their home. Daniel looked up at Walt like he was his whole world, which, Sam supposed, he was – apart from his mum, of course. Sam wondered what she was like. Probably a wafty free spirit, living on an island with a fisherman whom she allowed to take Daniel paddle boarding.

Walt bent to pick up a particularly round pebble and gave it to Daniel to squeeze into his tiny palms. If she were mother to such a cutie, Sam thought to herself, she couldn't imagine letting him leave her sight. She bit her cheek. Walt clearly wasn't all that bad. And she couldn't forget Judith telling her about his help the previous night.

She tried to weigh up what would be less awkward: ignoring what had happened and pretending she was having a normal, leisurely dip or raising it head on. Walt lowered Daniel to the sand, holding his arm as he patted his feet on the shoreline and laughed at the tiny splashes. She took a deep breath. The last thing she wanted was for him to have even further evidence that she was some stuck-up, ungrateful city type.

'Thank you,' she called. 'For looking after me last night. I hear I was in a bit of a state.'

Walt looked up as he held both of Daniel's hands up high whilst he jumped in the water. 'No worries,' he said.

'I didn't mean to be a liability.'

He shrugged. 'You'll become an island folk hero with all that money you put behind the bar. It was pretty funny actually.'

Her ears pricked. 'Funny how?'

He picked Daniel up under his arms and swung him over the surface of the small waves.

'I don't know... you running around like a space cadet in that silver dress and doing that chant and singing those songs at the front to everyone.'

'*Singing* to everyone?' She almost slipped off the rock as a small current pushed her forwards.

'Your Fresh Prince rap. Very impressive.'

She groaned as she remembered the pony-tailed man earlier. *Fresh*. God.

'Well that's great. Excuse me while I let myself sink.'

'Ah, don't be so dramatic. You weren't nearly the drunkest person there. Not even top ten.'

'Really?'

'Don't you remember Jack doing the worm?'

'Jack? I'm surprised he's nimble enough to get on the floor.' She was starting to feel the cold and tried to wiggle her toes to keep moving.

'He isn't. It was in the middle of *Sweet Child of Mine* – like an enormous performing seal.'

She laughed but it came out as her teeth chattering.

'Want a towel?' he asked.

Both of them looked down as Daniel giggled with delight at his feet getting wrapped in a clump of seaweed.

Sam's leg twitched. Was Walt being nice or was this just another miniature jibe at how unsuited she was to island life?

'I'm ok,' she stuttered. 'I'll do one more minute.'

'Come on. You're almost blue. Where's your stuff?'

A light wave pushed her forwards, and she realised she could no longer feel her feet. The idea of being warm again was suddenly overwhelmingly appealing. She waded towards the shore, arms still wrapped over her bra, and nodded towards where she'd left her things.

'Somewhere on the left there,' she stammered. 'On a rock.' But she stopped as she said the words. The rock had disappeared.

'Where?'

'I... But it was right here.' She walked in a circle on the stoney sand.

Daniel picked up a handful of the seaweed and giggled as he threw it back into the water.

'Well done, little man,' Walt said. 'Did you pick it up?' He turned back to Sam. 'The tide? We've got one of the largest in the world here. Look.' He pointed at the dark water line high up on the rocks. 'Take that.' He motioned to a towel on the front of the board. 'And I think...' He broke off as he waded with Daniel in the shallows. 'What's that, Danny? Is it a shoe? Can you get it?'

Daniel carefully bent down to retrieve a seaweed-adorned sandal and held it up like a trophy.

'Is that yours?' Walt looked back again at Sam. 'And look, Danny, there's another one. Can you grab it? And that very soggy top floating there? Good boy. Good boy!'

Daniel beamed with pride as he collected the other items.

'Shall we give them back to the lady?' Walt asked in a soft voice. 'She didn't realise how far the tide comes in and lost her things.' He turned again to Sam. 'You bring anything else?'

'Just my clothes. I guess there's no sign of them.'

'Bad luck. Just wear the towel.'

'Thanks,' she mumbled, wrapping the fraying fabric over her shoulders. 'Normally I'm actually quite a capable person.'

'Sure.' Walt bent to hoick Daniel onto his hip again.

She slit her eyes, unable to read if he was being sarcastic. She pulled the towel closer. 'When do you need this back?'

'Whenever. I can just collect it from the cottage.'

She shifted her weight to the other foot. 'I'm not staying there anymore. Well, not for the moment.'

He brushed some sand off Daniel's arms and looked back over his shoulder. 'Can't live without a curling tong?'

She winced internally. Like Judith, Walt didn't seem like the kind of person who understood the appeal of Egyptian cotton sheets and designer bath oil. 'Caspar Rowe invited me to stay at the hotel. For free. And it was such a generous offer…'

Daniel stared straight at her. Sam resisted the urge to go and tickle his tummy and ask for a cuddle.

Walt turned. 'You're joking?'

She tilted her head. He had done all that work on the electrics, but that didn't mean she was obliged to live amidst the dust bunnies and dodgy sofa springs.

'You shouldn't be supporting that place,' Walt said.

Something in the atmosphere soured, and the hairs on her arms bristled the way they always used to when she realised that she'd got to the crux of a thorny story, revealing the rotten heart within. Typical. Of course Walt would have a personal vendetta against anything new or progressive. He was probably short-sighted and desperately jealous of Caspar. 'I'm not paying for it, so I'm not exactly *supporting* it. And why would it matter if I was?' she said.

'Because he's an arsehole.'

'Don't you *work* for him? Two standards much?'

'Worked,' he replied, deadpan.

'Oh, come on. How anti-enormous potential for economic growth can you be? Don't you want things like reliable electricity and proper medical facilities?'

'Not in exchange for what Caspar Rowe's got to offer.'

'It's a boutique hotel, not a nuclear power site.'

'I wouldn't expect a Londoner who's been here five minutes to understand.'

She arched her back. There it was. The little insult she knew he'd been holding in. Well she took no shame in being a Londoner rather than a country bumpkin, and he needed to know that she was not the type of person who took well to being told she shouldn't have an opinion. She crossed her arms. 'And I wouldn't expect a narrow-minded odd job man to understand economic potential.'

He took a step back. Her eyes widened. Rather than give her the high ground, the words stung like venom in her throat. Perhaps she did just sound like some uptight city type. 'Sorry, I didn't mean...'

He held Daniel closer as he started to squirm. 'No, *I'm* sorry,' he curled his lip, 'for clogging up your private beach resort. We won't block your view any longer.' He bent to pick up the rest of their swimming gear and slung it over his other shoulder like battle spoils.

'Come on,' Sam said. 'You know that's not what I meant.'

'No, no,' Walt replied without turning round, Daniel

fussing and starting to grizzle. 'We get the message.' He pushed the paddle board back into the shallow water with his foot and carefully set Daniel down. 'Keep the towel. Complimentary from the resort.' He turned away from her and bent to tighten Daniel's life jacket and tuck their things under the board's strings. Then, without looking back, he picked up the oar and pushed them off towards the horizon, heading back to the next-door bay.

'Dick,' Sam muttered to herself as she kicked the sand, her heart racing in anger and a headache setting in again like a helmet of pain. 'Why such a fuss about a hotel?'

CHAPTER 17

She spent the rest of the day in The Rowe's garden, accompanied only by a large pitcher of water and a platter of eclairs Caspar had left in the fridge. Partly it meant she could escape any further awkward encounters with people who recognised her from the previous night and partly she wanted to spite Walt by enjoying herself there enormously, thank you very much.

Whichever way you looked at it, the grounds were stunning. Pairs of wooden sun beds with plump cushions encircled a large round pool, which spread out like a mirror amidst the wall of grass. Around this wound a wooden canopy entwined with pink and purple roses and a thick, low hedge of lavender, all overlooking a gentle slope which spread out towards the sea, a kitchen garden growing on one side and a yoga pavilion on the other. Sam felt sure that people should be able to see that such a carefully set out space could only add to the island's appeal.

Keen to avoid going inside until she was absolutely confident that she wouldn't be tempted to watch *Martin Makes Mornings* on catch up, she stayed out until the sky faded from blue to pink to a heavy, velvet black, encrusted with the brightest stars she'd ever seen. It was only when her teeth started to chatter in the dark cold air that she took herself off to bed, having managed to quickly stash the TV remote in another room, and planned to spend the next day alone in the garden doing exactly the same thing.

But in the morning, just as she had selected a different, hopefully more engaging, political tome to accompany for her the day, the doorbell rang.

She ignored it, assuming whoever it was would want to see Caspar, but then it rang again. And again. And again.

It continued until she'd flung the door open as quickly as she could only to find Olive, happily giggling to herself as she went to press the buzzer once more.

'I said stop it,' Nixie said and hoisted Ash up above her hip. 'It is naughty. *Nein.*' She batted the chubby fingers away before looking up, her concerned frown cracking into a wide smile.

'You *are* here,' she leaned in to give Sam a hug, who returned it with a wary squeeze. 'Hello!'

'Did you come for the flip flops?' Sam said hopefully, worried that Nixie was there to remind her of further embarrassing drunken antics that she'd prefer to keep hidden in the dark, hazy recesses of her memory.

'Flip flops? I forgot about those. Wait, Olive! No!'

Olive had run through her mother's legs and into the hall where she was straining to reach up to pull a hydrangea from the large glass vase on the round table.

'Leave it!' Nixie shouted and lunged forwards, but Olive jumped from her grasp and grabbed the flowers, sending the vase teetering forwards. Sam's arm shot back and managed to steady it. A handful of petals floated to Olive's feet.

'PRETTY! Flowers for Olive!'

'No!' Nixie said. She bent down to her level, wobbling slightly as she also held onto Ash. 'We do not run in people's houses and grab things. You could have broken that vase and made Sam very sad. That was naughty.'

Olive crossed her arms and pouted in response.

'I am sorry.' Nixie straightened up. 'This was not quite what I had planned.'

'Don't worry,' Sam said and smiled nervously. 'Do you want to come in? As in, beyond the hall?'

'No, no.' Nixie shook her free hand out in front of her. 'This place...,' she peered into the living room, 'is not prepared for Olive. I came to see if you wanted to spend the day with us.'

'Oh.' Sam almost jumped. She was still getting used to such easy familiarity with people she'd only recently met.

'Nothing too exciting. I just thought you might fancy seeing a bit more–,' Nixie bent forwards to hold Olive back before she opened a cupboard door, 'of the island. Leo is on conference calls all day, playgroup is cancelled as the woman who runs it is away and Olive is in a particularly...*curious* mood at the moment. And she loved spending time with you at the races. So I thought, well...'

Olive gave a wide toothy grin as if in agreement. Sam couldn't help wondering whether she was expecting to be presented with another £25.

'But I understand if you are busy. Or if you would rather spend your day in peace.'

Sam glanced out the windows in the adjacent room to the glistening pool and quiet loungers beyond. She really hadn't come to Sark to spend her time surrounded by babies and toddlers.

But then she felt a small sticky palm tugging down on her own.

'PLEASE! Olive likes Tin Foil Lady!'

She looked down at the wild mess of curls and expectant round cheeks and placed her book down on the table. If nothing else, she'd be firmly away from the threat of the TV.

With the four of them on two electric bikes, Sam on one of Caspar's and the children strapped into a carrier on the front of Nixie's, their first stop was to the dairy to watch feeding time. Olive appeared to know every cow by name, squealing with delight as they swished their tails and looked up at her from heavily lashed eyes. After sharing a milkshake from the machines downstairs, they headed for a wooden playground, where Olive then almost threw up the milkshake on the zip wire. The next stop took them speeding down a long hill, too fast for Sam to do more than give a cursory glance to the fateful café whizzing past on her left and slowing down only to let a shire horse and its carriage pass.

'MINT SAUCE!' Olive shouted as they came to a stop, pointing a pudgy finger into the field of sheep next to the road.

Sam and Nixie put their feet down either side of their bikes. 'Ah,' Nixie said as she leaned forwards and ran a hand through Olive's matted hair. 'I suppose it could be. Though we don't know which field Mint Sauce actually lives in.'

'I do!' Olive pouted. '*That* one.'

Nixie and Sam peered at the flock of sheep, each of which was difficult to distinguish from the others.

'Really?' Nixie said.

'YES,' Olive said. 'Mint Sauce is small. And her face is brown. Not white. And one of her ears is a funny shape.'

Sam looked closer. 'Had you met her before the race?'

'*YES*,' Olive said, as if it was the most ridiculous question she'd ever been asked. 'Mint Sauce was born last. Farmer Toby said. She is always later than the other sheep because she is small, but they are FAT and she is not. So they get tired and she WINS.'

Sam and Nixie looked at each and laughed.

'She will not try and read a single world with me, but all the time talking to everyone. The farmers must tell her all about the animals,' Nixie said.

'Reading is silly,' Olive scowled. 'I know EVERYTHING.'

Nixie rolled her eyes and they remounted the bikes, pushing up a hill until they reached a granite manor house with picnic tables and umbrellas lined up outside.

The inside revealed itself to be a small chocolate shop, with three busy women pouring thick brown liquid into silicone moulds behind transparent plastic blinds on one side and rows of neat, colourful bars and boxes on the other. Sam smiled to herself as she watched their fast hands stirring and pouring in unison. This tiny industry seemed so unlikely on the cliffy outcrop of the island where the front garden looked out across miles of empty sea.

'You can have three single chocolates or one hot chocolate,' Nixie said. 'Not both.' She swiped Olive's hand away from picking up a large tray of truffles. After a little foot stomp, Olive pointed to three white strawberry creams as Nixie ordered two coffees.

Sam stroked her fingers across the pastel bars and boxes lining the shelves. In the early days of *WakeUp!*, one of their prime sponsors had been a toothpaste company, and several segments were contractually dedicated to oral hygiene and the best diets for perfect teeth. The message from one of the guest dentists, a Ken-doll of a man in a white coat and with a whiter smile, impressed itself very keenly upon Martin, who subsequently banned refined sugar from their flat, denouncing it as the enemy of a good figure and good teeth. Sam had protested that this seemed extreme but when'd she brought an Easter egg into the house a few weeks later he ceremoniously dumped it in the bin. Soon after, Erin had brightly but piercingly commented that maybe, just *maybe* Sam would better fit into the samples sent to them if she dropped a couple inches here and there. Sam noted that she preferred the sharp but forgiving trouser suits she'd been wearing for years, but Erin sipped her green tea and sniped that perhaps Sam didn't realise that the more light-hearted the TV show, the more demanding audiences were of hosts to look physically 'neat'. So, to Erin's delight, she agreed to aim to squeeze into some altogether tighter and trendier looks. Her efforts were half hearted until the start of the fertility battle. Out went surreptitious Kit-Kat trips to the corner shop and in came spinach and steamed fish. And certainly no more Easter eggs. Depressingly, not only had the strict diet not helped her get pregnant, but she'd bloated to the size of a small sumo wrestler from all the hormone injections anyway.

Now her fingers stopped on a medium-sized navy lid

speckled with silver stars and swirly writing. The chocolates in the open tray above gleamed like tiny pieces of polished ebony. Chocolate so dark must surely not be so bad for you, Sam reasoned to herself. Practically a health food. With a tingle of pleasure, she quickly snapped up the box and paid at the till.

Olive led the procession to the picnic table outside, her small plate of treats held reverently in front of her. Once there, she proceeded to pop them in her mouth like grapes and declared that she was going to play by the tree.

'Go ahead, Olly,' Nixie said. 'But no snails to bring home today, please.'

Nixie took a gulp of her coffee and positioned herself so that both Olive and Sam were in her sight. 'I reckon that gives us ten minutes of quiet. Maybe twelve.' She smiled as she put Ash onto feed and tilted her head momentarily towards a slit of sunshine which slipped in behind the umbrella.

Sam curled her palms around her mug and looked out at the strip of sea beyond the field. With just two other tables filled and the only other neighbours an apple tree and the house behind, it really was peaceful.

'So,' Nixie caught her gaze, 'the IVF?'

Sam jerked backwards as if she'd been slapped. 'What?'

'Oh. I am sorry, you mentioned the other night? I did not mean to...'

Sam shook her head sharply, desperate to free herself from the ridiculous nerves that set in whenever it was mentioned. 'It's ok. I just...I haven't had that much to drink in a while. My memory of the evening's a little hazy. How much did I say?'

'Just that your transfer did not work.' Nixie readjusted Ash's head and put her hand out onto Sam's arm. 'I am sorry. I also had a miscarriage before Olive. I know it is not like what you have been through, but I know that feeling of waiting. It is hard.'

'Mm.' Sam shuffled in her seat. 'Did...' she started to peel off the end of a fingernail, 'did I say anything else? Or just about the transfer?'

Nixie sat back and shielded her eyes from the sunshine. 'You said that your boyfriend had been a dick for writing you out of your own show and, even though you know he did it just to help you relax, you cannot help feeling pissed off. I am afraid that I do not watch much TV, so I had not heard of it all. You also said that you used to work in political television, which you preferred, and you showed me how to use the grill questioning technique on Jack to admit that he fancies Judith De Carteret.'

'Right.' Sam flushed. 'Woah.' She held onto the edge of the picnic bench. 'Well that was a lot. Blimey. I'm sorry for offloading.'

Nixie shook her head. 'No problem. It sounds stressful.'

Sam twisted her lips. She looked around at the other groups absorbed in their teas and chocolates. 'Nixie,' she leaned in, 'did I say any of this to anyone else? I know it sounds ridiculous, but because I've been on TV, sometimes gossip magazines...'

'Oh no,' Nixie said and sat Ash up on her knee. 'You did do that 'He is a dick' chant for a while, but it was only after that I asked you who it was about. No one else heard. So have you decided? I do not mean to be rude, but this boyfriend of yours does sound... *challenging*. And kids are not an answer to a relationship. They can be a problem, but not an answer.'

Sam could only groan in reply with her hands over her eyes. 'I chanted 'He's a dick'? Were people watching?'

'Of course!' Nixie laughed. 'Everyone loved it! But they thought it was about the island ownership proposal, not your boyfriend.'

'The what?' Sam looked through a slit in her fingers.

'Oh, it does not matter.' Nixie jiggled Ash as he started to fuss. 'The point is what you are going to decide. It is a big moment in your life.'

Sam grimaced. She couldn't get over the image of her chanting to the crowd. It would be a nightmare if it got out.

No doubt she'd be billed online as the scorned woman, bitter and twisted that she'd been dropped from her post. And Martin wasn't a dick, of course he wasn't. It had all been in her best interest. She repeated the point over to herself, unsure why it left such a heavy feeling in her stomach.

Before Sam could formulate an answer to Nixie, Olive rushed over, gabbling at a hundred miles an hour about how her new friend – a worm – HAD to come and live in her bedroom.

'Absolutely not,' Nixie said. 'I told you before.'

'You said SNAIL,' Olive pouted. 'Not WORM!'

'Same thing.'

Nixie's comment did not have the intended effect. Olive's lip wobbled dangerously, and Nixie apologised that she should get everyone home before the eruption of a tantrum. The women drained their coffees and cycled back at pace.

Sam plastered on a wide smile as she hugged them goodbye, noting to Olive that worms really did prefer damp soil to cosy beds. But, as she and Nixie laughed and warmly agreed to meet again ahead of the festival, all she could think about was how right she'd been right after that fateful morning walking out of filming. Her life was a mess. *She* was a mess. The best thing for it would be to get into bed, hide from the world and never come out again.

❋ ❋ ❋

The phone was ringing when she walked through the front door. Caspar was due to return the next morning, and the call could only be for him, so she let it continue as she headed upstairs to retreat under the covers. What had happened to her? When had she become the kind of person who got uproariously drunk in a field, led group chants and spilt her life's secrets to near strangers? This couldn't go on. She had to get a grip.

The ringing didn't stop. Sam sighed and slunk back downstairs again. Just as she was about to unplug the phone at the wall, she decided otherwise and picked it up.

'Caspar isn't here right now. He'll be back tomorrow.'

'Babe, is that you? Who the fuck's Caspar?'

'Louise!' Sam slunk back against the wall, winded by the shock of the familiar voice. 'How did you get hold of me?'

'More like what kind of *Castaway* bullshit have you been playing at? I know you wanted some time off, but not full digital isolation. I'd been trying to get in contact for bloody ages until I managed to get that useless secretary to work out how to check Martin's recent caller IDs. Honestly, getting a Gen Z-er to do anything. It's *exhausting*.'

Sam felt almost choked with relief. 'It's so good to hear you, Lou. I broke my phone. Still waiting for a replacement.'

'Well, there we go. The mystery of the century solved.' There was a long pause before Louise added in a lower voice, 'It might not have been such a bad thing.'

'What do you mean?'

'Look, hun, I'm going to get straight to it; it's been a fucking whirlwind since you've been away.' She paused again. 'Hang on – you didn't answer my question. Who's Caspar?'

'Oh, just the guy I'm staying with. No one important.'

'The *guy* you're *staying* with?' Louise rounded her mouth over the words as if Sam had just admitted to an elopement.

'He owns the hotel.'

'Are you *sleeping* together?' Louise hissed.

'Jeez, Lou! No! As in I'm staying in his hotel. Not like *with* him. Of course.'

'Oh.'

'What do you mean 'oh'?' Sam straightened her neck. Something about Louise's tone was off.

'I mean… I don't know. A new man on the scene might have made the news easier.'

'What news?'

There was a pause.

'Look. Regardless of what I think of him, I take no relish in saying this. But I'm glad to be the one to tell you rather than you reading it in the press,' Louise said.

Sam exhaled. 'I know about the show already. I've spoken with Martin. Doing it behind my back was a total arsehole move, but I've been considering it and I actually think his heart was in the right place.' Saying the words out loud felt good – made them feel more solid in some way, more believable.

'It's not that.'

'It's not?'

'Are you sitting down?'

Sam edged her back down along the wall until she reached the wooden floor. 'What's going on?'

'I'm just going to say it all at once.'

Sam's limbs felt weak. What now? Some other awful story about her smeared across the tabloids? An exposé on every detail the press could grasp at on her IVF?

'There's photos of Martin snogging someone else. The little shit.'

Sam blinked. *What?* Her stomach flipped. She dropped her head against the wall, her jaw slack against her neck. She couldn't speak, couldn't move.

The room seemed to tilt. She bent her head down over her knees. Of course the whole new show bullshit hadn't been to protect her. How could she have been so naïve? 'Nina?' She managed to whisper. She knew she never should have left the city. Nina had probably been waiting for this moment for years – ready to swoop in to snatch Martin back up in a weak moment.

'Heh?' Louise said.

Sam cleared her throat. 'With Nina? He's kissed Nina.' The name was like acid on her tongue.

'Nina? Christ no. *Keira*. The new producer.'

Sam flicked her head back in surprise, hitting it against the wall. 'What?'

'The fucking arsehole. Trying to curry favour, no doubt. The whole presenter change crap smacks of smutty bullshit from the two of them, which, by the way, is totally fucking illegal, and there's no way they can just write you out of the show.'

Sam felt as if someone had slit her open from her throat to her pelvis, and she had stepped out her body to look down on it from above.

'Babe,' Louise paused, 'are you ok? I wondered if you knew when I saw that video of you but then I realised the timing was slightly out. I'm sorry. I really am.'

'I, urm.' The words stuck like flour in Sam's throat. 'What video?'

'The 'He's a dick' video? It's done the rounds on social media. God, that was such a genius move. You look so happy and relaxed. I don't know where the hell you are. Looks like some God-awful tent. But all those local people chanting with you – makes you look fun and part of the community, not like some snobby urbanite. It's perfect. *YouNews* love it – thank God. And the public have lapped it up – all the headlines today are that you've been shafted off the show unfairly by Keira trying to elbow you out the way to make room for lover boy's ego. And all that crap about you being a diva – I mean, firstly,' she tutted, 'what the hell do people expect? That you just walk into top roles by being some simpering wallflower? But now people think that Keira and Martin leaked it to make it not look so bad that he'd moved on. Now you're the suffering, misunderstood victim who can come back as a bad ass phoenix rising from the fucking ashes. It's perfect, babe. I mean I know it's shit. But it's also perfect. Well fucking done.' She paused. 'But I mean actually, like, *are* you ok?'

Sam traced a line in the grain of wood with her finger. It was all she could do to keep herself from streaming into a puddle of limbs. After the initial shock, one thought ran cold in her veins. 'The IVF. What now?'

'I know,' Louise scoffed. 'There's still been murmurings

about whether you're pregnant or not. We can quash those quickly – just say it was all hearsay in the first place. And – not that I needed confirmation – but it really hammers home what a total cretin of a human being Martin is, hey? Playing the nepotism game. At your fucking expense. Eugh,' she spat. 'He disgusts me.

But Sam wasn't listening. All she could think about was the egg. The remaining fertilised egg. His egg. She almost whimpered as the realisation rushed through her. She'd have to go through it all again. The egg collection procedure. With a donor. She felt faint at the thought.

'Anyway,' Louise continued, 'there's lots to consider. I've got a call with *YouNews* in a minute. Just try and focus on prepping for the new role. Put Martin on the shelf.'

Sam felt shaky as she was consumed with incredulity. The effort, the money, the injections. She'd have to go through it all again. On her own. Nausea swept through her chest, and she slunk further to the floor, unable to hold herself up.

'Babe?' Louise said. 'You alright?'

Sam couldn't speak. She let herself slide down until she was lying with her back on the floorboards. Her breath came in gasps as her chest tightened.

'Hun? Seriously. You ok? Do you need me to come over there?'

A stifled bleat escaped from Sam's throat. Her thoughts were suddenly painfully, horribly clear. She didn't want Martin – could hardly care less. He could put his tongue down however many producers' necks he wanted. But she still wanted a family. A baby. And she'd just lost her best chance at having one.

'I've got a meeting in a few mins,' Louise said. 'I wouldn't take it, but it's *YouNews*. They want to move fast. I know this whole thing's shit, but it might be good for you in the long run. I don't mean to be insensitive – I really don't. I know it's caused you a lot of fucking pain and heartache – but it feels like a sign. Like a turn back now – this isn't your path sort of thing?

Anyway, I might just be chatting shit, but don't let Martin get to you. He's an insecure little dickwad sidling up to whichever side his bread's buttered on. You were always better than him. By far. Don't waste your thoughts on the wanker. Promise?'

Sam mumbled a non-committal reply, her voice thick with a sob.

'Hun,' Louise added. 'I love you. I miss you. Things will get better. Call me anytime. *Anytime*. But please, do not try to contact him right now.'

Sam straightened. It took a few moments for her voice to break through. 'Surely –'

'Absolutely not,' Louise barked. 'Not at the moment. You'll say something you'll regret, and then the little weasel will call up the tabloids.'

'But I need to tell him it's over.'

'I'll tell him. No fuss – just a message. Then let's get you home tomorrow, wait until you're composed, and you can skewer him in person until he squirms like some pathetic prey stuck within a lion's teeth. Ok?'

Lying back flat on the floor, her thoughts jumbled like tissue in a washing machine, Sam could only nod silently to herself in return and reach up to her box of chocolates on the console.

CHAPTER 18

It was past eleven o'clock when Caspar walked in the front door. It had been a long but successful few days with his lawyers, and he'd been looking forward to a celebratory night cap. He had a silky pinot noir tucked away in the bar, and he could almost taste its dark cherries and earthy spice as he put his hold-all on the floor and went to turn on the lights.

'Ow!'

'What!'

'Shit.'

'Who's that?'

He smacked the light switch and looked round – hands posed to fight – before he saw the body of a woman huddled in a ball on the floor.

'*Sam?*'

'Urgh,' she groaned, rubbing her eyes.

He put out a hand to help her up. 'What are you doing? On the floor? In the dark?'

She breathed out heavily as she took his hand and stumbled up.

He clocked her puffy eyes, red cheeks and a strange brown rim around her lips. 'Is everything ok? Did you fall and hurt yourself? Tell me where.' He looked frantically around. 'I'll get the new builders on it in the morning. On the staircase? Have you broken anything?'

'No.' She limply flapped a hand away. 'I'm fine. Well, *physically* fine.' She wiped her eyes and mouth and tried to tuck the empty box of truffles behind her with her foot. 'It's just my boyfriend. *Ex*-boyfriend.'

'Ah,' he exhaled and put a hand to his chest. 'That's alright then. The last thing I need right now is to be sued for an unstable floor or something.' He rubbed the back of his neck before glancing over her crumpled sundress and hair tousled from the wind of the bicycle. 'Ex boyfriends I can deal with. Fancy a drink?'

'I don't think so.' She stretched out her neck. 'I should really get to bed. Christ, I'm sorry for being in a heap on the floor. I just couldn't bring myself to move. That probably looked…' She grimaced. 'I don't know. I wasn't thinking.'

'Don't apologise.' He placed a hand on the small of her back. 'Break ups. We've all been there. Come,' he nodded towards the bar, 'just one glass will take the edge off, and you'll sleep much better than without.'

She sighed. She was exhausted but her mind was like a merry-go-round. To distract herself from the deep, crushing baby-related pain, she'd thought about Martin and Keira instead, managing to wind her indifference up to raging umbrage. She knew she was just displacing her fear and sadness about another transfer onto them, but she didn't care. She turned over and over on how long it had been going on and why and where and when and what on earth she would say when she saw him. And, of course, she'd spent a decent amount of time imagining how she would torture him appropriately. Ripping up his suits with scissors felt too cliché. Plus he got most of his clothes for free through work. Maybe stealing his favourite watch? Though he'd know it was her because she was the only other person who knew where he'd kept it. Or something that would ruin his image for the show? Cutting off a chunk of hair, or shaving an eyebrow or painting his forehead with a fake tan cock in the night…? She gave her head a sharp shake.

'Alright then. Just one,' she said.

Caspar was right. The pinot noir was very good. He was one of those people who insisted on tasting it properly – sniffing it first to take in the aromas and then taking time to tease out the different layers of fruit and earth and spice. It was the sort of performance she and Louise would usually laugh about, but now it helped take her mind away from at least the sharpest shards of despair.

'Let me show you how to hold the glass properly,' he said and placed his hand over her own. She flinched at his touch and pulled back slightly, only then realising how close they had been sitting on the sofa.

'I won't bite.' He caught her eye. 'Look, here on the stem.' He guided her fingers down. 'Like this.'

And soon one glass turned into another and she went back to not thinking about how she was holding the wine or releasing different flavours, but just taking great mouthfuls and splurging all her questions on whether it *was* all just down to nepotism and, if not, why Martin would choose Keira – who was *fine* but nothing exciting and had an odd short fringe and always wore black and never seemed to smile – particularly when he could have gone off with someone like Nina – or Erin even – and whether she was the first person he'd cheated on her with or whether it had been going on for years – and whether it had been in their flat, in their *bed*?

Her whole body felt jittery with anxiety, and her knee wobbled as if in spasm.

'Because if it wasn't enough to ruin my professional life,' she took another large gulp, 'now he decides to piss all over my personal life, too. One fell fucking swoop.' She swept her glass in front of her like a wand casting a spell.

Caspar caught her wrist just as the remaining pool of wine was about to tip onto the velvet sofa. His grasp was firm but gentle, and he slowly took away the glass and placed it on the coffee table before placing a hand down on her quivering knee.

It was hot and heavy and tickled against her skin. Something burned warm in her chest, and she suddenly jumped out of her racing thoughts and into awareness of the heat of his large body next to her own.

'You're ok.' Caspar nodded, his expression serious. 'You clearly don't need an idiot like that in your life.'

She shook her head, the tight coil of anger loosening within her chest, her lips and tongue now thick with the alcohol. Something pricked in her stomach as she looked down at the hand still on her knee.

'I just –' she started, but she didn't know what to say. She just hadn't expected it? She just felt small, stupid, taken for a fool? She let her forehead drop.

'It doesn't matter.' Caspar bent his head, catching her gaze. 'What matters is right now. Not yesterday, not tomorrow.'

She nodded and exhaled, closing her eyes as she sunk back into the large cushions behind her. It was true. Save calling Martin or Keira and screaming blue murder at them only to see her words quoted in some tabloid tomorrow, at this moment there was nothing she could do.

'And right now,' Caspar edged closer, 'things are good. I sealed a big deal today. And you're here. We can celebrate it together.'

'Really?' She sat up slightly, noticing that the room was starting to tilt as she did so. 'What kind of deal? I know I haven't really talked about my prosesh –' She laughed and covered her mouth with her hand, '*professional* life, and now I just do rubbish like Britain's best cow!' Caspar raised an eyebrow, and Sam cleared her throat. 'But I love hearing about that kind of thing.'

He peered at her through slanted eyes, his hand still warm on her knee.

'Honestly,' she nodded quickly, her head light, 'I used to be a political journalist. Quite a good one, actually. It was only because Martin...'

'I know,' he laughed. 'Of course I know what you do for work, Sam Elton. You're a pretty familiar face.'

She frowned. 'You knew?' She was finding it hard to order her thoughts. Every part of her mind and body felt slower to connect. 'But you never said?'

'I didn't need to. I figured maybe you didn't want to be recognised. I mean why else would you be here? That's the beauty of the island: its privacy, seclusion. No one needs to know what's happening. It'll be what The Rowe's all about. You've been our first celebrity guest on a retreat.'

'Do you think other people have recognised me all along?'

'I doubt it,' he snorted. 'Most of the locals wouldn't recognise the British prime minister.'

'It *is* hard to keep up these days,' she said and bounced her knee, her thoughts now whirling in the wine.

'Stop.' He squeezed her leg still. 'You can relax now. Forget about him. About everything.'

She sat back again into the cushions and closed her eyes. Her spinning head sunk firmly back. Caspar was right. If she could try and get some sleep tonight, she'd feel better about hatching a plan to confront Martin in the morning. And possibly Keira. Both at the same time? No. Straight after the other? Martin first? She took a deep breath and tried to imagine doing an exercise Issa often touted: out with the dark energy, in with the light. Out with the dark energy...

It was then that she felt a finger slowly trailing up her inner thigh.

She flicked her eyes open, her heart leaping into action. It wasn't what she'd expected.

'Everything ok, gorgeous?' Caspar looked closely at her with his icy blue eyes.

'I, urm.' She squirmed slightly and shuffled backwards from the hand. 'Today has been,' she grimaced, 'a lot. I'm flattered, honestly, but I'm just so angry with Martin. And sad. And scared. I don't think...'

Caspar leant back slowly and took another sip of his drink.

She fumbled to pull down her dress where it had risen up. 'It just doesn't feel like the right time. Not so shoon. I mean soon.'

He smirked. 'Now's the perfect time.' He put down his glass and rolled up the white sleeves of his shirt, revealing a large watch and layers of thin fabric bracelets that Sam recognised as subtle confirmation of an expensive gap year or similar 'travelling' experience. But she couldn't help noticing his thick, toned arms.

He moved slowly closer and ran a finger along her collar bone.

She took a sharp intake of breath. If *this* happened it really would mean things with Martin were over. And, yes, he really was an absolute arsehole, but he was an arsehole with whom she not only shared a TV show and a flat, but a frozen fertilised egg.

She tried to subtly inch in the other direction.

Caspar's other hand crept forwards under her dress.

'Go on.' His breath was hot and sweet and against her ear.

'I don't –'

He gently stroked her inner thigh.

'Honestly–' But she faltered, her thoughts filled with Louise saying that another man would make things easier... Maybe a bit of fooling around *would* make things easier? Take her mind off things. And Martin needn't know. It wasn't like it meant anything. And what right would he have to be cross anyway? He was the one who'd been shagging around. Throwing her future out the window.

Caspar's fingers stroked the fabric of the top of her underwear, and she thought about just how large, black and grannyish her pants really were. But then her body sparked, and she forgot to care. It had been so long since she'd felt desirable. Like someone had *wanted* to touch her, rather than doing so because it fit a fertility schedule. Maybe she needed this?

'Urm,' her cheeks flushed as she managed a shaky exhale, 'I'm out of practice.'

His lips travelled across her ear and cheek. Every inch of her skin felt like it had been lit. But something in her didn't quite sit well. She hadn't officially ended it with Martin. Maybe he had some perfectly plausible explanation. Maybe he still wanted to go ahead with another transfer. Her face tightened. Of course he bloody didn't.

And then Caspar's hand sunk lower, and he kissed her eyes shut. His hand slipped below the fabric of her dress, skimming across her bra until he reached gently underneath. Flush with nerves and sensation, she tensed her arms, gripping onto the seat pad.

'Let yourself go, Sam,' Caspar whispered, his lips hovering above her own. 'I want to celebrate with you tonight.'

He kissed her neck, her shoulders, her breasts, first softly then hungrily. She could feel him hot and thick against her thigh, and a ripple of pleasure pooled between her legs.

'Forgot everything,' he said, more forcefully now. 'Tell me how much you want this.'

She hesitated and bit her cheeks. Caspar pushed back her underwear to rub his thumb against her. 'Tell me,' he rasped into her mouth as she arched her back and rocked her hips into him.

'I –' But the words and her inhibitions dissolved into the warm evening air.

CHAPTER 19

Sam woke up in her room to a dry throat, a stomach like a ship lost at sea and a sinking feeling of dread. The other side of the bed was empty, but Caspar's almond scent still seeped from her pores. She scrunched up her face in shame, remembering the night only as a tangled mix of hot, sweet breath and drunken limbs.

What had she been *thinking*? She buried her head in the pillow. Yes, it had felt good – electrifying even – but this was not her normal behaviour. Was it still technically cheating if she hadn't yet spoken to Martin? Or did she have free licence if he'd already thrown himself at someone else? She tightened herself into a ball. She shouldn't have made things more complicated than necessary. It would have been far simpler to wake up sad, alone and desperate to speak with and then kill Martin. But now she wasn't just the victim.

She flopped on her back and looked around the room. There was no sign of Caspar. Unsurprisingly. He'd probably slipped off in the early hours when he remembered what a mess she'd been blubbering on the hall floor. At least all her things were in the room; she might be able to pack up and sneak back to the cottage without an awkward confrontation in the corridor.

She glanced at the time on the room's retro-style radio. Just past half 7. Another lie-in, but she was still tired. Her eyes were swollen from yesterday's tears, and her head throbbed as if she'd drunk a vial of poison rather than a few too many glasses of pinot noir. She sunk down into the sheets, closing her eyes for a few seconds before she could bring herself to get up and face the world. Perhaps she might even get another hour of sleep.

But, as she flipped her pillow to the cold side, she noticed the brushed gold handle of the door moving. Shit.

Caspar's head emerged, his thick blonde hair ruffled in different directions.

'Morning,' he said. 'How are you feeling?'

Sam wasn't sure on what tone to take. Should she be brisk and business-like? Give a curt nod and pretend like last night hadn't happened? It wasn't that she didn't *like* Caspar. He was no doubt a Hooray Henry, but he clearly also had vision and direction, qualities she admired. And now, as she pulled the sheets up over her chest, it was impossible to ignore the way in which the morning light caught the golden hairs of his arms and that impish, knowing curve to his lips. But he might just be checking in to see when she was leaving. After all, it wasn't like she'd woken up to pillow talk and a morning kiss. And nor had she wanted to. Had she? Surely it had been a one-off thing. A mistake. An unthinking reaction to an unexpected situation. Caspar held her gaze, his eyes wide and dancing.

'Fine,' she said and gave a tight smile, trying to ignore the slight tingling between her legs. 'Don't worry, I'll be –'

'I know, I know. You're trying to run away from me as quickly as possible.' Caspar dropped down next to her on the bed, kicking his boat shoes off across the room. He leant over, placing his torso above her, his shirt hanging loose onto the sheets. She held her breath. This was ridiculous. She'd had a few drinks last night. She'd been upset – in shock. She was angry with Martin and wanted to get back at him in some way. Break even. But there was no excuse now.

'There was something I thought you needed.' His voice was low.

She swallowed, so keen to ignore the part of her that was imagining him pulling back the sheet and lowering himself onto her body. She gave her head a short, sharp shake.

He smiled again and leant back, picking something up from the floor. 'Close your eyes. Hold out your hand.'

She did so, her brain struggling for control of her short-circuiting body. He momentarily held her palm in his own long fingers.

'Here.'

She felt the weight of a small, metal rectangle.

'A phone!' Sam grasped it to her chest. 'Finally!' She wriggled up, being careful not to let the sheets slip down. 'God. Thank you.'

'I'd far rather keep you locked here in my sex cave, but you know,' he shrugged, 'I figured you might need some contact with the outside world. A chance to tell that ex of yours where to stick it, perhaps.'

Sam rushed to turn it on and login to her online account. Once she did so, she'd be able to access all her numbers, her messages, her emails. She'd be back. No more isolation on this tiny rock. 'How much do I owe you?'

He laughed. 'Take it as a fee for your services.'

'*Services?*'

'The design advice. And confirmation that the chicken in that dish perhaps is a tad too hot.'

'Ah.' She turned her attention again to the bright, flashing screen. Her heart pumped with adrenaline. Now she could speak with Martin, organise transport, check in with Louise. It was amazing to think how cut off she'd been over the past few days.

Her fingers hovered over the screen. A dark, menacing itch willed her to check the tabloid websites and her social accounts to see what else Keira had leaked and gauge the reaction. She hadn't considered just how cocooned she'd been from online noise until that moment. It had been a strange sensation, living for her actual emotions rather than always checking how actions had been publicly received. She wondered how differently she might have behaved over the past five years if she hadn't always had one eye on the online response. Would she have cared so much about making things work with Martin? Would she have been so keen for a baby, to join in with the ubiquitous pumpkin patch, Santa's grotto and bunny ears photos? Her chest felt tight. She still wasn't sure who she'd be when she re-entered 'real' life. She wasn't even sure if she wanted to re-enter real life.

'All ok?' Caspar tilted his head.

'Yep.'

'Sure?'

Sam wrinkled her nose. 'You know,' she held up the phone. 'I know this sounds ridiculous, but I'm not quite ready for this. The posts, the comments, the speculation… Tomorrow, maybe. I just need a bit more time to get my head in the right place.'

'Good idea.' He smiled, taking it from her hand and slipping it onto the side table. 'I might be able to help.'

Without saying anything else, he scooped her forwards and kissed her on her forehead, lips, neck, chest and then lower and lower until she closed her eyes and lay back on the pillow, and the reasons for having the phone – to contact Martin, to speak with Louise, to check reactions to her departure from the show – suddenly melted into irrelevance. It felt like there was nowhere else – and with no one else – that she could possibly need to be.

The mobile was returned to its box. When the hotel phone kept ringing later that morning and Sam explained that it was probably Louise trying to speak to her about a new job, Caspar simply pulled out the cord and went back to frying rashers of crispy bacon for breakfast. And after he'd made a few calls himself, tying up what he'd said were a few loose ends on a big deal, they spent the morning wrapped up in each other – in the bed, the hot tub, the cool stone floor of the kitchen.

She felt bewitched. After years of sex on schedule,

dictated by the results of her peeing on ovulation sticks, being touched by Caspar's giving hands and strong, warm chest was like shedding an armour that she hadn't realised she'd been wearing. She felt fresh, youthful, *sexy* – not just a barren vessel empty of eggs.

The afternoon brought one of those perfect summer skies as fresh as lemonade and with the sun powdering the fields in white gold. As Caspar made some more calls, Sam strolled smilingly around the garden in a towelling robe covering her underwear, dizzy with passion. With Caspar having kissed every inch of her, she felt drunk on his touch and sank gently into a sun lounger as she awaited his return. Stretching her limbs out in the sun, it was as if she'd been gifted a new body, one which was lithe and fresh and had never been punctured with injections or opened with speculums or prodded under sedation by shockingly long needles. And it was whilst lying on the lounger, contemplating her new-found good fortune, eyes closed against the bright light, that she heard the click of a camera.

'Don't move,' Caspar held up a finger. 'You look perfect.'

'Hey,' she smiled, 'what's that?'

He held the camera out to his side. 'My second greatest passion next to the food. Though I haven't used it in ages. Just haven't felt inspired. But you...' He walked forwards and sat at her feet. 'I want to capture you from every angle.'

'Absolutely not.' She laughed and lightly held up her hand. 'I spend my life avoiding being photographed.'

'Not today.' He snapped another before tugging open the folds of her dressing gown. 'Today you're my muse.'

She grimaced as she covered her eyes and he clicked again.

'Go on,' he stroked her toes, 'pose for me.'

'No!' she kicked him away and wrinkled her nose in mock disgust.

Caspar ran his fingers along her legs. 'Go on,' he repeated, a cheeky glint of challenge in his eye.

'No!' Sam kicked him back again but then stuck her tongue out like a sassy six-year-old.

'Ha!' Caspar clicked. 'Got you!'

He leant forward and kissed her. 'Five more?' He whispered in her ear. 'I want to remember this day – this feeling of you – always.'

'Always?'

He smiled. 'When you're ancient and wrinkly and haven't got any teeth left and your boobs are dragging on the floor, I want to be able to show our great-grandchildren some photos to prove what an absolute goddess you were.'

Great-grandchildren? Sam knew he was just pissing about, but she couldn't help flushing with pleasure. Perhaps this was what everything had really been leading up to? Maybe the saga with Martin was life's way of getting her here. She felt herself melting under the weight of him. 'Just one,' she whispered back.

'Three.'

She laughed and wriggled out from underneath him and ran towards the pool. 'Better be quick!' She dived into the cool water and pushed her arms up into a neat handstand before emerging spluttering at the surface where she quickly adjusted her bra.

Caspar grinned and sat on the edge, dangling his feet in the water.

'Did you get it?' She coughed. 'Can't say I've done an underwater handstand in the past decade, but I reckon that was alright.'

'Bellissimo!' He kissed his fingers.

'Now your turn. Hand it over! I'm not going to be anyone's muse unless they'll also be mine.'

'No way.' He raised his eyebrows and shook his head. 'Scoot.' He kicked slightly at the water.

Sam waded towards him. 'Yes way,' she laughed. 'Pass me a towel and strike a pose, Mr Rowe. Show me what you've got.'

'No!' Caspar stood up as he wiggled his forefinger. 'You'll have to catch me first.'

He ran with the camera in his hand into the wide expanse of grass outside the bar. Sam pulled herself out the pool, dried her hands on her robe and sprinted after him, giggling with abandon as he teased her by running towards the tree and back, taking a sharp right then a quick left, poking his tongue out as he slipped past.

She turned only to find that he'd already twisted towards the other direction and, as she turned again, he ran up behind her, wrapping his arms around her waist to scoop her up and then have her fall on top of him to the grass.

'I win.' He reached up and kissed her, holding up the camera for another shot.

'Not fair!' She held her hands over the lens. 'It's your turn.'

'How about I promise that you can take the next shot. But not before I do this.'

He quickly pulled her down on top of him as he lay back in the grass. Sam screeched, but he kissed her deeply before running his lips along her neck.

She took a deep breath. He pulled at her bra to kiss lower, and she felt him reach into her underwear, pushing his fingers against her.

She felt alive, electric, uncaring of how far her sighs of pleasure might carry in the fresh afternoon air.

He kissed her neck and reached round to unhook her bra. He then reached both hands round onto the small of her back and quickly pushed her back and forth until she moaned.

'God,' she exhaled, 'what are you doing to me?'

But, instead of replying, Caspar quickly jumped up, letting her roll face first the ground, and snapping a photo before she turned around.

'What! You arsehole!' She laughed and kicked in his direction. 'Was all that just to lull me into a false sense of security?'

'Don't pretend you didn't love it.' He winked.

She lunged forwards but he danced back before running towards the bar.

She hooked her bra back on and sped after him, shouting and laughing as she approached.

'Password?' He stood at the door, his large body filling its frame.

'Caspar's a little shit?' She panted slightly.

'Correct!' He laughed and picked her up from the waist, spinning her round until they both landed in a heap on the velvet sofa.

'My turn. Hand it over.'

'Ugh.' Caspar gave a mock groan. 'One minute. And then I get my other shots.'

'One.' She wrinkled her nose. 'If you're lucky.'

He slid himself up, passed over the camera then pranced around the room in a host of silly poses, pretending to growl, scream and strut about before taking a bottle of beer from behind the bar and using it as a fake microphone.

She howled with laughter and clicked away, running up to kiss him between each ridiculous shot.

'Ok, my turn, my turn.' He took the camera from her. 'I'll just take one more…' he smiled cheekily, 'if you do something stupid with the bottle.'

She rolled her eyes. 'Like what? More singing?' She held one foot up and put the bottle against her mouth.

'No,' he ordered. 'On the bar.'

'Really?' She rolled her eyes.

'Yes, or I get to take another two photos after this one.'

She scoffed before jumping up onto the marble surface and spreading her legs wide, the bottle covering her crotch. 'Like this?' She laughed.

'Ha! Yes!' He snapped quickly before throwing the camera down onto the sofa. He quickly reached towards her, moved the bottle to one side and wrapped her open legs around him, kissing her slowly on her mouth and neck and chest before carrying her upstairs.

CHAPTER 20

Caspar left after breakfast the next day for negotiations with new builders in Guernsey. The previous firm had pulled out at the final hurdle, and he needed the finishing touches completed on the indoor pool.

'So sorry, gorgeous,' he said. 'I'll see you later to pick up where we left off. Will you be ok waiting?'

Sam nodded and smoothed down his shirt collar. 'Yes,' she smiled, 'I'll be fine.'

And, as he closed the front door behind him, she realised that she meant it. She'd hardly thought about Martin or Keira or *WakeUp!* or tabloids since the previous morning. It was like something in her brain had switched off to the pain, numbed instead by her newfound physical pleasure. She knew it was all so ridiculously fast, but it felt like a door of possibility had opened again. Caspar offered a hopeful new direction. And, despite Louise's warning that she should wait to confront Martin in person, she knew she was ready to speak to him today. To firmly close the lid on him for good.

But not right yet. First she needed to clear her mind completely. Get into the same headspace she once cultivated before grilling politicians – calm, focused but ruthless. No emotion.

She started by taking her book out into the morning sun of the garden and curling up on one of the loungers. The early morning air was bright but still crisp. It was, she realised, as she blankly scanned the words of a chapter titled 'The West's Loss of Faith in Liberalism', the perfect day for a run.

Bar the recent expeditions on electric bikes, she hadn't exercised properly for months, not since starting the IVF injections. The heavy stomach from egg stimulation and fatigue from hormones hadn't exactly inspired rapid movement. But as she took her first steps across the gravel in her plimsolls – not having packed proper trainers – and took a deep breath of the clean air, she felt like she could keep going to the other side of the island.

After that initial burst, she eased into a steady pace, keeping focused on the sharp colours of the cottages in the bright air and the trilling of blackbirds in every hedge. It couldn't be more different to her London commuter run, dodging in and out of crowds and trying to remain focused on whatever topical podcast she'd chosen to drown out the sirens and traffic. The only place she now saw any people was in a bustle outside a house on the Avenue. The group was holding clipboards and flags, and Sam figured they must be there to finish planning next week's festival, an event that, after the sheep racing debacle, she'd try her best to ignore.

She shook her head to clear her thoughts and strode past the high street down a long hill towards the top of the path to Dixcart bay. She pushed away the memory of the awkward encounter with Walt and losing her clothes to the tide, focusing instead on her surroundings. The scenery turned lush with ferns, the path mottled with shade beneath the leaves, before she pushed up another hill, arriving on a coastal path with views out across the channel to France.

After moving steadily forwards, she emerged, panting but exhilarated, onto a wild headland dotted with sheep. Below her, the waves swelled against the angular assortment of wet rocks, now glittering against the rising sun.

Her chest heaved red and she stopped for a moment, stretching out as she drank in the view. She couldn't imagine now why she'd been so keen to leave the island so quickly. It was sublime – breathtakingly beautiful. No view of an endless grid of city lights from the top of a soulless glass building could compare.

Taking a deep breath, she realised that she felt ready. She let her thoughts be solely filled with the sound of water before heading back to the hotel.

After showering, she slipped into a dressing gown and perched on the edge of the sofa, the new mobile in her hands.

'This is it,' she said to herself and murmured her old pre-interview mantras: *'Be stronger than your excuses; If it doesn't challenge you, it doesn't change you; The more you do, the more happens to you.'*

He picked up on the first ring.

'Martin. It's Sam.'

'Sam?' She heard a clattering sound on the other end of the line as if he'd just tripped over. 'Jesus, Sam! I've been trying to call for ages. I'm assuming you don't know about that bullshit text from Louise? God, she's such a stirrer. Look, it really wasn't how I wanted the news to come out. Honestly. I know I've fucked up. Are you ok?'

'Fine.'

'Really? Shit. I feel like such a twat. Trust me when I say it was a one-time thing. I'd been such a mess with you leaving.'

She took a deep breath. She wasn't going to allow herself to get angry. 'Leaving?' she said.

'Going to that island. You don't know how hard it was for me, babe. You walked out and I didn't know when you were coming back.'

Sam gripped the edge of the sofa. 'That's not quite true.'

'Excuse me?'

She paused. 'You were the one who encouraged me to stay here. To recuperate before another transfer.'

'Look, I know I've been an idiot, but it's been fucking stressful for me.'

She could have screamed, but she gritted her teeth. 'Has

it?'

'Just when I thought I'd finally sorted everything out – you pregnant, me with my own show. New producer, perfect timing. And then that bloody test faded. It fucked me up.'

He paused. She didn't reply.

'And then,' he spoke more slowly. 'I don't know. You went off. I had to sort everything out. I was worried about the show – they could have axed us after your outburst. I needed to do something to make sure the new production team kept us – or at least me – on board. There were lots of late nights in the studio office. Keira was there. I thought I'd just flirt with her. You know, sell myself a bit. Show what an asset I was. But she practically threw herself at me one evening after a late meeting. And I don't know. She's younger. Different. Made me feel sort of… myself again. When there'd been so much going on.'

'Right. So this is my fault. Of course. Any other excuses?'

He sighed. 'Shit, look. I know. It doesn't look good. And if it's any consolation, it couldn't be worse timing for it to come out with the new show. Ratings are bloody plummeting.'

She couldn't stop her lips curving into a small smile.

'Sam,' he groaned. 'I'm sorry. Look, I did it for us. For the show. You know how these things work. You've got to keep people on side. If I slip up a few times with some women falling at my feet, it doesn't mean anything.'

She'd been about to confess about Caspar. It would put them on an even footing, allow for a balanced conversation about next steps. But something Martin said lingered like a bad smell.

'A few times?'

'Look, babe,' he cleared his throat, 'I want you home.'

'Martin, what did you just say?'

'I said I want you to come back. Go back to how things were.' His voice softened. 'Come on, sweetheart.'

'Before that.'

'What? I don't know. Christ, Sam. Are you listening?'

'You said 'a few times'?'

'Huh. Oh, well – you know, *hypothetically*.'

She pursed her lips. 'Really?'

'For fuck's sake, babe. Things have been tough. I'm trying to make amends here. I want things back to how they were. Everyone's saying the show worked better when it was us together. And – I've been thinking – we can just try and run as normal with a set up that's less stressful for you. Later starts, fewer meetings. I'm sure Issa will have some ideas.'

She paused. She wanted to make sure her words came out correctly and hoped the fluttering of her heart didn't come through in her voice. 'Martin, is this even about me anymore?'

'Huh?'

She peeled off the end of a fingernail. 'Do you actually want us to be together?'

'That's what I'm saying, isn't it? Come back, rejoin the show, we'll do another transfer.'

'And that's what you want? With me?'

'Jesus,' he exhaled, 'this is the kind of mind game that messed me up in the first place. Of course that's what I want. We've been together five years, haven't we? I didn't do it for a bit of fun.'

A thought rose within her. It had been festering in the pit of her stomach for years now, blistering, unacknowledged but unabating. She'd never before really wanted to know the answer.

'And if I took on the *You News* role?

He huffed.

'Would you still want me home then?'

His voice hardened. 'You can't be serious?'

She ripped off the end of another fingernail and took a breath to steady herself. The words that had been hidden for years, like the rotting contents of an unopened drawer in an otherwise pin-neat fridge, were finally ready to come out. It was a truth she'd always known but had never wanted to admit. It had been there when she'd first dominated a conversation to demolish a politician's argument on *Real News* and she'd been surprised to see Martin frown. It had been there when he'd sent her outfits that he wanted her to wear on their dates. It had been at their signing of the *WakeUp!* contract, Martin cheering as Sam shakily held the pen, her fist white with nerves. It had been in his smug smile from reading the reviews praising their good-cop bad-cop duo on set. It has been there when he'd tightly held her hand in the car to the television awards. It had been in every perfect smile he flashed when the two of them were near cameras, in every comically knowing look he feigned when interviewees talked about difficult spouses, in every time he'd refused to put sugar in her tea. And it had been there most potently, like a fetid smell lurking in the corner, when she'd first agreed to try for a baby. 'It'll be great,' he'd whispered, 'to show everyone we're a proper family. The ratings will skyrocket.'

She swallowed. Her mouth was dry.

'I don't think you want to be with me, Martin. Not really. I just fitted the right roles in your head. It's not me you care about; it's how we look as a couple.'

He scoffed. 'Oh, come on. You're being ridiculous.'

'Am I?'

'Yes,' he spat. 'I've been incredibly patient with your whole IVF thing. I've always supported you. And I didn't *have* to, you know.'

She narrowed her eyes. '*My* IVF thing?'

'Well, it's not like *I* needed it.'

Her stomach twisted. 'How magnanimous of you.'

'What's that supposed to mean?'

She straightened her back and gripped more tightly onto the sofa. 'Martin,' she said slowly. 'I think in your mind I've become some sort of nuisance. A barren problem to fix to make things look better again.'

'Oh, come on–'

She stood up. 'I don't think you give a toss about who I actually am.'

'Jesus, woman, talk about an overblown reaction. It was one kiss. Are you just going to conveniently forget that I'm the one who gave you the career you wanted and then the one who's given you the chance to have a family?'

'Actually,' she looked calmly out the window at the wide expanse of lawn, 'I don't want my career to have anything more to do with you. And,' she gulped, 'nor do I want your children. I knew Louise sent that message. Now I'll send her round to collect my things.'

Blood rushing through her chest, she quickly hung up and turned off the phone.

She felt sick.

So that was that. All gone. She sat back down, numb and unsure what to do next. Should she be sad? Angry? She lay back amidst the layers of cushions on the sofa, noticing the white sun momentarily covered by a cloud, and tried to name her unfamiliar feeling she felt rising in her chest.

She tried to cry, thinking it might help, but the tears wouldn't spill over. Instead, she felt only a wave of utter exhaustion. Whether brought on by the run or the call, she didn't know, but she nestled into the cushions and let herself sleep.

* * *

Hours had passed when she finally woke up, head groggy as the golden light of the early evening poured in. She made herself a tea amidst the gleaming metal of the industrial kitchen and checked the clock on the oven. It was past six. She blanched, not expecting to have slept so long. She hadn't realised, she considered as she padded back to the living room, just how tired she'd been from everything. It wasn't just today, but the past few weeks, the past year. Every day had felt like a battle – either against her body, or her mind, or the papers or Issa or now Martin. Her early twenties had been exciting, invigorating – she'd wanted to get up each day. She was hungry for experience, desperate to prove what she could do. But now life had a before and after point: before the appointment with Mr Thomas and after. And life after had felt like wading through mud; every solution had brought with it a different set of problems. For years she'd woken up in the morning only to think about where she was in her cycle, and anytime that she wasn't ovulating or in the two-week-wait felt like days to simply bear, not live. She was constantly counting down time, but then thinking about her future was like staring into a great, dark, unknown abyss.

But then it had all brought her here.

She stared blankly out of the window for a few minutes, a cross of confusion etched into her forehead.

It was only then, her eyelids still heavy, that she felt the strange feeling again and realised what it was. It was lightness. She felt at peace. It was like the previous few months – years – had been a cold, dark veil of mist that had lifted, and she was now finally free. The last couple of days had shown her what it was to just enjoy being in her own body, not worrying about the turmoil of life outside the island. And that had brought with it unexpected clarity.

She knew she no longer wanted Martin in her life. Not now; not ever. And she didn't want Keira. She didn't want the show. She didn't want po-faced models or people who'd eaten their sofas or Britain's best cow. She didn't want to live life on an endless diet just so that she could fit into Erin's chosen tight, sticky leather skirts and clingy crew-neck jumpers. She didn't want to spend her mornings sitting on a sofa with a fake smile etched permanently on her face beneath an inch-thick layer of make-up.

And suddenly, overwhelmingly, she realised that she didn't want to go through with a donor transfer on her own. For the next few months at least, that door was closed. Her body and mind needed a break. The prodding, the hormones, the waiting, the disappointment, the constant pain of seeing prams and babies and pregnant bellies. She wasn't closing the door on it forever, but it wasn't something she could deal with now.

She needed to live. And Caspar had shown her that her body was still alive. Perhaps Louise had been right: perhaps it was a sign. Her life *was* supposed to take another path. To follow a different plan. But it wasn't the plan Louise had mapped out for her.

Because now there was Caspar. She knew it was madness, rushing forwards in great leaps, but it just felt right. Natural. She could live here with him and run this gorgeous hotel and have friends like Nixie and prove stubborn locals like Walt wrong.

She bit her lip. The reminder of Walt and the altercation on the beach jolted her slightly, so she brought herself back to the idea that there'd be fresh air and sea and light and Caspar's strong arms against her body. And then maybe, when she was ready, they'd try and fertilise new eggs. Or she might even have a miracle pregnancy. A fresh start.

That would be all she ever needed, she thought to herself and smiled. And as the rays of sun streaked the enormous glass windows, it felt like the beginning of something various and beautiful and new.

But then the doorbell rang.

CHAPTER 21

This time it wasn't one of Olive's long, giggly calls, but short, sharp and impatient, and Sam immediately stood to attention.

She quickly opened the door, expecting it to be one of the new builders, but was surprised to see Judith instead.

'Judith!' She pulled the dressing gown closer round her chest. 'Everything ok? I'm so sorry I haven't fed Trevor D recently. I should have said. Things have been…' She laughed lightly, 'all a bit crazy.'

Judith gave her a slanted look. 'She's here,' she shouted over her shoulder. 'I told you.'

Sam leant out the door so she could peer down the lane. Behind Judith was one of the island's horse and carts being driven by Jack. And as the carriage came closer, Sam could make out a familiar figure in the passenger seat.

'What in God's…?' she muttered to herself, and gingerly picked her way barefooted on the gravel towards the carriage. Because there, draped in a floating white dress, resplendent as Mary herself entering Bethlehem on a donkey, was Issa.

'Sam!' Issa called, stretching her arms out in front of her now, frankly, enormous stomach. 'You're here!'

'*You're* here.' Sam frowned. She had about hundred questions, not least how such a pregnant woman was allowed to travel.

Issa held onto the side of the carriage as Jack brought the horses to an abrupt stop and rushed round to help her clamber out.

'Thank you,' she almost whispered, putting her hands in prayer position. 'You've been such a kind couple to me.' She smiled solemnly.

'We're not –' Judith stepped forwards.

'Our pleasure.' Jack stood in front of her, returning a toothy grin. 'You should have said yer had yer sister coming, Sam.' He looked back at her. 'I'd have had the carriage all ready. You can't exactly put a woman in that *condition* in the tractor trailer. The baby might drop out of her and roll down the hill.'

'She's not my –' Sam winced as she tiptoed another few steps in the gravel.

Her throat tightened. For the first time in a long time, she'd felt positive about the future. The last thing she needed was Issa there to drag up the past. Unless, she bit her fingernail, was she there for some kind of emergency?

'Oh, Sam.' Issa launched herself forwards, lodging her bump between the two of them as she pulled Sam into a tight embrace. 'It's *so* good to finally see you.' She held on for such a long time that Judith and Jack gave Sam a wave, dropped an enormous suitcase by the door and headed back in the carriage towards the Avenue.

'You've no *idea* what I've been through.' Issa squeezed her arms closer, and Sam widened her stance to avoid pulling them both to the floor.

Sam tapped Issa awkwardly on her shoulder. 'Issa, what –' she started and slowly managed to peel herself back and took a step up towards the front door. Her jaw clenched as she suddenly felt nervous. She'd been asleep for hours. *Had* something happened? Maybe it really was an emergency. Was Martin ok? Had he been wracked with guilt and done something stupid? 'Is everything alright?' she said.

'Oh God.' Issa stepped forwards and put her head in her hands. 'It was *awful*.' She was struck by a great sob and almost tottered back against the hedge. Sam took Issa's arm in one hand and her suitcase in the other and led them into the hotel living room where Issa sank heavily into the sofa.

'What's wrong?' Sam asked and perched next to her.

Issa placed a hand on her stomach. 'Well, first,' she sniffed, 'I had to charter a *private plane* to that other island because the stupid airline wouldn't let me fly pregnant. And I didn't want to tell Clive...' She paused and wiped away tears. Sam noticed with a jolt that her skin was a much duller grey than when she'd been dropping from the sky in a hot air balloon and her usually thick, luscious hair was limp and unwashed. How bad could the news be?

'So I had to pay for it on my *own* credit card and then I had to take this *tiny* public boat stuffed full of people, and I tried to at least make the most of my time and take some tranquil clips for social media of me with the sea in the background – you know, run some posts on how island hopping in the British Isles is the eco-friendly version of Croatia or something – but there were dogs barking and children running around and screaming babies and...'

'What's happened? Is Martin ok?'

Issa coughed back another sob and placed a thin hand on Sam's arm. 'I *knew* that's what you'd say.' She took a tissue from the coffee table and blew her nose loudly. 'Worried about him, and not yourself. Typical!'

Sam tilted her head. She opened her mouth then closed it again.

'Martin's *fine*.' Issa gave a sharp laugh. 'Absolutely fine. Of course he is. Still leering over that *producer*.' She wrinkled her nose. 'Last night they were swanning in and out of restaurants and nightclubs together. I mean *nightclubs*. What is he thinking? Just because the new woman dresses like a teenager in a Goth-lite crisis doesn't mean that he isn't forty. It's ridiculous.'

Sam sat up. She felt like she'd been punched in the stomach. It was one thing Martin making a mistake after a late meeting, but this was clearly far more. It was like she'd walked out of the set and disappeared from his mind completely. Years combusted as one door had clattered shut behind her. She blinked slowly. It didn't matter now anyway, she told herself firmly. She had Caspar. 'We spoke this morning. Ended things. I wasn't sure...'

'I know.' Issa gave a watery smile and shifted towards her. 'He's been an idiot. And you don't need to worry anymore. Because I'm here now. For you.'

There was a pause.

'For *me*?'

'Of course.' Issa took Sam's hands in her own. 'I thought you were, you know, pregnant. Everyone did. It was all in the papers, online, the works. But then,' she sat up, 'I found out what was happening with Martin and Keira and then I found out today after he told me things between you were over,' she made a noise of disgust and shook her head, 'you really *had* been going through IVF, and it wasn't just some tabloid rumour. I was so angry with him, Sam. Furious. That short-fringed, army boot wearing new girlfriend of his isn't *mother* material. And to realise that the whole career-woman act you'd been putting on for years was just a front. I should have known!' She squeezed her hands and then added in a lower voice, 'I mean Nina had always suspected that you weren't *that* serious about it all or you would never have left *Real News* in the first place, but,' she raised her eyebrows, 'to have it made so clear to me. That of course you didn't really care about your job and that all that time you'd been *desperate* for a baby. Just like I'd wanted for you all along! And no wonder you'd never warmed to me, which I always thought was odd.'

Sam held a hand up, ready to protest.

'No, it's ok.' Issa smiled. 'I understand. You were *jealous*. Of course you were.' She laughed like a small bell. 'I had everything you wanted. The house, the children...'

'Issa, it's not –'

'And then Martin went and left you for that woman!

Barren! Without the chance to use any more eggs! Awful, *awful!*' She hit one of the cushions and dramatically shook her head.

Sam flinched, 'I wouldn't...' but Issa quickly wrenched her into another hug.

'Shh.' She stroked Sam's hair. 'Don't torment yourself anymore. I rushed here as soon as I'd spoken to him. Everything's going to be ok. I've got a plan.'

Sam tried to move away, but Issa suddenly shifted back, letting out a strange whimper and holding the sides of her stomach with both hands.

Sam jumped up. 'Christ. Are you in labour? Shall I call...?' She looked hopelessly around. There didn't seem to be an ambulance other than the tractor she'd seen outside what appeared to be the GP surgery. And she really, *really* didn't want to have to explain to Caspar that someone had given birth on his custom white furniture.

Issa's contorted face quickly relaxed as she batted a hand away and leant back against the cushions. 'No, no. It's nothing. Braxton Hicks.'

Sam sat tentatively down on the edge of the sofa as if any sudden movement might send the baby shooting out.

'Don't worry about me,' Issa said and smiled serenely, putting a hand to her heart. 'I'm here for *you*.' She closed her eyes. 'Though I am quite tired.' She shifted onto her side. 'I might just nap for a few minutes. And then I'll tell you how I'm going to fix everything. It's been quite a day.'

Issa was still asleep on the sofa by the time Caspar got home an hour later. Sam had spent the time pacing the hotel corridors, unsure quite what to do with herself. She'd thought about calling Martin and giving him hell about lying to her about Keira, but the logical part of her brain wasn't sure what it would achieve. She didn't want to be with him anymore. Despite their united front on the *WakeUp!* sofa, it had been a long time since they'd properly felt like a couple. As the IVF treatment had worn on, in every moment out of work Sam had been consumed by research: what she should be eating, how she should be sleeping, bathing or exercising, the meaning of every bodily twinge. If she was being honest with herself, and now really was the time to be honest, Martin had mostly become a sounding board for her questions and musings on data. Instead of taking the walks along the river they'd once made part of their post-filming routine, there was usually something that Sam had wanted to get home to test, whether it was pregnancy or ovulation or base body temperature. And she'd lost interest in dates and holidays and dinners; they seemed like an unnecessary distraction from the main focus. The whole experience had hollowed out their relationship to a shell. And if he'd now found someone that made him feel even half of how she felt with Caspar, then how much could she blame him? So she'd just walked and wondered and considered how on earth she'd get Issa to leave as soon as possible until she heard movement from the front door.

'Hang on,' Sam whispered as Caspar walked in and kissed her on the cheek, 'trust me when I say I don't *exactly* know why, but my ex-boyfriend's sister is here. Asleep on the sofa. So pregnant that she might actually burst.'

'Who?'

'Issa. Martin's sister. I think she's here to console me? It's all been some big misunderstanding.'

Caspar tried to peer past her.

'I'll get her to leave as soon as possible.'

'So she's not aware that you've spent the past few days with me?'

'Not yet.'

'Or that you've found another, more effective way to forget about a good-for-nothing ex?' He grinned and reached to slide his hand up her thigh.

'Stop.' She suppressed a laugh and batted him away.

'Oh, come on.' He kissed her neck. 'Don't pretend you don't want it.'

Sam felt herself momentarily melt into his touch but

then stood back and shook her head. 'Caspar,' she hissed. 'She's right there. She could wake up at any moment!'

'So let's get her upstairs. Then I can do what I've been thinking about doing to you all afternoon.' He looked straight at her and reached a hand forward to trail a finger inside the edge of her bra.

'*Stop!*' She took his hand and held it in her own. 'Come on. At least help me get her stuff upstairs.'

He rolled his eyes and followed her towards the sofa. 'But then I'm going to bend you –'

'Shh!' She placed a hand over his mouth. 'Look, she's stirring.'

'Issa,' Sam whispered, perching on the armrest. 'I think we better get you up to bed.'

The heavy body shifted slowly, like a walrus on the shore.

'Clive?' She muttered. 'Is that you?' I'm sorry –'

'Issa,' Sam repeated, carefully tapping her on the shoulder. 'It's me. Let's get you upstairs.'

Issa groaned. 'Sam?' Her voice croaked as she rubbed her eyes. 'How long was I asleep for?'

'Not long. It's ok. There's a proper bed waiting.'

Issa stretched out as Caspar pounded downstairs to wait by the doorway, tapping his feet as he did so.

'I'm so sorry,' she yawned. 'I'm supposed to be here for *you*. But things have been so full on with the three kids that I've just…' She stared blankly out the window. 'I'm so tired. All the time.'

Caspar strode into the room. 'Right. I've taken your suitcase up and the bed's ready, so why don't you go and make yourself comfortable?'

Issa flicked her gaze between Sam and Caspar and blinked several times. 'Who's this?'

Sam blushed. She wasn't quite sure how she should label Caspar. They hadn't discussed being boyfriend/girlfriend yet, so she couldn't dive straight in. And of course it was extremely early days, but it felt like it would be something so much more. Should she call him her *lover*? But that was just ridiculous – as if he were some 25-year-old Greek beach boy who clambered into her room late at night, glistening with olive oil. Though she couldn't exactly call him her friend – unless accompanied by an enormous wink.

'Caspar Rowe.' Caspar struck out a hand. 'Hotel proprietor.'

Issa sat up and let her bird-like arm be shaken. 'Oh, excellent. Could you have someone send me up four extra pillows – I always need more than anyone provides – and some rosehip tea?' She smiled sweetly and yawned again. 'And a fresh fruit bowl if there isn't one already, but with passion fruit swapped out for apples. And extra shampoo – there's never enough in those tiny bottles. And a room away from any main roads, so it's nice and quiet. Although...' she paused, cocked an ear and tittered, 'that might not be a problem here.'

'The thing is, Issa,' Sam said quickly, 'the hotel's not quite open yet. I'm not really staying here as a guest.' She put a hand on Caspar's shoulder.

'Let me show you to your room,' Caspar stepped forwards, putting an arm out to help Issa up. 'I'll have everything with you by the morning.'

Sam crossed her arms. 'I'm sure Issa doesn't really need passion fruit, do you? You're lucky to get something as exotic as a banana on this island.'

'No, no,' Caspar looked back at her and winked as Issa leant on his arm. 'She's a guest, and she'll be treated as such, starting with a quiet evening to herself upstairs.'

Caspar housed Issa in an enormous suite, insisting to Sam as he stroked her hair on the sofa later that evening that everyone through the door needed to be treated like a critic.

So it was not without surprise that Sam looked out the window the next morning to find Issa lying on her side in the wet grass of the lawn.

'Shit,' she muttered as she struggled to push open the

heavy sash window. 'Issa! Are you ok?'

Nothing. She leant further outside. Issa's limbs were stone-still, but the movement of her chest at least showed that she was breathing.

Sam rushed down the stairs and out the back door, almost slipping on a rug in the corridor. It was only once she'd launched herself onto the grass, red from running, that she noticed Nixie lying on the ground, too.

'Hello?' She panted as she stepped tentatively forwards. 'Is everything alright?'

'Welcome,' Issa murmured without opening her eyes. 'Join us.'

Sam looked down at Nixie who flicked open one eye and smiled.

'Issa is taking me through a *breath work* class.' She gave a knowing nod.

'Right,' Sam said. 'Well.' She dropped her shoulders. 'As long as you're both ok.'

Nixie propped herself up on one elbow. 'I came to check if you'd heard the news,' she whispered.

'What news?' Sam bent down to better hear.

'Join us, Sam,' Issa repeated without moving. 'Let yourself be guided by the breath.'

Sam twisted her lips and looked around. She'd never been good with stuff like this. Her mind was usually full and whirring – either with what angles to take in questions, how to structure new segments or engage with guests or anything and everything related to IVF. Lying on the floor and failing to think about nothing had only ever seemed pointless. But perhaps now that she'd left all that behind things would be different. Plus Caspar had the last of his meetings and wouldn't be back until the evening again.

She sat down, imitating Issa and Nixie by lying on her right-hand side.

'Begin by noticing,' Issa intoned. 'Notice each breath – the energy of Gaia, of Mother Earth – entering the nostrils, travelling down to the lungs and expanding the belly. Notice each breath as it moves out of the lungs and back out of the nostrils. Invite your mind to follow the breath only, clearing other thoughts.'

Sam took a series of inhalations but was quickly out of sync with Issa's deep snorting. For a woman of such small stature, she could make an impressive amount of noise through her nose.

'What *news*?' Sam whispered again to Nixie.

'In,' Issa purred. 'And out. If your mind wanders from the breath, notice it. Then return. Do not judge yourself. Guide your awareness back to your breathing.'

Nixie shifted herself closer towards Sam. 'It is complicated,' she whispered back. 'I will tell you after this.' She paused. 'Do you think Issa would be good for the festival? People love this sort of thing. It could help sell a big batch of tickets.'

'And back to the breath,' Issa spoke over her. 'Notice if any other body parts, such as a hand or foot... or mouth, are moving,' she paused, 'and stop them.'

'Isn't the festival in a few days?' Sam whispered back. 'I sort of thought she might leave today.'

Issa cleared her throat. 'And focus on the breath. Taking a deep inhalation into the lungs. In *silence*.'

Sam shifted position slightly and tried to focus. In and out. In and out. *Notice a thought.* She really didn't want Issa staying with her. It was sweet – though a bit odd – that she was there, but having another person in the hotel might put a dampener on things with Caspar. *And let it go. And return. Breathe. Notice a thought.* How long would she be staying? A day? A week? It surely couldn't be that long or the baby might come. And surely Clive wouldn't want her there so close to her due date? Could she get her to leave today? This morning?

'Imagine you are a rose, taking in the energy of the sun. Each inhalation brings in light and energy. Allowing your petals to spread open.'

Sam shuffled uncomfortably.

'Remain in peaceful stillness,' Issa directed. 'You are a rose awakening to the sun.'

Sam turned to the other side. 'I'm sorry.' She sat up. 'I'm not in the right headspace.'

Issa opened one eye and looked at her with a veneer of disdain.

'Look, I just... How long are you planning on being here for, Issa? I'm doing fine, you see. Really fine.'

Issa pushed herself up to seating. 'I'll be here until my intuition tells me, Sam. At the moment I'm sensing a very... uptight energy.'

Sam narrowed her eyes.

'What Sam means,' Nixie tucked her legs underneath her, 'is whether you'll be here for the island festival. It's in four days. You could do a breath work class and meditation and...'

Sam did her best to eyeball Nixie. *Four days*. There was no world in which she wanted Issa there for four days. Four hours was already pushing it.

'Oh,' Issa's face softened, 'well. That *would* be of interest. Thank you, both.' She reached forwards and patted Sam's knee. 'How thoughtful. I could also do a workshop on natural remedies for children and releasing your inner moon goddess and,' she paused, 'I recently did a course on Feng shui. Would that appeal?'

Sam opened her mouth to a neat zero, but suddenly the unmistakable shrieks of Olive rushed into the garden.

'MUMMY!'

Olive ran towards them, throwing herself onto Nixie, who fell backwards with an 'oomph'.

'Daddy said he's too busy working to take me to the dairy for feeding time and I said it's NOT FAIR and I said *we* always go and he said it's because you don't work so you have to take me then and I said YES.'

Nixie turned to see Leo waiting sheepishly by the garden gate with Ash strapped to his front. 'Olive,' she said slowly, 'this was supposed to be a quiet morning.'

'I didn't WANT to!' Olive pushed her chin out and crossed her arms.

'*Olive*,' Nixie said sternly. But Olive responded with the same threatening wobbling lip that had weakened Sam before the Mint Sauce bet.

'Fine.' Nixie moved Olive onto the grass as she stood up. 'I don't have the energy to battle a tantrum. Sam, I will try and come round later or tomorrow. Issa, it was lovely to meet you. I will send details about the classes soon.'

Sam smiled sympathetically but noticed that Issa hardly looked up from the ground.

After Nixie had managed to coax Olive away from the excitement of the sun lounger and swimming pool and out of the back gate where Leo promptly handed Ash over, Sam sat closer to her.

'Are you sure that's the only reason you're here? Because of your intuition?'

'Yes,' Issa said quickly.

Both women sat in silence.

'Really?' Sam said.

Issa pulled out a handful of grass out and threw it across the lawn.

'*Yes.*'

Sam stood up and looked out at the deep sky in front of her. The blue was slowly being overtaken by a patchwork of grey clouds. Something wasn't right. If she could find out Issa's actual motivation, then she could potentially solve whatever was wrong and get her back home.

She went to turn back into the house but was stopped by the noise of a small sob.

'Well, no,' Issa hiccuped. 'I suppose not.'

CHAPTER 22

It didn't take long for Issa's whimpering to morph into a full throttled wail.

'Issa?' Sam sat back down on the grass. 'What's wrong? Is it Martin?' She gingerly put an arm around her bony shoulders. 'I get it. He let us both down. But, you know,' she gave her a squeeze, 'I'm actually really happy now. You might have guessed that things have sort of *happened* with Caspar. It was all so quick – just after I heard about Martin and Keira. And it's been great. Amazing, actually. It's like… like I've been given a new body.'

But she was interrupted by a fresh howl, like a fox screaming in the night. She recoiled. Not Martin, then. Maybe it was the pregnancy? But surely Issa loved being pregnant? What with the social media shoots and long, swirling dresses and, for goodness' sake, the hot air balloon baby shower entrance, she didn't *appear* to Sam to be stoically struggling through.

She twisted her lips. 'Is it Clive? Martin did mention that he's up in London a lot whilst you're down in the Cotswolds. Has it been difficult?' She paused. 'Is he seeing someone…?' She really couldn't imagine it. Martin always called him a walking briefcase.

'Not Clive,' Issa wailed. 'He's…' she covered her eyes with her hand, 'an *angel*.'

'Of course,' Sam said quickly. She really hadn't seen that much of Clive over the past few years, and he was hardly even present in Issa's social media accounts, only popping up in the Christmas and Easter shots when she hired a professional photographer. But, when she did see him, he was innocuous and well-mannered, asking polite questions about the show's ratings and murmuring approval at Martin's bombastic responses. His wardrobe of identical blue shirts and specialism in corporate law didn't scream perfect match with Issa the self-styled moon goddess, but, Sam recognised, he afforded her not only stylish homes, but annual trips to Val-d'Isère and St.Barts, a handful of staff and an unlimited credit card. So she could probably put up with a lack of variation in the wardrobe department.

Issa slumped forwards over her belly and let a pool of tears fall into her lap. 'It's the *baby*.'

'Oh.' Sam sat up straight. Surely she wasn't the best person for Issa to come and complain to about popping out another child? If not one of Issa's mum friends who regretted having a third or fourth after they'd just had a fresh seagrass carpet installed, then at least Nina could be there to roll her eyes about paint-splattered handprints on new-season silk. And especially now that Issa knew why she didn't have children, wasn't it just a bit... cruel?

'I can't have it. I can't.'

Sam raised an eyebrow. 'You'll be alright. What's one more when you've got three already? It'll just melt into the background.' She glanced at Issa's stomach. 'And isn't it a bit late to do anything about it anyway?'

Another wall of tears broke though Issa's frame just as Sam noticed the new team of builders start filing in the back gate towards the indoor pool. It didn't feel like the sort of conversation they could have in front of an audience.

'How about a walk? Nowhere far. It might help clear your head? I went on a run the other day and I don't think I could have felt better after a year in therapy.'

Issa looked like she was considering another wail but then sniffed and nodded before laboriously making her way up with Sam's help to standing. Sam guided her along the road towards the garden where she'd first met Caspar. With no Mrs Pedvin in sight, she tucked their entrance fee into a money box by the gate and led Issa towards a bench under a rose-entwined canopy. Sam looked up at the intertwining white and pink petals and breathed in the sweet air. It was hard to imagine any problems existing here; the trellis-laced walls appeared talismanic, encasing only the almost magical beauty.

'Isn't it peaceful?' Sam almost whispered, watching the water trickle up from the small fountain at their feet. 'Like stepping into a dream. I thought you might find it soothing.'

Issa blew her nose on a large leaf.

Sam slowly sat down, worried that any sudden movements might jolt Issa further out of sorts.

'How's your garden getting on in the new place?' she said, awkwardly tucking a foot underneath her in an attempt to seem more approachable. It was an age-old interview technique: get your subject to relax into some inane questions before getting too heavy. 'Any...planting done this year?'

Issa shrugged and held her temples in her hands.

'Or, urm,...plans for a pool?' An outdoor kitchen?'

No response.

'How did your feng shui course go? Where is it you're supposed to put the bed again?' She really hoped Issa opened up soon; her bank of suitable topics was pretty slim.

'The baby's not Clive's.'

Sam's head snapped back. Issa covered her face. A razor blade of silence hung in the air.

'Sorry. Did you just say...?'

Issa averted her eyes for a few seconds then looked straight at Sam. She blinked slowly. 'I'm not carrying Clive's baby.' Her shoulders dropped as if she'd thrown down a great weight.

Sam wanted to baulk and implore Issa to share every

detail about what had happened and, most importantly, with whom, but her time at *RealNews* had taught her to remain calm in the face of scandal or revelation lest the subject clam up entirely. If they'd chosen to reveal their biggest card, the details would usually follow. Granted, Sam was used to these sorts of conversations being about cash for access or expenses or bullying accusations rather than an illicit love child, but she figured that the same rule applied.

A butterfly landed on a rose in the trellis and both women silently watched its bright blue wings as the declaration diffused into the fresh, morning air. Sam managed to cross her legs and clamp her mouth shut as Issa mentally ran over her packaging of the preceding events.

'He usually works three days a week in London,' she finally started, running her fingers along the arm of the bench. 'So I'm on my own some nights. And it's fine. Noemi deals with the children, thank God. And it's not like I have a lack of things to do or people to see. There's so many Londoners in the Cotswolds these days it's *suffocating*.' She ran a hand through her hair. 'But I was on my own one night and asked if Tino wanted to join me for dinner.'

Tino. Sam nodded. She should have guessed.

'I don't know why I did it, but he agreed. He's *such* a great help. And we shared a bottle of wine, and there was a moment when our legs brushed against one another under the table… But,' she placed her hands on her stomach, 'nothing else. Then the next day I was filming a few Pilates moves for a post. He offered to help with some positions. He's very nimble for a tall man, you know. He helped stretch out my abductors. I think we both knew what would happen next. It wasn't about emotions or long-term thinking. Just pure…animal.' She sighed. 'Like what you've got with Caspar at the moment.'

Sam inwardly flinched at the comparison between what she had with Caspar to Issa bonking the butler whilst her husband was at work.

'Our energies were in alignment. My social feeds were

full of comments on how much I was glowing and what my new skin care routine was. And I just couldn't get enough of it. Of him. But then it was Christmas.' She paused and exhaled. 'We had our annual Caribbean jaunt and Tino went back to Italy until the new year. I knew something was wrong when I threw up a green juice. Clive did, too. Made me take a test. He was bloody ecstatic when it was positive – had always wanted four. I was mortified.' She shook her head and brought a hand to her throat. 'I was sure we'd missed my fertile window, but, you know me, I get pregnant like…' She clicked a finger.

Sam gripped a fistful of her dress.

'And Clive was just so wonderful about it all.' Issa shook her head. 'Showering me in gifts as usual. I felt so stupid. I mean the sex,' she sniffed, 'was mind blowing. But look at the life I have with Clive.' She squeezed her eyes together as more tears formed.

Sam smoothed down her dress and put her hand again on Issa's shoulder. 'Could it be Clive's? I mean technically speaking.'

Issa wiped her nose with her sleeve. '*Technically*, but I know it's Tino's,' she snivelled. 'I tried to pretend. To both of them. To everyone. But I know. I had a 3D ultrasound.' She held her hands over her eyes before falling forwards into a choking sob. 'I'm sorry,' she muttered in fragmented gulps. 'It's so awful.'

Sam grimaced as she stroked Issa's back. 'I know I've not had an ultrasound before. I mean not one where there's been an actual baby to look at, but I really don't think they can determine the identity of the father.'

Issa sat up. 'Well, I *know* it's his.' She raised her voice, tears dribbling over her downward turned lips.

'Did you do some genetic testing? That one with the needle?'

Issa looked straight at her. 'I know because it's got *hair*.'

Sam was silent for a moment, unsure how to respond. A magpie swept close in front of them. She cleared her throat.

'Doesn't Clive have hair?'

'My other children were born *bald*,' Issa hissed. 'So I knew. And Clive will know. And so will Tino. Everyone will. It'll come out covered in dark, Italian hair.' She shook her head as she wiped away more tears. 'So I can't have it.'

'Right.' There was a pause. Sam shifted back on the bench. 'I don't mean to be insensitive, but surely you *have* to at this stage?'

Issa looked at Sam with wide, watery eyes. 'Isn't it obvious?' she said.

'Isn't what…?'

Issa took Sam's hands in her own. 'I've got it all planned out.'

Sam furrowed her brow. 'You're going to give it a haircut? Ask the midwife to do a quick snip before it's brought to you?'

Issa rolled her eyes before turning directly to face Sam. 'No, silly. I'm going to solve everyone's problems. All at once.'

Sam itched to pull her hands away. There was something about the conversation that made her feel hot and uncomfortable. She couldn't imagine how Issa was going to use her new baby as some sort of family panacea. Maybe she'd have a slot on *Martin's Mornings* on the genetic possibility of one sibling being born hairy in a family of shiny baldness.

Issa smiled, her eyes still wet with tears. 'I've thought about it really hard.'

'Right.'

'This is the best solution.'

'Ok.'

'I know you'll try and talk me out of it. For my sake. But I want you to know that I'm sure. One hundred percent.'

Sam wasn't sure what to say. She nodded blankly. Issa brought Sam's hands onto her stomach.

'Sam,' Issa beamed through her tears, 'I'm giving the baby to you. And Martin.'

Sam's mouth fell open. She pulled her hands back.

'What?'

'For you to keep. To bring up as your own.'

'*What?*'

'I knew you'd be surprised.' Issa gave a slightly manic laugh as she wiped her cheeks. 'I can't have this baby. I can't. It'll be the end of my marriage and – honestly – three children is enough. And you so *want* a baby. And so does Martin. Well at least he will once he gets this ridiculous woman out of his system.'

'Issa –'

Issa spoke quicker and higher, taking up Sam's hands again. 'Everything has fallen into place. It's fate. Most of the papers seem to think you're pregnant anyway. You could have had the baby here. Just tell Caspar I'm your surrogate and that it had all been planned for ages and you need to go back to your boyfriend. I know you're all sexed up for the moment, but it won't last. Martin's not going to hold a brief rebound against you.'

Sam pulled her hands back. '*Issa* –'

'And I'll tell everyone that I had a stillbirth. No one would really know. And, look, I know this sounds bad, but there's a massive market for fertility issues on social media these days. I could become a sort of spokesperson.'

Sam stood up and put a hand on the trellising to steady herself. 'Stop.'

'I know it's a big surprise.'

'No.' Sam was dizzy with shock. 'It's mad. I'm not having your baby. You're not *pretending* you had a stillbirth.'

Issa cocked her head. 'But it's the perfect plan. I know you'd prefer to have your own, but isn't this the next best thing? When Martin told me what had happened, I just knew –'

'No.'

'But it solves so many problems.'

'*No.*'

Sam blinked slowly then sat back down, her limbs stiff against the wood. Issa's mouth started to wobble again.

'I thought you'd be so pleased,' she said quietly.

Sam pressed her lips together. 'It's very...' she paused as she forced herself to think of a more polite phrase than was running through her head, '*thoughtful* of you. But there's no way I'm doing this. It's *your* baby.'

Issa's thin shoulders slumped forwards and her eyes once more filled with tears. 'But I *need* you to,' she said in a small voice. 'I can't have it. I had it all planned.'

'Whether the baby's got Italian hair or not, you won't want to just give it to me.'

'It's the only solution.' Issa slumped forwards, curving her torso over her large bump.

Sam grimaced to herself. This was not what she'd imagined when Issa had turned up at the door. Perhaps it was a sign for her to be grateful to be finally out of the Bailey family. She just now needed to calm Issa down, get her thinking straight and convince her to go home.

'Come on.' She put a hand on Issa's back. 'Let's walk a bit more. Clear our heads. In fact,' she went to stand, 'I've got a good idea. There's someone I'd like you to meet.'

CHAPTER 23

The wind picked up as they made their way down the hill towards Judith's cottage. Tiny petals of jasmine danced in the air as the grass swished at their feet.

'It's beautiful,' Issa said as she momentarily stopped for breath, leaning against a tree. 'The Cotswolds are lovely, of course,' she looked across the valley to where the fields met the sea, 'but this is so quiet. Like going back in time.' She paused. 'It would be so perfect for children.'

Sam pointed towards the shed, keen to change the direction of conversation. 'He's in there. I think you'll like him.'

'I hope not. The last thing I need is someone else to take a fancy to.' Issa waddled behind her, but her words whipped away in the breeze.

As they approached the shed, Sam was surprised to hear a voice coming from inside. It was calling Trevor D 'little guy' and 'buddy' and offering him a bucket of feed.

'Oh my God,' Issa squealed back to Sam as she put her head round the door. 'He's precious!'

Sam hung back. 'Maybe we should pop by later instead,' she said. She had a feeling she knew who else was there, and it wasn't someone she wanted to see.

'Absolutely not.' Issa's eyes glinted. 'Hi, little one!' She beamed as she walked towards where Walt was petting Trevor D. 'Aren't you the cutest?'

'He's not had the best start,' Walt said, straightening up. 'His mother didn't take to him. But he's coming along well.'

As Issa cooed and stroked his fur, Sam hovered around the back of the barn, hoping to sink into the shadows. The last thing she wanted was another awkward exchange or ridiculous telling off from Mr High & Mighty, especially since things with Caspar had progressed.

'Oh, Sam!' Issa cried out, ruining her plan. 'He's just the sweetest thing!'

Walt turned.

'Hi,' Sam said quickly as he looked at her. 'Sorry. We won't be a minute. I didn't realise you'd be here.'

'I was just leaving. I need to pick up Daniel.'

'Great.'

There was a pause. Sam twisted her fingers behind her back. Walt crossed his arms.

'Weren't you supposed to be going back to London?' he said.

'I was.' Sam searched for a way to summarise the events of the past few days without giving him any actual information. 'Circumstances changed.'

'Right,' Walt said. 'Well. I'll be going.'

But as he stepped firmly towards the door, Issa burst into another howl of tears.

He stopped. 'Is she ok?'

'Yes,' Sam tried to say as lightly as possible, keen for him to leave. 'This happens quite a bit. Hormones. Nothing to worry about.'

'Really?'

'My children *love* donkeys!' Issa wailed. 'Clementine asked if we could have one in the field, but I said she'd have to wait until she was old enough for a horse, but she was so disappointed. God, I'm a *terrible* mother!' Her shoulders shook as she threw both arms around Trevor D's neck. He widened his eyes at the commotion.

'You're sure?' Walt said.

'Sure.' Sam batted away the comment, hoping Issa's tears might subside. When they didn't, she padded over, awkwardly bending to place a hand on her shoulder. 'You're a great mother,' she tried to whisper. 'You've got lovely children. And you'll be wonderful with your new baby. Thousands of people follow you online to get parenting tips.' She wasn't sure that this was strictly true; most of Issa's posts seemed focused on the interiors of the house or recent additions to her wardrobe with the children artfully decorating the scene, but it seemed like the right time for some tactful embellishment.

Issa looked up and shook her head at the ceiling. 'And I haven't even told Clive where I am. Everyone probably thinks I'm *dead*!'

'You haven't?' Sam raised an eyebrow in alarm. A heavily pregnant woman going missing could well be within the interests of the police.

'The boat's in the harbour if she needs to get back,' said Walt. 'How pregnant *is* she exactly?'

Sam bit her lip. The prospect of returning Issa straight home that afternoon had significant appeal, but she didn't want to be responsible for a baby being delivered in the English Channel.

'No.' She plastered on a smile. 'It's ok. We'd better be going.'

Walt raised his eyebrows. 'To the Rowe? You're not seriously still staying there?'

She exhaled. This again? She felt sorry for Caspar having to put up with what must be constant sniping. 'I don't understand why it's such a big deal.'

'I wouldn't expect you to.'

'What if they don't even notice I'm *gone*!' Issa screeched. Trevor D baulked and shook her off as he trotted towards his hay in the corner.

'That's very unlikely,' Sam said and knelt beside her.

Issa slunk into her lap like a rag doll. She tried to dab her wet nose with her sleeve, and Sam looked up to see if Walt could find her some tissue. But he had already gone.

'Charming,' she muttered to herself before turning again to Issa. 'Judith lives in that cottage we passed. Let's get you cleaned up there. Then we'll head back and give Clive a call. He'll be waiting to hear from you.'

Issa opened her mouth to protest but then nodded, let Sam help her up and leaned heavily on her arm as they headed down the hill.

Both women were silent until they approached the cottage, where Issa sniffed and give a heartfelt sigh.

'That man was very good looking. In a sort of rugged, never-done-any-manscaping sort of way. You're spoilt for choice round here.' She ran a finger around one of the yellow roses next to the door.

Sam snorted. 'Walter is not someone I'd speak to out of choice. He's bitter and rude and...' To her annoyance, she could feel her cheeks redden. She didn't know what it was – whether the memory of the seagull incident or the simple fact that he was so small-mindedly anti-Caspar – but there was something about the man which caught a nerve. 'He's not someone I want to waste my time on. And, anyway, he's taken. He's got a son.'

'Shame,' Issa said, sniffing the rose as some of its petals fell to the floor.

Sam rolled her eyes as she went to ring the bell, but Judith let them in before she had even pressed the buzzer. She pulled both women into close hugs – made slightly difficult by the fact that Jeremy was wrapped around the back of her neck like a boa constrictor.

'I saw you coming.' Judith bustled them onto the linoleum tiled floor. 'You've heard the news then?'

'What news? Actually, hang on.' Sam pointed towards Issa. 'Would you mind if she cleaned herself up in your bathroom? Mild crisis. But fine now.'

'Of course not, my love.' Judith ushered Issa into a toilet behind a wooden door with an iron latch. 'Take as long as you need. You've never seen such a mess when I was pregnant. I remember getting set off by a particularly sweet looking doily once.'

Issa shuffled down the corridor and Sam smiled gratefully as she followed Judith into the kitchen. It was small but cosy, lined with wooden dressers heaving with glasses and a low-beamed ceiling on which hung baskets, hops and copper saucepans.

'Take a seat.' Judith brushed some paperwork into a pile. 'Don't mind the mess. Walt's just been reading through all the plans this morning. I'll just be a tick. Kettle's boiled.'

The top document caught Sam's eye and she was surprised to see it was an architectural drawing of The Rowe. Before she could look any closer, Judith set down three teas on top of it followed by a cow-shaped jug of thick milk and a plate of chocolate shop truffles on a blue and white china plate.

'Not for you, Jeremy,' Judith scolded as he jumped up onto the table. 'You've had your breakfast, and you know you're not allowed chocolate.' He scowled back and spread himself between the women, looking up at them with scorn.

'What's this?' Sam crossed her arms as she nodded at the pile. 'Why is Walt so interested in the hotel?' She could have guessed that he would be trying to cause further problems for Caspar, no doubt nosying into every minor detail to see if he could pull him up on some petty retrospective planning issue. She knew what these pathetic busybody types were like.

'So you've heard about what's going on?' Judith said.

'What do you mean?'

'The blasted island ownership plan,' Judith tutted as she sat down. 'I never thought it was serious, but the bugger's got everything lined up to go through. I know there's nothing to be done. It's just...' She sunk her head into her hands.

Jeremy swiped quickly and successfully at a fly. Sam eyed him nervously and shifted back in her seat.

Judith sat back up, her shoulders heavy. 'I know we'll be alright. The island's survived occupation before. I just keep telling myself to think of Dame Sybil, letting those blasted

Nazis know their place.'

'*Occupation*? Judith, what *is* going on?'

'Oh, she was ever such a woman,' Judith sniffed. 'Told the Nazis that she was still the Seigneur – the leader of the island – even when they came and started trying to bark orders about. I made sure Walt named the boat after her, see. Strong woman for rough weather. And I don't mean to compare Caspar to the Nazis.'

'Sorry what?' Sam almost spat out her tea.

'I'm sure he can't be all bad deep down. You've been staying there, so he must be sort of alright. Course his uncle could be a trouble – making his cleaning ladies cry when they hadn't dusted under the beds and whatnot. But by and large he kept himself to himself. Nothing like this.'

Sam held a hand out in front of her. 'What are you talking about?'

'I told you. *The island ownership plan*,' Judith said.

Issa padded back round the corner. Sam couldn't help noting that she was clearly one of those maddening people who had the ability to howl like a toddler but then appear freshly gleaming only minutes later – no evidence of the blotchy skin or puffy eyes that had plagued her own face for hours in recent weeks.

'Didn't you know?' Judith said.

'No, and what's Caspar got to do with this?' Sam said.

'It's awful!' Judith shook her head. 'No-one actually believed it would happen, but it's going through next week. He's gone and bought the freehold.'

Sam sat upright. After Issa's revelation, she was struggling to organise other thoughts. Nothing seemed to make sense today. 'The freehold for what?'

'The island, of course.'

Sam had to consciously close her mouth. Her brain felt jumbled like a knotted ball of wool. It couldn't be right. There had to be some miscommunication somewhere. She shook her head slightly and straightened her back, looking over Jeremy's piercing gaze.

'How? It's full of residents.'

'Same way that anyone buys anything else, I imagine,' Issa piped in, taking one of the chocolates. 'By paying a lot of money.'

'And knowing the right people,' Judith added. 'Apparently he wants it to be a private resort. Very luxurious. With a helicopter pad and a spa and all sorts. And no locals. He'll own the freehold, so he'll force sales of each lease until everyone's gone.'

'I can see it.' Issa nodded as she bit into a truffle. 'A sort of Maldives of the British Isles. You know, it did actually remind me a bit of Croatia on my boat trip.'

Sam bristled. 'But surely public land isn't for private sale. You can't just buy people's homes.' Her mind whirred with possibilities, trying to filter for what seemed logical or at least possible. There had to be some form of misunderstanding. 'Unless, of course, everyone's agreed to take the money and move?'

'Of course not! We're all bloody miserable about it. But there's not a whole lot of laws on that sort of thing here.' Judith took a sad sip of tea.

'And Caspar definitely knows people are unhappy?' Sam asked.

Judith's face darkened. 'Of course he knows.'

'Right.' Sam cleared her throat, trying not to show how shaken she was by the answer. It really didn't sound like Caspar. Did it? He was clearly passionate about the hotel, but pushing people out of their homes? Surely not. 'Has there been some sort of campaign?'

'We've been trying.' Judith sighed. 'But we only took it seriously when it was too late. We'd raised over ten thousand pounds to fight him after the sheep racing. But it's a drop in the ocean compared to what we're up against. And Walt's been trying his hardest, bless him. He read through all the plans and documents available. Trying to look for any details to stop it.' She pulled her cardigan closer. 'Got us all there at the committee office on the Avenue the other day to protest. Everyone on the island, pretty much. But no one in power's interested in listening. It's too much money to say no to apparently.'

Sam stood up and paced towards the other side of the room. She couldn't sit still; her limbs felt jittery. 'How many people live here? Five hundred?'

'Maybe more since all them European technology whizzers arrived.'

Sam looked out the window at the wide daisy-speckled fields just as a majestic heron soared in the air above. Below its wide wings, Walt was crossing from the barn to the path, Daniel bobbing happily on his shoulders.

'And you're *sure* that Caspar knows the level of disquiet in the community? It just seems really unlikely...'

Jeremy arched his back before plonking himself on Judith's lap. 'Walt got over three hundred signatures on his objection letter. Caspar's had it delivered to him. By hand.'

'Three hundred.' Sam blinked quickly. She felt heavy with dread, as if she'd swallowed stones. 'I'll talk to him. Something can't be right.'

CHAPTER 24

Caspar wasn't in when they returned, and, as Issa was in keen need of a nap, Sam spent a few minutes walking though the hotel.

She had grown to greatly admire the building. Each room was fresh and bright, the wide windows pooling light across sleek furniture, and yet the faux fur rugs and clever nooks made it feel cosy rather than intimidating, somewhere where you could both lock eyes over a cocktail or relax over morning tea. She had started – tentatively – to imagine a life there. To imagine a life with Caspar. And she knew her mind was moving quickly, but there was something about him that was addictive; his touch had taught her body how to feel and his presence had renewed her hope for the future.

But walking across the wide corridors now made her cold with discomfort. The idea that the luxury of the hotel came at the expense of an entire community seemed ridiculous. She was desperate to ask Caspar what was really going on, certain that there would be some reasonable explanation.

But first, she knew that she needed to put Clive out of his misery. She momentarily roused Issa to locate and unlock her phone. 57 missed calls from Clive. Shit. She retreated to the bar to finally get back to him.

'Issa!' Clive almost shouted as he picked up on the first

ring. 'Thank God. Where are you? Are you ok?'

'It's Sam.' She perched on the navy sofa. 'As in Martin's...'

'Sam? Oh. Are you with her? Is she ok?'

'She's fine. She's here. In Sark.'

Clive almost groaned in relief before giving a sharp exhalation. '*Sark?*'

'The channel island. Near Guernsey and Jersey.'

'Christ. I tried everyone. Martin, Nina, Cassie, Lula, Tamara, Zor...' He swallowed loudly. 'Can she speak?'

'She's asleep. But she's ok. I just wanted to let you know as soon as possible. I'll get her to call you again when she wakes up. But there's no need to worry.'

'Hang on. Why is she there? What's going on? She's full term. She shouldn't be travelling.'

Sam twisted the tassels of a cushion between her fingers. She was hoping to be able to skirt around the explanation as much as possible. 'She came to look after me. After the whole Martin and Keira thing. She's... she's been very kind. She was worried about how I was doing.'

Clive scoffed. 'So worried that she chartered a flight whilst nine months pregnant, for God's sake? Are you serious? I didn't even think you were close.'

Sam ran her fingernails together. 'I don't know how best to...' she trailed off, not sure how to phrase what to say next. 'I think Issa feels quite...stressed. She's not exactly her normal self.'

'Well I know *that*.' He snorted. 'I'll come and get her in the morning. The kids can stay with Noemi.'

'Great,' she chirruped, more perkily than she'd intended. The sooner she got Issa off her hands, the sooner she could solely focus on Caspar.

'And Sam,' Clive added. 'Sorry to hear the new contract fell through. See you tomorrow.'

Sam crossed her legs as she looked at the blank screen. New contract? She frowned. But she didn't have a new contract with *WakeUp!* The problem was that Martin and Keira had essentially torn up her old one. Anyway, she shook her head, she'd let Issa know that Clive was coming and try and get the hair nonsense out of her mind. Or at least work out a way to explain what had happened with Tino. And then the whole, ridiculous nonsense episode would be over.

The sound of Caspar pushing open the front door and slipping out of his loafers echoed through the hall. Her mouth went dry.

'Sam,' his voice carried along the corridor, 'are you in?'

She poked her head around the door. 'Over here,' she whispered and put a finger to her lips, 'Issa's asleep again.' Her hands started to jitter. She had years of experience in confronting people over ill-founded plans, relishing the verbal poking until they exposed flaws in hubristic projects, but she deeply wanted Caspar to just laugh it all off as a big miscommunication. Let them return to the easy life of the past few days.

Caspar quickened his pace. 'Then let's see if we can wake her up with your moans.' He laughed as he grabbed her by her torso.

'Wait!' She tried to wriggle back. 'I want to talk to you about something.'

Caspar kicked the door closed behind him and pushed Sam down onto the sofa. 'No waiting. I've been thinking about this all day.' He started kissing her collarbone and reaching down to her jeans.

'Seriously, hang on!' She put her hand on his chest. 'Let me talk to you first.'

He raised an eyebrow and pushed back a stray hair that was covering his eyes. 'Right now?'

'Right now.'

He sighed as he sat back and ran a hand through his hair. 'Make it quick.'

She smoothed down her top, 'I was speaking with Judith today –'

'Judith de Carteret?'

'Yes, and –'

He shook his head.

'What?'

'Nothing. I just can't imagine you'd hear much of interest from that old biddy.'

She flushed. Her heart beat through her ears. She'd asked countless difficult questions, but she'd never cared so much about the answer. Her fingers crossed behind her back as she wished that it could all be some big misunderstanding. 'She's not... Look, she mentioned the island ownership plan. That you were buying the freehold of the island?'

'Bet that's got her knickers in a twist.' He smirked. 'I can't lie, I'm bloody pleased. The entire place a private resort. Total luxury. All those Londoners who look for seclusion and the wild by jetting halfway across the world. We'll have it here and with all the comforts of a five-star hotel. I'd been waiting to tell you until everything goes through next week, but I'm actually glad. I thought maybe...' he beamed, 'you might want to be involved with the launch? Some celebrity presence could drive the PR.'

'Oh.' Sam grimaced. Her body felt weak. She'd so desperately wanted him to say that Judith had clearly caught the wrong end of the stick. That *of course* it couldn't be a private island – because how could it? Her voice wobbled as she continued, 'Apparently the islanders aren't happy about it? There's been some sort of petition?'

He draped a languid arm over the back of the sofa and laughed. 'The islanders wouldn't know a good thing if it hit them in the face. Sometimes in life you've got to fight for your vision. I already own most of the rental property here. This was inevitable.'

Sam slit her eyes. Nerves sat heavy in her stomach like a cold toad. His answers were so far from what she'd expected. She could only hope he had solutions to the problems that she'd simply overlooked. 'Won't it damage the community?'

His face darkened. 'What do you mean?'

'You know. The upheaval. If it's a private island, won't they all need to leave?'

'And?'

'*And?*' She furrowed her brow. Her disappointment was twisting to irritation. 'Won't that cause major damage?'

His voice hardened. 'Where's this coming from?'

'What do you mean?'

'This sanctimonious 'look after the community' bullshit. I didn't think it was your style.'

'My style?' Her scalp started to prickle.

'You don't know these people. Why care?'

'Well, I know some of them. And I think it's natural to care.'

Caspar scoffed as he sat forwards, bringing his hands over his knees. 'Give me a break.'

Sam swallowed. She wasn't the kind of person who could let this sort of thing go. 'It sounds like a big deal. Apparently Walt has had a petition signed.'

He rubbed his temples.

'Five hundred people live here,' she added. 'It's not insignificant.'

'Yes,' Caspar snapped. 'Five hundred people without a hospital, decent school or public services. When they'll all be rehoused on a neighbouring island with all those things on offer for free. Or they can work for me here. It's plain logic. And, for God's sake, don't listen to any of Walt's nonsense. He's got some stupid personal vendetta against me.'

She crossed her arms. Part of her wanted to just forget the conversation had ever happened, but the reporter in her wasn't going to back down. 'But surely if they'd wanted to leave, they could have done so before?'

'Jesus.' He rolled his eyes and pushed himself back against the sofa. 'Isn't this all a bit rich?'

'Excuse me?'

'You seem to be enjoying the hotel for yourself well enough.'

She gripped the arm of the sofa. 'What's that supposed to mean?'

'You know what it means.'

'Then maybe I've made a mistake.'

He curled his top lip. 'What?'

'I thought,' she used her tone typically reserved for unreasonable politicians, 'I was still staying here because of us. Because of what we had. Not because I was just 'enjoying' the facilities. You're sounding like a right arse right now, you realise?'

He laughed again then held her gaze. She looked back but flinched. The conversation was like unpeeling fruit to find it rotting inside.

'What?' she said.

He smiled. 'Is this just a thing?'

'Huh?'

He moved towards her. 'You like arguing?'

'No I don't *like* arguing. I mean I do at work. Sometimes. But not at home.'

'Really?' He raised his eyebrows as he moved forwards, holding his body over her own.

She looked up, trapped between his arms. 'What are you doing?'

'Is this all just some elaborate foreplay?'

'No! Of course not.' She wasn't sure what, but something had shifted. She felt dizzy, disoriented. Her head pounded.

He leaned down towards her. 'You're so sexy like this.'

'Caspar.' Sam whipped her head away from his approaching mouth.

'Come on,' he whispered in her ear. 'I love seeing you feisty.' He dropped his hips down and reached to take off his belt.

'*Caspar.*' She tried to move away, but his full weight was now on top of her. 'Stop.'

'Go on,' he breathed heavily into her neck. 'Berate me. Tell me off.'

He squeezed her breast and went to push down his jeans.

'I said stop.'

'*Go on*. Use that voice again. Tell me how bad I've been.'

'Stop!' She writhed underneath him, but he held his position. 'I don't want to.' She closed her eyes tight, swallowing back the beating of her heart in her throat. Her limbs froze.

'Really?' He bit her neck, scratching the skin with his teeth. 'Why so frigid and coy all of a sudden? Come on.' He ran his tongue around her ear.

'No.'

He paused and positioned his face over hers, his blue eyes narrowed, before quickly sitting back and running a hand through his hair. 'What's the point in now playing the prick tease?' He smirked as he did up his trousers. 'I thought with you staying here we had an understanding.'

Her stomach dropped. She flicked her head round to face him. 'What did you just say?'

But he was saved from answering by the sound of Issa's voice calling to ask whether Sam knew if her passion fruit had arrived yet.

'You know what,' she took a shaky breath, 'I don't need to hear that again.'

'Jeez, gorgeous. Lighten up. That could have been fun.' Caspar reached over to stroke her leg, but she had already opened the door and pushed it firmly shut behind her.

CHAPTER 25

Sam felt like she was in automatic mode.

Prick tease... an understanding? Really? Was that what Caspar thought of her? That the sex was somehow in payment to stay there? Her hands gripped into fists. She'd never been someone who'd had casual sex. Before Martin, she'd had a handful of few-month-long relationships, starting with the only boy in her politics A-level class who didn't interrupt her in debates and then with a couple of other journalists in her early career, but never one-night stands. It hasn't been from lack of desire, more from lack of time. When she had to be up for early morning reporting segments, she hadn't fancied needing to traipse across the city in last night's heels or having to shake someone awake to pointedly tell them to leave her flat before the first tube. They'd once done a segment on *WakeUp!* on app-based dating with its complex unwritten rules and lingo of ghosting and fading and roaching and breadcrumbing and she had never felt more thankful for Martin's existence.

She'd just assumed that Caspar had wanted to sleep with her because he liked her. Because he saw something worth pursuing. Not because...what? She was *present*? Willing and available? And there she was idiotically sprinting ahead to him fertilising her eggs.

She wanted to vomit. Her limbs seemed to move independently of her brain as she gathered her and Issa's things together. Caspar didn't try to stop her from going and seemingly didn't leave the bar. The only thing that held her back was the question of whether she should take the phone he had bought for her, which still lay gleaming in its box. In the end, the practicality of having means of contact outweighed the moral high ground of leaving it in the room, so she slipped it into her bag and rushed outside to meet Issa, whom she'd told to wait by the front door.

Issa went quiet as they trampled further over the fields towards the cottage. Sam hoped it might be tactful silence in a stressful moment until she saw the discomfort etched on her face. That discomfort morphed to horror as it became clear just how small and crumbling and very much not luxury five star hotel the cottage really was. Things didn't improve when they went through the already open front door, the doormat suspiciously grey with short, coarse hairs. Sam couldn't deny that the sad brown sofa and cobwebbed hearth felt shabbier than ever in contrast to The Rowe. But, as she'd explained to Issa, staying with Caspar was simply no longer an option. Plus they would only be there for one night, with Clive due to take them home tomorrow.

'Tomorrow?' Issa's eyes widened as she gingerly leant against a peeling kitchen unit. 'But what about the baby?'

'That's the point. You're about to give birth.'

Issa put a stiff hand on her stomach. 'I told you. I can't.'

'You have to.'

Issa blinked several times in quick succession. 'The plan only works if you pretend to give birth here.'

Sam sighed and put her hands on the counter. 'Please. Listen. Whatever happens. I was serious. I am not *taking* it from you.'

'So you don't want –'

'Christ, Issa.' Sam turned and held her upper body over the unit. 'Firstly, it's not a case or want or don't want. It's not an option. And secondly, I've thought I've wanted a lot of things recently. It doesn't mean they're right for me. Following my gut hasn't exactly led me to a bloody good place.'

Issa tilted her head.

Sam closed her eyes and gave an exasperated sigh as she turned. 'Sorry. I'm just... I don't know. Pissed off. Nothing's where I thought it would be.'

'Hmm,' Issa made a small noise. 'When it's all about the sex it doesn't usually last long. It's probably for the best.'

Sam focused her mind on a hay bale out the window to stop herself from picking up one of the rattly old saucepans and throwing it against the wall.

'You know we can't leave tomorrow anyway?' Issa sniffed. 'The festival's not for another three days.'

'The festival?'

'You know? Nixie is setting me up with some classes. I've already posted about them, so I can't let people down.'

'We're leaving tomorrow. We have to.'

'We don't.' Issa met her gaze with a surprisingly fixed glare.

Sam rubbed her forehead. 'Well let's see what Clive says.'

'But the plan–'

Sam's voice came out louder and sharper than she'd expected. 'There is no 'plan'. *Please.* Just stop. My time here is finished. I want to get–' She was about to say home when she realised with a twinge that her and Martin's flat wouldn't be her home anymore. It wasn't that she particularly liked it – with its dark leather and industrial fittings –, but the prospect of not having a place to call her own seemed oddly terrifying. She exhaled and added more quietly, 'I want to get back on track. Get my life in order.'

'Without a baby?'

Sam wanted to scream, 'WITHOUT A BABY.' But she took a deep breath and looked at the hay bale again.

Giving up on the imminent prospect of parenthood felt like removing a knife from her side. It had to be done, but she didn't know how much damage there'd be from the bleeding. On the one hand she'd never felt so furious at the uncontrollable, fickle nature of fertility. She wanted to shout, scream, tear the room apart. Rip each cabinet from the wall and set fire to them on the floor, use each utensil to tear wildly at the peeling wallpaper, savage the sofas with the knives, exposing their white, springy flesh. On the other hand, she just felt quietly sad, in a gentle mourning for a life she'd still not experienced. She wanted comfort, ease: to be tucked quietly into bed with a hot chocolate on the side table and Ella Fitzgerald on the radio.

Her mouth went dry. The words scraped her throat. 'Without a baby.'

'Huh,' Issa made a small noise and looked to the side. 'So things aren't over with Caspar because you're getting ready to bring the baby back to Martin?'

'No.'

'And you wouldn't consider bringing up the baby on your own?'

'No.'

'Even with a nanny?'

Something flicked in Sam's brain. 'Enough!' She pounded her hands against the countertop. 'All of this talk about the plan and you giving me your child is fucking insane! Stop! You can't just make your mistakes go away like that.' She snapped a finger. 'Talk to Clive. Take some goddam responsibility. The fact of the matter is that you'll love this kid, and you need to make a stable home. You had an affair. Own your behaviour. I'm not some baby stealing fairy fucking godmother who'll make it magically disappear.'

Issa stood limply, her blue eyes wide.

Sam sighed. 'I'm going back to bed for a bit. I need some time to myself. Please just leave me be. Unless you go into labour or something. But don't ask for anything ridiculous like exotic fruits.'

'I won't,' Issa murmured. 'The baby's not dropped yet. We've got at least a week.'

Sam didn't reply as she ploughed upstairs, each footstep

heavy with disappointment. As she closed the curtains against the bright sunshine, she felt like she was closing the emotional gates she'd only recently opened. All those tears, all that vulnerability, now just felt like a colossal mistake. Where had it all left her? Without her home, without her job and with a stupid, weak mind that had built Caspar up into some romantic hero who'd save her from all her problems. She couldn't understand how she'd been so blind to what he really was: a shallow ex-city boy who figured she was easy knicker-dropping picking. And, like a total idiot, she'd not only proved this true but convinced herself that this seeming God to women was about to change her life.

She dropped onto the bed, pulled the covers tight around her and brought her legs into a tight ball. Everything was so far from what she'd imagined when Louise had showed her the information on Sark. The island had seemed so full of promise, somewhere that she could recuperate and find calm and clarity. But nothing was how she'd planned. How she could have fallen out of the mess with Martin and into such blind stupidity with Caspar she didn't know. Ever since that first faded line on the pregnancy test, it was like her emotions had the control seat of her brain and her usual rational, logical approach had been kicked out the cockpit.

When they'd started the IVF, she'd assumed that she could carry on as usual, the drugs and procedures taking place during lunch breaks or quiet afternoons like some extended dental treatment. She hadn't realised how much it would mess with her head. It was like being a ship in an endless storm at sea; yes, she could pull the ropes and control the rudder, but at some point she would let the next rolling wave tip her over.

Her mind flashed back to the morning she'd had crab sandwiches with Caspar at the monument. What had that inscription read? Something about being in the sea and losing your path in the great waters. Well it was right. She needed stability, normality, dry land.

There was a knock on the door.

'Please not yet, Issa. Unless it's an emergency, I just need some time by myself.'

Another knock.

Sam scrunched her legs up into a ball. 'Not yet!'

But the door gently opened, and Issa nudged in, belly first. 'Can we talk? Just for a minute?' she said.

Sam pulled the duvet up around her chin. 'Look, I'm sorry I lost my temper, but I don't think there's anything else to say.'

Issa shuffled over to the bed and perched on the opposite side for a few seconds. 'Do you mind if I sit? My back's killing me.'

Sam didn't reply. Issa heaved herself against the pillows.

'There *is* something else to say,' Issa almost whispered. She let out a long breath. 'I'm sorry. And I will tell Clive.'

Sam flicked her eyes open but didn't move a limb.

Issa rested her hands on her stomach. 'You're right. Of course I want the baby. And I do need to take responsibility.'

Sam shuffled around so the two women were lying side by side. 'Really?'

'Really.'

'So where did this 'the plan' thing come from?'

Issa spoke slowly, 'I was scared. I am scared. Clive genuinely might leave.' She brushed her eyes. 'And I really thought giving the baby to you and Martin might help all of us. I could go back to normal. And you get a family. I've never really done a big charitable act. I thought this could be it. Figured it could be my big legacy sort of thing. I hadn't really considered you saying no.' There was a pause. 'Will you adopt?'

Sam flinched. She'd been asked the question many times before by well-meaning acquaintances whilst bouncing their own gurgling babies on their laps, blind to its insensitivity.

Unsure how to word her complex feelings into a coherent response, she always said 'maybe' as brightly as she could muster and steered the conversation in a different direction. But now she realised that her answer was different.

She clenched her jaw as she thought about Nixie jiggling a grizzly Leo on her hip whilst Olive's lip wobbled. 'No. I couldn't do it on my own.'

She felt sick with grief. A future of empty arms and a darkly silent flat loomed like a grey sky ahead.

Issa frowned. 'But you've put yourself through so much.'

'When I was younger, it never crossed my mind that I might not be able to have children. I took the option for granted as I focused on my career. And then I couldn't do it. It was like some special club that everyone around you swans into, but you can't access. I'd always had control over my life. Every job I wanted, every story, every pay rise – I fought for and achieved. But however hard I fought, I couldn't win this. My choices and my efforts were redundant. And now I know. This is the end. I'm not *ever* going to win this. I've lost, and I can't do it anymore.' She closed her eyes. She wasn't sure where the words had come from, but they seemed to be the niggling voice of truth that had been squatting, ignored, in the back of her mind.

Issa's hand slid across the bed and clasped onto her own. 'It doesn't have to be the end,' she whispered.

Sam exhaled heavily. 'It does. I feel like I've been losing my mind. I'm this person who walks out of sets, leaves home, spits in people's faces, does drunken chants, sleeps with dodgy men. I don't recognise myself. The drugs, the dashed hopes, the painful, endless, heart-twisting waiting. Adoption would just prolong the miserable wait for years. I'm not even surprised that it broke my relationship with Martin. I just didn't realise that it might break me, too.'

There was a pause. A flutter of breeze caught the closed curtains. Sam felt winded by the finality of her own words, but in a strange way she also felt free. She was giving up. There was no fight left in her anymore. It felt like drowning – sinking calmly beneath the waves of regret and sorrow and loss rather than struggling so much to keep afloat.

'So why not fight Caspar?' Issa said.

'Excuse me?'

'Isn't that what you used to do? As like… a journalist? Uncover secret information to stop stuff happening? I mean I know that Nina's always saying that no one actually wants to read mind-numbing stories about expenses or policies or whatever, but wasn't that your sort of thing?'

Sam's eyes traced the flock pattern on the peeling wallpaper. 'Not anymore. Not since I started *WakeUp!* And anyway, Walt's tried. They've already raised a petition. It wasn't enough. He thinks he's right; they think they're right.'

'At least it would take your mind off things. Give you some time to heal? Discover your authentic self? One of the first lessons of my breathwork session is the importance of creating emotional distance from tragic events.'

Sam turned her head slightly, distracted by a small glinting object on the dresser next to the windowsill. It was the London bus keyring that Louise had given to her that day at the harbour. 'It's a local issue. It's best left to local people. I appreciate the thought, Issa, but it's not for me to fight.'

CHAPTER 26

The two women spent the rest of the day in quiet but amiable companionship, visiting the local food shop, cooking pasta for lunch and feeding Trevor D. Issa even managed to keep quiet about the state of cottage, though Sam couldn't help smiling when she caught sight of her silently pulling a face when trying to select the least ragged of the very ragged tea towels.

Without explicit agreement, both steered conversations away from anything about children, men or future plans and instead made brief, uncontentious comments on the beauty of the island and the pleasant weather. It was a bit like living in a dull period drama, but a banal afternoon was exactly what Sam had wanted. And despite Issa's gushing about the gorgeousness of the daisies and the honeysuckle and the bell heather, the quaintness of the carriages and the heart stopping wildness of the cliff top views, Sam still felt she was mentally ready to go home.

She knew she'd be lying if she said she felt better or improved in some way since leaving; the prospect of not immediately preparing for another transfer still felt like a hurricane had swept away the building blocks of her life. But she was at least starting to be consumed by her old, comfortable numbness to emotions, as if her mind had been injected with mild anaesthetics. She finally felt like she could rationally consider next steps and return to the possibility of taking on *YouNews*. Logic dictated, she told herself once she was back in bed in the evening, that no child meant she should redirect her efforts towards her career. Return to pick up the pieces of Part B. Which was why, early the next morning after she'd managed to read an entire chapter on the impact of AI on voting security, she'd decided to finally call Louise.

'Lou!' Sam paced to the other side of the room. 'Hi!'

Silence.

'Can you hear me? It's Sam. I've missed you!'

A cold, sharp voice cut through the line. 'So this is how you want to play it?'

Sam put a hand on the windowsill.

'Play what? Have you been calling? Shit, sorry. Caspar unplugged the hotel phone, and I've got a mobile now, but I just didn't get round to...'

'Caspar. Of course.'

'Look, I'm sorry I haven't been contactable, but things have been hectic.'

Louise snorted.

Sam lowered her voice, 'Honestly. Issa turned up at the hotel, can you believe it? *Issa*! And it gets crazier – she wanted me to *take* her baby because she's worried it might be Tino's and not Clive's. It's like living in a telenovela.'

'I'm not interested,' Louise snapped. 'I'm interested in not sitting back and taking it as you ruin your career. Your job is my job, remember. And I get a say in things, too.'

'What are you on about?'

'You can't be fucking serious.'

'Come on, I said I'm sorry. It's been busy. You can't have needed me that much. I know you're getting the contract sorted, but I've only been off grid for a couple of days. And being here hasn't *exactly* been what I expected. But I have clarity now, and you were right. I want to get back into work. Properly. At *YouNews*.'

Sam exhaled. There was no going back now. The

decision was made. She swallowed back a stubborn lump of regret.

'Fat chance.'

'I'm sorry?' Sam sat down on the bed. Louise didn't take any nonsense; it was one of the reasons she liked her so much, but this reaction was ridiculous.

'Look. Babe. I love you. I get it. You've had a rough break up. You want to feel confident. But this is not the right way to go about it. You don't need some shoot to give you self-worth.'

'What are you talking about?'

'The shoot.'

'What shoot?'

'What *shoot*?'

Sam crossed her arms. 'What shoot?'

'Lord,' Louise whistled. 'You better not be serious. Hang on. Check the link I just sent. *This* fucking shoot. You know, the one where you're flogging a hotel through soft porn. The one which has made *YouNews* retract their contract offer to avoid you bringing their brand into disrepute.'

In a horrible flash of realisation, Sam knew what she was going to see before she saw it. Her heart beat in her ears as she put the phone on speaker to check the link.

And there they were. The pictures Caspar had taken of her when they were messing about with his camera. The double spread was captioned, 'What's got Sam Elton so excited? Visit The Rowe to find out.'

'Oh God.' She stumbled back, almost knocking over a lamp.

Because there she was. Captured from behind on the grass, her underwear pulled up over one bum cheek. And not gracefully tucked into a handstand in the pool, but coming up for air before she'd adjusted her bra so that her nipples were almost visible.

Her blood ran cold, and she fumbled around for a surface to steady herself.

'Come on, hun,' Louise pressed. 'What in hell were you

thinking?'

But Sam couldn't talk. She could only shake her head as she flicked back and forth between the photos. She felt the sudden urge to wash herself, to scrape every inch of that day with Caspar from her skin. She tapped on to the gossip pages of the main tabloids. It was worse than she'd imagined. The photos of her nipples zoomed in on for all to see and beneath them thousands and thousands of comments.

'Sam,' Louise added, 'talk to me. What's going on?'

But Sam just scrolled through row upon row, a vicious pain tightening her throat: 'filthy whore', 'Martin's better off without that slut, 'how classy. NOT', 'she wants that bikini ripping off'.

She tried to explain but could only moan like a wounded animal and sink to the floor. 'I didn't…' she choked. 'He didn't…'

'He didn't *what*? How did this happen?'

Sam tucked her legs up to her chest and heaved into her knees. How could he do this? God, that was it now. Those photos would never go away. She would never work as a presenter again.

She dropped the phone to the floor and cried until she rasped for air.

CHAPTER 27

'I've hardly touched my phone since I've been here.' Issa sighed to Louise as she stretched out her back. 'Other than to promote my breath work class, of course. You know, I always was a bit suspicious of Caspar – almost too attentive; smacks of desperation – but the house and scenery are gorgeous. I've just been enthralled by the whole thing. I'd told Nina that she should run a travel piece on the island as a newfound retreat, but I suppose she'd better not now. It's a shame really. It could be fabulous. But, you know, I really hadn't even seen the photos.' She tutted and passed the phone to her other ear. 'It's shocking really. I honestly thought Sam was being attacked when I heard her screeching up here, but this isn't much better.' She placed a hand on Sam's still quivering shoulder. Sam stared darkly at the wall in front of her.

'I'd ask Nina to run an article on consent or something, but she's always saying the more politicised editions don't sell as well.' Issa twisted her mouth into a sympathetic grimace. 'Anyway, I'll look after her. Clive's coming over in the morning.' She paused and inspected her nails as she listened. 'Yes, I suppose you *could* come with him. Help her through.'

Sam wiped her eyes and looked round to where Issa was sitting over her. 'No,' she mouthed. 'I'm coming home. Tell her to stay.'

Issa covered the phone's microphone. 'It'll be good for you. Get the backup troops in.'

Sam furiously shook her head.

Issa ignored her as she shifted over on the bed. 'Yes. That's right. Gatwick.'

'There's no point,' Sam hissed. 'I'm leaving.'

'Mmhmm,' Issa nodded, batting her away, 'you catch a quaint little ferry on the other side.'

Sam reached over to squeeze Issa's arm. 'Tell her...'

'Oh for goodness' sake.' Issa put the phone on loudspeaker and dropped it into Sam's lap. 'You speak to her. I need another pee.'

'Sam, I'm coming,' Louise's voice crackled. 'I want to look this arsehole in the eye.'

Sam rolled over. She was so tired. It was like living under a weighted blanket. There didn't seem to be any point to anything anymore. She'd lost her personal life and her career. And it had all been her fault. Her own poor judgement. Anything else she did would likely cause more mess.

'What we need is to totally discredit him,' Louise said. 'Show *You News* that he's a slimy, untrustworthy git so they drop the disrepute claim. Turn it all on him.'

Sam looked out the window. The sky had faded to grey with a light film of rain. She could just about make out a dark figure crossing the fields and heading towards Trevor D's shed. It was probably Walt, carrying out the afternoon's feeding duties.

'Are you even listening?'

'Hmm? Oh.' Sam dropped her head on the pillow. 'Not really.'

'For God's sake, babe. Snap out of it. This is important. I asked what you've got on him. Anything that could make a story?'

Sam exhaled. 'I don't know.' She closed her eyes.

'Christ. Earth to Miss Elton. Who are you and what have you done with my best mate?'

'Nothing's going to work, Lou.'

'Of course something is going to work. Pull yourself together.'

'I don't have the energy.'

'Then find it.' Louise paused. 'Where are you?'

'In bed.'

'Sit up.'

Sam didn't move.

'Go on.'

Sam propped herself against the fading floral headboard. She stared at the second hand of the clock on the opposite wall. It was all she felt she could do: wish away the time until she was able to face the world again.

'Focus. What dirt have you got on this man? Other than the photos, what's he done that could create some unease?'

Sam sighed. 'Loads of stuff.'

'Good. Great. Like what.'

She kept staring at the second hand. Another minute gone. 'I don't know. Things.'

'Sam! Come on!'

She closed her eyes. 'I'm sorry. I'm not up for this right now. Please.'

'Make yourself up for it. If we're going to get *You News* back on board, we need to act before they find a replacement.'

Sam looked again at the clock. Another minute. She knew there was no point putting up a fight when Louise was in this kind of mood. She'd hound her for an answer like a hunting dog. 'He's buying the island.'

'He's *what?*'

'He's buying the island to turn it into an exclusive private resort.'

'But don't people live there?'

'Yes.'

'And they've agreed?'

'No. He hasn't got popular consent.'

'You're not serious?'

'Mmhmm.'

'Bloody hell,' Louise whistled. 'That is a proper story. Morally bankrupt millionaire shafts local population from island homes. Fantastic.'

'It's not fantastic.' Sam's voice was flat as she watched the clock's second hand pass twelve again.

'You know what I mean. It's exactly what we need. He really is a proper dick. Christ, you know how to pick them.'

'Seems that way.' The rain was intensifying. Sam saw the figure leave the barn and head back out again across the fields.

'Look, I'm coming tomorrow. Start getting a skeleton feature together. We need something ASAP. I'll work on where we can run it. Bring the fucker down, hun. Your career depends on it.'

'Sure,' Sam mumbled in reply as she ended the call, sliding back down into the sheets.

She had no intention of running about gathering a story on Caspar's island takeover. Yes, he was an arsehole, but she was the naïve idiot who'd jumped into his bed and let him take the photos. Now she had to live with the consequences.

She spent the next hour in bed, staring numbly at the raindrops shimmying down the windowpane. She watched as they twisted in thin lines, waiting until they merged into one another. She would have stayed there all afternoon if it hadn't been for Issa requesting use of the bed for a nap.

'I'm sorry, darling,' Issa drawled, her eyes heavy. 'I feel like an absolute whale and I'm not confident the sofa won't collapse from beneath me.'

'It's fine,' Sam said as she smoothed her rumpled t-shirt.

It wasn't fine. She didn't want to get up. Not now, not ever. But she wasn't about to deny a heavily pregnant woman a rest. And the rain was easing, so she could at least mope about on the cliff paths.

Outside the air was fresh, still damp but with a light breeze pushing away the clouds to reveal glistening slivers of late afternoon sun. She drifted across the field until she reached the narrower path where the salt of the sea blended with the herbaceous scent of cow parsley and sweet gorse. Uncut hedges spilled over onto the dirt path, and she waded on, pushing through the bushes in a way that reminded her of squeezing past the crunch of bodies on the Tube.

As she headed uphill, she soon reached a turning for a wider stone path lined with quaint granite cottages. So focused on protecting her own privacy, she usually hated the idea of nosiness, but her distracted brain couldn't stop herself from peering into each building. Besides, she reasoned to herself, this was Sark. Everyone knew each other's business, except, of course, from her knowing anything half useful about Caspar and his plans.

The first cottage to the right was garnished with a pink, blooming rose and white clematis, framing the wooden door like icing on a cake. The house name – 'Belvoir' – was hand painted on a wooden post adorned with limpet shells around the border. Two pairs of wellies stood neatly at the door, and Sam imagined an older couple slipping them on to potter about in the garden. The opposite house was whitewashed with primrose yellow shutters and a gleaming matching bench. Behind an open shutter, she spied the leaves of the day's papers on a wooden kitchen table held down by an open butter dish and bowl of apples. Next door, their neighbours had left the front door open, and from it danced the familiar tones of Radio 2 accompanied by the clatter of cooking and shouts for children to come downstairs for tea.

Sam had never met her neighbours in London. She'd heard some of them a handful of times, returning late at night and pacing on the ceiling above. But their warehouse-style block housed at least fifteen or so flats, and she didn't keep track of the different people rushing in and out each day. Perhaps she might be able to point out one or two vaguely familiar faces, but the other flats could well all be short-term rentals or holiday lets. She certainly couldn't imagine one of the neighbours keeping their front door open all afternoon.

She walked on a few paces and was faced with a neat playground filled with wooden apparatus. Three unaccompanied seven or eight year olds – she assumed from the next-door glamping site – were hollering with ecstatic glee on the zip wire.

It was funny, she shrugged to herself as she paused and leant onto the playground's wooden fence: when she'd arrived on the island her overwhelming impression had been of its remoteness, its emptiness. But she couldn't have been more wrong. The children's screams pierced the cooling air as the girl in the group was thrown up high at the end of the wire and she yelped with delight. Yes, it was small, but small didn't mean empty. It was compact, close-knit.

And yet that arsehole was going to evict everyone.

She shook her head. It was like chopping down an ancient wood to graze fat cattle. Yes, it could be luxurious – with sauna complexes, glass-roomed restaurants and indoor-outdoor pools – but at what expense?

She frowned as she carried on walking until she approached the crossroads leading to the Avenue. The layout was familiar enough to her now to know that to her left was a cricket pitch and the primary school and a café and the dairy and B&Bs and to her right was a bank and bike hire shops and small supermarkets and the museum and pubs and stables. There was, she felt with an irk, the ingredients of a rich community. She bit her lip. It *was* a story worth exposing, regardless of her personal issues with Caspar. She just wasn't the right person – or in the right mental headspace – to take it on.

Instead of turning, she decided to walk straight on towards the tops of the tents in what she assumed must be the festival field. As she approached, she could hear a cluster of voices on the wind and the heave of a tractor running larger items across the grass.

The field set up wasn't exactly Glastonbury, but it was coming together. She stood by the gate and watched as a group of young men heaved hay bales into circles for seating areas and festooned the canvas walls with lanterns. There was a large marquee – presumably for music and the bar – a series of smaller tents for retail stands and a large tipi-style tent in the adjacent field, which ran clean down towards the cliffs. Perhaps this was where Issa's earth mother class or whatever it was called would take place.

'Evening!' a voice called, and she turned as a young family flashed behind her on bikes. Two toddlers were strapped onto back seats and waved cheerfully as they passed. Sam tried to return their smiles, but her mouth twitched with irritability. She gripped her hands into fists. How could Caspar just want to shut everything down?

The rumble of another tractor approached, and she looked down the lane to see Jack driving the vehicle, its cart laden high with kegs of beer and a sound system. He lifted his cap to the family on bikes and shouted a genial 'Cheerie.'

Sam took a sharp breath in. Where earlier she'd felt her stomach hold a cold pit of sadness and shame, its walls were now twisting into tendrils of bitter anger, wrapping themselves around her chest. Clearing everyone out for the sake of his own vanity project wasn't just distasteful but nigh-on barbarous. She kicked a stone from the dusty road. There might not be the most reliable public services, but people weren't exactly trapped here in misery. Nixie had said about all the technology people moving to the island. Surely they had come because it offered something positive, something they couldn't find elsewhere.

She started walking back towards the cottage, slightly faster now as her heart picked up pace. If the ownership plan or whatever it was called had gone through, it might now be too late. The more she thought about it, the more she was sickened by Caspar's arrogance in thinking that his lofty aspirations trumped hundreds of day-to-day lives.

Her throat felt tight. She hadn't felt passionate – properly so – about anything in her professional life for a while. It was an emotion she'd been numb to over the years at *WakeUp!,* where it was hard to get worked up about the best wines under a tenner to accompany a takeaway or a woman who woke up one morning with a Welsh accent. But she recognised the sensation from her days back at *Real News,* when every now and then there'd be a story so unjust, actions of a politician so crooked that she knew she'd fight to expose its filthy core and let it rot in the bright light of public knowledge.

She stomped back down past the crossroads and the playground and the granite cottages until she was at the top of the path looking down the hill towards Judith's house. Trevor D was happily grazing in the field, his ears flapping to the side and tail wagging, and she could just about make out Jeremy lying on his back, arms and legs akimbo in a pool of sun next to the rose bush.

A hot flash of anger lit up something inside. Regardless of her personal skin in the game, she was suddenly overwhelmed with the certainty that she couldn't sit back and let Caspar get away with this. She tightened her lips. She *was* going to fight him. And she was going to win.

But, though it pained her to admit it, she couldn't do it on her own. There was one person she would have to see first.

CHAPTER 28

It didn't take Sam long to find where Walt lived. The long July day meant the sun was only just beginning to drop as she crossed La Coupée, and she soon came across a dog walker who was able to point him out from the dozen or so houses. Perched almost on the edge of a cliff, the little stone building was sturdy and squat with a trim blue door and a pile of lobster pots outside. In front of it spread a blanket of fields down towards the sea, which was now shimmering silver in the lowering light.

Walt heard her approach before she could knock.

'Can I help you?' he asked, standing on the threshold.

He looked as tired as she felt riled up, with heavy wide eyes and his arms crossed over a t-shirt spattered in what looked like pumpkin soup. 'I can't fix any fancy hair equipment tonight,' he said.

Sam ignored the comment. However much she'd rather not come begging at his door, she needed him on board. Her blood was pumping, and jitteriness flooded her body. She just wanted to get what she needed from him and get going. 'I've changed my mind,' she said.

'You want your pregnant friend taken back after all? No can do this evening.'

'Not Issa.'

'What then?'

'On Caspar.'

'Good for you.' He stood back and went to close the door.

She rolled her eyes. He had every right to treat her like this after their conversation at the beach – she would have done the same – but she really didn't have time for it.

'Look,' she stepped forwards, putting a foot on the step, 'I've come to discuss the hotel situation.'

He raised an eyebrow. Unlike Caspar, who seemed now to Sam like a cheap inflatable in a swimming pool – brash and full of air –, Walt reminded her of the sea surrounding them: cold, serious and not to be messed with. She'd need to take a direct approach. Back in the days of *You News*, Louise had her use a power pose – legs slightly wide, arms crossed, chin high. She'd always thought it made her look like a politician with a poker up her bum, but she adopted it now, looking straight at him, gaze fixed, keen to show that she was in earnest.

'I want to help,' she said.

There was a pause. Walt tilted his head and placed a hand on the door frame. Sam tried to hold her pose, but her chin dropped and she tucked one foot behind the other. She wasn't sure why, but she was starting to feel a bit nervous.

'Help do what?' Walt said.

'Gah!' Daniel's voice called down the corridor.

'Just a minute,' Walt called back. He looked straight at Sam. 'It's not a good time.'

'But we need to act fast.'

'Gah! Bah!' Daniel shouted. He tottered into Sam's line of sight, palms splayed and covered in the same orange food on Walt's shirt.

'Just a minute, little man!' Walt repeated over his shoulder. He looked again at Sam and took a step back from the door. 'Another time.'

She hesitated, realising how ridiculous she sounded – waiting for all the paperwork to be signed and then saying she wanted to join the cause.

Walt moved to close the door.

'Wait!' She surprised herself by putting her hand out on his arm. She whipped it back. 'Sorry. Look. Just give me a minute. I have some ideas. It sort of feels like now or never.'

Walt exhaled then looked down to find Daniel clasping onto his jeans and giving Sam a quizzical look.

'Hey, buddy,' he said and leant down to hoist him onto his hip. 'I won't be long.' Daniel gave a wide smile as he held Sam's gaze before trying to reach for the wooden netting of a lobster pot ceiling lamp. She felt a tug in her chest.

'Aren't you and Caspar pretty cosy together?' Walt said.

Sam slipped her foot back behind the other. 'I made a mistake. I want to help.'

'Why?'

'Excuse me?'

'Why do you care? Aren't I just some narrow-minded odd job man?'

Daniel turned back to Sam, his eyebrows raised in expectation. She so wanted to reach for him, swing him up and watch him giggle as she kissed him on the nose. Instead she bit her lip. 'I told you: I made a mistake.'

Walt glanced at his watch and sighed before stepping back from the door. 'Fine.' He gestured for her to come in and pointed towards a small table in the kitchen covered in a tractor motif wipe-clean tablecloth. He set Daniel down on the floor and picked up the bowl whose orange contents had splattered on the wooden floor.

Daniel looked up with wide eyes, and something in Sam felt like it might break. She pinched her finger. She needed to focus. The future of her career depended on the next 24 hours.

'It's ok, little one.' Walt sat down and ruffled Daniel's hair. 'It wasn't very nice anyway. Grandma does a much better soup than me.'

He nodded at Sam to sit in the other chair. She tentatively did so, picking up a toy train from the seat, before casting an eye around the room. It was not what she'd expected. She'd had Walt down for a dweller in some sort of bleak man cave, complete with a tired leather sofa, TV on the floor and camping chair in the corner. But the wooden kitchen opened onto a bright and airy living space. Beneath the multicoloured plastic layer of children's toys, it was unquestionably stylish with pale furniture, rattan lamps and linen cushions.

'Wow.' She motioned around the room. 'This looks like it's straight out of a coastal living magazine.'

'Someone else decorated it. Nothing to do with me.'

'Oh. Right.' She winced. Of course. He wasn't a bachelor; he had a family, and a wife or girlfriend who probably took great pride in their home.

He raised an eyebrow. 'I thought you had some urgent idea?' Daniel reached up for the cord of a table lamp, and Walt swept him up in one fluid motion and placed him in a playpen in the living room. He rubbed his chin as he returned to the table. 'If I'm honest, I've had a crap day. I've got to get up at the crack of dawn to feed that blooming donkey again, and I could be doing without this. The deal's gone through. There's nothing to be done.'

Sam shook her head. 'I think you're wrong.'

He gave a thin laugh. 'I'm sure you do.'

She placed her hands awkwardly in her lap. That wasn't how she'd wanted to start the conversation off. She knew how to handle tricky exchanges – it was what she'd done her entire career – and it wasn't by starting by insulting someone. He had every right not to let her in at all. She'd need to prove she wasn't there just to mess around.

'I don't mean to be rude,' she said. 'I want to help stop the takeover. The island ownership plan.'

He stood up to wash up the dirty plastic plates. 'Let me guess. He's dumped you after a fling and you're seeking revenge?'

'No,' she snapped, then shifted back in the seat. 'Well, sort of. It's complicated, but I'm fully on board.'

'You've left your change of heart until too late. It's been

approved.' He turned his body as if to invite her to leave.

Sam had a feeling this was coming. Walt wasn't going to accept her help easily. She'd approached it all in the wrong way; he wasn't an easy man to read.

'It's never too late,' she said.

'It already is.'

'I mean who owns Sark anyway and can just have it sold off?'

'Do I really need to go over all this? What do you think I've been doing for the past year? It's over. We lost. Signatures talk but money shouts.'

'Humour me.' She crossed her legs. 'Who's sold it?'

He sighed as he placed the plates in the sink. 'Up and until now Sark's been a royal fief.'

'Uh huh.' She took out her phone and wrote down 'Royal Fief' in her notes. He surely had that wrong; the island wasn't exactly cutting edge, but surely it had moved on since the 10th century. 'Of course.'

He tilted his head. She tried to smile and look officious and competent, but her adrenaline was wearing off and doubt at how useful she could be was starting to seep in.

'So,' she lifted her chin, 'that means it was sold by…?'

He ran the plates under hot water and spoke over the noise from the tap. 'Well, technically the Bailiwick of Guernsey, but, ultimately, the king.'

She crossed her arms. 'Be serious.'

He turned and leant against the sink. 'I'm being perfectly serious. Fancy giving him a call? Tell him your ex-boyfriend is a bit of a piece of work and he should reconsider?'

He walked over to Daniel and passed him a crinkly book, which Daniel proceeded to shake like a rattle. Sam sat on her hands. The king? *Was* Walt just having her on? She couldn't tell. 'Well,' she cleared her throat, doing her best to appear unfazed, 'why exactly is the king selling an island to Caspar Rowe?'

'What do you think?'

'I'm asking you.'

'I guess having Royal fiefdoms isn't a great look in the modern world. Doesn't scream progressive.'

'But people were happy with the setup, no?'

'Doesn't seem to have mattered. Look.' He picked Daniel up again. 'When you're ready to call the king of England up for a chat, let me know. Otherwise I'm tired. It's been a long, rubbish day, and you won't want to cross the Coupée on your own when it's too dark.'

Sam looked out the window behind her. The sky was now a moody grey as the light drew in. It would be so much easier to head home now, curl up amidst the springs of the sofa and persuade Lou to wait for her back in London in the morning. But that would mean giving in. Leaving Caspar to sit back and get what he wanted. Christ. She couldn't let that happen. Even if it did mean coming up against the head of the nation.

'I'll be fine,' she said tightly. 'Now. Sark is attached to Guernsey, but the king needs to answer to the UK government, right?'

'I believe Sark honours the Magna Carta.'

She narrowed her eyes, still half unsure if he was taking the piss. 'How many signatures did you get on your petition?'

'Just over 300. Most of the island's permanent adult population.'

She wrote the figure down. 'You know, at 10,000 signatures, the UK government *has* to respond. At 100,000 it would be considered for a debate.'

'Great news,' he said drily, placing Daniel on the floor. 'Why hadn't I thought of finding 99,700 more people who've not only heard of the island but care enough about it to get involved in its ownership structure?'

She dropped her shoulders. This whole thing wasn't turning out to be as simple as she'd hoped. 'It's possible. We'd just want to gather them before parliament goes on recess in a couple of weeks.'

'Sure.' He nodded as Daniel headed in Sam's direction. 'I'll check tomorrow if I happened to have missed out a few tens of thousands of members of the population. Maybe they were all hiding down the pub.'

'Well, to start: how many people will be at the festival over the weekend?'

'A few. Probably 1000.'

'Is there capacity for more?'

He looked at her with his wide, dark eyes as if trying to work out what she was getting at.

'That festival gets advertised all year. You're not going to suddenly drum up double or triple the interest with a couple of sponsored social media posts,' he said.

'I might.'

'Sure.'

Daniel squirmed to be let go and wobbled over to Sam's feet. She passed him the toy train and ran her hands over his silky head before stopping herself. She needed to focus.

'Look.' She stood up. The light was now truly thinning, and she'd need to get back before the sky was entirely consumed in darkness. He was right: she didn't really fancy crossing that high, narrow path with black sea either side and only a phone light for company. 'I'm a political journalist. Sam Elton.'

'I thought your surname was Murphy?'

'It's a long story.' So much had happened since Louise had booked her that boat trip that she almost felt like she *should* have a different name – she was hardly the same person. 'Trust me. I can make this happen.'

She felt a surge of confidence as she said the words. In reality, she had absolutely no idea whether parliament would debate this kind of issue even if a million people signed the petition. Royal fiefdoms might lie far outside its remit. But at least she could do *something*, raise some awareness. Somewhere, someone of importance would care.

He stepped towards her. His dark head towered at least a

foot above her own, and she tried to hold a strong stance whilst looking up from beneath his stubbled chin. 'Really?'

'I've got some ideas.'

He took a deep breath. There was a pause. 'Fine.' He exhaled. 'I don't have anything to lose anymore except my patience. But don't drag things out much more than over the week. Please. I'm exhausted. If it is going to go ahead, we need to just move on.'

She was flooded with the sort of nervous excitement that she hadn't felt at work for such a while. Reports could take days or weeks to plan, but she didn't have the luxury of time. She needed it filmed in the morning and ready to post by the afternoon. This meant she simply couldn't do it all on her own. 'I'm going to need your help,' she said.

Walt squinted down at her.

'Do you know anyone who's nifty with a camera?'

He stroked his chin. 'Rio, I suppose. He's travelled all round filming surfing drone footage but is back here for the summer.'

'Perfect.' Surfing videos were somewhat different to the style of news exposés, but it wasn't the time to be picky. 'And can you gather some talking heads? You know, people who can talk for a minute or so about what the island means to them, its history, what they'll miss, etc.'

'Sure.'

'And,' she grimaced, 'can you be one of them?'

He dropped his shoulders. 'Do I have a choice?'

'Not really.'

'Fine.'

'Then challenge accepted. A hundred thousand signatures here we come.' She stuck out a hand. He shook it tentatively in his own.

CHAPTER 29

The next day went by in a blur. Sam had been up late the previous evening researching for the script. She met Walt and Rio on the Little Sark headland for some opening shots of her outlining the history and political position of the island – it really was a Royal Fief – and the current threat posed by Caspar's plan. She'd cringed when Rio had arrived, recognising him as the 'Fresh' ponytailed man from the beach. He'd been warm and polite, without any experience in news reporting, but keen to give things a go.

'That was good,' Walt said, nodding at her after the first confirmed take. 'Really good. Punchy.'

'You sound surprised?' She raised an eyebrow.

He reddened slightly. 'I mean. I didn't...'

'It's ok.' She gave a small smile. 'I'm joking. I told you I'm usually quite a capable person. And this is me. This is what I do.'

She couldn't help flushing with pleasure. Regardless of how amateur their whole set up was, it felt so good to be out there doing this. The weather was playing ball, putting on a veritable show of bright blue skies, but, more than anything, she felt useful, purposeful. Back in the driving seat.

Once they'd finished the first few clips, they headed to the Avenue to capture some footage of daily island life before moving onto the talking heads. First up was Jack and another carriage driver, both looking so proud in their flat caps sitting above the shire horses that it made Sam feel a little tearful. Their anecdotes about growing up on the island after the war and how it had changed but kept its character led well into an interview with the headteacher of the primary school, followed by the owner of the dairy (who needed five takes to avoid him swearing) and then Judith, who wanted a break from babysitting Daniel to give a few words on community spirit, complete with Jeremy glaring at the camera from her knee. The next batch took a different tone, with some of the recent German arrivals, including Nixie's husband, extolling the benefits of the island's economic and political system and giving a vision of its practical future.

And, finally, came Walt, who chose to sit in Judith's field with Trevor D amidst the daisies in the background.

'I'm not really sure what to say.' He ran his thumbs over his fingernails.

Issa, who had assumed the role of stylist, straightened his woollen jumper. 'Oh, it won't matter,' she said. 'You're really only in it to sex the whole thing up.'

'That is not true,' Sam hissed.

But she couldn't help admitting to herself that Walt did make for quite a sight with his serious, rugged jaw and heavy brow amidst the bucolic scene. He might well sway a good segment of the female population to sign the petition.

'Just talk about what makes the island special to you. And what you've already done to raise awareness. It only needs to be a minute or so,' Sam said.

Walt bit his lip. 'I'll try.'

Something twinged in her stomach. She hadn't expected him to be nervous. It was quite sweet.

'Ready?' Rio shouted. He counted them in.

'So…' Walt looked straight at Sam like she'd shown him to. She nodded with encouragement.

'I've lived on the island of Sark for a long time.' He paused.

She twisted her lips. He wasn't exactly a natural in front of the camera. There'd be no free and easy Martin-style smiles as he draped his arms over a sofa. Perhaps not a bad thing. She knew this was far from polished, but it was honest – authentic.

'I've been here most of my life.' He looked up momentarily at the sky. 'It's not for everyone. People more used to cities might not see the appeal. In the summer we fish and swim and have little festivals. It can be harder in the winter, but we all pull together for events in the pub and the harvest and Halloween and Christmas. We even do the nativity outside in one of the farm stables. This little fella,' he nodded at Trevor D behind him, 'will probably have this year's starring role.'

Sam smiled. She could imagine it. Perhaps Olive could be a boisterous angel and Daniel the little donkey.

He lowered his chin. 'It's not much. No fancy cinemas or shops or bars. But we're like a family. We look after each other here. We've tried to stop the ownership plan from taking place, but it wasn't enough. A small island only has so many voices. So we need your help. Our lives here might be very different to your own, but we ask you to help protect this way of living. Please use your voice to help keep our family intact.' He paused then flicked his eyes towards Rio. 'That alright? I'm not sure what else to say.'

'Yes, mate.' Rio grinned. 'Sam, as long as you're happy?'

She sat on her hands, feeling like an idiot. How could she have goaded Walt for not understanding economic potential? She must have sounded so callous.

'It's great,' she said. 'Perfect.'

Walt rubbed the back of his neck. 'I could do it again?'

'Oh my God!' Issa's voice suddenly cut through as she shuffled in their direction. 'Do not change a *word*.' She put one hand on Walt's shoulder and one on her stomach. Sam was sure she could see tears in her eyes. 'That was beautiful. The whole vision was so idyllic and pure. Almost spiritual. Just like I thought the Cotswolds would be. Before I actually moved there, of course. And, Sam, FYI, I've plugged the workshops for the festival on my feeds. I reckon it'll sell at least another few hundred tickets. The pregnancy's really helped with post engagement. That *Sark's the new Hvar* reel got about 20,000 likes.'

Rio looked impressed. 'What workshops are those?'

'An exclusive collection on how to release your inner moon goddess, including natural remedies, breath work and Feng shui.'

Sam did her best to suppress a smile and tried to nod along as if she herself had released her own inner moon goddess several times over. Walt glanced at her. She could have sworn he raised his eyebrows in knowing jest.

'And Nina's agreed to plug the video on the magazine's online edition tomorrow. If it's ready by then.' Issa nodded at Rio.

'Really?' Rio blanched. 'You think people will actually watch it? I've never really gone mainstream before.'

Issa's face tightened. 'Dark White is not *mainstream*.' She said the word in the same way she might have said 'excrement'. 'But it means the *right* people will watch it.' She turned back to Walt. 'It's far from being on brand and Nina usually steers well away from anything political, but I sent her a quick snap of you and she agreed you might be the new David Gandy, so you're in.'

He laughed awkwardly. 'Who's that?'

But before Issa had the chance to reply, Sam's phone rang.

'It's Clive and Louise,' she mouthed. 'They're here.'

❉ ❉ ❉

With Issa waiting at the cottage and Walt and Rio working on the edit, Sam met the new arrivals at the harbour at the bottom of the hill.

She knew they'd look like quite an unusual travelling pair, and she hadn't been surprised to see Louise step off the boat first in an oversized camouflage wrap dress and matching suitcase, her face barely visible behind enormous shield sunglasses, with Clive following in a gingham Ralph Lauren shirt, navy chinos and large rucksack. What she had been surprised to see was Clive turn to pick up a small child and then be followed by two more up the steps.

Sam rushed forwards. 'Over here! I didn't realise you were all coming.'

Louise pulled herself up the last step and almost fell into Sam's arms. 'Help me,' she whispered into her ear. 'It's been *hell*. Like my nieces and nephews on speed.'

Clive pulled the middle child back from the steps' edge with one hand and hooked the younger child further up his hip with the other. 'Clementine! Put that bloody thing back,' he said.

Sam peered over Louise's shoulder. Clementine had pulled a loose limpet off the wall and was licking its insides.

'Hi, Clive,' Sam said. 'Do you need any help?'

'God yes. Here. Take this one.' He thrust Ottilie over to her so that he could hold Clementine in one hand and Magnus in the other.

Louise took a step back from the group.

'I didn't realise the kids were coming?' Sam tried to keep her voice light. Where on earth was she going to house them? She'd already been planning to share the sofa with Louise.

'Nor bloody did I. Noemi pulled a sickie this morning. Something about a migraine. Probably a hangover. And Tino's back in Italy for the entire summer. Bloody Continentals. They think the whole world stops for July and August. The journey's been a nightmare.'

'It has,' Louise agreed.

The children all looked up at Sam with expectant eyes.

'Where's Mummy?' said Magnus.

'Mummy's in the cottage where we're staying.' Sam

looked round at the group. 'Though it's going to be a tight squeeze. A *very* tight squeeze.'

'I don't share rooms,' Clementine announced. 'It doesn't suit my temperament.'

'Lord,' Louise whispered.

'Let's worry about all that when we get there,' Clive grimaced. 'I hear there's no cars on the island. I hope we're not expected to walk up that hill?'

Sam led them over to the toast rack trailer. They all piled in, the children squealing as the tractor came to life and they chugged over every little lump and bump on the unpaved road. Louise looked like she was going to be sick.

'Caspar Rowe, eh?' Clive raised his voice over the engine. 'Issa tells me he's got his sights set on the island?'

Sam nodded, trying to extricate her hair from Ottilie's grasp.

'He's a piece of work. I know of him from early days in the city. Heard he got dropped after some questionable deals. Slunk off somewhere quiet. Didn't realise it was here.'

Sam's ears pricked. 'What do you mean by questionable deals?'

But they'd already arrived at the top of the hill. They decamped the whole entourage into Jack's horse and carriage, and the rest of the journey was filled with Clive ensuring each child kept all limbs within the vehicle and kept screeching with delight at the horse to a minimum.

Louise leant over as they neared the top of the field. 'How's the IVF decision going? Still a possible?'

Sam looked across the carpet of green to the expanse of sea in the distance. 'No.' She shook her head. 'That ship's passed.'

Louise exhaled. 'Thank Christ.'

Sam clasped her hands together. It felt strange saying it so casually. Like she was Sisyphus and Hades had suddenly removed the boulder from the hill. But that part of her life was now over. She'd been thinking about what Walt had said on the report about the island being like a family. She got it now. She totally did. People want to live in tight groups of other like-minded, supportive people. It was why people got married, why they put up with noisy, messy kids. It helped create their own little clan, created company, fostered bonds. And for most people, it was the centre of their life.

But she wasn't most people.

She'd grown up without a proper family, and she didn't need one now. She was a lone wolf. An island.

'I want *You News*. And to get this dickwad out of the island's business. I'm going to make it happen. We shot the report this morning,' she said.

'Really?' Louise grabbed her hand. 'Well done, babe. Well bloody done.'

The carriage soon came to a stop, and Magnus let out an extraordinarily ear-splitting cry. He had, apparently, decided that he wanted to keep going forever, and Clive had to coax him down as Sam, Issa, Ottilie and Clementine padded over the thankfully dry field towards the cottage.

'You're joking?' Issa said as she opened the front door. 'What on earth are the children doing here?'

'Mummy!' Clementine threw herself at Issa's legs.

'Noemi's sick apparently.' Sam set Ottilie down.

'But we're never going to all fit in this hovel.' Issa gestured around the living room. Her face paled as Clive approached. 'Oh God,' she murmured. She caught Sam's eye and spoke under her breath. 'Stay, please. I've no idea what to say to him.'

Sam cocked an eyebrow. 'You'll be fine.' And then more loudly so that Clive could hear, 'Louise and I will go straight out. Find another rental for the next few nights. There's no point waiting around and then finding some of us need to sleep in the kitchen.'

Issa glared at her. 'Hi, darling,' she said tersely as Clive stood up to the cottage entrance. There was a pause. 'I didn't mean to sort of run away.' She flitted her spare hand about in a light motion and bit her lip.

But Clive just set Magnus on the carpet and pulled Issa as close as he could – belly bump allowing – towards him. 'Whatever it is, I don't care. There's no need to explain. You're safe. The baby's safe. That's all that matters.'

Then he leaned in for a smacking great kiss, which Sam and Louise took as their cue to leave.

CHAPTER 30

The holiday rental agency on the Avenue was closed, with a sign blu-tacked to the window simply reading 'Full for Festival'.

'Urgh.' Sam slapped a hand against the clapperboard front wall. 'I should have guessed. Well I suppose it's good news for tickets.'

'Don't expect me to go anywhere near a tent.' Louise wrinkled her smooth brow. 'And nor am I sleeping on the kitchen floor.'

'There'll be something. We'll ask around.'

'Ask around?'

'If people need help here, they tend to ask each other.'

'Bloody hell. That's weird.'

'I know. Strange. People actually talk to their neighbours.' Sam wiggled her fingers in a mock spooky gesture. 'I imagine it's all hands on deck for the festival set up for tomorrow. Someone there is bound to be able to help.'

She had been right. The festival field was now a hive of friendly, hands-on locals, all keen to help with the set up, and it had only taken Sam a few minutes to find Nixie instructing her husband on how to space out banner flags and Olive wrapping herself in bunting. As soon as Nixie spotted them, she pulled Sam into a hug and then shook Louise's hand, unable to stop gushing about how glamorous she looked and how she'd once worn similar outfits in Berlin but was now lucky if she wasn't wearing her T-shirt inside out. It transpired that Nixie and Leo had three spare rooms – Sam figured that an international tech company salary probably stretched quite far on Sark – so they offered to house Issa and the family whilst Louise and Sam stayed in the cottage.

'Would you like to have some little friends to stay, Ollie?' Nixie bent down and started trying to unwrap the bunting from Olive's legs.

'YES!' Olive stuck up a hand. 'Because then I am boss because it is my house, and I can tell them what to do!'

'You're not wrong, hun,' Louise said. 'Make the most of it.'

Sam and Louise were soon roped into preparations, with both of them helping count out the endless bottles of beer and wine behind the bar.

'Absolutely none of these will be drunk by me,' Sam said. 'Not one.'

'Oh piss off. It's ages since I've seen you on a night out. I was looking forward to it.'

A voice came through from the other side of the loose canvas. 'So no storming the stage this time?'

Sam grimaced. 'Is that...?'

Walt pushed open the side of the tent. 'I seem to remember you caused quite a stir at the sheep racing. £400 behind the bar and then drinking most of it yourself.'

Sam flushed, but there was something in his tone that was lighter than before and the comment came across as him being in on the joke, rather than a criticism. 'This is Walt, by the way. He's been the one leading the campaign.'

Louise looked him up and down. 'Walt... Are you the one I booked the boat with?'

'Indeed.'

She raised her chin slowly. 'You're not exactly what I expected.' She gave a mock cough in Sam's direction. 'Bloody hell.' Cough. 'You didn't mention.' Cough.

He nodded, bemused. 'Editing's going well apparently. Should be finished this afternoon.'

'Great,' Sam exhaled. 'Nina will plug it as soon as it's ready.'

'And I'll push from as many different angles as possible,' said Louise. 'Don't worry. We're going to get this arsehole and crush him by the balls until he squeals. Anyone else as excited as I am?'

But Sam didn't reply.

Because, storming past the piles of cups and cardboard boxes and hot dog buns, was a figure she really didn't want to see.

'Caspar,' she whispered. 'Shit.'

'He's here?' Louise turned. 'Let me take a look at the fucker.'

Sam and Caspar locked eyes. His lips curled in disgust. Suddenly she felt nervous. And small. The memory of his teeth on her neck and his hot tongue in her ear flooded her with unease. How could she have let him in? With his silly quilted gilet and shaggy hair and affected walk. What had come over her?

'What in God's name do you think you're up to?' he said, trying to hold Sam's gaze as she ducked in the other direction.

Louise positioned herself between the two of them, hands pressed firmly on her hips. 'So you're the guy who thinks he can pull my client's image into disrepute.'

'Excuse me?' he said.

'Using explicit images without consent for a campaign? We could sue.'

He rolled his eyes. 'Is that what the stupid video's all about? I hear you've been filming the village idiots of the island.' He looked round Louise to Sam. 'Personal revenge? Bit spiteful, wouldn't you say? You can't deny you enjoyed it at the time. And you know I could have chosen something far worse. On the bar...'

Sam's blood ran cold.

'Caspar.' Walt pushed forwards 'It's time for you to leave.'

'Well, it's the Pied Piper himself,' Caspar sneered. 'Rallying everyone up. Feeling all high and mighty that you've got some C-list television star on your little campaign?'

'Hypocrite much?' Louise stepped closer to him.

'Enough!' Sam held up a shaking palm. She looked at Walt and Louise. 'I can deal with this.' She breathed through her racing heart. There was nothing about Caspar Rowe that needed to scare her.

'The news report isn't just about me.' She shook her head. 'It's about stopping a failed city boy thinking he can trample all over local life. So, yes, we have been filming people around the island. And, yes, it will be released this evening for all the world to see. Good luck to you, Caspar. Very soon you're going to need a new plan.'

She swallowed. Nina sharing the video would certainly help, but there was no guarantee that it would get anywhere near the views that it needed to convert to a decent number of signatures. Or that anyone outside the island would care. But she wasn't going to let him sense a whiff of doubt.

'Sure,' he said. 'I'll close my multi-million-pound investment project because of some tourist who happens to work on television and fancies herself as a community do-gooder.'

'Some tourist who's an award-winning political journalist,' Louise added.

'Right. With all that serious *journalism* she's been doing over the past few years.'

Sam bit her cheek. She couldn't exactly say it wasn't true.

'And Sam,' Caspar flashed a cold smile, 'I own that cottage you're staying in. As I do half the rental properties on the island. I want you out. Today. I'll change the locks this evening.'

'Not a problem,' she said quickly. 'The locks need some maintenance anyway.' She thought back to that first night when Trevor D made his entrance. 'As does the whole thing.'

He narrowed his eyes. 'Check out by 7pm.' And, with that, he turned to leave.

'I had a feeling he was the landlord,' Walt said. 'Total disrepair but holding onto all and any properties to keep his island stronghold. Typical.'

Sam shook her head. 'And he knew I was staying there when he let me stay at the hotel. I don't get it.'

'I do.' Louise smirked. 'Power play.'

Sam sighed. 'You're probably right. I clearly do know how to choose them. What time is it now?' She checked her phone. 'Five. Crap. That doesn't give us long. I am not going to be there when he rocks up all smug and throws our bags in the field. Sure I can't tempt you with a tent, Lou?'

Louise snorted in reply.

Walt scratched the top of his arm. 'You could, uh,' he shrugged. 'Stay with me? Daniel sleeps through the night, so he won't wake you. I know it's a bit out the way over the Coupée, but I've got a spare room. You can share if you like?'

Sam took a step back in surprise. He must have taken a liking to Louise. She opened her mouth to decline; it would be far too awkward to say yes.

'I don't –,' Sam started.

'Thank God,' Louise put a hand on his shoulder. 'Please.'

Walt glanced down and spoke quickly, 'If I'm honest, you're doing us a big favour with this news report. If it works. I owe you one.'

'Don't worry. We wouldn't want to trouble you – or your wife.' Sam said.

Walt frowned.

'What she means is absolutely, thank you,' said Louise. 'As long as the house is warm and dry and with a bed that's not a blow-up mattress on the floor, we're in.'

He gave a small laugh. 'It is. Hang on.' He pulled his phone from his pocket. 'Rio said he'd call when the edit was ready. It's him.' He paced a few steps in the other direction as he took the call.

Sam scraped a hand through her hair. She so hoped the report looked good. Professional. Everything hinged on it. She turned to Louise to allay her worries. But then she paused. Louise was clasping the edge of the bar, looking like she might collapse at any moment.

'What's up?' she put a hand on her shoulder. 'Are you about to faint?'

'Rio,' Louise stuttered. 'It's him.'

'Who?'

'Rio. You know: *Rio*.'

'I know his name, Lou. What are you getting at?'

'It's *him*. From Thailand.'

'*Rio* is Hot Taken Guy?'

'Yeees,' Louise hissed under her breath. 'Jesus. I never thought he'd be back here. Figured he'd be living in Bali or something with a hot influencer wife who only eats raw fruit and with four feral children.'

'I think Walt said he's back for the summer.'

'Shit.' Louise started patting down her hair and jacket. 'I am not bloody prepared for this. What's he like? Still hot? Still taken?'

'I'm not sure.' Sam shrugged. 'He's not really my type. Seems sweet. Still got a ponytail. No mention of an influencer wife.'

'God. He sounds gorgeous.'

'Everything alright?' Walt wondered back over. 'Shall we go get your things? Rio sent the report over. We can watch it back at the cottage before we go.'

'Just out of interest,' Sam smiled, 'is Rio, er, staying on the island with his girlfriend?'

'Huh?'

Louise elbowed her in the ribs.

'Rio? He's been flying solo for years,' Walt said.

'Do you think he'll be at the festival tomorrow?'

'The whole island will be at the festival. Maybe bar Mrs Pedvin. How come?'

'No reason,' Sam smiled, giving Louise a wink.

CHAPTER 31

The report was perfect. Just the right balance of fact and human interest. Sam sat back on the spring-filled sofa cushions with relief. There was a chance – even if a small one – that the plan might work. They just needed the story to be picked up by a big enough news outlet and for enough people to care.

'You smashed it.' Louise squeezed her round the shoulders. 'Well done, babe. I'll send it out to as many contacts as possible. See who bites.'

'I have to agree.' Clive nodded thoughtfully. 'It's high time that Caspar Rowe was smoked out the woodwork.'

'And the island looked *beautiful*,' Issa sniffed, somewhat overcome. 'Edenic.' She bent as far as she could over her belly to address her children sitting on the floor in front of them. 'Did you see the donkey, sweethearts? Wasn't he gorgeous?'

'You *promised* we would get a donkey,' Clementine said, 'and that was *ages* ago.'

'I think I said you'd need to wait for a horse,' Issa replied in a low voice.

'Issa,' Clive said firmly. 'I told you about the alpacas. We are not housing a farm animal in the garden.'

Clementine's lip started to wobble. 'But Mummy promised...'

'DONKEY!' Magnus trotted across the room and made a

large bray, shocking Ottilie to tears.

Louise put her head in her hands.

'You know, I think it's time for us to get going.' Sam stood up. 'Nixie's going to come round in a few minutes. Catch you at the festival tomorrow?'

'Of course. First workshop is remedy making,' Issa raised her voice over the growing din.

With Daniel asleep upstairs and his toys tidied into a wicker basket, stepping into Walt's cream and blue living room was like being cocooned in a Caribbean retreat.

'Thank God,' Louise ran her hands along the stone top of an oak console table. 'I can cope with this.' She closed her eyes. 'Sweet, sweet respite. In fact,' she turned, 'Walt, would you mind if I had a bath?' She pressed her hands to her temples. 'Today has been... trying.'

Walt showed Louise upstairs whilst Sam perched on the sofa. She couldn't deny that he had turned out to be more pleasant than she'd once thought, but she still wasn't sure that she was comfortable sharing his living space for the evening. A part of her felt like he was only being polite to get the report made and that he still saw her as a clueless city idiot. Not that it mattered if he did.

A clock made of distressed wood hung above a side table. Just past seven. She smiled at the prospect of Caspar being so smug at the thought of evicting her from the cottage only to find them having left without a trace. But it was also too early to excuse herself to bed, and Louise would be hogging the bathroom. She looked around. There wasn't even any sign of a television that she could sit silently glued to. No wonder Walt hadn't recognised her when they'd first met.

Her attention was caught by a series of photographs in silver frames. She got up to have a closer look. They were photos of Walt with a woman. A very pretty woman. Something pulled in her stomach. After all this time he'd still never mentioned his partner. Where was she? Upstairs? Shouldn't he at least have said something? Not that it made any difference, of course. She felt hot. Frustrated. But then she supposed she didn't exactly know that much about him. Not everyone's private life was plastered about for public consumption.

She picked up a frame. It must have been in autumn. The couple was walking down a road lined with orange-leafed trees, the woman clasping a tiny baby to her chest. Whilst Walt was looking down at the baby – Daniel, Sam supposed, the woman was laughing back at the camera, her eyes glittering.

'Everything ok?'

At the sound of Walt's voice, Sam dropped the frame back onto the table, where it clattered down with an ominous crack. 'Shit.' She picked it up to inspect the damage. The glass had broken, splitting across the middle. 'Shit. Shit. Shit.' She held it in her hands as if she might somehow be able to fuse it back together. 'I'm so sorry,' she turned. 'I'll have it fixed. Or buy another. Will your wife mind? I think it's just the glass.'

Walt took the frame from her, placing it down on the console table. 'Wife?'

She hesitated. 'The woman in the photo?'

'Sister,' he said.

She exhaled, unaware that she'd been holding her breath. It wasn't that she cared about his relationship status, of course, she just wasn't sure why she turned into such a clumsy idiot around him. 'And she's... Daniel's mum?' she said.

'Yep.'

Sam waited for a further explanation, but Walt didn't offer one.

'I can still get the frame fixed?' she said.

'No. No. I never really look at them anyway.'

'Oh. Why not?'

There was a long silence. She bit her lip. She hadn't meant to say anything. Her curiosity had just slipped out, unchecked.

He scrunched his eyebrows and placed the two other frames face down on the table. 'I don't know.' He hesitated. 'I guess it's not always helpful to look back.'

He tilted his head down, and Sam willed the ground to swallow her up. Had his sister died? And there she was storming in smashing up family photos. What was *wrong* with her? She went to apologise again but was interrupted by a gush of water from the bath tap upstairs.

She twisted one foot behind the other as Walt carefully placed the frame and broken glass in the drawer. It felt too rude to sit and put her feet up in his living room, but she couldn't just stand in the corner all evening like a lampshade. He was probably only being polite when inviting them over – just general island hospitality. It was tempting to make up some excuse and escape to Nixie's to stay amidst the herd of children, but Louise might never speak to her again.

'Sorry to be nosy,' she said with a wince. 'And to intrude. I suppose that now we have the footage, Lou and I can go back at any time. Probably the day after the festival. It won't be long.'

'It's fine,' Walt said. He leant against the table with his hands behind him.

'I'll look to see if there's been any dropouts in the hotels or rentals tomorrow. See if we can get out of your hair.'

'It's fine. Good to have some company.'

She caught his gaze. His eyes were soft. Serious. She'd certainly never considered the prospect that he might be lonely; Walt had seemed like he was almost a part of the landscape – wild and wolfish – and without need of anyone else.

He sat in the cream armchair and pulled a plastic figurine out from behind the cushion. Sam figured it would now be even more awkward for her to loiter in the corner so shuffled away from the wall and sat tentatively on the sofa. She wasn't sure how to sit – relaxing back felt inappropriate somehow, so ended up perched on the edge like a nervous interview candidate.

They fell into a heavy silence again. Sam willed Louise to

hurry up but could just about hear gentle acoustic strumming in the distance – she'd no doubt dug out some candles and done a full spa set up.

'Did you grow up here?' Sam didn't really know why she was asking. There was no reason why he should want to share with her anything about his life. And she wasn't sure why she was so interested, but there was something about this man – presumably close to her own age but living on a tiny rock and leading such a cut off existence – that she found intriguing.

'In this house?' Walt rested his arms on his knees.

'In Sark.'

'Of course.'

'Right.' Sam nodded as if a great mystery had been unlocked and then promptly stopped herself. Questioning was usually her superpower. It felt ridiculous how much Walt made her feel out of her depth. She squeezed her fingers together.

'So not in this house?' she said.

'No.'

Another silence dropped between them.

Walt opened and closed his mouth as is weighing up whether or not to speak. He crossed his arms before saying, 'This house is owned by my sister. I used to live in a place on my parents' land before they sold up and went to the UK. And now I'm here.'

Sam relaxed back into the chair. So she hadn't smashed a photo of a beloved dead relative. 'You know, I didn't have you down as a pale wood and wicker furnishings kind of guy,' she said.

'Meredith was an interior designer. *Is* an interior designer. Hence the,' he waved an arm about, 'stuff.'

'Blimey. How many interior designers does one island need?'

Walt frowned.

'I mean with Caspar. His ex-girlfriend…'

His face darkened. 'Same person.'

'Oh!' Her cheeks flushed. She really shouldn't have stuck her nose in. Her mother had always told her off for prying as a teenager – would tell her that she might not like what she found out. Perhaps she should slip out upstairs – pretend she'd heard Louise getting out of the bath.

But she thought about the photo. A horrible thought rose like bile in her throat. She had to ask. 'He's not Caspar's, is he?'

'Daniel?' Walt blanched. 'No.' He rubbed the side of his face. 'Thank God. No.' He sighed. 'We don't know his father. Someone from her travelling days. My sister's... I don't know. She's what you might call unstable. Always has been. She's in rehab. Caspar really didn't fucking help.'

There was a pause.

'I'm sorry.'

'It's not your fault.'

'I know, but...'

'Seriously.'

'He's an arse.'

'Yep.'

Sam shifted her position. 'How long have you looked after Daniel?' She inwardly cursed her motor mouth. Surely his response had been her cue to change topic.

'Past three months.'

'Wow. On your own? Must have been tough?'

He shrugged. 'Yes and no.' He twirled the figurine between his long fingers. 'It can be hard, but I love the little fella. He deserves more.'

'Is she coming back?'

'Maybe. We don't know.'

Sam thought about Daniel's round, red cheeks and curl of a smile. She felt a rush of sadness. The poor mite.

'So she lived here?' Sam had the distinct feeling that Walt would rather not say any more, but her curiosity hadn't been sated.

His worry lines deepened across his forehead. 'For a

bit. We were both off island for a few years – travelling and working in different places – but she came back when she got pregnant. Thought she'd clean up her act and make a stable home. I figured I'd come back, too. Help out. She'd built herself this fancy career with lots of fancy parties with high net worth clients. I'd only ever been fishing or crew on boats. So I figured I'd take up Sybil, Dad's old vessel. Things worked for a bit, but Mede fell hook, line and sinker for Caspar's charms. Thought it was the real deal – that she'd found a father for Daniel. She didn't take it well when she found out he wasn't serious – left for a bender in the UK and hasn't yet come back. I figured I'd stay to give the kid some stability – keep him in his home. For as long as we can stay on the island anyway.'

Sam bit her lip. All she could think about was how insensitive she must have sounded in their previous conversations. He had every right to think she was a pompous prick. She usually always knew what to say, the right kind of follow-ups to fit the tone of the conversation, but her brain felt limp.

'It's…' she started, not sure how she'd finished the sentence.

'A bit shit?'

'That's not what I was going to say.'

'I know,' he sat back. 'I don't mean it. Not really. Looking after Daniel is a privilege. I love it. But it's not always easy. We spend a lot of time picking broccoli off the floor or saying hello to every sheep in every field.' A small smile rose and fell. 'And it's clearly not ideal without his mum, but we're ok,' he shrugged. 'Most of the time.'

Sam hummed. It could hardly be further from her days being ferried to and from the studio in company-paid cabs, takeaway coffee in hand, dreaming of the distant prospect of a family life.

'Your day-to-day's a bit different, I bet?' he asked.

'That's not…' But she paused. Had her thoughts been so obvious from her face?

He narrowed his eyes. 'TV political journalist? Sounds like you've seen a lot.'

'And cocked up a lot. Lost my partner, lost my career. Made a complete fool out of myself with those photos.'

Walt furrowed his brow. 'I don't think anyone can call you a fool.'

'Many people are calling me far worse.'

She looked up. She could hear Louise pulling the plug out of the bath.

'I find that hard to believe.'

'Trust me.'

There was a pause. He rubbed the back of his neck. Sam went to get up. She pulled at her shirt collar, suddenly uncomfortably warm. Was he actually trying to be so nice to her? No. She was imagining things. Again. As she always seemed to be doing recently. It was nothing. He was clearly lonely, a bit angry and bitter about his lot and trying to make her feel a bit guilty for her earlier behaviour towards him. And he'd succeeded.

'Sounds like Louise is up. I better go wash, too. Get ready for the big day tomorrow.'

'Sure.'

'Night.'

'Night.'

She pushed open the living room door.

'Sam?'

She turned. Walt cleared his throat.

'For what it's worth, I think what you've done with that news report is pretty amazing.'

She gave a small laugh, but it came out more like a snort. 'It's just a report.'

'Seriously.' He caught her gaze. 'Thank you.'

'No worries.' Her voice came out much higher than she'd expected. Could it be that he wasn't guilt tripping her? That he was just being kind? 'Still a way to go yet.' And with that she headed upstairs, her head now full of more questions about the man than before.

CHAPTER 32

'Jesus, Sam, look at this!'

Sam grunted as Louise shook her awake the next morning. The room was bright white from the sunshine flooding in the open window, and she rubbed her eyes to register the phone held a few centimetres from her face.

'Give me a minute,' she mumbled.

'Watch! It's Martin!'

Sam blinked a few times and propped herself up against the pillows. As her mind returned to focus, she recognised the familiar studio on the screen and Martin looking serious as he bent forwards on the sofa, eyes flirting with the camera. She grunted and, keen not to see his smarmy face, heavy with foundation and faux interest, she rolled onto her side. Louise pushed her back.

'Listen!' Louise said.

'I know many of you have wondered where Sam's been over the summer.' His voice was slow and measured, as if he was delivering hard-hitting news to the nation. 'As she's stepped back from the show, she's been researching this *incredibly* important story about the people of Sark – a small island in the channel where their tight-knit life is under attack.'

Sam sat up. She couldn't have heard him correctly.

'Please sign her petition and help keep this unique and

vulnerable community intact.' He made a face like an orphan puppy on a dogs' home advert.

Louise gave a delighted cackle. 'Ha! I sent the report to Keira last night with a little note saying that if she had an ounce of guilty conscience for the shit they've put you through they should plug it. I didn't think she'd *actually* do it.'

Sam stared at the phone screen, speechless. Martin hated doing charity appeals – he always said that the money was in livening up people's days rather than bombarding them with drudgery.

'She really must feel guilty,' Sam mumbled.

'Too right,' said Louise. 'Let's check the petition.' She snatched the phone back.

Sam almost didn't want to know the signature count. She'd forced herself not even to imagine how much traction they'd get, feeling sure she'd only set herself up for disappointment. She cringed to think of herself swaggering over to Walt's, fuelled by indignation; she wasn't feeling nearly so confident anymore. There were so many causes, so many struggles – they were like a bee in a swarming hive. A plug from Martin and Nina *would* help, but she'd probably vastly overestimated the number of people who'd care about the plight of a few people mad enough to live on a rock in the channel. And then not only would Caspar bloody Rowe continue to throw his weight around, but she'd look like some arrogant idiot who'd wasted everyone's time.

'Bloody hell!' Louise said.

Sam frowned. 'Bloody hell good or bloody hell bad?'

'There's 30 bloody thousand signatures. No offence, babe, but I wasn't convinced that many people would give a shit.' Louise thrust her the phone.

And there they were. 30,748 signatures, all totted up on a little line. Sam refreshed the page. 30,749. A lump formed in her throat. People actually cared. The government would have to respond. The idea that they might get 100,000 signatures suddenly didn't seem so bonkers.

Sam blinked back a tear and, keen to hide her new-found soppiness from Louise, flicked back to the show to distract herself. She couldn't help smiling at Martin's familiar, angular face as he moved onto the next segment – on someone hatching a duck from a supermarket egg. He might still be a self-centred arsehole who'd caused so much crappiness over the past few weeks, but it was a decent thing for him and Keira to have done. 'You know,' she said, trying not to sound too overwhelmed, 'I both love and hate how that slime ball has so much sway over the viewing public.'

But before they'd had the chance to revel in their emerging success, they were distracted by the noise of what sounded like an entire school of children outside. Upon inspection from the window, it turned out to be just Clementine and Magnus led by Olive, who was marching purposefully in red wellies and round sunglasses. A weary Clive brought up the rear.

'Hide,' Louise barked, dropping to the floor. 'Quick.'

But for Sam it was too late.

'TIN FOIL LADY!' Olive shouted up to the window, hands splayed either side of her small but very loud mouth. 'YOU COME WITH US! AND DANIEL!'

Sam grimaced, her mind racing for an excuse that would be unquestionable to a particularly demanding toddler. She ran a blank.

'Hide!' Louise repeated. 'Before they're sure you're there.'

'Auntie Sam!' Clementine shouted. 'We can see you! Come with us to Venus!'

'Christ, they're like cryptic mind readers,' Louise hissed. 'Sorry, hun, but you're on your own for this one. No one saw me. I'm safe.'

Which was how Sam ended up with Walt, Daniel and a terrifyingly excitable clutch of children heading to the Venus pool, a natural tidal pool nestled amidst the rocks beneath the cottage. Clive apologised profusely for the intrusion; Issa was feeling a bit off, Nixie and Leo were still helping set up, so he'd been left in sole charge of children over one.

'My two are bad enough without throwing that little madam into the mix.' He pointed at Olive, who was trying to pull the tottering Daniel along much faster than his little legs could manage. 'It's reminded me to give Noemi a raise.'

Once they'd reached the path, there was much squabbling about who would make the biggest splash, all of which almost ended in tears when Clive declared jumping, diving and limpet eating banned. Clementine put up a good fight until they edged around the corner to find the green circle of water sunken within high walls of granite, and she declared the mission actually *quite* dangerous and that she would like Walt to show her how to do it first.

Once they were ready, Walt asked Sam to hold onto Daniel as he slipped in, dunking under the water and running a hand through his hair as he surfaced. She couldn't help noticing how different his body was to Martin and Caspar's — not smooth, plucked and sculpted, but tough and sinewy, with an angry scar etched across his chest. Daniel waved his arms and legs in excitement, and Sam hugged his torso close to her own.

'Want to join me, little man?' Walt swam towards them. 'Sam will help you in.' He gave her a soft smile and a nod as she gently lowered Daniel's wriggling limbs into the water and into Walt's hands. His fingers brushed her own and she flinched. He caught her eye.

She automatically went to apologise but was interrupted by the ear-splitting squeals of Olive as she launched herself – un-arm-banded – into the water. Sam immediately jumped in to grab Daniel again as Walt dived down to retrieve Olive, who appeared to be sinking straight to the bottom. Panic writhed in Sam's stomach like an eel. Clementine and Magnus lurched forwards until Clive tossed them back and tentatively readied himself to jump in, too. But when the screaming toddler emerged in Walt's arms, they realised that they were screams of delight, and Olive went to clamber out to do it all again.

'No way, young lady,' Walt said. 'Gentle entrance only.'

But the seed had been sewn. Olive threw herself forwards once more, giggling with glee, and her splash was closely followed by those of Clementine and Magnus, who'd taken advantage of Clive momentarily checking his emails on his phone.

Sam swept Daniel out of the frothing water and cuddled his cold body in a towel. Her heart pounded; he might have been kicked, she worried to herself, or have inhaled water or she might have lost her grip on him amidst the commotion. She could never imagine letting her own children do anything so dangerous. There was no safety equipment or a lifeguard or even any handles screwed into the slick rock. But her nerves subsided as the swimming trio screeched with joy and Daniel clapped happily within her arms on the sidelines, shouting like a trooper at each splash.

Walt caught her eye again and smiled, shrugging with comic defeat as Magnus hurled himself at him. She smiled back. He was a good guy, she decided. She'd been wrong about him. About lots of things. And as Clive relented to his children's pleas to join them, she held Daniel a little looser, closing her eyes momentarily to look up and soak in the morning sun.

Rounding the children up to go home resulted in more threats of tears than there'd been on the way down. As a successful distraction technique, Clive suggested a race back up the hill, apologising again to Sam and Walt for roping them in before jogging behind the three determined bodies tearing through the daisies.

Walt carried Daniel on his shoulders as Sam walked next to him. After the riot of the past half hour or so, the air was suddenly very quiet, punctuated only by Daniel shouting at the sheep.

'Thank you,' Walt said after a few moments.
'For what?'
'For looking after Daniel.'

'Oh.' Sam smiled up at the toddler. 'No worries.'

There was a pause again.

'You're good with kids,' he said.

She hummed, not sure what to say.

'Do you have any of your own? With your ex?'

The question made her wince. It always cropped up in innocent small talk, like a hidden pin piercing her toe.

'No,' she said quickly.

'Right.'

'Want them?'

She bristled. She'd meant to shelve all that pain, hide it away until it had lost its sting.

'Do you?' She replied.

'I've got this big boy now.' He jiggled Daniel on his shoulders, who guffawed in reply. 'Well, for now at least. You know, it was never on my radar. Working on the boats, travelling, not meeting the right person, hitting the wrong side of 35.' He grimaced. 'And I blooming hope Mede recovers but my God I've loved having this little fella.' He swung Daniel round and up in the air before trailing his feet down in the grass and letting him totter ahead.

Sam took a deep breath. Normally she clammed up in these types of conversations, keen to steer the focus in any other possible direction. But today she felt differently. She didn't know whether it was the growing warmth of the air or the open vista ahead or the way Walt had started to crack open or the knowledge that she'd soon be leaving and would never see the man again, but she decided to talk. As they crossed the flower-speckled fields, arms swinging by their sides, she talked about the past year – about her hopes and expectations and disappointments and defeat. He didn't offer any of the usual advice or quips about the benefits of her freedom or inquiries on whether she'd adopt. Instead he just listened and nodded and, by the time they reached the door of the cottage, she felt better somehow. There was a sense that she could now package up her experience and inspect it, rather than suffocating in its mazy folds.

'Thank you,' she said.

'For what?' Walt held Daniel up to push down the handle.

'For just, you know, lending an ear.'

'No worries.' He paused. 'And I hope you know that I forgive you.'

She frowned, her chest tight. What had she done now?

'If you've been under that much stress then the least you could do was spit in my face.' He smiled, and she shoved his shoulder slightly and laughed. 'And there was me thinking all you had to contend with was some seagull shit,' he said.

'What are you two cackling about?' Louise emerged from upstairs. 'We're going to be late for Issa's class.'

And so they all split off to get ready, Sam feeling an unexpected lightness in her step.

CHAPTER 33

Walt stayed behind to feed Daniel first, and the women headed for the festival only to find an entrance queue snaking round three roads. It was an eclectic mix: families with babies in noise-proof at headphones or toddlers in trollies; groups of teenagers in flower crowns and bejewelled faces; laid back couples and friends in socks and sandals; and glamorous women in white linen and statement jumpsuits.

'Is this a local crowd?' Louise asked.

For the most part Sam wasn't sure, though it was pretty obvious that Louise, sashaying along the unpaved road in wet-look baggy trousers and snakeskin boots, wasn't the standard island tourist – let alone resident.

'If not, then let's skip in at the front.' Louise pulled her along towards the ticket desk. 'These boots aren't for queues.'

'I'm not sure those boots are for fields,' said Sam.

'I think they look *brilliant*,' a voice said. The women turned to see Judith, staring down in rapture from behind the float and pile of wristbands. 'I can't remember the last time I put on a pair of heels.'

'Don't need them, Jude,' Jack said, squeezing her shoulder. 'You're glam enough in your wellies.'

'He's a shameless flirt,' Judith tutted as she stuck on the wristbands, her cheeks apple pink. 'Been pestering me all morning.'

'Have you seen Issa?' Sam asked.

'Is that the woo woo one doing kung fu?' said Jack.

'It's Feng sushi.' Judith rolled her eyes. 'And there are plenty of people here very keen to join her. It's been a real boost for ticket sales. Lots of people who aren't our usual type.'

Jack guffawed in agreement and nodded unsubtly towards a tall woman in a cashmere tracksuit heading to the opposite desk.

'They've moved her to the main tent for before the music starts,' Judith said. 'She's drawn quite a crowd.'

Sam and Louise headed over to the large marquee, out of which flowed tens of young women keen to capture the final minutes of Issa's advice on how to 'activate' your front door. Holding in their snorts of bemusement, the two women squeezed towards the front where they found Nixie and Ash and Olive, Clementine and Magnus cross-legged next to them, eyes glued to the stage.

'Issa is a miracle worker,' Nixie whispered, as Sam and Louise shuffled into the clutch of enraptured listeners. 'People are loving this!'

Sam gave a tight nod. She wasn't quite convinced of Issa's mystical abilities, but, looking around, she couldn't deny the enchanted looks on the faces of the crowd as they gazed up at Issa in a white crochet dress draped over her bump.

'And now,' Issa said, 'as we move onto the final workshop – a space for you to discover the energy of your breath – let us take a moment to feel the power of this special island. A place of healing, of forgiveness, of fresh starts, of serenity and harmony. A place that needs your protection through adding your name to our petition.'

Louise elbowed Sam in the ribs. 'Marketing gold,' she whispered. A woman with a large nose ring gave them a stern look.

'So let us manifest that protection and transition into the breath with a collective deep exhalation through the mouth. Three, two, one...'

The whole crowd released a rush of air at once, making Sam jump. It wasn't her usual scene, but she had to hand it to Issa: if this was going to lead to more names on that form, then she was all for it.

'We will now seamlessly transition to breath work.' Issa closed her eyes and put her hands in a prayer position. 'Allow yourself to sink gently to the floor. Let your limbs find a position of comfort.'

Sam thought about bowing out until, almost unbelievably, she saw Olive, Clementine and Magnus silently laid out next to each other like prostrate sunbathers. If Olive could give it a go, so could she.

'I'll stay if you stay,' Louise whispered. 'Some harmony and serenity might be good for my complexion.'

'Close your mind,' Issa's voice swirled around the tent. 'Seal off your thoughts.'

Sam lay down but tapped her finger against her side until Louise kicked her to stop.

As Issa started chanting various breathing instructions, Sam let her mind wander to what would happen next. If they got the signatures, would it be debated in parliament before summer recess? If it didn't, would it be too late? Would parliament even care? If it was on UK soil, things would be different, but the island occupied such an odd, liminal political space. And where would Walt and Daniel go if things didn't work out? To the UK or Guernsey, presumably. Or maybe somewhere totally new. Or maybe not if it meant leaving Judith behind. He'd been so earnest in the video. It was sort of endearing. And, she had to admit it, he did *sort of* look like David Gandy. In a rugged, fisherman I-only-wear-practical-clothing sort of way. She winced at the thought of Caspar and his sister. He must have thought she was such an idiot being taken in by him.

'Focus on your toes.' Issa's voice cut through.

Right. Yes. How had her thoughts ended up on Walt?

She'd probably never see him again after tomorrow. Focus on her toes. Yes. Big toe. Toe next door. Middle toe. Other toe. Little toe.

What had he said about her last night? *Amazing.* Well, the report was amazing. Not her, per se. She hadn't been quite sure how to react. Was he just trying to bolster her to get her to focus on the campaign? Or was it something else? Something more? She didn't know. Deep down, he might still think of her as some Londoner sticking her nose in. It wasn't an entirely unfair assessment.

'Imagine the colour blue,' Issa went on. 'Peaceful waves lapping the shore.'

How would Daniel find it having to move to a new home? He'd already had to cope with living away from his mum. How she managed to cope with not seeing his chubby little cheeks and earnest eyes everyday she didn't know. If she had her own... she stopped herself. It wasn't a helpful line of thought. That chapter was finished; she had to keep forging ahead. At least doing the report was of some help. The magic of distraction.

A drum suddenly sounded on stage. She flinched.

'Now let the sound go through your body.' Issa's voice was louder over the low, rhythmic beat. 'Let it enter every crevice. Let it push out those patches of dark energy.'

Another drummer joined her on stage and then four more. The deep, overpowering sound began to echo around the tent like an approaching train.

'Now come to standing,' Issa ordered. Sam opened her eyes. Issa herself was at the front of the stage, swaying with her eyes closed as she tapped a small drum next to her stomach. 'And let your body move with the music.'

Sam frowned as she looked around. Surely other people thought this was a load of nonsense? But the crowd had started to slowly rock as a single mass, following Issa's lead. She did a double take when she even saw Mrs Pedvin tapping her foot at the back.

'And exhale. Hah!' Issa snorted. The crowd snorted back. 'And let your necks loose. Your arms loose. Your jaw loose.' The crowd duly wobbled their necks like a clump of car bobble heads.

Sam went to smirk with Louise or Nixie, but both women were absorbed in the moves, eyes closed and moving with the crowd. She figured she'd better try and join in so put her head down and tried to let her arms swing. The drums became louder and louder, pulsing through her brain.

'Let your whole body loose!' Issa shouted. 'Let your limbs go! Let laughter out! *Breathe!*'

The crowd was whipping into a frenzy unlike anything Sam had experienced outside of a nightclub. Women in designer yoga gear were jumping on the spot and letting tears fall, others were shaking out hands and feet or lifting their arms to the tent's ceiling. She could hear Olive, Clementine and Magnus screeching in excitement as the drums resounded like thunder.

Suddenly she felt two hands take her own. She opened her eyes. It was Nixie and Louise, both laughing and holding her arms up as they wriggled like teenagers at a rave. Sam scrunched up her face but then tried to let her last niggle of awkward doubt out, shaking her legs and hips and laughing with them.

'Fellow seekers,' Issa now spoke over a microphone. 'I see you. I feel your power. And I feel the energy of this island like nowhere I've ever felt before!' The crowd roared back at her in agreement. 'And so without further ado,' she shouted. 'I let you go out into the world and declare the Sark festival officially open for MUSIC!'

She threw her hands up in the air as she swayed off stage and the drummers were joined by brass band members, who quickly snapped into a version of a well-known pop tune, sending the crowd squealing with unrestrained delight.

'This is INSANE!' Louise shouted over a trumpet solo. 'Ibiza eat your heart out!'

'Better than Berghain!' said Nixie, taking Olive and the other children so the group formed a circle, all laughing and dancing together.

'It's better than *anywhere!*' a voice said, and they looked round to find Issa shuffling towards them and taking Clementine and Magnus' hands.

And as they moved and shouted and screeched for what felt like hours and hours as hit after hit swirled round the tent, Sam could only bring herself to agree.

It was getting late in the afternoon when their little group dispersed. Issa had been a long time on her feet, the children needed feeding and watering and Louise declared herself in need of a drink.

Sam paused her as they wiped the sweat from their foreheads outside the now steamy, packed tent. 'Let's just check the signatures before we do anything.'

Louise opened up the page on her phone. '85,482! Yes, babe!'

Sam snatched the phone to check. 'Well thank God for Martin, Keira and Issa. There's a sentence I never thought I'd say.'

Louise shook her round the shoulders as she led her towards the beer tent. 'Reckon they'll do me a negroni?' she said. 'I need something to numb my blisters.'

'You'll be lucky to get a warm cider.'

'Like hell. There'll be gin somewhere.'

'And I told you,' Sam said, picking up the pace as Louise charged on. 'I am not drinking today. I've done enough damage recently.'

Louise pulled a face as they approached the bar. 'Come on. We *never* do this sort of thing. Let loose.'

'Nope. I've learnt my lesson.'

Louise rolled her eyes and poked her tongue out.

'I'll join you.' A voice sounded behind them.

They turned around. Louise stumbled backwards, putting her hands out against the bar to keep her balance.

'Rio!' Sam kissed him on the cheek. 'Thank you so much. I can't say it enough – the edit's great. You did a fantastic job.'

He shrugged, twisting his mouth slightly. 'Yeah. It's not bad, is it? And it's getting some incredible traction online.'

'I know! Not too far to go now.'

Rio frowned. 'Where's your friend's gone? I was going to buy her a drink. She reminded me of someone.'

Sam looked around. There was no sign of Louise.

'Hang on.' She raised a finger. 'Do *not* move.'

It didn't take long to find Louise round the back of the bar with her face in a portable fridge. Sam tapped her on the shoulder. 'What the hell are you doing?' she said.

'It's Rio,' Louise hissed.

'I know it is. He's single, you know.'

'Fuck.' Louise looked around. 'I have to hide.'

'In a fridge?'

'I'm sweating like an overweight rocker in a mosh pit!'

'He won't care!'

'Fuck.' Louise stood up, smoothed back her hair and fanned herself with her gold nails. 'Fuuuuuck!'

'Calm.' Sam placed her hands on her shoulders. Louise never got herself worked up over guys. 'Think about Issa's breathing techniques. Think about your toes.'

'Piss off.'

'Seriously, Lou. You look great. And he's here. You'll have to see him at some point. Plus if you hide for ages you'll look like a freak. We can still pass this one off as you having popped to the toilet.'

'Absolutely not.'

Sam raised an eyebrow.

Louise sighed. 'Fine. Shit. *Fine.*'

They walked back to the bar in silence as Louise applied and reapplied her lip oil.

'Found her,' Sam said, tapping Rio on the shoulder. 'Just in the toilet. Did you say you wanted to buy her a drink?'

Louise stood stony-faced behind Sam like a toddler

hiding behind her mother's legs.

'I did,' Rio replied, cocking his head to peer round Sam. 'Sorry – don't worry if you're not keen. You just remind me of someone. I hope you don't mind. Trust me, it's a compliment.'

Louise edged forwards. 'Rio?'

He frowned.

'It's me.'

'Excuse me?'

'Lulu.'

He stood back a step. 'Lulu?'

'Who's *Lulu*?' Sam pulled her chin back, but Louise was nodding, hands clasped behind her back like a nervous schoolgirl.

'Wow. I can't... *Seriously*? I had a feeling, but you look different. In a good way.'

'It's the hair.' Louise gave a high giggle that Sam had never heard from her before. 'I think I was in dreads last time we met. And harem pants. Times have changed.'

Sam did her best to keep her face neutral. Louise in *harem* pants. Christ. Times really had changed.

'Well,' he sheepishly looked her up and down, 'you look great. Fantastic. I can't believe how good it is to see you. Please – stay. Let's catch up. What can I get you? Cider? It's probably warm but it's a local brew.'

'Sure,' Louise nodded coyly, taking a gentle step forwards.

'And you, Sam?' he said.

Sam shook her head. 'Not for me. I'm going to head to the outdoor area for a bit. Get some fresh air.'

'See you,' Louise said without breaking Rio's gaze.

And neither of them really seemed to notice when she left.

The acoustic tent was situated in the far field, perched on a cliff overlooking endless sea. It was like a soothing balm after the wildness of the past few hours, with soft folk songs and the audience propped up against hay bales.

Sam leant back against a pile of straw and checked the petition. Over 100,000. They had done it. Or at least they'd completed a major step. She exhaled and closed her eyes, letting the music fill her thoughts. It had been a busy few days – few weeks – and she needed some time to be numb to it all. As the party heated up in the other fields, with yelling and clapping and the sounds untamed on the salty afternoon air, she let herself melt away, the time passing in a gentle hum until she was roused by the lights and sounds of a vast bonfire sending cracks into the darkening sky.

She watched as children's faces turned orange in the glow and giggling young couples stole kisses amidst the jumping sparks. And then, as the time went on, the lanterns round the site were lit, the air acquired a chill and people huddled next to the flames to watch the stars pepper the empty sky.

'Blanket?' A large figure loomed above her, holding out a woollen rug from a pile.

'Walt?'

'Sam?'

'Yes?'

'Can I?' He indicated to sit down next to her.

'Sure.'

He dropped down. She hadn't realised she'd been cold until she felt the bulk of his warmth next to her. His face was slightly loose and his breath sweet with beer. 'We always hand out blankets this time of night. You don't want someone who's completely sozzled sleeping out in the cold by mistake.' He leant forwards and tapped a hand on her knee. 'Though it looks like this year that I'm the sozzled one. If only slightly.' He smiled and wrinkled his nose. 'Sorry. Two beers and I'm rolling down a cliff these days.'

Sam laughed. 'It's ok. You looked after me last time.'

He waved a finger. 'I do *not* need looking after.'

'Have you seen Rio or Louise? Or both?'

He scrunched his nose. 'Hmm... yes. But I don't know

when. Or where. They were together.'

Sam laughed. 'That figures.'

She looked up into the evening air and shivered slightly. The sky was lowering to a deep blue, and she could just about see the white moon reflected in the sea. It was beautiful, and she felt a quiet sadness knowing she'd soon be leaving it behind and stepping into a new unknown.

'You're cold? Here.' Walt pressed a blanket to her. 'Take this.'

'Thanks. It's getting late. I should really be getting back.'

'I might as well come with you.'

'Oh no. You stay. Doesn't this go on for hours more?'

Walt waved a finger again. 'I have had enough.' He put his forehead in his hands, 'And I have to get up early to collect Daniel. And to feed Trevor C. I mean D.'

'I can always feed him tomorrow. Before I leave.'

He slowly cocked his head. 'Leave? Where are you staying next?'

'The island, I mean. We have what we need for the petition. It's over to the government now, so I should really be getting back.'

There was a pause. Sam looked over to Walt as he stared over towards the bonfire. 'Don't leave,' he finally said.

She caught his gaze before he turned away. His eyes flickered in the light of the flames. 'I'll miss you.'

She flushed. She didn't know what to say. He was drunk. Of course. So it didn't mean anything. *Obviously*. Though it was nice to hear – in the way that knowing all men weren't going to treat her like a leper after her public fall from grace. Not that Walt was all men. She shook herself back to focus. He was probably one of those happy drinkers, everyone his best friend a few beers in.

Which was why, she reasoned to herself, after they'd quietly walked home together, his arm sometimes brushing against her own, it was only right when they reached the front door – and didn't mean anything whatsoever at all – for her to admit (if only very quietly) that she might miss him too.

CHAPTER 34

Sam woke up to an empty house and a barrage of emails. As she flicked through her inbox, archiving the many messages praising the report and asking if she might be interested in making a guest appearance on a news channel/podcast/radio show, she felt grateful for having a clear head. It also meant she could remember exactly how the night ended, and she had nothing to regret this time – with Walt's brief goodnight peck on her cheek and lights out in separate bedrooms by 11pm. Thank goodness. Louise hadn't made it back at all, so Sam smugly doubted she'd be getting up in a similar state.

She had just about cleared through yesterday's influx when another message came through. She sat up.

Jeremy Nuttall MP

House of Commons, London, SW1A 0AA

Her heart leapt into action. This was it. She skimmed through:

The Parliamentary Under Secretary of State... yadda yadda...UK minister with responsibility for the crown dependencies... yadda yadda... response to petition... yadda yadda... discussed in parliament as a matter of urgency today.

Jesus. She took a sharp breath. Today. She checked the email again.

Not just today, but this morning.

She called both Walt and Louise. Neither picked up, so she sent excited messages urging them back. The parliament TV footage was due to start in twenty minutes. She wondered whether to rush out and try to gather everyone to watch together or just watch it on her own.

She bit off a nail and decided she should stay calm. There was no point whipping everyone up. The outcome might not be what they'd wanted and then it would be horribly anticlimactic with everyone together. This also meant she had time to get dressed, make a cup of tea and find a comfortable spot to watch.

And so she'd slipped into her jeans and T-shirt when there was a knocking on the door.

'Coming!' she shouted, expecting to find an abashed Louise on the front step. 'Give me a minute!'

The knocking increased.

'Alright.' Sam left her phone on the side to start buffering the live feed. 'What's the rush?'

'Nixie!' Sam was surprised to find her ashen-faced at the door. 'Did you get the message? I'm so nervous.'

Nixie frowned. 'Did *I* get the message? Did *you* get the message?'

'Huh? Of course – he emailed me this morning. It starts in 14 minutes. Come on in. We can watch it on my phone.'

Nixie shook her head. 'Not that message – whatever that is – it is Issa. She is in labour.'

'She's *what*?'

'Is Walt here?'

'No.'

'*Scheißen.*'

'How come?'

'I was hoping he'd know where Judith was. Apparently she delivered a baby during a storm in the 90s, which currently makes her the most qualified midwife on the island.'

'*Delivered*? Issa can't be helicoptered off to hospital?'

'Things are moving too quickly, and the GP's too

hungover from last night to be of any good. I guess at least we have you now.'

'*Me?*'

'All hands on deck. Come on. On the back of the bike.'

Sam chewed her cheeks as she tucked herself onto the back of the cargo bike, head woozy with adrenaline. 'Will she be ok?'

Nixie started pedalling. 'I don't know. She is panicking. Clive is trying to keep her calm, but she keeps repeating something about hair. None of us can work out what is wrong.'

'Ah.' Sam grimaced. She wasn't sure quite how she'd explain that one.

'Olive suggested we get in the farmer who delivered Mint Sauce, which is ridiculous, but we are lacking other options.'

'Do you know where Jack lives? I have a feeling I know where Judith might be.'

Jack, eyes bleary and arms crossed over his only half done up shirt, had put on a grand show of tutting and harrumphing that *of course* Judith wasn't there and what kind of woman did they take her for, etc., etc. He managed to keep the act going until Nixie shouted past him that Issa was delivering her baby 'RIGHT NOW' and needed help 'IMMEDIATELY'. Sam couldn't help making a mental note about where Olive got her voice from.

'Delivering the baby?' Judith hurried along from the end of the corridor, hastily dressed in yesterday's clothes. 'Goodness. Why didn't you say?'

Jack looked bashful as she squeezed past him. 'She asked me to keep quiet about her staying here,' he mumbled. 'Don't know why she's embarrassed. Perfectly natural for a man and such a looker of a woman –'

'Stop yakking. Get moving,' Judith commanded. 'No time to waste.'

She wasn't wrong. By the time the party arrived in Nixie's bedroom, Issa was screaming blue murder and Clive was a worrying shade of grey. Sam bit her lip; the atmosphere didn't feel right. Issa was so far from how Sam had imagined her to be in labour – less zen-like maestro and more hysterical banshee. It was unnerving.

'She's never been this bad before,' Clive stuttered. 'Magnus just slipped out of her in the water bath. It made paying for the Portland feel like a waste of money when she could have done it herself at home. But this...' he rubbed his head, 'God help us. She can't keep calm.'

'Well we haven't got long,' Judith declared as she stood up from between Issa's legs. 'All progressing nicely. Well done, love.'

Issa howled in reply.

'You know,' Clive said gravely, 'I don't think she actually wants me here. Could one of you give it a try? I've been with her through all the other births, but they weren't anything like this.'

Nixie and Sam looked at each other. A dark, twisting feeling gripped Sam's chest.

'Sam, you sit here,' Judith said, pointing to the stool next to Issa's writhing head. 'Nixie, you make Clive a sweet tea. He's looking a bit peaky and a fainting dad's the last thing we need.'

'Are you sure?' Sam said. 'I could make tea. Nixie at least has experience...' The sight of Issa reeling and thrashing was making her feel a bit peaky herself. Her heart was thumping. She wasn't good with blood and could usually hardly bring herself to watch *Call the Midwife*. Conception had been her focus for so long that she'd hardly thought about the actual experience of labour. It was hot and furious and like entering a different dimension.

'Sit!' Judith directed.

Sam nodded limply, took Issa's hand and tried to catch her gaze. Her eyes were wild and red and terrified like a nervous rabbit. 'You can do this,' Sam whispered. She tried to sound confident, but her voice was wavering.

Issa shook her head in a frantic movement. 'I can't have it. I can't...,' she said with desperation. She closed her eyes and squeezed Sam's hands. 'I haven't told Clive. He's going to know as soon as it's born.' She groaned as the next contraction gripped, baring her teeth like the fox that once chased Sam home in London. Her whole body contorted with pain as the noise ricocheted across the room.

'Breathe through it,' Judith shouted from the other end. 'You're doing really well. You're already in transition. Almost time to push.'

Sam felt utterly helpless. If something went wrong, she'd have no idea what to do. And then what? Judith wasn't exactly a professional. There was no hospital on the island. The thought crashed over her like a wave. She tried to control her breathing but found herself taking shallow gulps as she watched Issa, who had started loudly sobbing between deep animal-like moans. She dug her fingernails into her palm. She had to pull herself together. 'You're going to love your baby,' she said through chattering teeth. 'Not long now.'

Issa's face crumpled in fear and she let out a piercing moan.

Sam glanced down at Judith for some more words of support, but she was stoney-faced in concentration.

'You'll take it,' Issa gasped for air like someone drowning.

Sam squeezed Issa's shoulder with a shaking hand, trying to ignore her comments. 'Breathe.'

'Say you will. Promise me you will.' Issa's voice was tight and desperate, as if she was being choked.

Sam swallowed. She was surprised by how emotional she felt. Issa's earlier comments about her taking the baby had felt silly – just another Issa drama. But this was real and distressing – Issa's emotional and physical pain entirely consumed the room. 'You will love this baby,' she said firmly. 'Just focus on the moment.'

'Transition does funny things to women,' Judith said, still staring firmly ahead. 'I told poor Trevor that I wanted to hang him by his tie. I'd ignore anything she says.'

Issa clasped Sam's hands as she was wracked with another contraction.

'That's it, my love. Keep breathing. It's time to push,' Judith said.

Sam bent down so that she was face to face with Issa. She had to shelve her own anxiety and actually help. 'You did so well yesterday. It was incredible. You can do anything. And you can certainly have this baby. Now breathe in. And breathe out. Think about how you teach in your classes.'

Issa looked at her, her terrified face wet and purple.

'Breathe,' Sam repeated with more conviction.

Issa clenched her lips together and slammed her head from side to side.

Sam steeled herself and continued with the breathing mantra – over and over.

Finally, Issa closed her eyes and inhaled.

'And that's it,' Judith declared. 'It's time to push. Let's go, my love.'

Issa let the breath out in a great rush as she bore down.

'Go on,' Sam said through gritted teeth.

'And another,' Judith said. 'This is coming along well. A couple more and the head'll be out.'

Issa closed her eyes and crumpled her legs by her ears. Sam managed not to yelp as she crushed her fingers.

'Promise me,' Issa gasped.

'Not much longer,' Sam said, desperately hoping it wouldn't be.

'Here's the head!' Judith announced.

Sam whipped round. 'What does it look like?'

'Like a baby,' Judith snapped. 'Come on, Issa. Focus. You're almost there.'

'Does it have hair?'

'Not now, Sam. Come on, Issa.'

'Does it?' Sam went to stand to check.

'Sit down, for goodness' sake. It's bald.'

There was a pause. The comment hung in the air like

scent.

Issa flicked her eyes open.

Sam almost collapsed in relief. 'You hear that, Issa?' she said, rallying herself.

Issa looked at her and nodded, her wild face a contortion of pain and joy. 'Clive,' she whispered. 'Clive.'

And so as she groaned into the next push, Sam slipped out the room to find Nixie and Clive slumped in the corridor outside.

'She wants you.' She nodded at him.

'Really?' He frowned. 'You're sure? I thought she might kill me earlier.'

'I'm sure.' Sam smiled. 'Go on in.' She slumped down the wall to join Nixie on the floor, where she stayed, her body quivering with adrenaline and exhaustion, until a fresh cry resounded from inside.

It wasn't long until Judith popped her head round the door, her eyes bright and wet. 'Get the children. Their bonny little brother's arrived.'

CHAPTER 35

Leo popped open a bottle of champagne on the beach shoreline whilst Issa's family stayed back at the house.

'Well done, lass,' Jack gave Judith a squeeze after he'd knocked back his plastic glass. 'Done us proud.'

'My second baby.' Judith wiped her eyes. 'Never thought I'd do that again. It was lovely.' She dabbed at her cheeks. 'Really lovely.'

'And well done to Sam.' Nixie shakily raised a glass as Olive ran through her legs, splashing Ash in the sling. 'A natural doula.'

Sam laughed. 'I don't even know what this is.'

She looked out across the sparkling water and buried her toes into the sand. She was happy – ecstatic even – but also felt like an emotional dishcloth wrung out to dry. Another glass of champagne and she'd be asleep on the pebbles. Which was why, when Walt charged down the steps brandishing a slightly crazed look and Daniel on his shoulders, it took her a few seconds to piece together what he was talking about.

'It's been blocked,' he shouted across the bay as put Daniel down to run beside him. 'Pending further review.'

The little group frowned, and a small wave broke at their feet..

'Nothing blocked about this one, son,' Jack shouted back. 'Your nan said he was out in a few pushes.'

'BABY COME!' Olive shouted happily as she jumped over the next wave.

'Huh?' Walt rushed over.

Sam stepped towards him. 'Wait. What?'

Walt stepped into the water in his heavy boots, swooping Daniel up and over into Leo's arms. He grabbed Sam's shoulders, his quiet face split open with triumph.

'The ownership plan's been blocked. The MP just called. Said he couldn't get hold of you. They're reviewing the laws on the sale of fiefdoms to check they're robust enough or something. Could take six months. Doesn't mean he definitely won't get it, but it buys us a bit of time.'

Sam let out an indistinct noise. Christ. The petition. It had completely gone from her mind. 'You're serious?'

'I'm serious.'

'Oh my God!'

'You did it, Sam,' he grinned.

'*We* did it!' She jumped slightly and pulled him into a hug, the top of her head just about reaching his shoulder. And it might have been because she was tired or overcome from the birth or the news or even just the glass of champagne, but she couldn't help bursting into heavy, happy tears, sobbing a wet patch into his flannel shirt.

'Sorry. I didn't mean to...'

'Come here.' He pulled her into him again.

Surrounded by Walt's arms, she was hardly aware of the others, only just noticing Jack heave a squealing Judith up in triumph and Nixie and Leo swinging Olive and Daniel with both hands. It was a golden moment. The sun danced on their backs and the water sloshed happily at their feet. Sam breathed in the warmth of Walt's chest and couldn't remember ever feeling so serene.

Louise's voice called in the distance. Sam lifted her head. At the same time, Walt looked down at her and their noses collided. Sam went to laugh, but instead Walt's head jutted forwards. His lips brushed her own. Surprised, she went to pull back, but something stopped her. The butterfly-like kiss sent wings flapping in her stomach. Her body responded before her head could find a reason not to, and she closed her eyes and pressed back against him, quivering at the touch of his warm, salty lips. Sam suddenly felt desperate for more of something she hadn't known she'd wanted. The negativity of the past few months disappeared in a tingling, glittering bliss. In that moment, all the pain, loneliness, sadness and frustration made sense as a pathway to bring her here. For a few divine seconds, everything else disappeared.

'KISSY KISSY!' shouted Olive. She and Daniel ran laughing into Walt and Sam's legs. The couple sprung apart, missing each other's eyes as Walt looked down to Daniel. Sam put one leg behind the other, feeling like a silly schoolgirl. Was that a heat-of-the-moment thing, or a *thing* thing? He *had* kissed her first, hadn't he? Or had he not meant to kiss her at all? Was his head actually just passing hers when she launched at him? Oh God, that was probably what happened. Cursing her idiocy, she glanced across the beach to Lousie, who was accompanied by a smiling Rio.

'Hey!' She waved, eager for distraction. 'You two remembered each other then?'

'How could I forget?' Rio said as they approached.

'So cringe!' Louise rolled her eyes, but pressed herself an inch closer to his arm before walking over to Sam. 'Hun,' she nodded pointedly. 'Can I steal you a minute?'

The women slunk over to a fold in the cliff, leaving behind the bubbling group.

'Did I just see you and Walt...?' Louise nodded over her shoulder.

Sam batted the comment away. 'Tell me about Rio. How's it going?'

Louise put a hand on her chest. 'Honestly? It's been fan-fucking-tastic. I'm not letting that man out of my sight again. Ever.'

'That sounds serious?'

'I know.' Louise made a little screech of glee. 'I can't believe it.'

'So you're staying here for a bit?'

'Here?'

'In Sark?'

'*Sark*? Christ, no. Rio was only ever back for the summer. We'll head back to London ASAP. With you, babe.'

Sam felt like she'd been winded. Of course that was the plan, but it was hard to imagine just leaving everything behind.

Louise stood straight in front of her. Her make up was smudged and she'd obviously peeled off her lashes, but her features were still stern and focused.

'Hun, I just heard back from *You News*.'

Sam suddenly felt lightheaded. 'And?'

Louise's face cracked open as she shook her shoulders. 'They only bloody want you back!'

'You're *serious*?'

'Of course I'm serious! They've seen the report – which they love – and seen how untrustworthy Caspar is. They're thinking of running a series of exposées of dodgy landlords who wield significant power over small, local areas, with him as top bill. So of course they bloody want you. They also like the angle on non-consensual marketing images. Drag him right through the mud. The offer's reinstated in full. Production and development meetings start Wednesday.'

'Wednesday?'

'So we need to get going.'

'*Wednesday*.' Sam felt like her head was detached from her body.

'Isn't it great? No time wasted. They don't want to mess around. I can already tell you're going to love it there. No fluff. Full focus. Everyone on board.'

Sam pushed a piece of seaweed with her foot. 'Yes,' she said a little too loudly. 'I mean, yes. Of course. *YouNews*. Wow.'

'It was always part of the plan, huh?'

'Yep.'
Sam nodded. How could she forget?

CHAPTER 36

'Good morning,' Sam said straight into the low camera, hands folded over her magenta trouser suit. 'We have one key question today: how will the Autumn statement impact you?'

She strode across the studio, past the vast interactive panels and towards the curved chrome desk, where she was joined by the chancellor of the exchequer, shadow chancellor of the exchequer and a union leader. All three were sitting tensely on black swivel chairs, trying to hold appropriately serious but likeable faces.

'First,' Sam flashed an easy smile, 'we go to Tamsin Black, and ask her how *exactly* she would respond to criticisms that this statement is an unnecessary return to austerity. Tamsin?' Sam nodded in her direction.

She loved this part of the process. The guests were usually slightly jittery, not having settled into whatever spin they'd been told to plug, and liable to make mistakes. It meant that she could seem all nice and friendly with a wide smile and open stance, but then catch them on the back foot early doors and quickly move towards the truth.

The show's executives also loved her for it – that and the fact that *YouNews* had soared in the ratings over the past six weeks. Everyone agreed that Sam was a natural fit: a woman exactly where she needed to be in her professional life.

The show ran live for an hour. It was fast and interesting, with a mixture of brief on-location clips covering current events of the week and interviews with political figures. From the moment Sam woke up in her new flat round the corner, her bedroom overlooking the brown river below, to the time that she slipped her stilettos off in the taxi home from whatever event she'd been at that evening, she lived and breathed possible content, endlessly hungry for fresh scoop.

She was desperate to keep her mind busy. She didn't want time to look backwards at the whirlwind of the previous few months – or to consider whether she'd definitely made the right decisions along the way. Instead she wanted to be consumed in the endless, heart pumping cycle of research, meetings, filming and events, constantly rushing to keep up with the maelstrom of Westminster. She didn't want time to think about the lost prospect of starting a family – and she was happy to be able to use work busyness as an excuse to not have time to date. She particularly didn't want to be the nervous, emotional wreck that she'd been over the summer. She wanted to be Sam Elton again, experienced political reporter – informed, attentive and still with an acid-like ability to slice through spin.

No men in her life meant no distractions. She didn't even have Issa to try and avoid since her and Clive had decided to stay permanently in Sark. In the weeks after Arlo's birth, they had loved the open fields and clean air and bracing sea so much they'd decided to stay put, with Clive working remotely. Sam was happy for them – and overjoyed when Issa dropped her a message to say that they had put in an offer on The Rowe for use as a family home and for holding Issa's new retreats. Caspar, keen to snaffle up the cash and escape any further media attention by making himself scarce in some other quiet corner of the earth, had agreed to the sale. The message also had a photo attached of Clementine, Magnus, Ottilie and Olive playing with the latest addition to Issa's garden: Trevor D.

Sam had smiled at the image and then swiftly moved

back to addressing her ever-swelling inbox. It had been such a strange summer. In those very early days back in London, she'd unwittingly constantly replayed the memory of her last morning in Sark. With the fog coming in, she, Louise and Rio had taken the passenger ferry rather than have Walt risk the journey. They'd waved goodbye to the island and its inhabitants – to Issa and the family with Clive holding Arlo in a sling, to Jack with his arm around Judith, to Nixie and Leo and Ash and Olive and, finally – not without a painful twinge – to Walt, who held Daniel on his hip and solemnly held up a hand until he disappeared into the mist descending upon the cliffs.

But then came Wednesday's meeting with the production team, and life was busy once more.

And now, as she crossed her arms over her suit, she could tell that Tamsin Black wasn't quite sure where to begin. Why these politicians arrived expecting her to sweetly puff up their policies she didn't know. But it made for good TV.

'Austerity?' Tamsin winced. 'I'd say that's going a bit far.'

'Would you?'

'We're simply making sensible cuts to what was an unnecessarily inflated and unsustainable budget.'

The shadow chancellor of the exchequer grimaced.

Sam narrowed her eyes. 'So the implication is that the healthcare system is currently *over-* not under-funded?' she said.

'Well,' Tamsin squirmed.

Sam smiled. She was going to enjoy her morning.

And so she did – and even more when she wrapped up the show to find Louise beaming backstage.

'Well done, babe.' Louise gave her a hug. 'Killed it as usual. Bloody love the suit.'

'You don't think it's too… I don't know. Pink?'

'It's fierce. You're smashing it.'

'Are you picking him up for lunch?' Sam nodded over to Rio, who'd taken on a job as cameraman for the studio.

'Yep. But first I've got some news.'

'What's up?'

'Big news.'

Sam flinched. 'You're pregnant?' Despite everything, the question still hurt. She almost asked it on instinct, having found over the years that it was less painful to anticipate it than to be taken by surprise.

Louise snorted. 'God, no. Far more exciting.'

Sam felt a flood of guilty relief. She knew she should be able to feel pure joy if Louise did make The Big Announcement. One day, perhaps, it wouldn't hurt. But she wasn't there yet. The grief was still there, not the all-consuming agony of previous months, but a constant, niggling presence – like a blister on her heel. And she was coming to terms with the fact that it might just always be there, a part of her anatomy. She wouldn't have chosen for it to be that way, but she was coming to accept its presence. 'Go on,' she said.

Louise put a hand on her chin in a mock-pensive pose. 'So what would make your life complete?'

Sam frowned. Up until recently, her answer would have been, of course, a baby. But she couldn't deny that it came with caveats. She didn't want a baby from one of the embryos from her IVF with Martin. It just didn't sit right to have him in her life anymore. Then she was terrified of the arduous process of adoption – plus she was too close to her fertility treatment to be accepted by her local council as a prospective parent anyway. She also didn't think she could go through any more treatments alone. They were too painful, came with too many looming unknowns. And she loved her new job – it was invigorating and stimulating, and she felt useful and competent. But, deep down, she knew that she spent so much time absorbed in the studio because there was nothing – and no one – for her at home. Sometimes she remembered the kaleidoscopic summer with its sheep racing and donkeys and chocolate shop and beaches and cool waters, hot sands, cottages, cobbled roads, horse and carts, milkshakes, bicycles, cliff faces, warm ciders, roses and Olive and Judith and Nixie and Daniel and Walt. And it felt like a different life. And she missed it. Missed them. Missed him.

'Earth to Sam. What do you need to complete Part B?'

'Oh, Christ. I don't know.'

Louise took up Sam's hands, her eyes sparkling. 'This is major.'

'Right.'

'Huge.'

'Ok.'

'Enormous.' Louise squeezed Sam's fingers.

'Go on then,' Sam said. 'Spit it out.' She tried to roll her eyes in nonchalance, but she couldn't conceal the anticipation from her voice. Had Louise heard anything from people in Sark? Maybe Rio had been in touch with friends there. Friend.

Louise made a strange bleat-like noise. 'It's the journalist of the year awards. The Caspar Rowe landlords exposé has been shortlisted. We're only going to the flipping ceremony next week!'

Sam paused. 'Oh.'

'*Oh?*'

'I mean that's great. Amazing.' Her voice was weirdly high pitched. She could feel a lump in her throat. It was ridiculous, she told herself. This *was* great. It was something she used to really want. It just wasn't what she'd expected. 'I hadn't even thought about it as a thing,' she said.

'Well it is a thing. A big thing. You bloody deserve it,' Louise said.

'Right. Great!' She sucked a breath in, doing her best to look pleased.

Louise took a step back. 'What's wrong?'

'Nothing.'

Louse crossed her arms.

Sam sighed. 'I mean. I don't know. I already feel like I sort of used the exposée to get this job.'

'You had this job before. It was only because of that arsehole's photos that you didn't.'

'That's true.' Sam stepped to the side as the crew started clearing the cameras away around them.

She couldn't explain why she wasn't jumping up and down with excitement. Even if she didn't win, just being nominated for the award was the pinnacle of her career so far. The culmination of years of work and recognition that she was at the top of her game. And, even better, it was something she'd achieved without Martin. But for some reason she felt strangely hollow – as if her emotions had pooled out in a puddle on the floor.

Louise put her hands on her hips. 'Seriously. What is it?'

Sam looked up. 'I don't know.' She paused. 'I guess now it feels like that whole chapter of my life has closed. Caspar's dealt with. I've got the job. Nominated for the award. It feels strange – that's all.'

'Well try and work on a better acceptance speech than you've just given me. I don't want you standing on the podium and shrugging that it feels weird or whatever.'

Sam tried to laugh, but it came out like a strange chirrup. 'I won't!'

'Anyway,' Louise looked around. 'Where's Rio? He's taking me out for lunch and then we'll probably be in bed all afternoon,' she breathed.

Sam rolled her eyes. 'Lovely. Well I won't keep you any longer.'

'Trust me, babe. Don't.'

They tiptoed round the maze of wires and equipment until they came to where Rio was packing up his things.

He picked Louise up and spun her round. 'You're here!'

Louise gave such a bashful smile that Sam had to suppress a laugh.

'And I'm ready!' Louise sang back.

He gave her a peck on the forehead. 'Let's get going.' Then he looked up and clocked Sam. 'Want to join?'

Louise shot one of her Medusa stares behind his back.

Sam couldn't help feeling a twinge of envy in her chest.

It was ridiculous, she told herself off. She had the job. The nomination. Professionally, she had achieved everything she'd ever planned. Part B was almost complete. There *was* nothing else she needed.

'No, no.' She waved a hand. 'You two lovebirds go off and enjoy yourselves.'

Louise blew her a kiss as they turned to leave.

'Hey, Sam,' Rio glanced back over his shoulder. 'You know that Walt's here, right?'

She felt like she'd been slapped. 'What?

'Walt. You know – from Sark.'

She tried and failed to swallow back the lump in her throat. 'I know who he is.'

'Arrived yesterday. Something to do with his sister.'

She felt like she'd been set adrift. Walt was here? In London. And he hadn't told her he was coming? She twiddled her fingers around each other. Why was she so nervous?

'He's not staying that far away at the moment,' said Rio. 'Do you want the address?'

'No,' she said more quickly than she'd intended.

Louise eyed her with suspicion. 'Why not?'

Sam blinked. She wasn't sure why not. Because she wouldn't know what to say? Because he hadn't told her that he was coming? They'd never got the chance to speak properly after that kiss. The day had been so busy with celebrations and packing and meeting Arlo. There just hadn't been a moment to themselves.

Rio shrugged. 'Think about it. Sorry we need to rush off.'

'Go!' Sam waved them away. 'Enjoy lunch. And afters.'

Louise gave her a ridiculous wink as they slipped out towards the studio exit.

Sam went to collect her bag. She wasn't going to think about it. She didn't need to. Life was about looking forwards, not back. Even if it was back to someone who, if she was truly honest with herself, had been in her thoughts for weeks.

CHAPTER 37

When she pushed open the double fire door, the heavy metal clanging shut behind her, what she saw almost made her scream.

'Sam,' Walt jerked backwards as she teetered on her heels. 'Sorry. I didn't mean to shock you.'

She gulped for breath. 'I didn't expect...'

'I know. I'm sorry. I guess it's weird me just turning up like this. I was going to call, but... I don't know. It's stupid.'

'No.' She shook her head, her surprise mellowing to flushed pleasure. 'I'm glad you're here.'

She had so many questions that she wanted to ask. How was the island? Had Jack kept Judith sweet? Was Olive still bossing everyone about? How was Trevor D putting up with carting round Issa's kids? Had Issa been caught naked moonbathing or the like? How was Nixie? How was Daniel? How was *he*? And – her chest tightened – why hadn't he been in touch?

She opened her mouth to speak but then stopped herself. Walt's usually broad, stable frame was twisted and twitching and, she noticed with a jolt, he had damp eyes. 'Are you ok?'

He looked at his feet. 'It's Mede.'

Her pleasure at seeing him, like the rush of riding a bike down a hill, sunk into fear. Her head felt light, and suddenly she felt old pain bursting out of fresh pain like a hydra spurting a hidden head. She was nineteen and back in her childhood kitchen, nursing a cold, weak tea on the sticky plastic of the faded tablecloth, waiting for the ambulance to take away her mother from upstairs. The floaty, floral woman of Sam's early youth had taken her last bottle of vodka to bed, her cheeks pale and mottled, her nose red and her lips blue. Sam never saw her again. She distinctly remembered watching the digital clock on the cooker change time, could once more hear the dripping of a loose tap. She'd been alone, so alone. And utterly helpless. There was no world in which she'd allow herself to feel like that again. And so then it had begun: the napkin plan, the chasing jobs, Martin, the trying for a baby. But the memory was still there, hidden beneath it all. She looked up at Walt's face, creased in worry, and took his hand. She couldn't let him feel the same way. 'I'm so sorry,' she whispered.

'No, no.' He shook his head and rubbed at his eyes. 'It's fine. She's fine. Better. Much better.'

'Oh.' Sam snapped her hand back. She'd just read him wrong – not for the first time.

But then she looked at him again, standing alone on the London pavement like a lost whale in the Thames, and realised something. Her stomach dropped. 'Daniel.'

He nodded as he looked down. 'Back with his mum. Where he should be. They're doing well. She's got a sponsor and lots of support around her. I'm really pleased.' His voice wobbled. 'They don't have that kind of help at home. Drinking island with a fishing problem and all that.'

'Oh Walt.' Sam pulled him into a hug. His heavy shoulders still smelt of the sea somehow – of salt and metal and cold waters.

'It's fine,' he repeated. 'Happy for them.' But he buried his face in Sam's hair and gripped her chest close to his own.

'Anyway,' he sniffed as he pulled back and brushed his face. 'I wanted to see you. I felt like you'd understand.'

She nodded, wiping her own cheeks with her sleeve.

This time he was the one to reach out for her hand.

He paused before speaking. 'I'm going back to the rock in the morning, so I might as well say it. God, I've missed you, Sam. You're the only person I wanted to see. Ever since I dropped that little tike off the other day, I just wanted to be with you. Rio said you were here...'

'So why didn't you come?'

'I did! I mean, I sound like a stalker, but I tried yesterday, too. Waited by the main door until the cleaning team arrived. Figured I'd try the fire exit today.'

'Why not just come in? Or message? I have a phone these days!'

'You don't want some yocal turning up at your big fancy new job.'

'Yes, I do!' She blushed at the forcefulness of her words, but she realised how much she meant them.

His eyes settled on her face, his expression serious. 'Really?'

'Really.'

He smiled and gently took her hand in his own. Sam felt like she was floating. His heavy palm felt both safe and electrifying, and she longed for him to hold his body against her own. She paused then inched closer, feeling the warmth of his torso beneath his white t-shirt and slipped her other hand into his, intertwining their fingers. He stroked her skin with his thumb and the hairs on her arms stood up, her body awakening to his like a meadow in the sunlight of spring. Her heart pounded as he slipped a hand into the small of her back. She slowly looked up, fearful that a sudden movement might break the moment's spell. He bent his head towards her, close enough that his rough stubble brushed against her cheek, and as his hot breath tickled her neck, a bolt flicked through her: she knew that she wanted this man. She knew it like she knew she was standing on the earth – as something elemental, essential.

The body she'd once hardly recognised as her own now felt fully engaged as every inch of her trembled under his touch. His soft lips pressed against her ear as he whispered something she was too intoxicated to hear, and she had to clasp a fold of his shirt to keep herself steady. She'd been wrong before. She could see that now. She didn't want to be an island, floating alone in the sea. What she wanted – needed – wasn't to get pregnant, but to give herself entirely to someone. But it didn't have to be with a baby. Instead, the person she wanted this with was Walt. He could be her everything.

'Is that a yes?' he said.

'Hmm?'

'Will you come?'

She leant back, smiling in a golden haze of smittenness. 'Sorry. What did you say?'

'Will you come back to Sark with me? Not forever. I mean – unless you want to. For a bit. For however long you want. I think we might, you know, have something. I think we should see what it could be. Unless you need to stay for work, of course.'

Reality dropped like a castle gate. Sam let go of his hands.

'What? No. I mean. I'm sorry. I need to stay.' She stepped back. What had she been thinking? Of course Walt couldn't be her *everything*. She liked him a lot. Really a lot. But she had her career, the awards, everything she'd worked for. She wasn't going to give up on herself again.

'Right.' He gave a tight nod. 'Of course. Well.' He looked around as if wondering which direction to take before heaving his bag over his shoulder.

But then she caught sight of the flowing river behind him and was flooded with the memory of them in the water that afternoon. She gave her head a sharp shake. What was she saying? Her thoughts shuffled like aligned jigsaw pieces revealing the picture. Life didn't have to be one thing or another. She couldn't let him go.

'Wait.' She grabbed his arm. 'Hang on. I didn't mean....'

Walt looked down at her, his eyes wide with hurt and

hope.

'I need to be here. I can't leave my work. Not again. But I want you to stay. With me. At least for a bit.' The words had tumbled out without much thought, but she'd never felt more certain. They could get to know each other. Properly. Slowly. On her turf. She'd let him in.

'In London?' He looked around.

She turned his chin in her direction, a wave of clarity washing over her.

'Here. In London. If you can. With me. You can see Daniel, and we can have some time together. The two of us. And I finish filming the series in a couple of weeks and then...' She blushed. She was jumping ahead of herself. 'Do you need to rush back?'

'Well there is the annual scarecrow festival this weekend.'

'If you see my hair in the morning, it'll be like being there.'

'Then the apples need to be taken down from the tree.'

'They'll be food for seagulls. Stop them nicking muffins off unsuspecting tourists.'

'And I'll miss the Jack-o'-lantern procession down the Avenue.'

'I'll blow another fuse so we have an evening by candlelight.'

Walt laughed. 'Well alright.' He put his rucksack down and his hands on her waist. 'You've persuaded me. I'll stay a while. You always were a stubborn thing.'

She laughed, and there, on the crowded street under the low sun of an autumn afternoon, they kissed.

THE END

ABOUT THE AUTHOR

Janey Grange

Janey Grange writes fun, uplifting fiction that explores the complexities of life and love.

After a decade in London, she returned to her roots in the beautiful Channel Island of Guernsey, where she now lives with her husband, baby daughter, and grumpy orange cat.

An English teacher and assistant headteacher by day, she spends her evenings writing when she really should be catching up on sleep.

Inspired by her own fertility journey, her debut novel, Part B, delves into love, loss, and new beginnings, making it perfect for anyone seeking a heartfelt escape.

PRAISE FOR AUTHOR

'Such a good holiday read and genuinely funny.'

'Very human and believable'

'Made me snort with laughter... thoroughly entertaining.'

'Brought tears to my eyes... subtly and beautifully written.'

- READER REVIEWS

Printed in Great Britain
by Amazon